The Wandering

Also by Intan Paramaditha

Apple and Knife

The Wandering

A Red Shoes Adventure

Intan Paramaditha

Translated from the Indonesian by
Stephen J. Epstein

Harvill Secker
LONDON

1 3 5 7 9 10 8 6 4 2

Harvill Secker, an imprint of Vintage,
20 Vauxhall Bridge Road,
London SW1V 2SA

Harvill Secker is part of the Penguin Random House group
of companies whose addresses can be found at
global.penguinrandomhouse.com

Penguin
Random House
UK

First published by Harvill Secker in 2020
First published with the title *Gentayangan: Pilih sendiri petualangan
sepatu merahmu* in Indonesia by Gramedia Pustaka Utama in 2017

A CIP catalogue record for this book is available from
the British Library

penguin.co.uk/vintage

ISBN 9781787301177 (hardback)
ISBN 9781787301184 (trade paperback)

Typeset in 10.5/14 pt Stempel Garamond LT Std
by Integra Software Services Pvt. Ltd, Pondicherry

Printed and bound in Great Britain by Clays Ltd, Elcograf S.p.A.

Supported using public funding by
**ARTS COUNCIL
ENGLAND**

This book has been selected to receive financial assistance from English PEN's
'PEN Translates' programme, supported by Arts Council England. English PEN
exists to promote literature and our understanding of it, to uphold writers' freedoms
around the world, to campaign against the persecution and imprisonment of writers
for stating their views, and to promote the friendly co-operation of writers and
the free exchange of ideas. www.englishpen.org

Excerpts from Franz Xaver Kroetz's commentary on his play *Request Concert*,
translated by Peter Sander; and Anne Sexton's 'The Red Shoes' from *The Complete Poems*,
copyright © Linda Gray Sexton and Loring Conant, Jr. 1981.

Penguin Random House is committed to a sustainable future for our
business, our readers and our planet. This book is made from
Forest Stewardship Council® certified paper.

MIX
Paper from
responsible sources
FSC® C018179

For the one who gave me a mirror and a pair of red shoes,
before the coming of autumn

Prologue: Demon Lover

Beware the gifts you accept, or so said your elders. But it's too late. You ask for the package: a present that comes with a curse. Demon Lover has granted you a pair of red shoes.

Demon Lover arrives as you're desperately contemplating flight. It's a night just like all those nights before, when you felt as if your limbs were lashed to the bed. Those nights when your mouth was sealed tight, though it was your ears that you wished were plugged. But, alas!, far from fighting the racket, they funnelled it into your eardrums, cramming, jamming noise into networks of blood vessels that slowly hardened to the onslaught: the buzz of televisions, the cries of street vendors, roaring motorbikes, blaring car horns, the clack-clack-clack of trains. Distorted by mosque loudspeakers, raucous calls to prayer marked the passage of time. Occasionally, you'd get a bonus – Islamic singing from frenzied matrons or a sultry dangdut performance on Independence Day. The scorching weather had grown claws and was raking them across a blackboard.

All this chaos mocks those who place hope in a dynamic rhythm. Some cities move faster than others, forever reminding you to board quickly as they won't stop for long: a train, a train, you're looking for a train. But here, you know, you're going nowhere.

You've grown roots, you're gathering moss.

You believe that certain settings can lure people into suicide. Reading teaches you that such places tend to be beautiful and bewitching: the River Seine, the Golden Gate Bridge. Jakarta, though, is so hot, so dull, so ugly, its face too foul to provoke action. But Jakarta is where you live, in this city full of thwarted suicidal urges.

You can't move. Perhaps this is what it means to be possessed by the devil. On those earlier nights, you'd close your eyes and pray to anyone who would listen. You'd count, hoping your life would change when you uttered *three*. But nothing changed. Bursting with rage, you'd rail at the universe. If a demon wanted to devour you, so be it, you thought – at least you wouldn't be so bored.

Maybe demons need an explicit invitation. And so, tonight you go to bed naked, and start to count. Before you reach three, the light in your room flickers and goes out. The window opens.

And there he stands, at the foot of your bed.

Gaunt, stooped and aged, his body abounds in scars so fresh that he reminds you of a child covered in itchy scabs, the result of falling again and again from his bike. Haphazard tufts of feathers adorn the creature – they sprout from his chest, his cheeks, his ears. His eyes glow crimson, radiating hunger. You hold your breath. Feeling a chill, you pull the covers up to your neck.

Are you going to rape me?

He grins, displaying rows of browning teeth, some sharp, others rotting. His slobber wets your big toe.

Or maybe you want to eat me?

He doesn't move. His crimson eyes merely fix themselves on your body in a passionless stare. He is neither a rapist nor a devourer of flesh.

Come here.

You are in command, so he obeys, and lies down beside you. You don't know why you're doing this. Perhaps you're possessed; perhaps you simply don't want to stay here, to live this life. You caress his long fingers, drawing them to your neck. His lips are cold, rough. As your tongue hooks his, his scrawny frame writhes in a state between pain and arousal, startling you.

Once you have coupled, you know that he worships you. You look at him in amazement as you wipe the sweat from your brow. The night is stiflingly hot. He lavishes kisses upon your feet, then draws near to your face again, to your ear, whispering in a foreign tongue. Yet you understand his words.

Make me your slave.

It's too cramped in here, you say. I don't have space for a demon.

Then I'll visit every night, he promises. I'll give you anything you ask for.

Anything?

Every night from then on, you hope and pray for this devil to slip into your rented room, eager to know the magic of his charms. His adulation makes him a formidable lover. You're famished, and nibble at him like a rat gnaws on bread.

You're not sure if he is some random shaitan or the Great Iblis himself, but you have a demon to call your own. What pet name shall you bestow upon him? Devil Dearest? Beelzebaby? You settle on Demon Lover.

He courts you like a suitor from days gone by, regaling you with roses and chocolates. Not the most useful gifts, you think, but sweet, because you're addicted to the lovemaking. Being as ancient as he is, he has many tales to tell. You've heard most of his stories but still he beats his chest proudly when you ask about everything from the slaying of Abel to his involvement in the First and Second World Wars. When it comes to the temptation of Joseph by Potiphar's wife, however, he denies involvement.

'Sorry,' he objects, 'but women have been demons since the dawn of time.'

You fuck him like crazy but soon tire of his presents. Before a month passes, you discard the drawerful of dried roses and complain that his chocolates are making you fat. Demon Lover prefers a curvy, voluptuous body, but you don't care. You want a more substantial display of his devotion.

'Are you really going to grant whatever I desire?'

Demon Lover nods, then returns to lavishing kisses upon your feet.

'OK,' you decide. 'My sole wish is to get the hell away from here. I want adventure. Give me money, visas and a one-way ticket. I don't want to come back.'

With a vaguely condescending smirk, he shakes his head.

'What's the problem?' you ask.

'Your wish is too specific. Ask for something more abstract, like success, or happiness.'

'Sorry, I can't. You and I might interpret them differently.'

You pull your feet away. Reclining on the bed, you take a slender volume from the bedside table and use it to fan your face. Screwing in the tropics requires negotiation with heat and humidity.

You grumble to him: 'I'm bored.'

Demon Lover flashes a knowing smile.

'I've realised that from the start. That's how women are. From Madame Bovary to Palupi.'

'Palupi?'

'Yes – a remarkable character from a famous film. An Indonesian classic from the sixties.'

'Why was she bored?'

'She married a poor author with integrity.'

'Ah. That would have bored her senseless all right.'

You study your neatly trimmed toenails. You've already done everything there is to do. Cut your nails, have sex, fan yourself.

'You're a little different. Palupi didn't have her very own devil.'

'But I'm still bored.'

'You've never been overseas?'

Of course, the new low-cost airlines mean that anyone can go to Singapore, Kuala Lumpur, even Manila, after saving up a little. But those cities are too close. It wouldn't be all that different from visiting Jogja.

'I want to go further, to stay away longer. I don't want to be just a tourist. I want to live in Paris. Or New York. I'm almost twenty-eight and I've never been to New York. It's a tragedy.'

Demon Lover squints and then snaps at you. His voice is slow and raspy.

'What a sad, spoiled brat!' He pauses, as if his words have led him to an epiphany. 'I'm sorry, but you're pathetic. Twenty-seven is a sacred age.'

'Oh, please. Stop. Don't tell me you're going to start blathering about Jim Morrison and the Twenty-Seven Club. How clichéd can you get.'

He looks at you with pity in his eyes.

'If you haven't accomplished anything by the age of twenty-seven, give up. Accept your fate.'

You glare, and order him out. Demon Lover doesn't want to quarrel. He refuses to go but makes another offer: 'How about a round-trip ticket?'

'I already told you – I don't want to come back.'

'That complicates matters.'

'How? Why? You're a prince of darkness, aren't you?'

'We'll need a contract.'

'Fine.'

Demon Lover snorts, annoyed, then lectures you. Don't you realise you're bargaining with a devil? Didn't you learn anything from the story of Faust and Mephistopheles?

The jagged contours of his face become even sharper. You understand now that he has been reluctant to grant your wish because he doesn't want you to leave. There's no place like home for nailing someone down.

'Don't get all moralistic on me. Just grant my wish.'

His face changes, saddens. Demon Lover grows pensive.

'Don't I satisfy you?'

'Baby, when it comes to sex, I'd give you a nine out of ten.'

As you say this, you feel surprised that a devil can be so lacking in self-esteem. But hasn't this always been true, since the beginning of time? Arrogance has served to disguise low self-esteem – the catalyst for envy, the root of evil.

'How will I be able to reach you while you're travelling?' asks Demon Lover. He looks despondent.

You stare at him, stupefied.

'For God's sake! Stop snivelling. Since when does a devil need a visa?!'

You wake the next morning at 10.30 to recorded Quranic recitation blaring from mosque loudspeakers. It's Friday, so you can be sure that the chanting will carry on until the afternoon prayers, and that there's no telling where the verses will begin or end. The rumble of passing motorcycles continues its assault on your ears. You massage your forehead. Your skin feels oily. At that moment you make a discovery: a pair of glittering red shoes beside your bed.

It's absurd to come upon such elegance in the harsh glare of day, amid the surrounding din. You get up from the bed, and kneel beside it to study the shoes closely. There you find a letter:

Darling,
    As you wished, I'm giving you a pair of magical shoes that will take you on an adventure.
    Their owner was a witch, but she is long dead.

'Second-hand shoes?' you grumble. But no matter. It seems this witch had a pretty badass sense of style, and after all, lots of adventure stories start off with an heirloom from someone who's passed on.

The letter continues:

I warn you, these shoes are cursed.

Adventure, or more precisely, wandering, will be your eternal lot. You will find shelter, but never home. Where you come from, wandering spirits can only rest peacefully after a dukun chants mantras or a kiai pronounces the Sūrat al-Fātihah. But let me emphasise that no dukun or kiai can help you – I'm running this show, and I'm cursed too.

Perhaps all this is what you're after. You've got your one-way ticket.

You'll hear many stories, and you'll collect gifts. One gift per story, more or less. You can choose your gifts and your storyline as you see fit.

Sometimes you may ask yourself how you got to a particular destination. Maybe it will be the result of magic, but during a long journey, one often asks such questions.

I've enclosed our contract. I recommend that you read it.

You put the letter down to look at a sheet of paper dense with rows and rows of print so fine it's barely legible. Of course, you don't read through it, no more than anyone reads the terms and conditions of a website. You can't even decipher what language the contract is in – Indonesian? Arabic? Hebrew?

I hope you're happy with your choice. If you want to go home you'll lose everything. Your home will not be what it was. There will no longer be a place for you here. Regrettably, there will be no place for you there either. If you return home, our contract will be null and void, and, in accordance with my own destiny, I'll wander hell until I find a new heir for the red shoes.

If you accept this contract, put the shoes on, which will indicate that you've signed on the dotted line.

Truly, I adore you. But I am Iblis – Devil – so any gifts I give are cursed. I cannot love you any other way.

Will you put them on?

Unfortunately, you've already made your choice – you'd decided even before the contract was drawn up.

You slide your feet into the shoes. First the left, then the right. They're a bit tight. But you see your reflection in the mirror and admire how the shoes flatter your legs. Suddenly you feel a terrible pain in your head. Your body shakes, your chest pounds. You feel faint. Everything goes black.

The Wandering: A Red Shoes Adventure

You find yourself in a taxi. You're no longer wearing a nightgown but a leather jacket, and a scarf wreathes your neck. Enthusiastic drumming from the car stereo assails you, making sleep impossible. The music – not dangdut but a Hindi song – urges you to sway along in time. The cab is stuffy, pungent with the aroma of cooked onions, making you sniffle. You lower the window for air and peer out at the avenues and concrete overpasses whizzing by. Occasional rows of red- or brown-brick buildings catch your attention. You have a feeling you're not in Jakarta any more.

Actually, you're en route to John F. Kennedy Airport, ready to leave New York.

Where have you been until now? Why are you in this taxi? What are you leaving behind? And where are you going? You don't remember arriving in New York. Damned Devil. He didn't even give you a chance to enjoy the city.

You rummage in your bag to look for a passport. You find a little green booklet stamped Indonesia. Shit. Couldn't he at least have given you a new nationality?

A Schengen visa, issued by the German consulate in New York, is affixed to one page. The previous page holds a visa for the United States, category J1: 'exchange visitor', valid until November 2008, exactly one year from when you put on the shoes. And then after that?

You note the name of your visa's sponsor. Mirrodoor Cultural Council. Mirrodoor? Sounds more like a Tolkien character than a legitimate organisation.

'Heading overseas?' the driver asks in a thick Indian accent.

You nod.

'Berlin,' you say, surprising yourself with your answer.

'What time's your flight?'

'Nine o'clock,' you respond automatically.

'It's already seven. You'll be late.'

The driver steps on the gas, the rapid acceleration making you feel carsick. If he keeps going at this speed, you'll land in hell for sure. He moves to pass a 1970s Jaguar with faded green paint and rust holes filled with putty. A sticker in the rear window reads *Good girls go to heaven, bad girls go everywhere*. As you hurtle past, the cabbie glances at its driver, an elderly woman whose curls are flying about in the wind.

'Ha, Granny … ' His long sigh expresses a mixture of annoyance and empathy. 'I hope she makes it to heaven.'

Good girls go to heaven.

Good girls go to heaven, bad girls –

Go wandering?

A haunted spirit roams from place to place, accepted neither in heaven nor on earth, neither here nor there. Where is your home now? Maybe, like a ghost, you can only find shelter.

You strain to recall what you have been doing in New York, but can't come up with a single clue. No images are present in your head. No voices. Your memories falter after your discovery of the glittering red shoes and the letter from Demon Lover. Everything beyond that is dark. Is this what they call amnesia? You can trace events up to that particular morning. You remember how you came to know Demon Lover and much that occurred beforehand.

You can recall your childhood.

Everything is happening too fast. You need time to stop, to breathe and put your story in order.

So, let's pause. Let's go over why you insisted on leaving, though a justification isn't really necessary. Travelling is the most ancient human desire. Just ask Odysseus. Just ask your mariner ancestors.

1990: a black model train set became your favourite plaything. In fourth grade you loved playing with toy cars, miniature buses and trucks, hand-me-downs from your cousins, but trains were the coolest type of transport. Your parents thought you'd turn out to be a tomboy, but you liked dolls too. In your made-up stories, trains and dolls always went together. Your dolls – Barbie knock-offs bought at the morning market – wore nice dresses and nice shoes to board the train; only on rare occasions did you imagine your passenger as a moustachioed gentleman. You called your favourite train the Orient Express. You plucked the name from the title of one of your mother's books that you read on the sly. When you grew up, you thought, the Orient Express would take you on adventures to uncommon places.

But, in fact, everything about you is common. You come from a common family that live like the majority of common folk. Your father and mother met in Jogja, while studying at Gadjah Mada University. Your father is a Sumatran migrant from Lahat, whereas your mother is Javanese through and through, raised in Sleman. Although born in Jogja, you speak little Javanese. Your family moved to Jakarta when you were barely a year old. Your father worked for a private company, and your mother dropped out of university to become a housewife. They boasted of their prestigious alma mater, because studying there was their sole achievement. They lived in Jakarta as common people, with two kids who would grow into common people, doing whatever common people do.

1994: the term 'abroad' evoked luxury. At your junior high, only the children of executives could go 'abroad'. Some of your friends belonged to this bourgeois elite, and had visited Singapore several times. Back then everyone was crazy about brand names, and members of the bourgeois clique dressed from head to toe in what were seen as sophisticated labels: Levi's, Doc Martens, LA Gear, Baby G, Ocean Pacific.

Meanwhile, you felt content enough with an Osella shirt with a frog logo, and unbranded jeans from Cibaduyut purchased at the end of Ramadan, the time for a new outfit. Nobody gives a rat's ass about some of those brands now, but back then collecting items from abroad with labels in English mattered to that clique. They said that white people were used to holidays. Australians visited Europe, Americans went to Asia, and so on. Your parents didn't go abroad. Neither did your aunts and uncles, nor your neighbours. Back then, you'd bitch without bothering to reflect: Indonesia, we're really a pathetic nation.

Until you graduated from high school you were convinced you could escape the prison of mediocrity. You studied hard, you scrimped and saved. You imagined that every now and then you'd go to Singapore, just like the elite kids. Yes, of course, Singapore. Your imagination got stuck there. Japan? Too expensive. Cambodia? Inconceivable. America only existed on TV.

You latched on to the illusion that you weren't common when you became quiz champion of your elementary school and were selected for a capital-wide competition. Your father and mother were so proud. A dozen years later, as your circle of acquaintances expanded, you discovered that your achievement was in no way remarkable. Several of your friends had been champions and attended top Jakarta high schools, just like you. But their lives were entirely common. The older you were, the more obvious it became that you weren't special. You began to suspect that your failure to transcend mediocrity stemmed from a wrong turn in your life, when you didn't get into a top state university.

1998: your final year of high school. Students demonstrated, clamouring for Suharto to step down. Political turmoil set the country aflame, but you faced a different upheaval: your parents were moving back to Jogja. The financial crisis had spawned mass lay-offs, and your father did not escape. You didn't want to leave with them, so you studied desperately in order to be accepted to the University of Indonesia. Though hardly wealthy, you couldn't envision a life without the blessing of trips to Plaza Indonesia and Pondok Indah Mall, those monuments that defined the meaning of 1990s modernity. Our high school conceptions of cool really can be pathetic.

You applied for programmes in international relations and English literature. Your father and mother had studied engineering and didn't value the social sciences or humanities, but at your cram school you'd heard that graduates in those fields often found jobs in the Department of Foreign Affairs. You dreamed of becoming a diplomat so you could travel; your father supported the decision because it sounded impressive. International: global, not provincial. English literature, on the other hand … 'English' sounded important, just like 'international', but 'literature' made him uneasy. He didn't want his daughter to turn into some dreadlocked poet declaiming at Taman Ismail Marzuki. Mother defended you. She was convinced you could become an English teacher, or open your own school.

'It's a good choice,' she said. 'It'll give you options when you have a kid.'

In the end, Father agreed. But he also thought that someone with a certificate from the Juliana Jaya Sewing Academy could open a school just as easily.

Some friends, no smarter than you, passed the entrance exam. When you learned that you hadn't been successful, your mother held you tight and comforted you. 'Lots of smart kids don't get into UI.' Her sweet words did nothing to make you feel better. Even today when you think about your failure, you obsess over the details in your head: had you been careless in working through the questions? Had your exam sheet become so damp with sweat that your answers were illegible? Were you so overconfident that your responses were reckless? What hurt the most was that your older sister had been accepted to the prestigious Bandung Institute of Technology. She was one of a select few women who – to borrow your father's words – 'broke into engineering at Bandung'. Unstated, of course, was his assumption that mechanical engineering would prove too difficult for the female brain to grasp.

Instead, you ended up at an expensive private university and majored in Teaching English as a Second Language. Your father sold off inherited land to cover your tuition.

No miracle arrived to rescue you. Some of your friends continued their studies abroad, but your family wasn't rich. You taught at EGW, English for the Global World, a prominent language institute in Jakarta. You didn't open your own school, as your mother had hoped, but at least you brought home a decent pay cheque. Every year you applied for scholarships; every year you were knocked back. You could only look on enviously when Abidah, a fellow teacher, announced that she'd won a scholarship to Kangaroo Country (or, as you called it, Kylie Minogue Country). You'd never spoken to Abidah, but you couldn't restrain yourself when you ran into her straightening her hijab in the ladies' room.

'Hey, do you have any tips on winning a scholarship?'

She looked at you sympathetically.

'Strive and seek. Yes, sister,' she said, '*man jadda wajada*. Inshallah.'

Abidah truly was successful, at least within fixed parameters. When she returned from Australia she wrote a book called *Follow Your Dreams*, which achieved minor renown. She focused on *pesantren* students who made their way to overseas universities by repeating the mantra *man jadda wajada*: the earnest will succeed. The bountiful love of Allah, however, evidently extended only to the earnest, not the envious.

To add spice to your life you looked for a lover, but the guys you dated were all losers. You wanted a boyfriend like Marcus Werner, an English teacher and manager at EGW. You didn't get why everyone called him a 'native speaker', like the instructors from America and England, given that he was from Germany. All the female teachers angled for his attention, either because of his blue-eyed good looks or because of his expat status, which meant he earned much more than local staff. Later you and your friends learned he was dating a former student. One gossipy colleague couldn't hold her tongue. 'Now, that's one damn lucky chick. She didn't even pass basic-level English but she managed to rope herself an expat.'

After failing to snag a handsome expat of your own, you scouted other available options. From a trash heap composed of men in professions ranging from civil servant to Internet cafe proprietor, you eventually found one whose eccentricities set him apart. Yudi, a philosopher, or rather a wannabe philosopher, read books and name-dropped thinkers and artists unknown to you. At first you found this appealing, but before long you realised that his only ambition was having time to read and write. He was a little younger than you and, despite seven years of study, he hadn't graduated from university. After a quarrel with his parents, he refused to accept any more money from them and began to borrow from you instead. In time, he ended up staying with you in your boarding house, polishing off your bread and milk, and slipping packs of *kretek* into your shopping basket even though you didn't smoke. He quoted Marx, and in his company you felt exploited enough to have discovered your own personal form of Marxist alienation. You had to rise up and revolt.

The next stage of development after that Marxist's exploitation was, naturally, socialising. You hung out with friends and went about life without a boyfriend. But you were soon complaining once more about the monotony of your boarding-house existence. A tedious story, and it was yours.

You didn't know what you wanted, apart from not wanting to be yourself. You didn't want to live like your friends, your boss or your sister. Especially your sister. Immediately after finishing her degree she married a fellow graduate and became involved in a Muslimah fashion business (bye-bye, mechanical engineering!). Maybe there was nothing wrong with your sister.

Her husband held a good job with a multinational automobile corporation, and they had a mortgage, a car and a pair of sweet kids. The older, a girl, is named Nazwa Salsabila Azzahra. You keep forgetting her son's name. Naufal? Or is it Raihan? But you always remember the name Nazwa, at any rate. Maybe it should have been Nazwa Fatima Zakiyya. Or Nazwa Syifa Arrahma. Whatever. Such are kids' names in contemporary Indonesia.

Your sister looked happy, but you didn't want her life. There was no one you knew whose life you aspired to. You had lost interest in becoming a diplomat.

You wanted adventure.

'We're here.'

You gawk.

'Here's the terminal, ma'am.'

Ma'am? Why does he call you ma'am? Do you look old or something? You're not even twenty-eight yet.

The taxi driver pulls over without turning off the engine and hurries to open the door. His agile movements make you realise that you have no time to dawdle and daydream. Your past is too cumbersome to schlep around. Bye-bye, past, you say quietly. Happy rotting in hell.

You tip the driver. You don't know if two dollars is too little or too much, but you hope it's enough to show your gratitude for being shuttled to the airport in time. The driver says curtly: 'OK, thanks, have a good trip.'

As you drag your suitcase towards the doors of the terminal, you sense something odd, something amiss. You glance down. You're wearing black stockings and a red shoe given to you by Demon Lover. A single red shoe.

Shit. Did you leave the other one in the taxi? Impossible. It couldn't come off that easily.

Please don't let it be back in Indonesia.

You feel weak as you struggle to recall where you left the shoe.

Do you want to find out where you left it and what happened to you in New York? You might have to cancel your ticket and go back to the city (New York, not Jakarta). Maybe you should go to the police station and report the loss first, because who knows? Your shoe could be in the cab and the driver may be kind enough to turn it in. Or maybe you need to accept that Demon Lover was telling the truth. Sometimes we forget how we came to be where we are. Maybe you just need to keep walking with the one remaining shoe. No need to feel too regretful. You can always pick up a new pair in duty-free.

If you want to cancel your trip and return to your home (wherever that may be) in New York, turn to the next page.

If you want to report your loss to the police, turn to page 25.

If you want to continue your journey to Berlin, turn to page 29.

You're waiting at Sutphin Boulevard Station, which you've finally located after asking umpteen people and passing several shops. You took the opportunity to stop in at one for a pair of shoes. The store looked tacky and sold cheap merchandise. No big deal. Once you get downtown, you can shop till you drop.

The station, cold and gloomy, is packed with commuters waiting for trains. Some who are toting suitcases or large backpacks may well be like you, recent escapees from JFK. Everything rushes past in a blur, and you realise that you're staring. Standing there feeling drained, beside your own suitcase, you notice muddy subway tracks and walls tiled in a dull white, splotched with brown. A rat darts along the rails and disappears into the darkness. There's another one. It sniffs intently at the garbage, damp from a filthy puddle, then dashes after its companion. The pair of rats may be playing a little game of rodent tag. You observe with disgust. You try to turn in the other direction, but as far as the eye can see, there is only filth. Sticky black stains coat the platform. On closer inspection they turn out to be wads of chewing gum encrusted with layers of grime.

Your legs are exhausted but you can't sit: a homeless man, bundled in a thick jacket and sound asleep, has laid sole claim to the nearest bench.

The E train finally arrives. You drag your suitcase into a carriage and take a seat. This carriage, in contrast to the others, is quiet. Crumbs of food and newspapers are strewn across the floor. Your fellow passengers consist of a lone young woman, and a man who is snoozing away. Strange city. In the morning, most people are rushing about, but one or two resist the tide of activity and slumber on. You sit by the door. Before five minutes pass, the young woman gets up and strides quickly to another carriage, covering her nose with a tissue. A pungent stench wafts from the dozing man. You want to switch cars as well, but moving your suitcase would be too much hassle.

New York City is not as glamorous as you'd believed.

You exit at Jackson Heights–Roosevelt Avenue Station in Queens and are met by milling throngs of people. Their faces suggest East and South Asia, as well as Latin America, though nobody you've seen so far would be mistaken for Antonio Banderas. Street vendors sell shawls and wallets, reminding you of the maze that is Jakarta's Tanah Abang market. A truck emblazoned with the word 'tacos' is parked next to a loud middle-aged woman hawking her wares: 'Tamales, tamales!'

How is it that New York resembles a Third World city? You walk by small shops with signboards in various fonts: Ecuador Notaria, Foto y Video Digital, Compro Oro. You can only guess at what they mean. At a corner, you turn and pass a grocery store, a vendor selling colourful saris, and an Indian restaurant. You revise your earlier thought: New York is a mini-version of the world. After your long walk, perfumed by a chaotic jumble of smells, from meat and onions to burning incense, you end up in front of an old brownstone apartment building – yours.

You give the sturdy glass door a push and find a faded, white-lit lobby, its floor carpeted in tones of dull brown. On your left, a man smiles and offers a good morning greeting. He appears to be the building's doorman. Not far from him, a woman sits on a fraying beige sofa, dull as the carpet. She wears sunglasses and a long red coat, and seems to be staring straight at you. You pretend not to notice. You walk, a little hesitantly, towards the elevator. Suddenly she calls after you.

'Hello, Cinderella. Lose this?'

Her voice is soft but in the quiet of the lobby it rings out like the clang of a bell. You turn to her. She rises from the sofa and walks towards you. Her right hand clutches a chihuahua; her left holds a sparkly red shoe.

'Very nice.' She surveys the shoe with something akin to awe before giving it to you.

You nervously thank her.

'How did –'

'I found it in the lobby this morning,' she says. 'Take good care of it. You might not get it back if you lose it again.'

She pats your shoulder, smiles, then turns and heads for the door. All sorts of questions leap up in your mind. How did your shoe come loose? How did the woman find it? Does she live here?

You enter the elevator and press the button for the eighth floor. Your apartment is a one-bedroom, complete with a tidy cooking area, a small dining table with two chairs, and a futon facing a television. Not bad. You peer in at the bathroom with its matching orange carpet and curtains.

Not bad at all.

You open the door to your bedroom. The mid-sized bed, covered with a crumpled blanket, looks a mess. You open the wardrobe, and find some jackets and dresses hanging there. This is your home. How strange to think of a home. You can't remember living here, but the apartment is filled with items that you assume are yours.

You fling yourself onto the bed. It's ten in the morning, but you feel drowsy. Your eyelids are heavy, and there is nothing to hold you back from sleep. You are tempted to imagine that, as has happened in the past, you will open your eyes elsewhere.

Turn to page 35.

The Wizard of Oz

The main character in *The Wizard of Oz*, as we know so well, is not in fact the wizard, who is actually from Omaha, but a sweet girl who wishes to escape her tiny Kansas town. Aside from its occasional tornadoes, Kansas really isn't such a bad place; you can be content to farm, to raise livestock, to keep house there. In your spare time, you can visit your neighbours or sing with the local fellas. As long as your pup doesn't nip the meanest old maid in the neighbourhood, you can live in peace. But the girl, Dorothy, isn't happy. Our Dorothy is played by a pigtailed Judy Garland. She gazes longingly at a point off-camera, past us, the audience, to a place far away, somewhere over the rainbow.

One day a tornado uproots Dorothy's home and launches it spiralling to Oz, where it lands on an evil witch. We need not imagine how horribly the witch was squashed; we know that she is really most sincerely dead. Nonetheless, her feet remain unsquashed, protruding in a pair of beautiful sparkly shoes. Dear girl that she is, Dorothy certainly had no intention of killing anyone, but she accepts being hailed in this foreign realm as a hero who has toppled a dictator. Though initially hesitant, at the urging of the grateful munchkin masses who surround her, Dorothy dons the slippers that were so recently attached to the witch's corpse.

Dorothy's reasons for insisting on return to Kansas, shot in sepia tones, without a hint of technicolour, don't make a lot of sense. Going home demands disavowal. Nevertheless, Dorothy keeps repeating the mantra, 'There's no place like home,' in order to convince herself of her wish. Her subsequent adventures have nothing domestic about them. Though underage, she wanders in the forest with three men (oh, Uncle Henry and Auntie Em would have a heart attack over that). By the end of the story she has murdered two powerful women, the Wicked Witch of the East, whom she has dispatched through the agency of a random house, and her no less cruel sister, the Wicked Witch of the West. Even if accidentally, she hits upon a method of murder most foul, melting the Wicked Witch of the West until not a trace of her remains. The event is so swift, so apt, so unexpected. As her life ebbs away, the Wicked Witch manages to pose an existential question to Dorothy: 'Who would have thought a good little girl like you could destroy my beautiful wickedness?'

Witches everywhere face a grim fate. But so be it. Oh, what a world, what a world.

Again, Dorothy has no idea how she can get home, or anywhere. In a court of justice, beyond the realm of Oz, she might win her freedom on the grounds of temporary insanity.

Dorothy wants to go home, since going home is a shortcut for bringing turmoil to an end. But let us never forget! The shoes shimmering on her feet are inherited from a dead woman. The wizened faces of elder and younger sister witch haunt every step of the sweet girl who believes she can return home but whose legs have been cursed to walk forever. There is no end for witches, as we know: good girls go to heaven, bad girls go wandering.

Return to the page that took you to this story.

Malin Kundang, Faithless Child

Your ancestors were sailors.

Travel is the most ancient human desire, and, being a traveller, Malin Kundang had fidelity issues.

Can there be a fate worse than being turned into stone and set in the soil, forever remembered by schoolkids as a faithless child? Little Malin Kundang did not foresee his future, back then, back when he lived alone with his mother and enjoyed small pleasures like fishing and breathing deep the salty sea air.

When Malin Kundang grew older, a wealthy merchant invited the lad to sail off with him on his ship. Years later, Malin Kundang returned to his village with a magnificent vessel of his own, filled with valuable cargo, a crew and a beautiful wife. And though he had indeed returned, home was no longer the same. Nor was Malin Kundang the same. He claimed not to recognise his impoverished mother. Desperately hurt, she uttered a curse to turn him to stone.

At least that's the usual version of the story.

But Malin Kundang was more than faithless: he was treacherous. Loutish. Before his first voyage he'd had a lover he wished to marry. But in the middle of his journey – and it's a given that travel always changes someone – he met another woman. Malin Kundang thought she was more beautiful than any woman he had ever seen. Absurd as it may sound, he considered her very cosmopolitan. Later he discovered that this woman was a pirate. She stormed the seas and stole that which you cherished most.

Malin Kundang had a habit of abandoning others for something, or someone, new. Every encounter served as a bridge leading elsewhere, and Malin Kundang was addicted to making his way across to the other side. In the end, he left the kind, rich merchant for a more thrilling life with the Pirate Queen, even though all the villagers had believed he would return and bring them prosperity. But Malin Kundang never wanted to be home for long. If he hadn't turned to stone, he would have realised his dream to travel around the world.

When his ship dropped anchor, Malin Kundang knew one thing: his old village was no longer large enough to accommodate his longings. He felt pain. Although he hoped to bring along the whole village on his voyages, he wasn't Noah.

Every adventure demands betrayal.

Malin Kundang is now frozen and mute. He has returned, and, letting the days go by, he no longer goes a-wandering like an innocent, sweet child. Every night he thirsts for the waves, to go into the blue again. He even longs for seasickness.

You see? How difficult it is to speak of roots, of soil, and of oaths when your ancestors were sailors.

Haul up the anchor! Choose your own betrayal!

Return to the page that took you to this story.

You're determined to find the nearest police station and report your missing shoe. Who knows what you'll do in Berlin, but you can hardly go abroad if you've lost one of your magic slippers. After all, enchanted footwear is a lot harder to come by than a plane ticket. You search for hints of what to do and at last spot a sign that reads 'AirTrain'. Fine. You'll take your suitcase onto the AirTrain and find a police station.

The doors of the train open, and you board along with others who are shouldering backpacks and carrying large bags. Beside you sits a middle-aged woman. She looks friendly enough, so you address her.

'Where's the nearest police station?' she says, repeating your question back to you.

'Yes, I lost a shoe,' you say.

She glances at your foot, stocking-clad but unshod. Her face conveys sympathy.

'Mercy,' she murmurs. 'I'd just buy a new one if I were you. Was your shoe that special?'

'Oh, yes.' You nod quickly. 'Yes.'

'Actually, there's a lost and found office in every terminal.'

Suddenly you feel stupid. Lost and found. Of course. Why did you go looking for a police station and leave the terminal where the taxi driver had deposited you? You're in too much panic to be able to laugh at yourself.

'Just get out at the next terminal.'

You express your thanks and, as soon as the door opens, you leap off the train.

Turn to the next page.

You're lost. You walk back and forth until you arrive at a building which, with its arched white roof, resembles a beetle. Others pass by, but your surroundings are entirely too lonely. Is this really a terminal? Or a hotel? You won't know until you enter.

In front of you stretches a large hall with a domed ceiling and an alabaster spiral staircase. The design is minimalist, clean and sterile. Sunlight streaming in from rows of glass behind you makes everything sparkle. Not far from the entrance you spy an information desk. An oval noticeboard hanging above it is supposed to list departing flights, but no one appears to be going anywhere. There aren't any attendants at the desk.

Still wheeling your suitcase, you proceed to a room where a row of red velvet sofas and plush crimson carpet offers a stark contrast to the rest of the building. A waiting lounge?

'Welcome to the future.'

A man is sitting alone on one of the sofas. He looks at you and grins. When he gets up, you notice more clearly how tall and slim he is. Could he be a pilot? He wears sunglasses and his hair is neatly combed. This guy needs to go easy on the pomade, you think. He looks sharp in his grey suit, a bit over the top. He reminds you of a movie star from the sixties. Welcome to the future? Well, that's ludicrous, you think. Is this the future or the past?

'How did you get here?'

The man stares at you for a long time without removing his glasses, making you feel slightly flustered. You tell him that you're looking for a manned information counter. It's unlikely that he can help you, as there doesn't appear to be one in this terminal, or whatever it is.

'Don't worry,' he says, to your surprise. 'Come with me.'

You follow with your suitcase, trying to match his quick pace. You arrive at a long hallway with another red carpet. Like a conch shell, a curved white wall obscures what lies ahead. Light is coming from the other end.

'This is like a –'

'Spaceship?'

It's almost as though he reads your mind. Or maybe everyone who comes here says the same thing. Walking the length of the red carpet, you imagine yourself as a glamorous astronaut.

'But this is a terminal, right?'

'Yes. Built in 1962, inspired by visions of outer space. But, of course, you can see that for yourself.'

Then something curious dawns on you. The noticeboard has no departure schedule. There's no trace of backpacks, jackets, or snack crumbs on the velvet sofas. No one is coming or going.

'OK, this was a terminal,' you say. 'But nobody uses it now, right?'

'Oh, some do. Some indeed do use this terminal.'

His words and manner make you uneasy.

'Maybe I should go,' you say.

His face grows tense.

'You can't go alone.' His voice is a half-whisper.

You now find yourselves in front of a door. He glances around. Then, still in a low voice, he adds, 'It's not safe here.'

You don't understand.

He opens the door.

'The room behind this door leads to my ship.'

'Your ship?'

Before you understand what is happening, he pushes you in.

Turn to page 31.

'Hello, Cinderella. Lose this?'

The voice, though gentle, startles you; you're distraught as you search for your shoe. You turn to see a woman standing behind you. She's wearing dark glasses and a red jacket, cut just above her thighs. She is beautiful, at least with sunglasses on. Her right hand clutches a chihuahua; her left holds a sparkly shoe.

'Very nice.' She surveys the shoe, with something akin to awe before handing it over.

You nervously thank her.

'How did –'

'It fell from a taxi,' she says, as if reading your mind. 'Be careful not to miss your plane, gorgeous.'

She pats your shoulder, smiles, then walks past you.

You hurry to put the slipper back on. All sorts of questions leap up in your mind. How did your shoe come loose? How did the woman find it?

It sets in slowly just how stunning she is. Where did she get that red coat? You want one just like it.

You'd like to keep studying her, but you have no time. Wheeling your suitcase as fast as you can, you enter the terminal and scan for airlines that fly to Berlin. You're in such a panic that you run smack into a man.

'I'm so sorry!' you cry as you tumble. The contents of your handbag spill on the floor.

The man you collided with helps you up.

'Are you all right?'

You nod. The man smiles and kneels to help you collect your things. His hair is completely white. Always respect the elderly. Such was the injunction of your father, your mother and your teachers at school. You feel guilty seeing him stoop.

'Thanks. I'm so sorry,' you repeat over and over.

After an anxious and lengthy wait in the queue, you arrive at the check-in desk and hand over your ticket and passport. The employee examines both, and her eyebrows furrow.

'This isn't your passport.'

'What?'

The employee shows you the photo. A man. Dismayed, you explain that you have no idea how you wound up with someone else's passport. The employee shakes her head impatiently.

All of a sudden, a voice: 'Sorry, that's mine!'

The white-haired man waves your green passport. You approach him.

'Mixed them up.' He smiles.

You return the smile, hoping you've had your last shock for this first day of your red shoes adventure.

Turn to page 42.

The Third World Cannot Imagine Outer Space

You are not American. Where are you from?

Are you a traveller as well? I learned a great deal about you all before I journeyed here. Your wanderlust is rather extraordinary. This terminal was built from a desire for travel. To the moon. Yes, it is only a matter of time before you finally go to the moon. You will puff yourselves up with an absurd pride, perhaps even commemorate the occasion with the planting of a flag. So laughably primitive.

Ah, just a moment. Your mother tongue is not stored in my memory. I am tracking your geographic boundaries. Your territory is extensive, but your language appears invalid, I do not have a conversion program for it. My apologies. We will have to communicate in English.

As you can see, I am not of this earth. Think of me as a neighbour. Where I come from, we do not voyage with ancient ideas; we neither colonise nor proselytise. Here, however, everyone is eager to go elsewhere. Paradoxically, you are also fanatical about constructing fences and walls. You have different worlds here – first, second, third – because you believe that each new problem can be solved by applying a name to it. You all wish to travel beyond the outer limits, but you continue to draw those limits. Not everyone can leave, not everyone may enter.

We only journey from home when we encounter a disturbance. I hope we can get along as neighbours, but your behaviour concerns us. Our mission is clear: we come with a warning. Headquarters sent me here because you have truly diabolical notions about technology. We do not use nuclear weapons.

Your information and communication technology is backward, but it is sufficiently developed to spread rumours and cause the occasional hanging of a witch in villages. Are you a communist?

Since you are so primitive, you will destroy one another before long. Yes. Arm apes with bones and the ultimate result is mutual slaughter.

I told you this before, and I do not lie: it is not safe here. There is no hope for the planet. However, we have chosen several specimens to rescue. You are among them. We have to hurry, as my ship will depart soon. Y3A has prepared everything. You will get to know Y3A later. He is eight feet tall and seldom speaks. His eyes shoot lasers that have the power to disintegrate anything in their path. Fear not, however, for he is only in charge of security. You might consider him a policeman.

Ah, those eyes of yours. They convey signs of disbelief. You think I am boasting? Of course, you do not believe me. You come from the Third World. The Third World cannot imagine outer space.

Do you know why science fiction flowered in the First World? Those in the First World dominated technology. They imagined travelling to other galaxies because they could. When this terminal was built, based upon conceptions of outer space, the Third World was distracted by its own problems. There's a term you use to describe your situation. If I am not mistaken, that term is decolonisation.

I will save you, but you cannot travel with your body, for it will be useless on my planet. There is no point in putting you into suspended animation. You would not survive. Therefore, you need to be relieved of your primitive container.

'This will not hurt much.'
No. This guy is sick.

You're trying to remember what happened after he pushed you through the door. He must have knocked you unconscious. When you come to, you find your hands and feet bound. Your mouth is covered with duct tape so you can't interrupt his long diatribe. He is a space alien – at least that is how he understands himself – stuck in the 1960s when this futuristic terminal was in use, before humans landed on the moon, before the Berlin Wall fell and the Soviet Union collapsed. He still speaks of the Cold War even though 2001 has already come and gone.

You have to get out, but walls surround you. White, sterile. There are no cracks, no exit. He adjusts his gloves. Your bound palms break out in a sweat.

'This is merely part of the teleportation process.'

He approaches you and deftly laces his gloved fingers around your neck. You struggle to kick him, but he is too strong.

He wishes to extract you from your corporeal shell so that you can take off, like a rocket.

Ten. Nine. Eight. Seven.

You jerk your body as forcefully as you can. You're enraged. Your adventure must not finish here, so prematurely. You refuse such a stupid ending; you never even wanted a science-fiction adventure. Is he really an alien? Or just a lunatic, a serial killer who believes he saves his victims by transporting their souls to another dimension?

Six. Five. Four.

His lips are so close to your ears. What he says sounds familiar, like a line from a film or something: in space, no one can hear you scream.

Three. Two. One.

You think you catch the sound of a machine, a new beginning, another journey that takes you through the stars. No. That's your own voice, squeaking like a hamster that's been stepped on. You're stunned. There is no air. There is no sound.

Are you floating? What colour is the sky? There are no answers
to your questions.

> *Tell the world*
> *That I have arrived at its edge*

> Subagio Sastrowardoyo,
> 'The First Man in Space'

FINIS

A Single Firefly, A Thousand Rats

The cold-blooded killer puts down the book she is reading. *A Thousand Fireflies in Manhattan*? It's all very well to write about home from far away, but she doesn't share the nostalgia of her compatriot Umar Kayam. After all, she is a cold-blooded killer. So, she crafts her own plot featuring a woman who dies without ever seeing a single firefly.

From her own far-off location in space and time, the killer spies Epon and her strange habits. Yes. At the stroke of midnight, while her husband slumbers, Epon will leave her house and head to the cemetery to see the firefly, for Epon believes that this firefly – a shimmering female who transforms herself to attract a male, only to prey upon him later – appears nowhere else. Of course, Toha, her husband, will grow agitated. In the peaceful, tight-knit village of Cibeurit, women do not roam about in the dark and especially do not visit the cemetery. His wife could be thought a devotee of black magic.

A few nights before a sad event, Toha will ambush Epon as she tiptoes out of the room.

'Where are you going? Why are you creeping around like a mouse?'

Epon, heavily pregnant, will return to bed without seeing the firefly.

Even as her life reaches its end, Epon will never have seen a real firefly. But a tiny baby will be born into the arms of Aunt Icih, a healer and midwife. The baby will be a girl, lovely, as if gifted with gleaming wings. A beautiful firefly, Epon will murmur before she dies. Our killer agrees, although she also has her eye on a firefly in another graveyard.

*

The cold-blooded killer is still skulking around Cibeurit, which remains indistinct and fragmented in her mind. She knows that Toha named his daughter Maimunah, and though nothing connected Maimunah and fireflies, all the villagers agreed that she glowed.

At thirteen, Maimunah began to attract the attention of Cibeurit's young men. Yet many were reluctant to approach her because she was too tall, or at least taller than average for girls of the village. Her childhood friends nicknamed her Longlegs. Single men felt inferior before her, worried about being ridiculed as midgets by jealous rivals. They also worried when imagining Maimunah ten years hence, remembering that the girls of Cibeurit tended to plump up after marriage and their first child. After passing her prime, Maimunah would be a large, tall woman, an amazon. Even now she was imposing.

Feeling no different from other women, Maimunah walked without slouching, her back straight and chest out. Her long wavy hair danced to the swaying of her hips. She always spoke her mind. Toha began to fret because his daughter feared nothing. With her provocative walk, she could be raped by goons on her way home from bathing in the river. Now, none of the lads in this peaceful village were hooligans. But chaos could arrive with transients, like the gangs of criminals who would wander from forest to forest stealing and violating innocent girls before vanishing. The sight of Maimunah's wet tresses was sure to awaken their hunger. And it was the end for a girl if she lost her virginity.

At seventeen, Maimunah grew tired of being the centre of attention. She welcomed her admirers but would soon grow bored with them. They didn't want to know anything about a woman beyond what was to be found inside her bra. Maimunah preferred to spend her time at the house of Aunt Icih, who, in Maimunah's eyes, possessed extraordinary knowledge. Every day Aunt Icih grappled with spreadeagled legs, the darkness of the womb and clots of blood beneath women's sarongs: women living; women dying. From the dukun, Maimunah came to know how her mother had looked before death snatched her away.

'Your mother said you'd be beautiful, like a firefly.'

'Where can I see a firefly?'

'I've never seen one myself, but your mother said a firefly dances in the graveyard.'

History repeated itself. Like Epon, Maimunah went in search of the glowing insect. However, it was not a firefly that she met but Jaja, the cemetery watchman. He rarely showed himself as he was often mocked. He was a little man, no higher than Maimunah's waist, dark-skinned and bald with a bristly moustache. Hair covered his stubby hands. The movements of his tiny body were so nimble that the village children dubbed him a giant rat. The Rat King. The adults forbade their children from making fun of others since that was not the nature of the people of Cibeurit, but none of them were eager to linger with the watchman.

The first time he encountered Maimunah, Jaja simply looked up for a moment from the grave he was digging. He enjoyed his work so much that saliva would collect at the edges of his perpetually open mouth.

'If you become a corpse, you will be just as ugly as me,' Jaja said, wiping the spittle from the corners of his lips.

Perhaps because radiance didn't dazzle Jaja, Maimunah found him more interesting than her peers. It was rotting flesh that enchanted the man, not fresh meat. Whereas Aunt Icih held the secrets of life beneath the stained red of women's sarongs, Jaja knew of all that was destroyed, decayed and porous. He possessed the key to the world of the dead.

Toha soon learned of Maimunah's odd relationship with the graveyard, like her mother before her. His face turned white when a few people reported Maimunah's intimacy with the watchman. That couldn't be allowed. It was time to act decisively for the sake of his beloved daughter's future. Toha offered Maimunah in marriage to Suparna, the village head, as his second wife. In his forties, Suparna owned acres of rice paddies and a jeep. Suparna understood Toha's anxiety and, as befitting a resident of Cibeurit, was prepared to come to the aid of a neighbour; thus, he opened his arms wide to save Maimunah's honour.

The day before her marriage, Maimunah approached Jaja and regarded him with a bitter expression on her face.

'Take me away,' she whispered.

Jaja knew he would never be able to make Maimunah happy and so he murmured: 'I only take away the dead.'

For the sake of peace, the young girl married. She lived in a house big enough to hold both her and Euis, Suparna's first wife. Each week, Suparna spent three nights with Maimunah, while the rest of the week belonged to Euis. Maimunah helped Euis care for her three children in accordance with the traditional ways of Cibeurit women.

The killer is still keeping watch, sipping her drink and refining her plot. A killer's instinct always winkles out the openings into any shelter. She smiles, well aware that when Maimunah was not with Suparna she met Jaja at the cemetery.

Maimunah went out at night, even after she was with child. The villagers caught whiff of her dark affair with the watchman. Several people claimed to have seen a tall woman and a little man entwined in the bushes. The residents of Cibeurit were not prone to gossip, but acts of abomination needed to be dealt with. When Maimunah gave birth to a baby boy, the uproar was inevitable. Aunt Icih, the dukun midwife, offered her praise: 'Handsome.'

But the baby was not handsome. Its body was small, hairy, almost rat-like. The rumours of Maimunah's affair must have been true. Damn it to hell! Suparna punched the wall until his knuckles bled. He gave Maimunah, the sinner, one night to leave his home. How shameful to have a baby that resembled a rodent. A bastard child, no doubt!

The next day, the entire house was awakened by Euis's screams as she found a plague of rats pouring from the room of her husband, who was spending one last night with Maimunah. Hordes of black, slimy animals rushed out between her feet. Hundreds, maybe even a thousand of them, running amok. Maimunah was nowhere to be found. There was only Suparna, dead, in horrific fashion. His flesh had been shredded, as if gnawed on throughout the night. Blood and tufts of fur covered the ulcerations that were his eyes. The rats scurried about.

The predatory rodents quickly spread throughout Cibeurit into the wells, the jars, the stores of rice. The inhabitants had no opportunity to grieve for their village head as, in no time at all, the close-knit, peaceful community was attacked by plague. Corpses lay at every corner. No one was buried because Jaja had vanished, as if sucked up in putrid air or dissolved in a puddle of vomit. Cibeurit was hemmed in by the stench of rats. The stench of disease, of death.

The long-legged woman and her lover were never found. The inhabitants of Cibeurit believed Maimunah had gone off with the Rat King and cursed the village. Those who escaped death formed a pact to forget, and they wandered like a gang of rogues. The kinship ties of Cibeurit dissolved. Aunt Icih, one of the survivors, told this tale to the pregnant mothers who came to her. Destiny's decree allowed her to live and to become the keeper of a secret, though she was never able to answer the question the mothers asked:

'Who sent those man-eating rats?'

Turn to the next page.

You stare at the ceiling, your body rigid, haunted by the image of thousands of rats padding over feet, ready to attain the thighs. Deafening rodent squeaks and the stench of human carcasses surround you.

Two o'clock.

You take quite a while to realise that you are still where you were. You are lying alone. You are in your bed, in your apartment. You are in Jackson Heights, New York. You feel a need to fix your location, to name names. You want to confirm that everything is where it belongs, before you fall asleep.

Just a dream.

Just a dream that causes the corners of your eyes to water. You don't understand why you experience such a story so vividly, a story that is so distant and foreign, so incomprehensible. Isn't it simply a series of fragmented, random images that appeared because you saw rats chasing each other on the subway tracks? But the dream agitates you, maybe because it felt so real, maybe because it made you cry. You aren't sure which.

You don't know who you were in the dream. If dreams allow us to become others, which role was yours? The village girl? The watchman? Or someone else?

Who asked the question at the end of the story? Was it Aunt Icih, or was it you?

If you want to know who sent the killer rats, turn to page 61.

If, on the other hand, you think curiosity could kill cats, turn to page 75.

You're standing in line once more, in the cabin of a plane, waiting to reach your seat. You remain patient even though your progress is delayed by other passengers cramming their bags into the overhead compartments. One man is grumbling loudly enough for you to hear. 'What kind of moron goes against the flow in such a narrow aisle? He's holding everything up. Does he really have to take a piss right now?' You don't understand why the man is so short-tempered. If he can't deal with the inconveniences of a cramped space, he should fly business class. But perhaps he travels a lot and is sick of these petty irritations. You, on the other hand, have scarcely ever been on a plane. For you, this is all part of an exciting adventure.

You make your way slowly to row 32. You have been assigned 32A, next to the window. The seat beside it is empty. But, from 32C, a familiar face smiles up at you. A white-haired gentleman greets you warmly.

'We meet again.'

You apologise as you force him to stand so you can reach your seat. Once settled, you fasten your seat belt and flip through the airline magazine. Before long, the flight attendant announces that the cabin doors have closed and that you will be taking off soon.

The white-haired man turns to you. 'It appears that the passenger between us isn't coming.'

You lift your eyes from the magazine and glance at the vacant seat. You look around, scanning for empty places. The plane is otherwise full.

'Maybe a last-minute cancellation,' you speculate.

'Anything can happen. Maybe he died suddenly.'

You frown. What a horrid supposition.

As if reading your mind, he smiles again and says, 'I'm sorry. I'm not as young as I once was. Anything could happen to me too.'

You regard his face, then counter politely, 'You look very healthy.'

You're not just making small talk: he does look hale, even handsome. You can't guess his age. Seventy? He could stake a claim to fifty. Soon the flight attendant pushes the drinks trolley along. You choose orange juice with ice, and the gentleman next to you asks for water.

'Do you live in New York?' he queries as he lowers his tray table.

You intend to say yes, but then shake your head because you don't know what you were doing in New York before the taxi took you to the airport. You can't very well tell him about Demon Lover and the red shoes that upended your life, so you make up a story about visiting your sister. He nods, and asks where you come from.

'Indonesia. At least, that's what it says on my passport.'

Your answer possibly sounds sarcastic. You're still a bit annoyed with Devil. Visa status: 'exchange visitor'? What the hell does that mean?

He laughs. You don't sound proud to call your country home, he comments, but you don't respond. What should you share with a temporary travel companion? Jakarta's sweltering heat, made all the more oppressive by noise and pollution, your longing for the Orient Express, or one simple word: boredom? And soon you'll be thirty.

'Are you from New York?'

'Call me Muhammad.'

The man – Muhammad – doesn't answer your question. He only says that he hasn't returned home for a long time. His family is scattered around the world and he is currently on his way to Berlin to visit his grandson.

'Now, as far as passports go,' he returns to the previous topic, 'I treat a passport like a marriage certificate, or any other document that's no more than rows of letters and numbers. It doesn't decide who you are, who loves you, or who waits for you.'

You nod in agreement. You don't need an official slip of paper to live happily with someone.

'But we can't just throw a passport in the trash because we feel like it,' he continues. 'A passport ties you down, determines what is possible for you and what's not.'

'And you can throw a spouse away just like that?'

'You know the answer.' He blinks. 'A passport is worse than a marriage certificate. You can choose a husband, but you can't choose where you were born.'

'It's a curse. But at least you can go abroad.'

'Ah, yes, they do say that international borders are more relaxed these days,' he replies. 'But that passport of yours may experience things differently.'

He fumbles in the small backpack at his feet and draws out a box from which he removes a transparent sphere, a snow globe of crystal. Inside you see a miniature cottage, complete with chimney and garden, just like in a fairy tale. Muhammad shakes the little ball, setting a flurry of white particles into motion.

'In a snow globe world, you don't need a passport,' says Muhammad. 'A round little world – all for you.'

'Yes, but it's confined in glass.'

If you lived in a miniature house, you'd probably be jumping around every day, straining to break the glass walls imprisoning you, desperate to escape. But, of course, after that there'd be no snow. How sad. Look, this miniature world is beautiful.

'It was a gift for my grandson. You can take it.'

You decline gently. How could you steal a child's happiness? Like other kids who grow up in the tropics, you've always longed to see snow. You have yet to witness it, but you'd rather wait for the real thing than admire it in a toy.

'I have another one, with the Empire State Building,' he says, half forcing the gift on you. 'He wants something that has more of a New York flavour. Take this one.'

Seeing the sincerity in his face, you take the snow globe. Your fingers make contact with his, dry and cold.

'Thank you.'

You shake the ball and watch the snow flurries inside the glass. The longer the sphere sits in your hand, the more enthralling it becomes.

'Do you like it?'

You nod shyly.

'Do you know the story of Snow Red?'

On planes, we rarely escape a travelling companion who entraps us with tales. You have no choice but to continue on to the next page.

Snow Red

And you all know, security
Is mortals' chiefest enemy.

Macbeth, Act 3, scene 5

On a winter's night, when all your eyes see is an endless blanket of heavy snow draped over cars, houses and withered trees, Snow Red will appear, like a droplet of fresh blood. Cold weather makes those forced to leave home scurry along, all huddled up, but Snow Red, with her cowl, and her long scarlet dress trailing over the ice, stares straight ahead, dragging her feet in slow steps. Sometimes she shows up in the company of a person or two hastening homeward, but not all can perceive her. She only comes to those who long for her, waking the dozing and the dead. So when your time comes, hold your breath and look the other way; pretend you do not see her, and she will pass you by, just as you pay no heed to the minutiae of your own life.

Unless you long for the contrary.

Berlin, 1977. Helga recounted the legend of Snow Red as Ismail, engrossed, sat staring out the window from his desk. It was Ismail's nightly routine, like brushing his teeth. Helga forgot when this ritual had begun, though they had been married just a month. Sometimes Helga felt their marriage had already lasted decades, not because they had come to know each other so well, but because they no longer asked why they had developed certain habits. Perhaps silence was a recipe for happiness. Though Helga understood what had happened, it was never enough. The only thing that could save them was the future.

She threw her arms around her husband from behind and whispered, 'Be careful. You're going to fall for a beautiful woman who likes to roam about in the snow.'

Ismail turned and kissed Helga on the lips. He smiled happily, as if he were being surprised by the arrival of his wife, back from work earlier than expected. But Helga had been home for hours. She'd cleared the table, washed the dishes and changed into her nightgown.

Helga was six when Oma told her the tale of a woman in a red dress who went wandering on snowy nights. Helga remembered Oma as a petite woman with waves of grey hair cropped short, big brown eyes and angular features. Oma was not actually Helga's grandmother, but she asked Helga to call her Oma. At first it was Oma Rachel, and eventually just Oma. She lived next door to Helga with her son and daughter-in-law. They had no children in the house. When she was lonely, Oma would invite Helga over to sample whatever she baked (Helga especially liked cherry pie), and then she would play the piano or sit in her rocking chair, knitting and telling stories. No one could tell stories like Oma. Her brown eyes would grow wider and wider when she came to the suspenseful parts, an invitation to belief. Helga had grandmothers by blood from her father and mother, but now, at forty-two, she only remembered one Oma.

Her memories of Oma were also memories of the woman in the red dress. Helga never tired of the tale and asked to hear the story several times. On each retelling different details emerged. Snow Red, so people had named her, was able to bewitch others until they became lovesick and allowed themselves to be abducted. Those who received the kiss of Snow Red, male or female, would disappear the next day, leaving behind all their possessions and loved ones. The kiss of Snow

Red was the first and last they would receive from her. They said that whoever Snow Red kissed would follow her amid an army of demons, her worshippers. When her long dress swept the ground, it meant Snow Red had marked out her choice. The victim's forehead would be branded with an invisible X, but we do not know at whose bidding: did Snow Red desire her victim, or did her victim desire Snow Red?

Fearing for her own safety, Helga asked: What if Snow Red wants to kidnap me? Don't worry, said Oma, Snow Red does not kidnap children. Helga didn't believe her, but Oma gave her a crystal snow globe. Helga's eyes sparkled. She saw snowflakes land on a little house that reminded her of Hansel and Gretel's gingerbread cottage. 'Take this ball wherever you go. Oma will always pray for you.'

Helga felt calm but then worried about Oma. What if Snow Red kidnapped her?

Oma stroked her head and told Helga not to worry. Oma was happy, so she would not go. Snow Red only came to those who longed for her.

Oma, Oma, promise to hold your breath if she comes.

Helga remembered how tears had welled in her eyes as she spoke. Oma nodded and smiled warmly. But when the world is too big for us, adults often have strange thoughts that we can't fathom. Oma had promised, but still she went away.

'Is Snow Red so extraordinary?' asked Ismail.

Helga was pensive for a moment. She had always thought so in her childhood. Humans able to move other humans must be very strong, and it seemed that Snow Red was beyond human. Now, as an adult, Helga saw there might be more to the tale.

'I think she's the type of woman that wives always fear.'

Helga's calm, sweet observation met with the glimmer of a smile on Ismail's lips, which made them both believe they were being teased by the other.

'Don't worry, she won't be attracted to me,' said Ismail.

What he didn't say was, 'Don't worry, I love only you.'

Helga wasn't surprised. It wasn't because they were now past the age when one burns with love. The only thing in Ismail's mind that smouldered, never charring, was a city. In this city, there were abandoned houses, soldiers brandishing weapons, and a row of trucks filled with anxious adults and children, ready to flee for the border.

Their marriage was an unspoken pact of mutual salvation. Ismail, a year younger than Helga, had fled to Europe when Lebanon became unbearable but, even before the civil war, Lebanon had not been his home. He was a Palestinian refugee. He was treated with sympathy but struggled to find work. With no passport to his name, he roamed far from his home-land like a ghost. But ghosts have no need for a country. They don't have to be driven off the land because their feet don't tread ground; Ismail, however, was a human being, and he needed to carry around his name, a letter of passage, a stamp. He, Ismail Saleh, was a man without a country, *staatenlos*, who had gone to Europe with a *document de voyage* issued in Lebanon.

Helga had roamed from city to city – Paris, Brussels, Amsterdam – only to return to Berlin. She found it more fitting to call herself a refugee than an adventurer, even though she knew she had no right to the term. It was inappropriate. Helga didn't really know what she was taking refuge from. Perhaps all her failed relationships, or perhaps something else that she could not fully grasp. What was clear was her friends' declar-ation that, given all the men who had disappeared from her life, marriage had been a crazy decision. Ismail drifted into her life as so much debris. She didn't know how to save him, nor did she hope Ismail would rescue her. But Helga believed they were bound together by a desperate plan to find shelter in a home.

Helga worked as a librarian, leaving home at eight in the morning and returning at six. Before this, she'd gone through job after job, but this one made her feel a bit useful. Libraries were a pillar of salvation for humankind, a stronghold against oblivion (although of course, thought Helga later, they went up in flames all too easily). Ismail had not yet found a job, so he whiled away his time at home writing poetry – or so he said. Helga had never read any of her husband's compositions. On the kitchen cupboards Helga would attach lists of chores for Ismail: shopping, taking out the rubbish, going to the laundry. Without a list, he lacked initiative to take anything upon himself, but he did complete his duties well.

After work, Helga would collapse on the couch and turn on the television. Sometimes Ismail would make her tea, but he never sat with Helga to keep her company. He refused to watch the news. At 7.30 they had dinner. They didn't have a lot to talk about because as a librarian Helga met few people, and Ismail rarely left the apartment.

'Some more soup, dear?'

Helga never tired of such questions: 'Would you like to eat now, darling?' 'Do you want more?' 'What shall we cook tomorrow?'

At a certain age, we make up our minds to stop being children. For Ismail, that time came when he was twelve, when he and his family were forced to abandon their home. Seeing how sad his mother was, Ismail began training himself to hold back his emotions. He didn't whine if he wanted something and had grown so accomplished in his self-control that, even now, he wouldn't ask for food if he were hungry.

Helga always cleaned her plate. After all, she was a child of the Second World War. Her parents would grow furious if she didn't finish her meal. Out there, they said, many people had no food. So Helga learned to devour everything. To the last bite. She didn't complain – that would have been disrespectful. Even now, Helga felt a need for self-discipline. She had become ever more adept at the art of cooking precisely the right amount to avoid waste.

She was among the fortunate, and Ismail never asked for food when hungry.

One night, when the lights had been turned off and Helga had closed her eyes, she heard Ismail whisper: 'I see her.'

Helga's eyes opened. A question was on her lips, but something prompted her to keep silent and wait.

'From the window. I saw her walking slowly, with a dog at her side. Her red dress was blowing in the wind. The dog was white as snow. And very strange. It had three heads.'

Helga didn't answer, and pretended to be asleep.

That night Helga tried to hide the sound of her shallow breathing. She didn't know if her husband was delusional or joking, but she struggled to cling to facts: Snow Red didn't exist.

She had learned this truth one afternoon, when she had found Oma's house empty. Snow Red had kidnapped Oma and her family, she'd thought. Oma had broken her promise. She hadn't held her breath as Snow Red had passed.

But then the neighbours had told her the truth and Helga had stopped believing in fairy tales: Oma and her family had left on a train. Helga was devastated. If Oma had been kidnapped by Snow Red, she wouldn't have had time to buy a ticket (at six Helga knew that you needed money for the train). Oma must have wanted to leave. Snow Red wasn't real.

Ismail didn't say anything the next day, but from then on, for longer and ever more often, he would stare out the window. Helga had to remind him to move from his desk and get ready for bed. Ismail claimed he was trying to do housework conscientiously, but he kept returning to that same spot, to the corner, as if awaiting a lover. He took to bringing a bottle of whiskey along. Helga remembered how Ismail had stopped drinking when they'd begun dating seriously.

Helga was reading a book in bed, a small lamp by her side, when from his desk Ismail said softly: 'I see her. No, she sees me.'

Ismail had his back to Helga. His head was turned to his right, as if he were bewitched by something outside. Helga put down her book.

'Snow Red,' muttered Ismail.

That was the first time the name had passed Ismail's lips since Helga had told him the legend long ago.

'The woman,' Ismail continued. 'She's standing outside and gazing up. She knows I'm looking at her.'

Helga rose in a huff, and walked towards the window. She peered below, but saw no one.

'You have to stop drinking,' said Helga accusingly.

'I don't know how long she was looking at me,' Ismail babbled, as if not hearing Helga. 'She smiled, then turned away and kept walking.'

'Oh, really? Was she pretty?'

'Very.'

With a venomous look, Helga opened Ismail's desk drawer – *her* desk drawer – and removed a pack of cigarettes. She pulled one out, returned to bed, and broke the promise she'd made a year ago to quit smoking. She found herself oddly jealous. She had never expressed her love even when she'd asked Ismail to live with her, but now she was jealous of a woman whose existence was likely confined to her husband's imagination.

Snow Red officially became a third party in their marriage. 'She' was always between them, sometimes explicitly, sometimes knocking in silence. 'She' was there at dinnertime, when the two of them no longer knew what to chat about, pressing up against the closed doors, darkening the television screen. Now it was Ismail, not Helga, who turned on the television, sitting upright on the couch and searching for his native land in the news.

When she was still a child, Helga envisioned Palestine as Paradise. In a book of Christian tales, she saw a picture of palm trees in a vast expanse of sand. The description of Palestine made her forgive Oma for leaving without saying goodbye. If that's where Oma had gone, she must be happy. Don't we all yearn for Jerusalem?

'Do you know who took over your house?' Helga asked her husband.

A few years ago, Ismail's uncle had visited, and found a Polish family occupying their former home.

They offered his uncle something to drink and were very polite. The baby they had brought from Europe in 1948 had grown into a beautiful woman.

'They're not thieves,' said Ismail. 'Their daughter, Ilana, was very beautiful.'

Ismail faced the television with blank eyes. Helga knew she could leave at any moment without Ismail being conscious of it, but – whether due to foolishness or faithfulness or neither – she chose to remain fixed at her husband's side. Ismail walked to the kitchen cupboard, removed the umpteenth bottle of whiskey, then returned to his desk. 'She', Snow Red, crept from the corner of the room to their bed, and slipped under the covers. Sometimes Helga thought she heard the sound of breathing between them. Slumber had yet to overtake Helga when Ismail, in a fitful sleep, called out a name. Helga couldn't catch it clearly, but delirium made his body tremble. Her husband was dreaming of 'her'. The Other Woman is never so dangerous as when she has a name.

Continue on to the next page.

'And then?'

The white-haired man next to you stretches his arms and yawns. Your question has a slightly demanding tone.

'I'm a little drowsy. I think I need a nap.'

'A nap?'

Your voice rises. You sound like you're protesting.

'What's the matter?' Muhammad laughs. 'Are you afraid I'll die in my sleep?'

You shake your head quickly. Don't be stupid. Your fellow traveller has the right to sleep or to do whatever he wants, of course. He's not obligated to finish his story, and you don't have to pout like a spoiled brat, abandoned while Daddy sleeps. But really, unfinished stories always arouse your curiosity.

'OK, I'll continue my tale.'

'Oh, you don't need –'

'Scheherazade postponed her death by telling stories.'

You're silent. His remark is unpleasant, but you'll have to get used to his dark humour for the next few hours.

You ask again, 'Is your story really true?'

The man beside you smiles enigmatically.

Turn to the next page.

Ingrid and Helga would meet at the library after work. Ingrid was an old friend, born to a devout Catholic family. But about ten years before, she'd announced that she had become an atheist. Ingrid rejected God but she believed in much else that, for Helga, couldn't be proven empirically. That evening she invited Helga along to visit her psychic.

'Ah,' Helga sneered. 'You're so full of contradictions.'

'Your marriage is even more full of contradictions, especially considering we're approaching the Age of Aquarius. Maybe it's because you're a Taurus. Your element is earth. You feel a need to plant your feet firmly on ground.'

Ingrid's fortune-teller was a middle-aged redhead who went by the exotic-sounding name of 'Esmeralda'. Helga knew it certainly wasn't the name she was born with. Esme, so Ingrid addressed her, had started her career by approaching people in the park and admonishing them politely: 'I'm sorry, but I can't help noticing that your aura is very dark.' Esme felt a compulsion to apologise, as if she were sorry to possess knowledge of ill fortune. Then, if the person she approached was keen for advice of a spiritual nature, she would bestow a card upon them with her address and phone number. Ingrid had been one of the recipients. And maybe because the Age of Aquarius was dawning, Esmeralda never lacked for clients.

Helga had often heard about Esmeralda's predictions, but this was her first visit with Ingrid. The room where Esme practised her art was painted dark blue and hung with colourful drapes. She wore a loose white blouse, adorned by a

Tosca-green pebble necklace. Ingrid paid rapt attention as the tarot cards were laid out and as Esme, with a solemn expression, began her reading. Helga heard vague phrases like: 'you need to be careful in making decisions', and 'someone will come along and change your life'.

Of course, those who don't take predictions seriously know such sentences can mean anything.

After making her predictions for Ingrid, Esmeralda turned her gaze towards Helga. Helga steeled herself for an invitation that would begin with something like 'your aura is dark'. But Esmeralda did no such thing. It was Ingrid who prompted Esmeralda to give Helga a tarot reading. Helga didn't refuse. She felt a need for consolation, although in her experience fortune-tellers had never proved consoling. Not believing in prophecy is one thing, but to hear that a bitter future awaits is another.

The cards were dealt. Esmeralda asked Helga to turn several over.

'Something refuses to depart and perhaps cannot be forgiven,' said the soothsayer.

She turned over another card, and continued.

'Crossroads. A choice must be made. Someone will go far.'

'She's certainly moved around a lot,' Ingrid replied. 'Next.'

Esmeralda contemplated the card for a long time, and then looked at Helga.

'This card is important for you,' she said. 'The goddess of the moon. She roams at night. I prefer to call her the goddess of enchanters. Witches pray to her.'

Feeling a bit silly, Helga asked, 'Do you think I look like a witch?'

'I think you're at a crossroads.'

They began to argue about this goddess of bewitchment. Christianity, said Esmeralda, had purged symbols of powerful women and replaced them with new ones. Old women came to be considered evil, bad, and associated with witches. Although Helga was not religious, she was raised by parents who gave her Christian storybooks for children. She no longer read them, but she also refused to believe pagan legends.

'I'm sure you'll meet her before long,' said Esmeralda. 'Hecate.'

The fortune-teller didn't feign an especially dramatic air. However, at that moment, Helga felt her body tense up.

The name, so present and warm, was not unfamiliar to her. She was reminded of the nights she heard Ismail's voice repeating something beside her, almost in a hiss.

At the end of their meeting Esmeralda gave Helga a piece of advice. 'Be nice to the three-headed dog.'

Ingrid and Helga took the train home together from the fortune-teller in silence. Helga had no desire to speak.

On Saturday Helga asked her husband to go shopping. Perhaps a new tablecloth and curtains would liven up their apartment. Ismail looked preoccupied, but Helga kept asking him for his thoughts on what they needed around the house. Ismail picked cheap, low-quality goods over items that would last a long time. His choices disappointed Helga. The mentality of a refugee, she sighed.

Or was her husband preparing to leave her?

Helga tried to remember if Oma had paved the way for her departure by purchasing second-rate furnishings.

Shopping that particular day, however, wasn't too bad. They found a new restaurant in Kreuzberg. That was enough for someone who had low expectations. Helga now understood how couples survived: investing in things that could be done together – like shopping or raising children – to forget their sense of mutual estrangement.

Later, at home and when night fell, Ismail called to Helga softly. His face was pale.

'She wants to kiss me.'

The two of them were watching scenes on TV of truckloads of soldiers and people passing by.

Ismail spoke as if they both had a grasp of the same reality. Helga didn't turn towards him. She refused to believe. She was aware of the madness of her decision to take on a man who'd become human debris. She also understood that Ismail had never been truly sane after he was forced from his homeland. But she was unable to accept this other madness.

'Don't ask me for permission to have an affair,' said Helga. 'It's humiliating.'

If madness had crept into the house, let it be her husband's alone. Helga rose from the couch but Ismail grabbed her by the arm.

'The first kiss,' he said, 'is the last.'

Helga sat back down. She held Ismail and stroked his hair. Her imaginings of Snow Red returned to frighten her. She cursed her own thoughts. Perhaps she had indeed become the sort of silly female who was convinced that another woman – a magnetically attractive woman – wanted to run off with her husband. She shouldn't worry, unless Ismail really was eager to be made off with.

But Helga never knew her husband's true desires.

'What do you want, Ismail?' she whispered.

Ismail did not answer. The question made Helga feel more and more powerless. She thought she knew the answer, but that knowledge was insufficient. Inappropriate.

Ismail fell asleep straight away that night. He didn't talk in his sleep. Helga thought something must have been wrong with the room's heating because she felt cold. Snuggling deeper under the covers, she kept watch over her husband's expression. In stark contrast to the previous nights, Ismail looked calm. Helga sighed out of a mix of relief and fatigue. Little by little her eyes grew heavy then closed.

Helga dreamed she was walking along a snowy pavement with someone else. She was once more a six-year-old who had to look up to see an adult's face. Oma was holding her right hand.

'Are we going to take a train, Oma?' she asked.

Oma stopped and turned to her with a strange smile. She drew Helga's left hand towards her and placed something in it. A snow globe.

A heavy snow was falling. Helga stuck her hands in her coat pockets. That's when she saw her. A red colour, so fresh, crept forth, and then slowly tore away the carpet of white snow. The figure became clearer and clearer. Yes, it was she, Hecate. In a red dress and long cloak trailing behind her, she walked with her dog, that uncanny three-headed beast. Later, when Helga awoke, she would forget what Hecate looked like, and whether she was old or young. She would only remember that in the dream the woman's beauty had been threatening.

Oma was no longer holding little Helga's hand. She had departed with the train, leaving Helga alone. Holding back tears, Helga clutched the snow globe in her pocket. Hecate drew nearer. Helga looked down. The woman stopped right in front of her and remained motionless. Helga forgot to hold her breath. She even tried to steal a glance. Hesitant at first, she gradually grew bolder. Hecate smiled at her. She wanted to say something. Suddenly, from behind Helga, someone ran up and threw himself at Hecate's feet, wrapping himself around her dress. Hecate took off her cloak and covered him with red.

Helga felt she knew him.

The snow was still thick the following morning. A crowd had already gathered when Helga went downstairs. Ismail had thrown himself from the ninth floor, hit a car, and was lying on a carpet of snow that absorbed the red, a red that now seemed muted and dull. The dress of Hecate, in Helga's dream, had blazed scarlet.

Helga didn't extend her lease the winter after Ismail's death. She wandered back and forth from the bedroom to the living room, which was crammed with piles of cardboard boxes, and busily sorted items for removal. She wouldn't keep much. Ismail had left nothing, and Helga donated all her husband's clothes to a charity. When emptying the closet, Helga opened the drawer where she kept her valuables and carefully removed an object. The snow globe.

That evening, the train had taken Oma to Auschwitz. You don't need a ticket to travel on the train of death.

Helga never told Ismail how she, a little six-year-old girl, had been unable to stop her beloved grandmother from boarding a train, just as she could never return the home Ismail had been deprived of. She was only a spectator. She hadn't been expelled from home or forcibly herded away, but she was cursed because she had memories, and the eyes of a witness.

Ismail surrendered himself to Hecate when Helga began to place hope in the future. But Helga couldn't complain, because what she'd done had not been appropriate. Hecate, Snow Red, was the goddess of the crossroads. The goddess of those who have no home. She remains with those who seek refuge, those who are often lost among adventurers and fugitives.

Helga would leave the day after she packed. She gazed at the vast carpet of snow from her window, clutching her crystal globe, praying to Hecate.

Turn to page 67.

May, the cold-blooded killer, has satisfied her appetite for destruction. She closes her small notebook. Yes. Satisfied. Her story is complete.

She parts her long wavy hair, which dances to the swaying of her hips. Her eyes fix on the large crystal globe hanging from the ceiling, at the hundreds of little orangey lights that revolve around it, like planets. A great writer who favours nostalgia over murder would certainly interpret this sparkling as akin to fireflies.

The woman doesn't think she will put the finishing touches on her story in this Chinatown nightclub. She sips her drink again. Like many women of Manhattan, she is partial to cosmopolitans. Vodka, Cointreau, lemon, cranberry. She has always seen herself as a cocktail, a mishmash. Gado-gado is a hodge-podge too, but gado-gado signifies home, a native village, a longed-for place. It doesn't mean a journey.

On a journey, a pack of criminals murders and leaves a trail. It's not easy, when one of your feet becomes ensnared, to search for the other shoe that's been left behind who knows where. May knows that one shoe has been abandoned in the village of Cibeurit, so she finishes off that close-knit, peaceful village before it destroys her. She kills off the place and the memories lovingly, as if slaying Father. In New York City, with the remaining shoe, she survives, like the thieves. Summon up the places of your past, then destroy them! Distant places, indistinct, remembered in fragments.

May's intention to exit the nightclub is stayed by a glittering figure. A firefly? Near her table sits a man with a bushy moustache wearing a gold robe. A sparkling cap covers his head. May squints, trying to convince herself she isn't drunk. The man is no stranger. How short his legs are: dangling, not reaching the floor. May shudders, struck by a flash of realisation.

The little watchman. He has made an appearance in this city, not as a butt of jokes as in Cibeurit but as a petty rajah. The Rat King. May notices that he is holding a staff tipped with a crystal globe like a mirror ball.

May's heart pounds. She thought Cibeurit had been obliterated, but its characters live on, forcing their way into her hiding place. They have found her out. Cleverly, he has disguised himself as a fortune-teller. Though a little afraid, May wants to ask him a question or, more accurately, to demand an answer, as when Maimunah whispered to her lover, 'Tell me what the future holds.'

But the man remains motionless, preoccupied with a martini, and doesn't glance in her direction. May gives the shirt he is wearing a once-over. The words 'Little Johnny' are printed on it. She comes crashing to earth.

She finishes her drink, laughing at herself for believing that remnants of Cibeurit have suddenly appeared in a Manhattan club. What a fool. Everything is wrong. He is Johnny, not Jaja. Swallowing her disappointment, May turns her attention to the crowd on the dance floor. The club-goers cheer when the DJ they've been waiting for mounts the stage. He is also bald, but tall and wears glasses, with a rather creepy smile. The music throbs like the raucous cries of thousands of famished rats. The clubbers pump their arms in the air, entrusting their happiness to the skilled hands of the DJ.

The man next to May disappears. Now Little Johnny is onstage, beside the DJ, dancing with an extremely leggy blonde. May takes a breath, feeling a second slap. Johnny and the statuesque woman are part of tonight's show.

Perhaps Longlegs is his lover. For some reason May is jealous, wondering why she is always the odd one out in a *ménage à trois*.

At that moment May understands that she is a firefly, swirling like a disco light, never touching down. It's time to go. She weaves through the crowd of dancers, looking for the exit. She passes the club's bouncer; some people are still queuing up to hear the bald DJ's set. She wants to run, to rush, to damn the fireflies, to await the attack of plague that obliterates all.

But she is a cold-blooded killer, and she is haunted.

On the Chinatown sidewalk, now growing quiet at one in the morning, something stays her steps. Not a firefly but Little Johnny standing before her, wiping away the spittle at the corners of his lips.

The watchman who only takes away the dead.

In front of the man with the bushy moustache, May stands like a statue. She cannot believe what she hears.

Where have all the rats gone?

Turn to the next page.

Where have all the rats gone?

The little man with the moustache challenges your gaze, his right hand on his hip; his left clutches a wand topped by a miniature mirror ball. You shake your head nervously. Little Johnny looks disappointed and paces back and forth in a rage.

Dreams have led you here, to a Chinatown sidewalk at one in the morning. You took the R train to Lower Manhattan, seeking an answer. Who is the killer who sent packs of rats to destroy the village?

Wait. You didn't take the R train. You took a taxi. No, that's not right. Did you come by train or taxi? Your head is dizzy. You forget how you got here. Maybe everything you're seeing is a dream. Like the nightclub.

A sudden terror descends upon you. The music of the DJ reverberates in your ears. But you can't recall where you were sitting and what drink you ordered. If the nightclub was a dream, why has Little Johnny suddenly appeared before you? Are you also a pawn, like Jaja, Maimunah and all the Cibeurit villagers?

This is too hard, too hard.

Little Johnny grumbles, pacing all the while.

Why are you so spaced out? You're shitfaced, aren't you? Who – ?

You turn to your side, unsure whether he's been speaking to you.

You, my lady, are drunk!

You gape.

Think carefully, Little Johnny says. He taps his temple patronisingly. Give me a proper answer!

In front of you is a spectacular view indeed. You glance at those trooping towards the subway station. Hair of multicoloured hues. Feet in boots, feet in stilettos, all clattering along. Everything looks real. The people hardly seem to be apparitions.

This mean Mr Moustache asks his question one more time, and you shake your head once more. The man looks furious. He stomps his feet and brandishes his wand at you.

Give me a proper answer! he repeats. Where did the rats go?

You take a step back, feeling threatened. Panicking, you answer: They're in the subway station, waiting for you.

Waiting for me? His voice thunders.

He looks left and right, as if seeking traces of the rats.

Then he asks again, more quietly, Waiting for me, or waiting for you?

Little Johnny squints. You don't answer. The night air grows colder. You stand motionless in front of him, for a long time, until at last he withdraws his wand, slowly.

Good girl, he says.

A smile spreads slowly across his face.

Since you're a good girl, I'll give you a gift.

His expression no longer looks fierce, but his words still stun you.

One gift per story.

You study the diminutive man in front of you.

Who are you? Where have we met?

We met on the run. But, hmmmmm, who was on the run? Me or you?

With a handkerchief, he busily polishes his mirror-ball wand as if he's planning to give it to you. Suddenly he laughs, and pulls it back.

Just kidding!

Sorry, no gifts, he says. This belongs to the show. Go look in a Halloween costume shop if you want one.

You're silent. Who'd want such a weird present, anyway?

Little Johnny then beckons you to come close. You do as he wishes, a little hesitant. You bend slightly. He whispers in your ear.

Don't look in the mirror for too long at midnight.

Little Johnny pats you on the hip, then turns around, making you feel as if you've just been harassed, but, then again, he's too short to be able to pat you on the shoulder. You're still bewildered, but he's already waving and walking away. You call out, asking him what he means. Without turning he replies, his voice cheery, almost teasing:

Because you never know whose face will appear.

Proceed to page 76.

The cursed tale is over before the plane lands, but it takes you to Dorotheenstadt Cemetery, where Muhammad has arranged to see you again. At eleven in the morning, there's a chill in the air, but the sun's rays warm your face. You stroll past rows of beautiful tombs and monuments shaded by tall trees. Your jacket brushes against lush golden foliage that will soon fall, as your feet tread piles of leaves in varying states of decay – dead, drooping on the grass, withered brown. Your reason for accepting Muhammad's invitation takes you by surprise. You don't need a tour guide, let alone an elderly one. But he has seduced you, inevitably, with a story.

Maybe you'd like to see the places Snow Red visited, he said.

His voice rang gentle and polite in your ears, combining sincerity and a temptation that promised adventure. You agreed to rendezvous at a gravesite that happens to be near his family's home. He is particularly keen to meet by the tomb of Bertolt Brecht. Finding the playwright's resting place isn't difficult. At the cemetery entrance a plot map shows visitors who is buried where. You recall how before you and Muhammad parted, he had torn a piece of paper out of his notepad and jotted something down. He folded the sheet and gave it to you: in case anything happens, he said. You had put the piece of paper in your jacket pocket, unread.

You've never read or seen a Brecht play, but you've heard about him from your ex-boyfriend, Yudi the Exploitative Marxist. Brecht's name came up once when you were hanging out in your room, listening to the Doors.

'Hey, did you know that Brecht wrote "Alabama Song"?'

'No, I didn't. Hey, how come the chips I bought last night are already gone?'

'I'll get more later. Anyway, about "Alabama Song" …'

Yudi never replaced your chips, but he never missed a chance to show off what he knew. You've forgotten Yudi's lecture about Brecht and Kurt Weill, but the memory of him as a walking encyclopedia of culture remains clear enough. Come to think of it, he was more like a walking Wikipedia of culture than a philosopher. There's no doubt that your relationship with him had its minor benefits. But the day you kicked him out of your room (in the middle of a cup of coffee – your coffee, of course – and smoking a cigarette that you'd coughed up the money for) was one of the most gratifying days of your life. OK, let's just move on. *Show me the way to the next whiskey bar.*

For half an hour you linger by the grave of Brecht and his wife, Helene. Two young men and a woman arrive and regard the tomb solemnly. They chat for a moment, then the woman opens a heavy-looking rucksack and extracts a pair of red boots. She comes over and asks you to photograph the three of them, along with the boots, which she places beside the tomb. The three then depart without taking the boots. Very nice red boots, you think. Why are they leaving them behind? Are they an offering?

Your mother said that making off with grave offerings was tacky, if not exactly taboo. You replied: But my Quran teacher said Muslims aren't allowed to worship graves, it's idolatry. Mother looked shaken to hear your words but quickly nodded. Until she turned forty, your mother didn't really have much grasp of religious matters. Your grandfather kept a kris in the house as a talisman, and only decades later, after your sister protested, did Mother realise that treating the dagger as a spiritual object ran counter to Islam.

Offerings can lead to idolatry, and now here you are, contemplating foul play with footwear. But before you can set your dastardly plan into motion, an elderly couple arrive.

They also want to be immortalised in front of the tomb. As the husband sets down flowers in reverence, the wife scrutinises the boots.

'Honey, look!' She calls to her husband in English.

'Those boots are still in great condition. Why would someone leave them here?'

The husband's question is the same as yours.

'You've gone senile. *Mutter Courage. Mother Courage and her Children.*'

'Ah!' the husband cries out, his memory apparently jogged. 'Devoted fans, I guess.'

You have no idea what they're talking about, but their conversation keeps you from engaging in your petty theft. Red boots and Brecht share a meaningful relationship, whatever it might be, so the boots are best left undisturbed. Besides, you've got your own shoes. Maybe someday another woman will steal the boots from the tomb and refuse to part with them. So be it. That will be another adventure.

Offering free photography service at Brecht's gravesite starts to get tedious. You go around with your camera to snap portraits of other tombs. A lot of famous people are buried here, even if you only recognise a name or two. Hegel, yep. You've heard of him, thanks once more to Yudi.

You make your way back to Brecht's tomb, but Muhammad has yet to arrive. Not coming or not able to come? You're growing restless. At 12.30, you stow your camera in your backpack and get ready to leave. You don't know if it's appropriate to feel anger towards that sweet old man, but let's face it, you're really pissed off. You decide to go back to the hotel and call him. From your pocket you remove the folded slip of paper that, foolishly, you've yet to look at.

There is no phone number. All you see are three bewildering letters:

XXX

You're stunned. XXX? What the hell does that mean? Kisses? Or worse, some sort of dirty joke?

Now you're really angry. Muhammad, for whatever reason, has been unfair to you. Honestly, leaving you waiting for more than an hour without giving you a phone number isn't funny.

As you're busy mentally cursing the old man, out of the corner of your eye you catch someone, or something, flash amid the trees. You turn, but nobody's there. You grow uneasy. All of a sudden you feel you're being watched. There's no reason to feel dread at such a beautiful gravesite on a sunny day, you think. Besides, even if the grave is quiet, you're hardly the sole visitor.

You head for the cemetery gates, trying to act naturally, but a voice startles you. Its source is not especially close. Is Muhammad playing with you? You turn around. Behind you stands a bronze statue of a man of imposing height, dressed in opulent baroque style, complete with waistcoat and knee-length breeches.

'Waiting for a prospective lover, miss?'

You gasp. The statue is solid and mute. Two seconds later you realise that it isn't the statue talking, but a figure hiding behind it.

Devil.

With a sprightly leap he descends to you. The way he's dressed makes it difficult to recognise him. He looks sharp in a black suit, as if he's just come from a funeral. In his right hand he carries a long black umbrella, folded neatly. A round black hat perched above his brow keeps him incognito, until you study his crimson eyes. He doffs his hat elegantly, then greets you with a smile. He looks quite handsome. For a devil, that is.

You didn't suspect that you'd see him again so soon. Too soon. His presence is unwelcome. With no regard for your stand-offishness, he tugs your hand until you have no choice but to follow him. He pushes you up against a century-old marble grave. His skinny frame presses against yours from behind. He grabs your hair and begins to kiss your neck, while his wrinkled hands expose your skirt and stockings. Your heart thumps. You're anxious but aroused as you imagine eyes upon you, eyes of the living and eyes of the dead.

Fifteen minutes later, Devil sits next to you, taking drags on a cigarette as you straighten your dishevelled clothes. Your chest pounds, you feel hot; he can always surprise you, thrill you. You're still panting when he says softly, as if to comfort you, 'Your boyfriend won't be coming.'

He pulls out a folded newspaper from his black coat. He spreads the yellowed print and draws your attention to a small column, seemingly insignificant.

'I don't know German.'

You look at the rows of letters while Devil translates for you a news excerpt about a man who committed suicide by jumping from the ninth floor. You understand only the name and date. Muhammad Ismail Saleh. 1977.

A leaf falls on your hair. Its dull, dry pigments mock you, reminding you of endings. You crumple the leaf.

You gaze into Devil's crimson eyes, seeking answers to questions that are not yet clear. He stares back at you intently, as if wanting to share your grief. You feel a momentary urge to embrace him, but then the look in his eyes grows stranger and stranger. His lips lift a bit, betraying a sneer.

'I don't understand.'

He pats your shoulder. 'There's nothing you need to understand other than that you're not the only haunted wanderer.'

Devil removes something from his pocket and places it in your palm. The Empire State Building snow globe. The crystal globe that Muhammad gave you is still in your backpack. What sits in your hand was intended for Muhammad's grandson.

'I pinched it from the old guy,' Demon Lover confesses.

'Bastard!'

'Don't you want a present?'

'Devil!'

'At your service!'

You slap Devil and claw at his face. You want to pour out all your anger on him, destroy him, murder him again and again. He does not respond. Eventually you grow tired. It's no use hurting him. He was wounded before his fall.

'*Unruhig sitzen wir so, möglichst nahe den Grenzen, wartend des Tags der Rückkehr,*' says Devil, as he dusts the dirty patches from his trousers.

Seeing your confusion, he adds, 'Brecht. "Uneasily we live, close as we can to the border, awaiting our day of return."'

You sob and sob, for who knows how long, like a little girl. You cling tightly to the gift you received from Muhammad's story, or rather, this new gift you rejected that ultimately became yours anyway. After the shoes, now a crystal snow globe. You swear that this is the last time you'll keep a hand-me-down from the dead.

*

Hush, little baby, don't say a word,
Papa's gonna buy you a mockingbird.
And if that mockingbird don't sing,
Papa's gonna buy you a diamond ring.
And if that diamond ring turns brass,
Papa's gonna buy you a looking glass.

You wake, exhausted, alone in your hotel room, and glance at a clock on the wall. Ten in the evening. You've just woken from a long, chaotic dream that you have no desire to piece together. Is what happened at the grave also part of it? You hope so. You reach for the camera next to you, but, alas, what you remember happening not only did happen, it's been digitally archived. The camera holds pictures you took of graves that afternoon, including Bertolt Brecht's.

You ponder the series of events. Demon Lover left you sobbing in the cemetery. After all, he is a devil. Man turns away from God, but Devil must turn away from you before you turn away from him. You stumbled out and wandered aimlessly along Chausseestraße until you finally grew weary and boarded a subway train. Arriving at the hotel, you sat down in front of a computer reserved for guests. In a search engine you typed 'definition XXX'.

Alcoholic beverages.
Pornography; a type of X rating applied to some porno-graphic films.
A warning or danger signal, or symbol for doubt/the unknown.
The code for 'of unspecified nationality'.

You went back to your room, removed your jacket and hurled yourself onto the bed. Your head rang with Muhammad's voice – or Ismail's – and his talk of passports. From inside your bag you took the two snow globes, the gift from Muhammad and the loot from Devil, and shook them both firmly. Look how the lovely snow churns in a raging blizzard. Snow globes fascinate us because we long for worlds that can be contained. You stared at the ceiling of the hotel room, as if waiting for snow to descend. But nothing fell, nothing tumbled, there was nothing but your eyes growing heavy and swollen. You imagined someone comforting you with 'Nina Bobo', the lullaby from your childhood.
Hush, little baby.

After languishing in bed for a while, thirst sets in. Sluggishly, you stir at last and pick up a bottle of water from the table. Your eye catches something curious, a cardboard box, like a parcel sent by mail. You're positive that the box wasn't there before.

Too many surprises. Can one more surprise make today any worse? You take a small pair of scissors and open the package. Beneath layer after layer of newspaper, you discover a hand mirror engraved in silver. A short cord allows it to be hung.

Papa's gonna buy you a looking glass.

A plain white card is affixed to the back of the mirror. You tear it off and read:

If you accept this make-up mirror as a gift from me, hang it behind the door. For everything that comes to you is both mirror and door – you see yourself every time you want to travel on.

Don't you wish to keep viewing yourself while on your journey?

A game of Devil's, again. A gift as well as a curse. But the mirror is very nice.

Everything that comes to you is both mirror and door.

Mirrodoor. Of course.

If you accept Devil's gift, hang the mirror behind the door and turn to page 77.

If you reject it, return the mirror to the box and flip to page 89.

You don't want to know who sent those murderous rats. There's little point in uncovering the secrets of a story from a dream. Will the knowledge change your life – offer a sign, perhaps? You don't care. The red shoes have become yours, and you can damn well choose where you will go in them.

You get out of bed and go to the kitchen. Hungry, you look for something to eat in the fridge, but its contents are depressing – —a half-empty carton of milk already past its expiry date and a bunch of plastic bags that contain wilted vegetables pooling in moisture. Shit. You grab your keys and slip on your shoes, ready to go out in search of fast food.

In the lobby, the doorman smiles at you again. This time you return a friendlier smile. A strange day. Too much has happened. But at the same time you feel you've missed many events. Maybe you're muddled because of the time difference, a jet lag of sorts. After all, the red shoes have escorted you to another continent, even if you didn't arrive by plane.

This is a new day, a new adventure. You, an English teacher who's never visited an English-speaking country, are now in New York. Celebrate!

Proceed to page 79.

Little Johnny's advice rings in your ears as you brush your teeth and see your face reflected in the bathroom mirror. 11.55 p.m. Yesterday was really bizarre. How is it that you ended up on a Chinatown sidewalk, meeting such a mysterious man and asking a nonsensical question about rats? You deposit your toothbrush in a plastic cup on the edge of the sink. Was it yesterday? Or a few hours ago?

You feel light-headed. A jumble of memories come to you at random and then disappear. You cannot trace them. You wash your face with warm water and dry it with a towel. While staring in the mirror, you consider other possibilities. God forbid that Devil slipped you some hallucinogenic drug. You look to see if medicine bottles lurk behind the glass, but discover only moisturising cream and a few vials of perfume.

Maybe the time difference has left you addled, a jet lag of sorts. After all, the red shoes escorted you to another continent, even if you didn't arrive by plane.

11.59. Time is running out. You hurry to turn off the bathroom light and climb into bed. In the end you do take Little Johnny's advice to heart. Don't look in the mirror at midnight for too long.

You never know whose face will appear.

This advice may be useful in the future.

You open your laptop because you don't feel tired and begin to plan the tourist sights you want to visit in New York. You don't fall asleep again until 4 a.m. No doubt about it, you think. This has to be jet lag.

Proceed to page 79.

You take the mirror and hang it by its cord on the coat hook on the hotel-room door. Maybe a spectacular scene will greet you any moment now – a quaking of the floor, a flash of light, billows of white smoke, etc. A few minutes pass. Nothing. You catch your face in the mirror. Your eyes are swollen from crying and oversleep. You look a mess.

You sit back on the bed. The clock shows 10.30. Only half an hour has passed. Time moves so slowly. Feeling cold, you curl up under the covers. Strangely, you feel sleepy even though you've just woken up. Maybe you're still jet-lagged. Your eyes close slowly. In a state between sleep and wakefulness, you imagine you hear the lullaby 'Nina Bobo'.

Hush, little baby, don't say a word,
Papa's gonna buy you a mockingbird.

The chirping of birds wakes you in the morning. With great effort you force your eyes open. The sound seems to be coming from a digital alarm clock beside your bed.

A clock. You don't remember any digital clock in the hotel.

You force yourself up and then sit on the bed, rubbing your eyes repeatedly. Why has your room changed? You're on a different bed, with floral-patterned sheets. You open the window, look out, and conclude that you aren't in a hotel. In fact, chances are you're not even in Berlin. You walk to the wardrobe and discover jackets and dresses that seem to be yours. Opening the door, you find yourself in an apartment fitted out with a small dining table, a futon facing a television, and a tidy kitchen.

You hurriedly don your shoes and dash to the elevator. You're looking for an exit. After walking a few blocks, you see a string of shops with a grocery, an Indian restaurant, and a vendor selling colourful saris. You wonder where you are. It wouldn't be funny at all to abruptly find yourself in Mumbai. You turn and come across a boulevard. Small stores by the side of the road carry signboards with all manner of lettering: Ecuador Notaria, Foto y Digital Video, Compro Oro. Where exactly are you? South Asia? Latin America?

Passing crowds, busy traffic, and a row of street vendors, you arrive at a train station. Now you understand. You have returned to New York. Devil's make-up mirror has brought you back.

Welcome to Jackson Heights, Queens.

Proceed to the next page.

You spend the rest of autumn and early winter in New York indulging in tourist life. Apparently, visa sponsorship from Mirrodoor Cultural Council comes with a $20,000 stipend. You consider yourself fabulously wealthy. You've never seen so much money in your bank account. You believe you should show this windfall the respect it deserves and spend, spend, spend, if only for a short while, the way that Faust celebrated his youth.

Every day you blow cash on seeing the sights. You feel like you're in a musical with a spotlight calling attention to each of your steps, accompanied by the crooning of Frank Sinatra. New York, New York. You want to be a part of it, and you even have just the vagabond shoes for it. And so, on your tourist itinerary you tick off the city's iconic symbols one by one: Times Square, Central Park, the Statue of Liberty, the Empire State Building, various museums (you learn too late that entrance is free every Friday at the Museum of Modern Art – but no biggie, because, hey, you're a rich girl). You ask anyone passing nearby, sometimes fellow tourists, to take your picture so you can capture yourself against different backgrounds: the bright lights of 42nd Street, Brooklyn Bridge, Van Gogh's *Starry Night* and the lions' pen in the Bronx Zoo. Ah, and of course New York is a city of trains, your favourite childhood toy. You take the train anywhere and everywhere: the F to Brooklyn, the C to Harlem, and the G, connecting Brooklyn and Queens. The G train isn't so reliable: sometimes it's there, sometimes it's not, suggesting how it got its name, G for Ghost.

Over time, you feel awkward interrupting others for shots of yourself. In New York, people walk briskly, as if in chase. More than once you stopped in the middle of the road to check the map, and the human flow behind you immediately erupted in irritated tsk-tsking. New Yorkers don't like to relax their pace for anything, whether it's a red light or ambling sightseers. Once you got told off loudly for standing on the left side of an escalator. Later you learned that the city's escalators have slow lanes and passing lanes. Yes, that's the flock you belong to: tourists who drive others crazy, like pigeons. Taking pictures is no easy matter. It's best to ask casual strollers or daydreamers for help. Finally you hit upon a way to memorialise your presence without depending upon the kindness of strangers: you snap pictures of your red shoes all over the city.

Your red-shoe photo shoots create their own narratives. Others pause on the sidewalk to say how beautiful your shoes are. At Times Square a swarm of camera-toting tourists follow suit with their snaps. They take pictures not only of the shoes but of you, the photographer, as you compose your shots in a variety of poses: standing, kneeling, bent over. At Grand Central Station, someone assumes you're working for a fashion magazine. Some ask where you got those fine red shoes.

Oh, I bought them on eBay, you lie.

You grow even prouder of your red shoes, which work their magic on people of all ages. You can vouch for how girls adore their sparkle. In fact, young girls often wear similar shoes. As you're photographing your shoes on a train, a little girl, about eight or so, sticks out her feet. She is wearing glittery red slippers, like yours, but without the high heels. Her mother tries to stop her from bothering you.

'Mommy, Mommy! She has Dorothy shoes too!' The girl tugs her mother's hand.

'Honey, your legs are in the way.'

'It's OK,' you smile.

'Are you a *Wizard of Oz* fan too?' asks the mother.

'You know the story, right?' the girl chimes in.

If you want to read (or reread) about *The Wizard of Oz*, turn to page 21, then come back here.

Have you just returned from page 21?

Fine, let's continue.

Yes, *The Wizard of Oz*. Come to think of it, your shoes do look like the ruby slippers worn by Dorothy, the pigtailed girl played by Judy Garland. As a child you watched *The Wizard of Oz* at the house of a friend from a well-to-do family. Her parents provided her with a decent collection of Western books and movies. You had a VCR at home, but your parents would rent Hong Kong martial arts films and Indonesian horror flicks, not Disney or other American movies. In the home you grew up in, kids were treated as having no voice, no tastes. As far as your parents were concerned, you and your sister had plenty of entertainment in the stack of VHS cassettes: *The Legend of the Condor Heroes* serials, and local B-movies about Sundel Bolong, a ghost who could polish off two hundred satay skewers and a big pot of *soto* without getting fat, thanks to the hole in her back. Only when you visited your friend did you understand that, in a different social class, a kid's tastes could be taken seriously. Your friend's room was filled with Disney cartoons that her parents hadn't just rented but bought. Your friend introduced you to international children's culture: *The Wizard of Oz*, Cinderella, Enid Blyton books, and Barbie dolls from Mattel, not the cheap fakes sold in the morning market.

'Do you want to go to the Emerald City too?' The little girl follows up with another question.

'Hmm, maybe.'

'Don't go back to Kansas. There are tornadoes!'

You and the girl's mother exchange smiles.

'You know, those ruby slippers don't belong to Dorothy,' the girl continues. 'They were the Wicked Witch's. She got killed when the house fell down from the tornado and squished her.'

'Hmm,' you mumble. 'Yes, the witch.'

'OK, OK,' the mother interrupts. 'But your shoes are from Amazon, honey.'

On your camera's viewfinder, the girl's legs are still in the shot. She obviously wants a photo of her little Dorothy slippers with your big Dorothy ones. You're no match for her pleading expression, so you take a picture and show her the result on the display screen. The girl practically jumps with joy.

Turn to the next page.

You're photographing your shoes against the backdrop of the fountain in Washington Square Park when a brunette approaches and asks if you were inspired by the film *Amélie*. She seems to be a tourist; she carries a large backpack and has a French accent. Unprompted, she goes on to relate how the film's protagonist, Amélie Poulain, wants to make her father happy. He had dreamed of travelling the world, so Amélie steals the gnome figurine from his garden and gives it to a flight attendant to take on her travels. She then sends pictures of the gnome, posed at tourist sights, from around the world.

'Are you taking the shoes travelling, like the stewardess took the gnome?'

You're silent for a moment.

'No. The shoes are taking me travelling.'

She laughs, and gives a thumbs up to show her approval.

From the brunette tourist (who turns out to be Belgian, not French), you learn that garden gnome abduction really is a thing all over the world. The modus operandi follows *Amélie*: a gnome is kidnapped, then taken travelling and photographed at famous locations, and the kidnapper sends photos to the owner. There are a number of groups dedicated to this, including the Garden Gnome Liberation Front. Your brow furrows.

'What's the point?'

The brunette explains earnestly: the kidnappers believe that gnomes should roam free in the wild, and not be enslaved in gardens.

These people have pretty weird ideas about freedom, you think. In your country, kidnappers take actual people, not garden gnomes, and the abducted are eliminated without being found. Most of the kidnappers have never been brought to justice.

Maybe in the West the law functions so well that people have time on their hands, you muse. Above all, though, you feel sympathy for those cursed to watch over a garden, whether they have voices or not. Anyone in that situation would long to be stolen away or given red shoes to take them on a journey.

A month after you learn about the garden gnomes, towards Christmas, an email message from your sister catches you off-guard. Its subject header is 'What's Up?' She also sends two other messages, both of which you delete right away. Your sister regularly forwards information from mailing lists she subscribes to. You don't need chain email, and the subject headers don't exactly arouse your desire to read on. The first is titled 'FWD: Mom and Entrepreneur, Why Not?' Your sister may well be a mother and a businesswoman who sells Muslimah fashion, but you aren't. Although she's had impressive career success, you regard her life as stultifying. She started out selling hijabs and clothing made by a small company in Tasikmalaya, and now she's dealing with distributors from Batam and Singapore. The goods in her shop are pricey and getting pricier. She had considered adding a category called 'High End Collection', but her husband quickly nixed that idea. In his words, 'That leads to *riya*. *Astaghfirullah*, let's not encourage ourselves or fellow Muslims to show off.'

The subject header of your sister's next email reads 'FWD: Is it Haram for Muslims to offer Merry Christmas wishes?' You ignore the body of the message; the issue comes up every December. How tedious. Some passionately cite scholars who forbid Christmas greetings, while others quote different authorities to refute them. Your sister takes the middle ground. Her husband, Malay and Muslim, works for a multinational company that has a lot of Chinese Christian employees (yes,

yes, of course they do, since Malays are lazy – you embrace the stereotypes without a second thought). Out of respect for his colleagues, your sister says: 'Merry Christmas for those who celebrate it.' For those who celebrate it. Annoying phrase. To you, the issue isn't even up for debate.

After deleting the email about Christmas greetings, you open a message addressed to you personally.

Hi Dik,
   How are you? We're all fine.

Instead of using your names, you've always called each other Mbak and Dik, Big Sis and Little Sis. You don't like being called Dik. It serves as a constant reminder that she is older and feels like she knows more than you. Even now that you've grown up and gone in entirely different directions, she still calls you Dik. And you haven't stopped calling her Mbak.

Why don't you ever write? Busy with school? Mom and Dad are thrilled you got a scholarship to America, but don't push things too far. Give them a call once in a while. They miss you and don't know how to use email. Oh, I just opened a Facebook account. You use Facebook, right?

Scholarship to America? Is someone spreading ridiculous rumours? You left without a word, but your family believes you're doing something important out there. Are these lies part of a red-shoe gift set from Devil?

I'm really keen to save up and visit. I want to take a picture in front of the Statue of Liberty. But you know how hard it is to get a visa for America these days, let alone with an Arab-sounding name like Abah's. One of Abah's friends has been waiting a couple of months. Alhamdulillah, another friend, managed to get his, but only after being questioned by officials for hours. Is Abah

supposed to change his name to Johnny or something?
Don't blame me if I can't see you. Blame your President
Bush.

'Abah' is your sister's husband. In the mid-1970s his parents,
inspired by boxing great Muhammad Ali, Muslim and American,
named him Muhammad Ali Akbar. Since your sister got married,
she's been calling herself Ummi and her husband Abah. As far
as she's concerned, Abah and Ummi are cooler terms than
humdrum old Papa and Mama.

I'm attaching the latest photo of Nazwa and Raihan.
Have a look! They're posing with this funny old man
statue. I forget his name. We just bought it at a florist's.
He's a cartoon character, right?
  Don't forget to send a picture of yourself at the Statue
of Liberty.

You open the attached photo. The image of your niece and
nephew, smiling like kid TV stars and flanking a figurine of a
chubby little man in a pointy hat, throws you off. A garden
gnome. How did he get to Indonesia, to your sister's house?
  The gnome has a surly expression. He looks like a crude
replica of one of the dwarves in the *Snow White* movie you
saw at your friend's house as a kid. His name is Grumpy, and
grumpy he is. His face radiates clear displeasure. Maybe he
doesn't enjoy watching over your sister's house. Maybe
someday an abductor-activist will rescue him. You're dubious,
though, about the possibility of activists stumbling upon your
sister's house in suburban Jakarta.

'Merry Christmas!'
  The doorman of your building greets you. His voice is
booming and cheery, like Santa Claus. Ho ho ho.
  You smile back sweetly. 'Merry Christmas.'

December 24th. Fresh decorations add life to the lobby. Under a fir tree hung with coloured bulbs, four garden gnomes stand guard. They range in stature from the size of a wine bottle to waist-high. You approach the figurines suspiciously. At the foot of the bottle-sized gnome, you discover a white envelope – and inside it, a Christmas card, highlighted in red and green, bearing the signature 'Demon Lover'. You smile. You don't celebrate Christmas, and you're pretty sure Devil doesn't either. But in New York, Christmas belongs to everyone: believers, agnostics and atheists; department stores (especially Macy's); and, very likely, witches and devils too.

You read the note from Demon Lover on the card.

Darling,

I still can't visit you in New York. Immigration control has been super tight lately, and I think my name is on a blacklist. The problem is I can't answer the questions on the visa application form. Here are some examples:

– Do you have mental or physical disorders that threaten or potentially threaten the safety or well-being of yourself and others?

– Are you a member or representative of a terrorist organisation?

– Do you intend to engage in espionage, sabotage, breach of export control, or any other illegal activity while in the United States?

As you can imagine, it's a real issue for me if I have to answer 'no' to all these questions.

You shake your head. Either Demon Lover has a lousy sense of humour, or he's an idiot to have forgotten that the devil doesn't need an advocate or a visa. You read the next paragraph.

Anyway, never mind. I don't want to burden you with my problems. I've sent you a Christmas present. I think gnome figurines are a hell of a lot more fun than baby Jesuses. Hopefully these four friends will keep a good eye on your building. Christmas is a season for sharing with neighbours, so don't even think of kidnapping one and taking it home.

Your beloved

You put the Christmas card from Demon Lover in your bag. Seriously. It's never been your goal to play rescuer. You leave the gang of four gnomes under the glittering tree and walk on to the elevator. After Christmas is over and the ornaments are stripped from the fir, the gnomes continue their faithful watch over the lobby. No freedom-fighting radicals show any interest in kidnapping them.

Flip to page 92.

Not all of Demon Lover's gifts have to be accepted, or so you decide. He should learn that you too can stage a protest. The next day you leave your hotel, and the package with the mirror, in search of cheaper accommodation. After paying your bill with your own personal demonic debit card, you take the time to check your balance at an ATM. 17,000 euros. You've never had the equivalent in rupiah, but considering that Devil might spring another surprise, you figure you'd better be frugal and prepare for the worst.

Maybe some sightseeing will brighten your trip. You buy a pair of low-heeled boots and put your red shoes in a bag. Devil's shoes aren't really designed for a tourist. Your heels chafe if you wear them too long. Wearing the simpler footwear, you stop at a little market and buy a kebab for lunch. After that you wander around Kottbusser Damm, past small shops sandwiched together, until you finally find yourself standing before an old movie theatre. At the entrance you glance at some flyers about screenings. Maybe watching a movie isn't a bad idea. Impulsively, you climb the stairs and buy a ticket. You join an audience that numbers fifteen at most.

The film you chose haphazardly is slow-paced, and the way it ends leaves you questioning its meaning. Or, to be more accurate, thinking, 'You've got to be kidding.' You didn't really enjoy the movie and even dozed off at one point. Afterwards you rise from the red velvet seat and walk out amid the handful of spectators. They seem to know one another, and may well be friends of the film-maker. You feel out of place. You want to leave quickly, but your steps are slowed in the lobby by a beautiful woman who smiles at you. You feel you've seen her face before. You nod politely and keep walking, but she approaches you.

'Sorry to bother you, but may I ask where you're from?'

You frown. If she were a young man and less attractive, you wouldn't pay her any attention. Such questions tend to come only from lonely guys who can't find themselves a partner (you firmly believe that all the good men are taken). If you say 'Thailand', they're sure to spout some cliché like 'I knew it. Thai women are so beautiful.' But the woman standing before you is too elegant to be compared to a man with zero value on the dating market. Perhaps she has other intentions.

She seems concerned that her question may have offended you, but you answer nonchalantly. She looks more excited.

'I guessed right. My friend is planning to film there.'

She calls a woman with hair dyed dark purple who is ordering a drink at the bar. The woman turns and walks towards you.

'This is my friend Yvette. She's been to Indonesia.'

Yvette's appearance captures your attention. Her cropped hair and bright red lipstick make her look like a beautiful boy, a vague combination of mischievous nymph and mysterious witch. Her movements are hurried, and her brown eyes regard you with curiosity. They have a slight slant. She's wearing a leather jacket and a black tutu skirt. You are taken aback by her shoes. Her legs are clad in knee-high red leather boots that remind you of the ones left at Brecht's grave. Are red boots in fashion?

Yvette greets you warmly and asks your opinion of the movie (good, you lie, trying to hide how much it bored you, since she is a friend of the director). She's involved in a lot of projects, a critic who also programmes film festivals. She has holidayed in Bali and visited Jakarta, where she met several locals involved in film.

In the middle of the conversation, the beautiful woman pardons herself because she has to go home and pick up her dog from her neighbour. Yvette waves goodbye, and you cast a smile her way, wondering where you've seen her before (is she a movie star? You don't even ask her name). Yvette soon invites you for a cup of coffee. You imagine this fairy-witch dancing in her skirt in the jungle. She may be an interesting companion, but you also want to walk alone.

If you're not interested in continuing the conversation over coffee, turn to page 97.

If you'd like to chat more with Yvette, turn to page 98.

The joys of Christmas and New Year pass quickly. It seems like yesterday when you would leave home in a thick coat and boots just to admire Macy's window displays. Mingling with the tourist hordes on 34th Street, you marvelled as Santa's toy train circled a forest blanketed in ice. The bluish glow turned the diminutive scene into a minor window-display miracle. Behind another pane, a fireplace warmed a home inhabited by figurines, beautifully dressed and ready to open Christmas presents. You felt as if you could smell the marshmallows, freshly roasted and dipped in chocolate. Amazing. You had become the Little Match Girl, selling your wares and peering in with envy. But outside, where you stood, was no less festive, and, anyway, unlike the Little Match Girl, you didn't die on your journey of adventures. Under the sparkling city lights, a sea of tourists flowed in and out of stores, laden with shopping bags. Hard-core New Yorkers might have been sick of it all, but not you. Not then.

January is a different story. Your honeymoon with the city has come to an end. No more Frank Sinatra crooning in your head, no more Jakarta blues melting away. In fact, you're freezing. The biting cold makes you reluctant to come and go. You shut yourself in your apartment with a stack of books, and only venture out when you have to buy food. Winter forces you to learn to cook. You're too lazy to deal with three layers of clothing whenever you want a sandwich from Subway or a box of fast-food lo mein. For the first time in your life, you experiment with recipes you find online.

Towards the end of January, the cold becomes even more bitter, and your lethargy reaches breaking point. You start wondering how long you can survive like this. You don't know anyone in New York. The one person that telephones you is old Mr Zhao, your landlord, who has come at the beginning of each month to collect the rent. Under the lease agreement between Mr Zhao and the Mirrodoor Cultural Council, you're responsible for paying him the $900 rent directly. He only accepts cash; no bank transfers or cheques. It makes you wonder if he's dodging tax. Why would a cultural council encourage a black-market rental? The organisation must be shady.

Because Mr Zhao speaks broken English, he brings his son Wei along to translate. On the first visits there's little to discuss besides the rent and maintenance issues. But after you offer them a taste of your home-made rendang (you finally succeed after several failed attempts), they try some small talk.

Wei is a thin, soft-spoken young man with dapper spectacles. He's in the last year of law school at New York University. When introducing Wei, Mr Zhao says the name with pride ('En-wai-yu'), but then shakes his head, his expression slightly pained. He adds in a brief staccato, 'Ek-spen-siv.' Mr Zhao has lived in New York for a couple of decades and owns a few apartments that he rents out, but apparently that's still not enough. He has to take federal loans so Wei can attend NYU. Wei himself works two jobs waiting tables. Mr Zhao utters several animated sentences in Chinese that Wei renders concisely: 'Lots of debt.'

But you've recently come to learn that in this country a job as a lawyer sets you up for life. You're not worried about Wei's ability to pay off his debts. He has a bright future.

Other than Mr Zhao, Wei and the doorman, you rarely meet anyone else in your building. Actually, there are two whom you've never seen but you hear often enough: your next-door neighbours. They are frequently noisy, especially at night. Sometimes you hear grunts, sometimes shrieks.

Once you banged on the wall. The noises stopped immediately.

But before long, the noises started up again, though not as loud as before. Oh, hell. You don't want to think about it.

It's your birthday soon. On February 1, 2008, you'll turn twenty-eight. Your life is still aimless, and growing ever more tedious. It becomes clearer to you that everyone needs a map and a departure point, even if we become traitors to our roots. But where to start? You seem to have a history here, in this city. Maybe you have lived here with another identity, but you remember nothing beyond a series of images of your home town: chaotic Jakarta, ever poised to fall into the abyss but never taking the plunge; your sister, mommy/industrious businesswoman; English for the Global World; Marcus Werner, the dream expat, and a host of loser potential boyfriends. You want to see it all wiped out, like a village annihilated by the plague. Like in the dream about the rats. But shit. You don't speak English in your dreams. When you became an English teacher at EGW, you once told your students: keep practising speaking and listening. The more the better, until all of a sudden one day – poof! – you'll be dreaming in English. Of course, that was idle boasting on your part. The only language you've ever dreamed in is your mother tongue.

You're staring out the window. It's snowing again. You've only seen it fall twice this winter. The first time you were thrilled, because you'd never seen snow before. You ran out and tried to make a snowman, but your fingers went numb. All you could manage were two snowy man clumps. This second snowfall, for some reason, depresses you.

In the whiteness of the morning, as the snow blankets the streets and buildings outside your window, you realise that something in your apartment has changed. A large mirror, even too large, now hangs on the wall, right in front of your bed. It wasn't there before. The mirror has an inlaid silver frame, exquisitely carved, like a mirror you'd expect in a well-to-do home from centuries past. It certainly doesn't go with your modest apartment. You're glad to be able to see yourself from head to toe, but something about the mirror is unnerving. Maybe it's the extravagant size, or its engraved frame, which reminds you of Medusa's hair.

You approach the mirror and examine it carefully. A scrap of paper is attached to its dusty surface.

A message from Devil.

Darling,

Happy 28th. This is my birthday present to you. I know you already have a mirror, but I think you need a bigger one to fully appreciate your beauty. If necessary, I'd give you a mirror several times over, because I adore you, and because every mirror is a door. Have I mentioned this before? Mirrors open doors to secret rooms – inside, outside, or somewhere in between.

This is a magic mirror. It can make you more beautiful. It can also show you who you really are. But the latter can be risky. If you truly want to know who you are, look in the mirror at midnight, and count backwards from ten. Just as an aside, however, I strongly discourage you from doing so. You shouldn't be too critical on a journey.

The message stuns you. If your lover doesn't want you to conduct midnight mirror experiments, he should just keep his damned mouth shut. Humans don't like being told what not to do, and Devil knows this more than anyone. Now you are tempted by danger.

The curvy, carved frame like Medusa's hair catches your eye. You feel there is something sly about the mirror, moving sinuously like a snake, coiling unhappiness around your apartment. Maybe you shouldn't keep it.

If you don't want the mirror in your apartment, turn to page 117.

If you want to know who you are and are willing to experiment, turn to page 151.

You're not interested in chatting with Yvette, or anyone else. You'd prefer to spend time alone and wander through Berlin with a guidebook in hand. A few weeks later, though, you're bored. It's time to go, but where? You enter a bookstore and see a rack of travel guides. There's 'Amsterdam', and next to it 'Zagreb'. They sound exciting. Maybe you can visit one of them.

If you want to go to Amsterdam, turn to page 204.

If you want to go to Zagreb, turn to page 214.

You and Yvette are in a small cafe. She orders black coffee, and you opt for a cappuccino. At the cash register, she hands over ten euros for both cups. You try to restrain her, but she insists: next time you can treat me. You're slightly amused. This is a random encounter, what kind of next time could there be?

Yvette removes her leather jacket and drapes it over a chair. Her collared shirt reveals broad shoulders and a protruding clavicle. She looks dashing, and her lips are oh so red. The cafe lighting, a tad brighter than the cinema lobby, makes visible the crinkles at the corner of her eyes. Maybe she's thirty-eight, forty, or more? The tutu skirt gives her an impish air. You pour sugar in your coffee and stir. She doesn't add anything to her cup.

The conversation about work continues. Several years ago Yvette became involved in friends' film projects as producer and screenwriter. You listen to her story enviously. As far as you can tell, she works when she wants and goes abroad occasionally. In fact, she's planning to go to Indonesia soon for a second time.

'To make a movie?'

'No, you could call it an early stage of research. Very early.'

You offer little white lies in response to Yvette's questions about yourself. Your biography should be simple, but you also need to hide how boring your life is. In your account, you become an English teacher who has used up her savings for a trip to New York, then Berlin.

Ah, how exciting; an adventure alone. Without a boyfriend?

No boyfriend. You're cagey about your relationship status: it's complicated. Things can be a bit messy when your boyfriend is a devil. Yvette says she always travels alone, sans boyfriend.

I've always thought of Western women as more independent, you say.

Travel is a new luxury for many women, she responds. In eighteenth-century Europe, women were always looking for ways to move on their own. The ones who wandered the streets as they pleased weren't considered good women. Some women wound up on boat tours to see faraway lands, but they tended to come from the upper class.

She looks out the window, observing the passers-by. You do the same. From time to time women in blazers and slick skirts zip past. You ask if in the eighteenth century any women travelled abroad on business. Yes, she says. Missionary business.

You are reminded of Snow Red. One could say she's a traveller too, though she doesn't go on tours. Nobody dares disturb her on the street, and she has very important business: abduction, if not spreading religion. You miss Muhammad. Ismail. Your face must look a little sad. Yvette asks if you're all right.

'Do you know the legend of Snow Red?'

Yvette shakes her head. 'Why do you ask?'

'It's not important. I thought you'd know because you're German.'

'Tell me.'

OK, here it is.

You want to start with the scene of little Helga at Oma Rachel's house, but then you feel you should drop the part about Oma Rachel and how the house was taken away. You don't know where to put it. You're not sure you can do it justice. Maybe you should recount the story of love between husband and wife that ends in tragedy because of a third party. Ah, no. This is no mere love story. They're not even in love with each other.

It's so hard to tell someone else's story, especially someone who narrates his own death.

Finally you choose what you consider to be the simplest path. Snow Red is a legend about a woman in a red dress who walks in the snow. It's said she kidnaps people. But that part is a bit ambiguous. You remember what Muhammad said: we don't know how things start – if Snow Red desires the victim, or the victim desires Snow Red.

Yvette listens intently. I've never heard of such a legend, she says. But maybe older people know it. She leans towards you and her eyes widen as she asks, 'If she comes, would you want to be taken away?'

'But she's not real.'

'You said she comes to those who long for her.'

'I don't know,' you say. 'Would you?'

Yvette has never fantasised about Snow Red, but as a child she imagined being abducted. She hated her life and hoped a kidnapper would rescue her.

'And?'

She grins. Her expression suggests a little girl hiding something. There was no kidnapper, she says. 'Unfortunately. Maybe I wasn't good kidnapping material. So I went and rescued myself.'

You laugh together. Watching the lines at the corners of her eyes, you think: not especially funny, but you're happy to share a laugh with her. She is also someone who wants to be on the move. Is she running away too, the way you escaped from your home town with your red shoes?

You don't want to overstep your bounds with too many questions. You just know that the woman before you is also a wanderer. She talks about the many cities she has visited, then asks about yours.

'Ah, yes, Jakarta. What do you think of Jakarta?'

Raucous. Frenetic. But going nowhere. A city that chugs along as it chokes on traffic.

Who loves Jakarta wholeheartedly? You didn't want to move to Jogja in the late nineties, because for you at the time fun only came from living among skyscrapers and going to the mall. But later you saw Jakarta as your fate, not unlike being Indonesian because you were born there, or being Muslim because it was the only religion you knew from your parents. Leaving Jakarta would have demanded sacrificing energy and emotion that probably wouldn't have amounted to anything. Like a masochistic lover, you couldn't move on. You watched Jakarta change quickly and in increasingly tyrannical ways. The din became your fault. It was you who was wrong for hating the motorbikes that clogged the streets and drove down the sidewalks. Your bourgeois aspirations kept you from empathising with those who rejected the pathetic public transport system but couldn't afford a car. You were wrong for hating the strident calls of the azan from loudspeakers every hundred metres. You should have been grateful for reminders to pray. You were wrong to be sick of cheesy music in the atria of second-class malls and in mini-marts. Everyone should enjoy being entertained while shopping.

Yvette is silent while you talk, but her eyes don't leave yours. All your petty complaints seem to hold meaning for her. Finally, she says, 'Juwita thinks just like you too.'

'Who?'

Juwita Padmadivya, she says.

Cafe conversations often move haphazardly, and it's impossible to map them out. But Juwita Padmadivya is a beginning. She represents a new chapter in both your conversation and your relationship with Yvette.

'Is that her real name?'

You knit your eyebrows when you first hear 'Juwita Padmadivya'. Of course, Yvette doesn't realise that there's a natural question about whether the name is genuine. A good name, overly pretty and a bit pretentious. It sounds more like a stage name than an everyday one. Still, you think of certain names as so common, familiar … banal. Names like Agus

Purwanto, Rizki Perdana, Dewi Utami, Tri Handayani. Sort of like Jane Doe and John Smith. These days, names like Budi and Siti have a classical quality because others, like Nazwa, Raihan and Salwa, have become so popular (you think of your sister's children). Juwita Padmadivya sounds odd. Although Juwita is certainly an Indonesian name, it recalls an earlier era, from the fifties when your grandmother was young, the days of singer Sam Saimun, who sounded like Nat King Cole.

I dub thee Juwita Malam. Juwita Night.

Juwita was a traveller but then decided to go back home. She was born in Indonesia and finished her education in America. She had worked there, before returning and making a film, her first and last work in Indonesia. At home and on the road, she was a stranger.

'I don't expect you to know Juwita,' Yvette says. 'She's a film-maker.'

'Sorry. I don't watch a lot of Indonesian movies.'

'I deal with lots of film people, and none of them know Juwita either.'

Through festival connections, Yvette had managed to meet some programmers and film-makers in Jakarta. Not many, but they seemed important enough in their respective fields. None of them knew Juwita.

'When was the last time you saw her?'

'I've never met her,' she answers. 'I'm looking for her.'

You pause, trying to understand Yvette's connection to this woman. Juwita is like a mysterious guest who knocks politely on the door, slides into a seat at your table, and before you know it, has taken control of the conversation.

Yvette's eyes are fixed on her coffee, now almost empty. You wait.

Next you learn that Juwita is a mystery. Yvette came across her in an odd way. Two years earlier, she had received a package with American postage from a Juwita Padmadivya, with a Connecticut address. Inside was a DVD without a cover. Yvette received many films for her festivals, but this package bewildered her, because it contained none of the information that should have come with it. She assumed that the film-maker had been in such a rush that she had forgotten to include it. Instead of the entry form, the sender had inserted a stack of printed email messages, written by Juwita Padmadivya to someone named Nadya Shafik.

'What did you do with the movie?'

'Nothing. I've just held on to it. I can't screen it because there's no signed release form.'

'Is it good?'

Yvette appears to hesitate. She glances at her watch and remembers that she is supposed to meet someone at seven o'clock.

'Shall we get together again tomorrow?'

You nod without giving it much thought. In this town you have no job, and you are keen to buy Yvette coffee in return. Maybe you just want to see her again. In front of the cafe, before you part, you finally say, 'I like your shoes.'

'Thank you.' She seems pleased by your compliment. 'I have a special bond with red shoes.'

Her words startle you. Me too, you want to say, but you restrain yourself. Anyway, you've left your red devil shoes at the hotel. Yvette waves and goes in the opposite direction. Before long you look back, stealing a glance at her purple hair, her sashaying black tutu skirt, and her galloping red boots. Where is this nymph enchantress going? Perhaps she lives in a tiny cottage in a forest full of wolves.

Turn to the next page.

Museums

Hi Dik,

How are you? We're all fine. Why don't you ever write? Busy with school? Mom and Dad are thrilled you got a scholarship to America, but don't push things too far. Give them a call once in a while. They miss you and don't know how to use email. Oh, I just opened a Facebook account. You use Facebook, right?

Steeling yourself, you finally read the email from your sister. Your family seems to think you've gone abroad to study. Who knows where they got that idea. There's a blank space in your head. You can't remember anything, that is, anything after when you put on the red shoes in your room and before you found yourself in the taxi heading towards JFK. How long was that in-between moment in space and time? Maybe it was the blink of an eye, or maybe it was also like a waiting room made of elastic. Inside that space you were able to say goodbye to your parents, as well as your sister and her children. Maybe your relatives came out in droves, like a carnival troupe, to see you off at hot and stuffy Soekarno Hatta Airport.

In-between moments. In fact you've often experienced them in situations that are hardly mystical. You never remember how you spent daytime during Ramadan. All you can recall is waking, grouchy, dazed and drowsy, for the pre-dawn meal and then the joy spreading inside you when you broke the fast in the evening: the aroma of coconut milk and brown sugar mixed into the dessert compote with its chill of iced fruits. In between, nothing stuck. Midday during fasting month was a time of waiting, a time in between, and so a time forgotten.

Are you planning to come to Indonesia for vacation this year? If so, I'd like you to pick up some goods for my store. OK, Dik? There are a few brands of bags and shoes that are hard to get from Singapore, and I've got some loyal customers who are incredibly picky. They're only after designer originals and won't buy knock-offs. If Dior made hijabs, they'd be the first to refuse fake Dior hijabs.

You skip the next few paragraphs because you're not interested in the details of your sister's Muslim clothing business. The way it has developed is actually pretty amazing, though. She started by selling headscarves and clothes more cheaply than the mall, and once her customer base grew, she branched out into other items: purses, bags and shoes. A year later she started dealing with distributors from Batam and Singapore, and little by little brought in more expensive goods. She thought about adding a 'High End Collection' to her catalogue, but her husband warned her that doing so could lead to *riya*: '*Astaghfirullah*, let's not encourage ourselves or fellow Muslims to show off.'

Not once have you and your sister called each other by your first names. Only Mbak and Dik, Big Sis and Little Sis. You were always treated as a unit. She's two years older than you, but your mom always bought you the same clothes until you were in middle school. Mom didn't want the bother. You grew up as very different people. At first, you're sure, this difference revealed itself in your musical tastes. She remained mired in the mainstream, while grunge tugged you to another world. Yes, your sister, devoted to Celine Dion, and you, the Nirvana fan – her heart would go on and on, but you always had a new complaint. In your parents' eyes you remained sisters who should always be together, everywhere. You hated it when she called you Dik. She always reminded you that she was older, that she knew more than you. But strangely, you've never been able to call her anything but Mbak.

Last week Nazwa went to the Wayang Museum with her school friends from Lentera Iman Elementary School. The museum collection is supposed to be quite good, but unfortunately not well maintained. Here's a picture of Nazwa for you.

You open the attachment and glance at your niece posing with some other children in front of the museum. Ah, kids in school uniform. Why do they look all the same?

You know, the teachers were going to tour Lubang Buaya. Can you imagine, like in the days of Suharto? I was the first to protest. I don't want pictures of torture leaving my child in tears.

The Sacred Pancasila Monument at Lubang Buaya, the 'Crocodile Pit'. You shudder at the name. When you were little, every schoolkid in Jakarta visited. The pit is where they discovered the corpses of the generals, the victims of the outrage committed by the PKI, the Partai Komunis Indonesia. Or so your teacher explained in the voice of a documentary narrator. You and your friends took diligent notes to make a report on your field trip. At least, it was called a field trip, although the term dark tourism would have been more appropriate. Black tourism for babes. The visit served as a warning to ten-year-old pupils that they could become helpless chicks at any moment; their fathers could be murdered and thrown into a pit.

So, don't let the communists rise again.

Sometimes you felt no need to listen to Teacher, as you'd memorised the contents of your history book word for word: the PKI masterminded a coup by kidnapping, torturing and murdering six generals on September 30, 1965. But General Suharto crushed this attempted insurrection and saved the nation from the communist threat. These events were relived in books, monuments, and the docudrama *Treason of the September 30 Movement*, which was shown on television every year. Under the New Order, the PKI rebellion was turned into an extravaganza of multi-media infotainment. Years later, you know that the whole narrative served as a tool to legitimise the regime (you also know an alternate narrative that has never been fully brought to light, of how millions accused of being communists were slaughtered). Even so, the images that rise in your head when you hear the word 'communist' are the hammer, sickle, blood and decomposing corpses.

The reasons your sister doesn't want her daughter to visit Lubang Buaya are those of your average, middle-class mother. She wants a healthy, beautiful world for her child, not one poisoned by trauma and images of horror. Her objections have nothing to do with ideology. The last time you saw her, she remained anti-communist.

You close your sister's email without replying and rise from the computer desk in the hotel lobby. Your sister, and your memories of her, always make you feel like you're on the run but that one of your shoes keeps catching on something behind you. You don't want to look back. You want to flee as far as you can, and not be caught.

At three o'clock you'll meet Yvette. Like Nazwa, you'll also go to a museum. Yvette has invited you to the Holocaust Memorial.

The sharp lines of the Holocaust Memorial make you uneasy. Perhaps everywhere is the same; sites that recall dark pasts never let people feel comfortable. But now you're rattled by order. You're surrounded by thousands of rectangular stones, arrayed horizontally like coffins, in neat rows behind and before you. The stones are grey, clean and uniform. You walk among them, on a narrow pathway, seeking a foothold on uneven terrain.

You glance at Yvette. It's truly unnerving when people place their memories in boxes, without curves.

'The design is deliberately disturbing,' says Yvette. 'Cold and clinical.'

The museum was built two years previously, in the vicinity of government buildings and embassies. Maybe we should be forced to remember straight lines and right angles, because memories are tangled strands vying to be drawn out. Humans hear so many stories. Maybe the strands in your head have become so enmeshed that you can't determine which stories to remember. You have to admit that your encounter with Yvette is making thoughts of Muhammad recede. Your grief begins to fade. But forgetting is an involuntary crime. You don't wish to forget Muhammad, so you have to hold in your memory what he has passed on: the story of Snow Red.

What would Helga say if she saw this concrete monument? Helga, child of world war, who felt that everything she did was inappropriate. Her memories were full of soft and delicate crannies, like Oma's cakes. But she could never reach what lay within. You feel you can see Oma's face here, among the grey concrete corners on either side. Oma boarded a train, but it wasn't Snow Red who led her away.

'Hey.' Yvette touches your shoulder. 'Let's go,' she whispers.

You nod.

Yeah, let's go. We all want to go. Muhammad wanted to leave with Snow Red because he was tired of seeking refuge, because he hoped that ghosts could help him return home. Home, though his house would never be as it was. You also wanted to leave, though you now realise how shallow your desires were. And Yvette – why did she long to be abducted?

You walk in silence, without speaking. Once you reach the road, you let out a sigh. Again you find yourself in a crowd, accosted by the hubbub of the street. Relief? An inappropriate emotion. But you don't want to feel alone. You don't want to be captured.

'Over there is the Brandenburg Gate,' says Yvette. You've been there, on one of your early aimless days, but you accept Yvette's invitation to visit again.

'This city is crazy about museums,' you mumble as you gaze at the bright blue sky sheltering the chariot atop the gate.

'Does Indonesia have museums like that?' Yvette asked.

'Like what?'

'Museums of dark history.'

Your sister's email comes to mind, and your memories of the trip to Lubang Buaya. Yes, a museum of dark history. Who could forget? They didn't let us. Maybe all these dark sites are connected. A close high school friend said the military called the PKI's attempted coup Gestapu, a jumbled acronym for Gerakan September Tigapuluh, the September 30 Movement, in order to recall the terror of the Nazi police. Gestapu and Gestapo, bloodthirsty older and younger siblings. In your head the voice of your friend rings:

But who are the real fascists?

Early in high school your best friend was Dian. Her full name was Dian Carolina Halim. You haven't seen her in years, but this visit to the past brings her back. Very strange. You wanted to run far, far away, but this new world catapults you to memories and names long buried, like Dian Carolina Halim.

'When I was a kid, my friends and I went to Lubang Buaya. They call it the Sacred Pancasila Monument. I don't know why they call it that – the name actually means Crocodile Pit. Maybe it takes a holy miracle to wipe out communists, like killing witches.'

You tell Yvette your story.

Unlike the Holocaust Memorial with its lines and angles, Lubang Buaya is filled with curves and details. You still remember a relief depicting the torture of the generals. Your teacher said it was proof of the savagery of the Partai Komunis Indonesia.

'Did I already tell you that bit?'

'Yes, you did.'

'I'm sorry, but I heard that line over and over.'

Teacher sounded like a broken cassette tape and probably didn't endorse his own statement, but you swallowed it whole. In the relief, side by side with the horror made manifest in violent bodies wielding hammers, a bare-shouldered woman was dancing, surrounded by men. Who is that? you asked Teacher. He answered quickly, as if wanting to stave off further questioning: Oh, that's a Gerwani, a member of the Indonesian Women's Movement, a communist supporter. Your teacher must have felt that the story of the Gerwani dancing naked before mangling the generals was too much for a fourth-grader. But the image on the relief was immortalised in *Treason of the September 30 Movement*, and repeated every year when it screened on television. 'Blood is red, General,' says a Gerwani, before slicing his face with a razor blade. Kids playing at school would repeat the phrase dramatically: Blood is red, General! When games got out of hand, cry-babies would run home tearfully to their mothers. Their mothers, in your imaginings, would be cooking in the kitchen. No razor blades for moms.

A woman dressed in red with blade in hand, however, is capable of anything.

The violent scenes always made you clamp your eyes shut. Fourth grade, fifth grade, sixth grade. After that you had no desire to watch *Treason of the September 30 Movement* again, but the agonised faces of the generals remained, cursed to be frozen in stone forever. Monuments and memories are grooved. Gothic.

For some reason you always connect memories of the PKI and Gerwani with an event that happened at school, before Suharto fell, back when you and Dian Carolina Halim were still best friends.

Students eagerly anticipated Year Two of high school because one year later they would enjoy the glory days of Year Three, when they became the most senior pupils in school, and girls could wear skirts as short as they liked without fear of being 'squashed' by the older girls. You don't know if kids even use the term 'squash' any more, since the English word 'bully' has become popular.

You and Dian Carolina Halim had just finished eating fried rice in the cafeteria when the most popular Year Three girls began creating a commotion. Hearing the shouts, you hurried to pay for your lunch and rushed to see what all the fuss was about. Dian was a quiet girl who didn't like parties, but she was always happy to peer, or rather peep, at pandemonium. You followed Dian, curious but shy. You hated the seniors from the popular clique, who could be so full of themselves. But they never squashed you – you weren't even a blip on their radar. You were nobody and your best friend was nerdy Dian, an innocent-looking bookworm who could never be a threat.

As her surname suggested, Dian Carolina Halim was of Chinese descent (her grandfather had changed his name from Liem to Halim in the sixties). Being Chinese in a good state school in the nineties meant being a minority, invisible, considered unattractive. You were occasionally mistaken for being Chinese as well – your skin was fair and you always walked at Dian's side. Sometimes you regretted that your best friend wasn't cool, but you'd immediately dismiss such thoughts because Dian was so nice to you.

'Those Year One girls are being squashed again,' Dian explained, unasked. 'The dynamic duo.'

A crowd of onlookers had already gathered. Here we are now. Entertain us.

'Linda and Ayu?'

Dian nodded. You'd never spoken to Linda and Ayu, but they were notorious around school for obvious reasons: they were beautiful, rich, and boys went crazy over them. That was enough to make them the most hated girls in Year One. The popular Year Three girls were always looking for reasons to squash them: for wearing shoes that were too flashy or skirts that were too short. At school, only seniors could show off brand-name shoes and wear miniskirts. This time, the reason was their underwear. Below their thin white uniforms, Linda and Ayu wore black bras.

'Oh, think you're hot, do you?' a Year Three girl shouted. 'Wear a black bra to school again, and you're fucking dead.'

'Don't go looking for attention!'

'PKI wannabes, huh?' added another.

You nudged Dian. PKI? What did that mean? Partai Komunis Indonesia? Dian shook her head. PKI: *perempuan kutang item*, she explained, a girl with a black bra. She was always trying to stay on top of the latest slang at school.

'Planning to be sluts, are you? You're already acting like Gerwani!'

'Yeah, Gerwani. They're lesbos.'

The word Gerwani was immediately met with howling laughter by the clique of popular girls. You remembered a bare-shouldered woman dancing on a relief at Lubang Buaya. Linda and Ayu looked down, their faces red. Ayu started to cry. You felt sorry for them, but your feet remained fixed in place. You kept watching, much as you watched *Treason of the September 30 Movement* when the generals were being cursed, tortured and then executed. Blood is red, General! No need to pity Linda and Ayu. Chances were that two years later they'd be doing exactly the same thing to pretty girls in the classes below them.

What happened was wrong. Very wrong. You shouldn't have been a bystander, just as you shouldn't have believed *Treason of the September 30 Movement*. But you only realised that a few years later, when you were a university student and met Dian Carolina Halim once more.

In Year Three you and Dian were in different classes, so you rarely saw her. When the May 1998 riots hit, Dian disappeared from school. Her father, afraid that she'd be beaten up or raped just for being Chinese, wouldn't let her out of the house. Dian was fine, but after that May's events she became more of a loner. She'd claim to be busy studying at home. She wanted to move to Jogja and attend Gadjah Mada University because she didn't want to stay in Jakarta. I hope you get in, Dian, you said. You heard rumours that state universities discriminated against ethnic Chinese. But Dian was accepted to study sociology at Gadjah Mada, while you were stuck at a private university in Jakarta.

Dian visited your house in early 2002. Her pale yellowish skin had grown sallow. She was interning with an independent organisation that documented the stories of former Gerwani, who mostly lived alone in sheltered housing. The organisation sought to present an alternative narrative of the past. Several times she used the phrase 'rectification of history'. Dian Carolina Halim, the bookworm, had become a left-wing activist.

'You remember that incident, don't you?'

The bullying at the school was part of New Order military culture, Dian said. We became used to violence because as kids we grew up watching torture in *Treason of the September 30 Movement*.

Our culture is a culture of torture.

In the living room, you mostly listened as Dian, who'd been quiet for so long, gave voice to her rage. She seemed to hate many things. She hated all forms of militaristic hierarchy in schools, including the hazing that happened during university orientation week. She hated how she had long stood by, watching students being bullied. She hated that she only came to understand years later how the myth of Gerwani as savage women was perpetuated. There were no nude dances, no razors in hand. The state feared smart women who were politically active.

In the middle of the conversation, your sister, who was back from Bandung for the school holidays, came over from her room.

'Hey,' she scolded. 'Don't talk about Gerwani so loudly.'

'Why not?'

'Informers could be all around us.'

'Informers?' Dian gave her a quizzical look. 'Suharto has stepped down, Mbak.'

Unlike you, Dian admired your sister. In Dian's eyes, not only did your sister get into Mechanical Engineering at Bandung, she was one of the first women to wear a headscarf when Suharto banned them in schools. Your sister spoke up for the right to wear the hijab with Muslim friends, and she was upset that your father forbade her to join the demonstrations against the New Order in 1998. Dian looked up to her for all this. To her, women who fought for the right to wear a headscarf were just as brave as Gerwani who rejected polygamy. But, in your living room, Dian was struck by something else: your sister feared a communist threat.

'Don't let communism rise again. Books are circulating now, written by children of PKI members,' your sister told Dian.

'What, don't let communism rise from the grave, you mean, Mbak?' Dian frowned. 'The thing is all the PKI members were wiped out – murdered.'

Your sister and Dian engaged in a fierce debate, while you, with allegiance to neither the right nor the left, remained silent. After that argument you realised that Dian's admiration for your sister had evaporated in an instant. And that was the last time you ever saw Dian Carolina Halim.

A museum exists in your head, a museum of ignorance. Entry is free, but you don't want to enter, because it displays all the stupidity of your past. Years later, after reading a book called *The Museum of Innocence*, you looked back and wondered about the right term to use. High school bullying: was that innocence or ignorance? There is nostalgia in the word 'innocent', whereas you really don't care to remember all the events that you consider ignorant.

How strange are journeys that prise open memories, events so distant you never think about them, items stored in a museum of ignorance. The journey makes you nervous. Perhaps the line between past and present is never clear. You're as unenlightened as ever.

Yvette continues walking beside you in her red boots, listening attentively to your story. You should have worn your demon shoes today, but you knew you'd be walking a lot, and your shoes aren't made for walking.

'Funny. I remember more about my home elsewhere,' you say.

'Like looking in the mirror?'

You turn to her. You feel like you're hearing someone else's voice, but it's just Yvette next to you, wearing a soft smile. Then you remember Devil's words: every mirror is a door.

'Yes, but each time I look, I see something slightly different.'

'I know. Your home will never be the same again.'

You sit on a park bench and buy Yvette a coffee. You didn't expect to reveal so much to a new acquaintance. You also didn't expect your journey to take you backwards rather than forwards. You feel you've run as far away as possible but have still been caught.

'Sometimes travel can revive traumas,' Yvette says.

Trauma? Watching the New Order's propaganda films, the girls who squashed each other at school, your communist-fearing sister and Dian Carolina Halim – you're not sure such memories can be called traumatic. Or more honestly, you don't know what to call them.

'Strange, but I don't feel traumatised.'

'Wounded?'

'Yes, maybe,' you say, and then sip your already cooling coffee. 'What about you? What do you keep in the museum in your head?'

'Not in my head,' she corrects, and taps the asphalt with her shoes. 'These are my museum. I walk with my wounds everywhere I go.'

On the road, it seems, people share the stories of their scars. That day you hear another tale, another bend in the journey.

You feel like a tourist moving ever further off the map, like an adventurer without an obvious storyline. But you have no fixed destination beyond a set of routes defined by tourist guidebooks. At an unexpected turn, Yvette reveals to you the origin of her red boots.

Continue to page 120.

You don't want to look in the mirror again. With the doorman's help, you lower it, wrap it neatly, and lean it against the wall. The mirror remains in your apartment, but at least you don't have to confront the carvings, that Medusa-like hair ready to strangle you. Instead, you order a plain black-wood mirror from Target. All it takes is a $15 purchase to check your clothes, shoes and scarf before leaving the apartment. No more irrational horror, no more anxiety from a sense of being constantly watched.

You can now return to the existential question that has been increasingly plaguing you: how does life go on? More precisely, how can you start living with a purpose?

Time to find a job and meet others. Besides, half the money in your account is gone. You've realised that $20,000 is not enough to live off for a year. How naive to have been thinking in Indonesian terms. You regret squandering so much. Perhaps Devil will send more money, but you doubt it. You believe he loves you, but he's also one cunning boyfriend.

Propped up in bed with your laptop, you start looking for jobs on Craigslist. You send out several applications to vacancies for English tutors for foreign speakers. The poor huddled masses of New York might be tired and desperate to learn English, but no one answers you. You're disappointed, but you get it. White people are trusted more in all sorts of areas, including teaching English. Who in America wants to learn English from a fresh-off-the-boat Indonesian? You start lowering your standards. Nanny? Nannying needs references, though, and you've never looked after a kid. You aim for waitressing jobs and contact a few cafes and restaurants. Unfortunately, waiting tables also demands experience.

As frustration sets in, Mr Zhao and his son Wei provide a glimmer of hope. When they come to collect the rent, you ask, with some embarrassment, if they know of any part-time work. Mr Zhao immediately taps his son's shoulder and they chat for a bit.

Wei turns to you. 'You can take my place in the cafe.'

'What? You don't need to do that!'

You're worried about Wei's source of income because you understand – at least from what Wei and Mr Zhao have said – that not every student at a private university is rolling in cash. But it turns out that Wei has been planning to drop one of his jobs so he can devote more time to his thesis. You glance at Mr Zhao, looking for a sign of agreement. The old man nods, which you interpret as support.

'Have you worked in a cafe before?' Wei asks.

'No.'

'Hmm. That makes it a bit harder.'

At Wei's suggestion, you add a small fib to your résumé and send it to the cafe manager. You write that you worked for a month at a Chinese restaurant in Flushing that belongs to Wei's aunt; she's willing to make up something on your behalf should the cafe manager call. You don't know why Wei and Mr Zhao are so nice to you, but you're thankful that you cooked rendang for them.

Less than a week later, you get a call from Tony Saverino, the manager of the cafe where Wei works. He asks you to come at ten the next morning for an interview. You jump for joy.

That night you try to sleep early, but your next-door neighbours are at it again. The festivities kick off with moans of 'ahhhh' and 'ohhhh' over and over. You put your ear against the wall, curious. The voices of a man and a woman, then panting, ever faster and louder. By eleven o'clock, their moans have taken over your apartment. The woman's hysterical shrieks make you feel like you're listening to the live broadcast of a sports event.

No doubt about it, this is a sex fest.

Dammit!

Amid your curses, you imagine – if only for a few seconds – the couple's antics in the next room. In your head they are changing positions energetically. The man probably has taut, muscular arms, like a porn actor, while his partner – endowed with a perfect body, of course – props her legs, wrapped in black fishnet stockings, on the man's shoulders.

How tacky can you get? Disrupting a neighbour's sleep, advertising carnal pleasures, especially to a listener who lives on her own like you? That's nerve for you. You block your ears, but the moans, punctuated by bursts of coquettish female laughter, grow more and more intense.

Unbefuckinglievable.

The rude couple need to be taught a lesson. You pound on the wall with determination. No reaction. You bang a second time, even harder.

The voices subside. Eventually, you hear nothing.

Your guerrilla attack has succeeded. As the clock strikes midnight, you howl with wicked laughter, like a villain. But let's not forget: villains lose in the end.

Proceed to page 139.

Shiny Red Boots and Lipstick

My father imprisoned me in order to care for a spirit. My body was a shrine inhabited by my mother's soul. Souls are always haunted, so they need a home to keep them from wandering everywhere. Father rejected religion, but lack of a religion doesn't guarantee that someone is any less spiritual or mystical. He seemed to believe that if I left, my mother's spirit would run away too.

My mother was called Yvette. She handed the name down to me, as my middle name. Father always called me by my first name, Gudrun. Mother's death came prematurely, and that's the main thing that pushed my father over the edge. She was diagnosed with cancer, and less than a year later it became terminal. Nowadays people speak of a fight against cancer, but back then, when I was eight years old, I didn't know if my mother fought or surrendered. The older I got, the more I realised that Mother wanted to leave us. She chose to die. My father knew that.

There was no return after Mother died. Previously, my parents had often quarrelled when she came home late at night. They would argue, Father would shout harsh words, Mother would cry, and before long he would be crying too (I picture him burying his head between her knees and sobbing). The words 'sorry' and 'worry' would end their arguments. Father was both anxious and jealous. He loved my mother so much that he tied her down.

But Mother managed to escape.

My father was a grim man, quick to anger, but Mother's death turned him into a monster. He realised that he was very much alone. Though still young, he would have to raise a child, only to be abandoned someday. Father was haunted by departures, deception and death. Because everything would come to an end, he decided to fortify his home against the outside world and the passage of time. Much as he tied my mother down, he locked me up. He wouldn't let me out of the house after eight o'clock. If I came home late, he would fly into a rage and smash things, only to sob later, overcome with regret. Unlike my friends who left home once they were in university, I stayed with Father until I was twenty-five. Does that mean I was a filial daughter or just a coward? I don't know. Maybe I simply felt too sorry for him.

Katrin appeared in our lives when I was thirteen. At first she only came on Sunday evenings, but as time went on she began to visit almost every night. Eventually I understood that she was Father's new girlfriend. I don't know where she came from originally, but my neighbours seemed to dislike her. Fräulein Else, an old maid who lived right below our apartment, always referred to her as 'that woman'.

'Is that woman with your father now?'

On other occasions, Else would observe that Father had chosen carelessly. 'That woman' certainly could not be compared with my mother.

Katrin always came to our house in knee-high leather boots. They were red, sombre like congealed cow's blood, but she'd polish them until they gleamed. When Katrin was in my father's room, I'd try on her boots. In the mirror, my legs looked so beautiful. Where did she go with those shoes? What kind of world had she seen?

Katrin was always nice to me. She probably wanted to serve as a nurturing mother figure, though I was more interested in imagining where she ventured in her red boots. When Father came back late, she'd cook dinner for me. Sometimes she'd help me with my homework. Maths was hard for her, but she tried.

One night, before Father came home, Katrin taught me how to put on lipstick. I couldn't take my eyes off hers as she applied it to my lips. The red made her lips appear plumper than they really were. I forget now how her face looked without lipstick. I don't think she was very pretty, but with lipstick on, her mouth seemed like a cherry. Suddenly I felt hungry.

That night we were too absorbed in doing my make-up to realise that Father had come home. He stormed into my room and tensed when he saw my face, colourful like Katrin's. He called Katrin's name and then told me to go and wash the make-up off. From behind the wall I heard arguing. Katrin shouted. Father responded, even more loudly, and soon Katrin began to sob. The door opened and Katrin rushed to pull on her red boots. She fled down our wooden stairs, never to return.

In front of the mirror, I didn't know what to do but remove the crimson from my lips. I didn't understand why my tears fell. I needed to hide my thoughts about ripe, red cherries.

Only as I grew older did I realise that my neighbours considered Katrin cheap. Perhaps Father thought so too, and he didn't want Katrin to teach me to become like her. I wasn't allowed to become a cheap girl. I reflected the image of my mother's face, the imagined graceful mother who had never left. But there was one fact that Father knew, though he refused to admit it. My mother escaped.

Mother had gone, died, fled, and I desired to become Katrin. I didn't want to be locked up, a shrine for Mother's spirit. I wanted red boots like Katrin's and to travel where I wanted. I had no interest in luring anyone, but my lips blazed crimson.

I kept wanting to run away but couldn't. I didn't have the heart: Father grew ever more dependent on me. And so, I imagined kidnapping scenarios. One day somebody would steal me away and give me red shoes that could take me anywhere. In my fantasies, my abductor had no face. Maybe I would be kidnapped by a gang of criminals or a crazed outlaw. Maybe even by the Devil. It didn't matter. I just needed a miracle to rescue me, to let me leave.

But the years passed, and no kidnapper arrived. So I decided my own fate. There was no abduction, just a departure. Before I left the city, I went into a shop and spent my savings on a pair of boots and blazing red lipstick.

Proceed to the next page.

At the hotel, you open your suitcase and remove your red shoes. Since becoming a tourist in Berlin you have worn your short boots; the red shoes have not greeted the world for a while now. You wonder what Yvette would say if you put them on.

Yvette. Her story continues to ring in your ears. You think over how, after she finished speaking, you asked a question.

'When exactly did Gudrun become Yvette?'

'When I decided to leave home,' she said. 'It makes me feel closer to both *Mutter Courage* and my mother.'

Yvette threw away the name from her father and used the one her mother had handed down. Perhaps Juwita Padmadivya, possessor of an unusual name of her own, resembles Yvette. Women who choose their own name, you think. Someday you'll have to read Brecht.

'But what happened to your mother's soul after you left?' you ask. 'Now it has no home.'

'Do you remember that old saying, good girls go to heaven?'

You nod. Then Yvette says that her mother always fought, in her own way. She isn't convinced that Mother is resting peacefully in heaven. Good girls go to heaven, bad girls go wandering.

'But because of that I don't worry about her,' she says. 'Mother's spirit follows me everywhere.'

How strange that you and Yvette share an identical longing for escape. But Yvette had no Demon Lover to give her red shoes; neither did Snow Red come to her. She chose her own shoes and her own adventure.

Although Yvette bought her shoes at a store, she was well aware that she'd inherited them from Katrin. Without Katrin, she'd probably never have wanted red shoes in her life. You stare at your own pair. Red shoes always seem to carry the traces of other women. Who wore these shoes before you? Where have your shoes gone adventuring? What kind of world have they seen?

Do you still need them?

Devil no longer comes to you. Nor do you expect him. You cradle the shoes in your hands. Perhaps their expiry date will arrive sooner than it should, but before then, you'll need to find the right time to wear them in front of Yvette.

That night you dream. Yvette appears as a beautiful witch, with locks of indigo, clad in a black tutu skirt. Her boots are red, inherited from a woman before her, just as your shoes were. She beckons you to enter a forest. There she lives, in a forest inhabited by wolves. You run to chase after her in your red shoes.

One week after your visit to the museum, you and Yvette dine at an Italian restaurant. She orders a bottle of wine to share.

'Is your boyfriend planning to join you?' Yvette asks.

'What for?'

'A holiday.'

You shake your head. You didn't expect such a question from her. Only once, as far as you recall, did you mention a boyfriend (though you didn't give Devil's name), but she appears to have noted that information carefully.

'It was just a guess on my part,' Yvette says. 'If you're really in love with someone, you never want to be alone.'

'I feel like I'm always shadowed by his presence, though,' you say. You continue, a little uncertainly, 'One way or another.'

Devil is not here, but you feel that he's watching you and occasionally appearing uninvited. He won't set you free. Please don't let him be lurking around, you think. You steal a glance at the window.

'Oh, a possessive man,' Yvette concludes.

'Is that typical?'

'I don't know, I just know my father.'

She laughs, then adds pepper to her food. She has ordered grilled aubergine and mozzarella, making you wonder how the two alone can satisfy her. The mince on the pasta on your plate smells wonderful.

'You haven't finished your story about the movie.'

Yvette frowns. Long enough for her to realise that you wish to return to a previous conversation. The visit to the museum and subsequent meanderings had made you both forget Juwita Padmadivya. Yvette wipes her lips with a napkin, leaving a trace of scarlet.

'Have you heard of *Request Concert*?'

You shake your head. She appears to hesitate. Several times she starts to speak, but cuts herself off. It's so hard to tell someone else's story, she says. Finally, she pulls a brown envelope from her bag.

'This is my interpretation of Juwita's film. You can read it later. I don't write in a typical style.'

It's late. You're tired and want to return to the hotel. Yvette insists on seeing you back even though you tell her she needn't bother. Yvette knows. I just want to walk with you, she says. You feel a little flushed, perhaps from the wine.

As you walk towards the train station, you come upon two figures dressed entirely in sleek black. They wear black hats. You can't see their faces clearly, but they seem to be women. They're working together to carry a gnome figurine. It looks heavy. Although they don't run, their haste suggests that they're keen to get away from something. Now and again they each look behind them, as if worried that they're being trailed. Yvette taps your shoulder.

'We're witnessing a kidnapping,' she whispers.

'A kidnapping? Who's being kidnapped?'

'Him, that old man being carried off,' she says. 'The garden gnome.'

'Why would anyone kidnap a garden gnome?'

You learn from Yvette of an ethical movement to save the gnomes. A society of activists who believe that garden gnomes should live in the wild, not be displayed in gardens to watch over plants. Without a decent wage, confinement to a garden amounts to slavery, and so they kidnap the gnomes and take them travelling. The gnomes are then photographed at famous places and the pictures sent to the owner.

'That's totally bizarre.'

'Yes, but who doesn't want to travel? It's the same for garden gnomes.'

'I want to travel too.' You pause for a moment. 'And I like red shoes.'

That night you feel chattier than before. You don't tell Yvette about Devil, how he suddenly entered your room and presented you with your shoes, but you speak honestly about many things. You tell her how you envied your sister because she studied in a prestigious engineering programme while you failed to get into a top state university. You even tell her about the toy train you called the Orient Express, the English for the Global World course, and how as an English teacher who had never left the country you longed to see the world. You've never opened up about so much to anyone, including anybody in that string of loser ex-boyfriends. Yvette also continues her own story, following her escape from her father. You wonder who else has heard these things. She's ten years older than you. Perhaps ten years ago someone was in your place, listening to her tale of shiny red shoes and lipstick.

About five hundred metres from the hotel, you feel your footsteps slow down. Maybe you're preoccupied with her story, or you want her to keep listening to you. You forget what you talk about in those last moments, but you feel like you're buying time.

In front of the hotel you gaze into each other's eyes. 'I still feel like talking,' she says.

You do too but just smile wordlessly.

'It's already late though, right?'

'Right.'

Your movements are awkward. Yvette leans towards you, as if she wants to say something. You tense slightly.

'Sleep well.'

Her voice is friendly but feels formal, like the voice of a telephone operator.

You wave and enter the hotel. You want to turn towards her once more, maybe to see if she has gone, but you suppress the urge. You ride the elevator to your floor in a swirl of emotions. Yvette didn't want the encounter to end there, but she didn't say so explicitly.

You should have invited her up. That's another matter, though, and you don't want to dwell on it.

You sit on the edge of the bed and think. About Yvette. About Juwita Padmadivya. You take out the brown envelope, open it, and begin to read.

Proceed to the next page.

Request Concert

Efforts to decipher Juwita Padmadivya and her experimental documentary have thus far proved unsatisfactory. I therefore offer the following argument: that Juwita's letters to Nadya Shafik, her friend in America and the editor of her film, are inseparable from a study of both the film's text and Juwita Padmadivya as text. In building a narrative about Juwita through two mediums, I myself inevitably play the role of another editor. I need not stress that based on the character of this work, with its cutting, pasting and rearranging, you are unlikely to ever locate Juwita.

*

March 23: First Attempt

INT. JUWITA'S ROOM, NIGHT.

JUWITA's *face fills the screen for several seconds. We see her make minor adjustments to the camera position before finally sitting to face the computer. From outside comes the piercing call to prayer from a mosque, slightly discordant. It merges with the buzz of motorbikes and trains.* JUWITA, *wearing a tight red T-shirt, begins typing. For fifteen minutes we view nothing but this shot, from the same angle, with only small variations such as her staring at the ceiling or scribbling notes on paper.*

January 28: Dear Nadya, I will fly out in a few days, on the 1st. I hate American carriers and their cold sandwiches, so since this is my last trip, I've narrowed my choice down to a few different Asian airlines. After everything is over, Taufik will send you a package via FedEx. I've given him your office address in Norwalk. My instructions should be clear (see my message 'Request Concert: Editing Directions'). After our decade of friendship, you'll know what I want. The main thing is to keep long takes. The audience should feel bored. All sounds must be diegetic, which means virtually no dialogue, just noise. You might want to cut parts that make me look fat, though. For the film's sake I'm putting on eyeliner every day.

JUWITA *picks up a cigarette from the left side of her desk, ignites it with a flick of her lighter and takes a deep drag. As she exhales the smoke she changes how she has been sitting so that her shoulders aren't as hunched. She crosses her right leg over her left while arching her back.*

February 20: It's impossible to infuse an Indonesian adaptation of Request Concert with a sense of calm. After so many years in America, I sometimes forget that peace and quiet are a luxury back here.

Toni, an Indonesian friend who was studying in Ithaca, had his mother come visit for a month. She kept complaining, and wanted to return home because it was too quiet. In Ithaca there were no cries of street vendors, no calls to evening prayers, nothing to mark the passage of time at all. Any longer and she might have hurled herself off the suicide bridge near Cornell.

It's not calm that needs to be captured on film, but cacophony. A constant din should be heard from outside my bedroom window.

INT. JUWITA'S ROOM, POV SHOT.

Desk: a laptop, a stack of papers, a cup of black coffee, a pack of Marlboros, an ashtray full of cigarette butts. Ash dirties the left side of the desk. Next to the ashtray, a beige envelope marked FOR TAUFIK. *Behind the desk, a bed with a rumpled duvet. The space where* JUWITA *finds herself is more reminiscent of a messy hotel room than a cosy home, with few marks of individuality. A transit stop.*

Further in the background, a closed door. JUWITA, *behind the camera, walks over and opens it. Other sounds are heard. A television is on. As our eyes follow* JUWITA *out of the room, we get a sense of the layout of her apartment. Kitchen on the right, sparkling clean, dry, in shades of pink. To the left, a single-door refrigerator and a dining table with two cream-coloured wooden chairs (identical to the one* JUWITA *works from in her room). Panning further left, we see an old brown sofa.* JUWITA's *living room. No one is there, but the sound of the television becomes clearer. A talk show. We arrive at a door that has been left ajar.*

February 10: I've found a room-mate to share the apartment. Retno Wahyuni, a high school friend, has moved here from Semarang. A bit of context: Semarang is certainly a vibrant city, but back when I was a frog in a well, I naively referred to everyone who didn't grow up in Jakarta as a hick. When we met up again, Retno was looking for a place to rent. She was married, but she said her husband was working in Kalimantan for a year. She was a little reticent about it, and I didn't want to pry.

Retno works for an ad agency, listens to U2, reads Murakami, watches Sex and the City (and has aspirations to become Carrie Bradshaw). She won't be any trouble to have around. In fact, she completes the concept of space in this film. Remember what I said about 'all-round somewhat' people? Given the logic of today's world, all the 'somewhat' elements in the film make it whole.

From behind the door we peek into a room. A woman works facing the computer, her back to us. We expect JUWITA *to enter, but she doesn't.*

March 23: Retno never complains about noise, but of course that's hardly exotic in Indonesia. She's always on the lookout for crowds. The door to her room stays half open, even when she isn't home. I don't know who she wants to invite in. Me?

She works in the bedroom with the television on in the living room. It's a ridiculous habit as far as I'm concerned, but here's her explanation: I can't stand working in solitude, and sharing an apartment with you feels like living in a graveyard.

The buzz is starting to get to me. My theory is that the constant hum becomes pollution in more than just real space. Glaring at the Internet is like listening to a night market – you can never be left alone. Oddly enough, your ears grow deaf to it all. Facebook is the worst (and I hear there's another site becoming popular called Twitter). Status updates every minute in cyberspace constantly shout to be heard, tugging at you to become part of a big family. You're not alienated so much as sucked dry.

Retno's Facebook posts from two days ago:
9.30: 'Late cuz of traffic.' (Ten likes; comment from friend A: 'Not using the busway?')
11.00: 'Rushing to meet clients, but the cab driver is taking me around in circles.' (Fifteen thumbs up; comment from friend B: 'Hang in there!')
13.00: 'Hungry!' (Three thumbs up; no comments.)

We return to JUWITA's *room, now much dimmer, lit by a bedside lamp. The camera is back in its original position.* JUWITA *sits on her bed, restless. She gets up and walks to the desk, then returns with a transparent bottle of sleeping pills and a glass of water. She cradles the bottle, looking hesitant. Slowly she taps out several pills. She takes a sip of water, but the pills remain in her palm.* JUWITA *stares at the camera.*

JUWITA *closes her eyes for a moment, panting. She puts the pills back in the bottle before placing it on the floor. She is lying on her bed, then gets under the covers, facing us. She closes her eyes again. Her lips are parted, and her breathing grows faster (although the noise outside the window makes it difficult for us to hear).* JUWITA *is masturbating. Shortly after, she falls asleep.*

*

March 24: Second Attempt

INTERTITLE

'The preparations for suicide do not violate the victim's mundane, everyday activities; and the act itself is performed with the same love of order, as neatly, as uprightly, and as silently desperate as the life which provoked it.'

(The above lines are from Franz Xaver Kroetz's commentary on his play *Request Concert*. Juwita appropriated these remarks for her video, which, obviously, was edited by Nadya Shafik and later by me.)

January 13: Darling Nadya, our era celebrates the middle class. Or rather, I mean, the mediocre class. Look around you and you will find a swarm of 'somewhat' people: somewhat clever, somewhat handsome, somewhat rich, somewhat famous. Put them all together to form a whole: a high achiever. Becoming good but not great is the norm. Everyone compromises and edges towards comedy.

Suicide in Kroetz's text is present at this point, for it is a continuation of – not a rebellion against – compromise. Kroetz's fictional protagonist, Fräulein Rasch, dies incomplete, endorsing her daily oppression, her confined boredom. Mute. Unlike Fräulein Rasch, I understand quite well the forces operating upon me. Unlike Kroetz, I refuse to act as a ventriloquist (OK, that's probably not the right word for a script without dialogue …): to offer criticism through the lives of others who, of course, are not as clever as the creator. I reject everything that is not complete, so I have decided to be both Fräulein Rasch and Franz Xaver Kroetz. My death will not disrupt order, but my work – which will naturally soon become famous – will serve as a repository of unbearable knowledge.

In this video I am your spectacle. You know that I am going to kill myself. You are waiting for it because that's the way it should be. But you are also me, the observer, borrowing my eyes, gazing at what I gaze at through my camera.

INT. JUWITA'S APARTMENT, MORNING.

The camera – apparently now placed on a chair in the kitchen – spotlights the bathroom door for ten minutes. The sound of a toilet flushing. The door opens. JUWITA *comes out with a book.*

JUWITA *at the dining table, facing a bowl of instant noodles and an open laptop (the song 'Suicide is Painless' is heard). She twirls the unappetising meal with a fork. She puts the noodles to her lips while staring at a point behind the camera. This scene lasts ten minutes. Without finishing her food,* JUWITA *shifts the bowl and lights a cigarette.*

March 24: I have to reconsider my ideas. The space in which I find myself right now, here, is not merely making me agitated, but triggering suicidal thoughts. This is not about claustrophobia, but rather about being in an enclosure with leaks, an enclosure that has opened cracks for loud-speakers, motorcycle exhausts, relentless television, online hysteria, everything that inhabits the city and coexists with you, kicking up a racket, causing congestion. The trap lies not in alienation, but in the crowd.

Request Concert was once staged in Indonesia back in the 1980s with the actor Niniek L. Karim. There are rumours it will be staged again. Unfortunately, it's possible that by that point I'll be gone. I'm curious how the protagonist's suicide will be framed: 'because' it's crowded, or 'although' it's crowded. But maybe being afflicted by din is only a problem of middle class intellectuals.

(After this Nadya Shafik seems to cut many scenes of Juwita's afternoon and evening activity.)

INT. JUWITA'S ROOM, NIGHT.

JUWITA *takes another cigarette. She stares at the ceiling as she exhales smoke. The voice of a woman chatting and occasionally laughing is heard.* JUWITA *turns to the side briefly and places the cigarette, still burning, on the ashtray. She grabs a beige envelope (which we know reads* FOR TAUFIK), *looks at it, puts it down again, then lifts the pill bottle. Again she cradles the bottle, and takes out some pills. We wait. Boredom sets in for us as spectators.* JUWITA *again looks to the side. She returns the bottle to the table, rises from the chair, and opens her bedroom door so that it is now ajar.*

March 24: I thought I heard crying a few minutes after I heard her laughing on the phone. I went to make sure she was all right. Perhaps just false sympathy, but circumstances forced me to listen.

Six months ago, Retno found out that her husband has a lover, a man. Apparently he married Retno to 'get back on the straight and narrow'. The situation reminds me of *Palace of Beauty,* an old Indonesian film starring Mathias Muchus, in which his character marries a woman for his family's sake.

Apparently Retno's husband – I forget his name, let's just call him Mathias – couldn't bear to live a lie and also came to the realisation that he had nothing to straighten. He ran away with his old boyfriend. Retno can't face the world. Now it's her turn to lie, and keep making a show of her happy marriage for those around her.

I don't know who the bigger idiot is: Mathias, who once believed that his salvation lay in heteronormative institutions, or Retno, now desperately protecting the very system that poisoned her.

(Juwita again appears on the screen after we're tormented by a lengthy shot of an empty room. Nadya Shafik has already cut it, perhaps from two hours to five minutes, but this does little to reduce the tedium of having to watch it.)

JUWITA *types for a few moments. Then she gets up, grabs the camera, and aims it at the laptop screen, which is opening Retno's Facebook page. A minute before, Retno has posted a status update: 'Can there be a couple as cool as Angelina Jolie and Brad Pitt? ☺'*

*

March 25: Third Attempt

INT. JUWITA'S APARTMENT, IN FRONT OF RETNO'S HALF-OPEN DOOR.
We hear the sound of motorbikes, and percussion accompanying women's prayer chants.

(This scene happens after the third suicide attempt. Because nothing occurs here except increasing repetition, I've cut it.)

JUWITA *pushes the door open slowly. There is no one in the room. The camera turns us into voyeuristic snoops. Retno's abundant room decor is chic. Below we see a small, bright yellow carpet that matches the cushions. Retno's bed is made up with light green sheets – slick, clean bedding against dark green pillows and duvet. Beside the bed sits a small dressing table. A mirror and rows of cosmetics (most sporting the Body Shop logo) are arranged neatly, as if in a store display. We see a framed photo of Retno and her husband in traditional Javanese wedding garb, gazing at the camera with happy smiles. Next to the dressing table are two levels of white shelves. Stuffed animals, large and small – teddy bears, pandas, rabbits, cows and pigs – on the first level, and a stack of women's magazines on the second.*

March 25: Retno wasn't home. I went back to my room and, for no particular reason, opened her Facebook profile. She'd made another new post: 'Really angry at the violence that an LGBT group has suffered lately.'

I've never seen her angry, or admitting anger. She has been drained or sad, but not angry. I wonder if this post was really written by Retno, victim as well as staunch supporter of the great big hegemonic fucking system. Maybe there's another Retno, a fragment of Retno, whom I imagine somewhat intact as a somewhat human being.

*

March 27: Ending

EXT. OUTSIDE JUWITA'S APARTMENT, MIDDAY.
JUWITA, *behind the camera, tracks the street outside her apartment. On the right side of the road we find rows of cramped houses, cigarette stalls and, at the end, motorbike taxis. We arrive at a T-junction. This road is narrower, but much more crowded. Cars, motorcycles, scooters and carts converge in two lanes. The camera highlights small ditches directly behind the railway tracks; convenience shops providing various services: photocopying, cell phone credit, silk-screening. A man's voice, catcalling, is heard behind* JUWITA.

INT. NIGHT, POV SHOT.

We follow JUWITA *into her apartment. As soon as the door is opened, we hear the sound of a television.* JUWITA *walks into the living room. Zoom in. Television: soap-opera scene. The camera moves towards* JUWITA'S *room, stops.* JUWITA *does not enter, but turns to the side. Retno's half-open door. We look back at her bookcase and her computer. The chair is empty. The camera pans to the left, stops. Retno's bed. A woman lies there, hands and eyes open. A very long silence. The screen grows shakier. An empty glass sits by the bedside, a pill bottle lies on the floor.*

INT. JUWITA'S ROOM.

JUWITA *at her desk, writing on a blank sheet of paper with a marker. Before we can decipher what is written, she dumps out some white pills, arranging them in two rows.* JUWITA'S *left hand, trembling, holds a glass of water. Her chest heaves. Her eyes are red, swollen. She looks towards us, glassy-eyed.*

She disturbs the rows of pills until we can make out what she has written on the paper. Then, confounding our expectations, she turns off the camera. Everything goes black.

The note reads: 'Et tu, Brute?'

Continue to page 153.

Café

The brilliant sunshine along the road to West 4th Street Station causes you to forget that it's only 3 degrees Celsius outside. At that temperature, your nose gets red and runny. Yes, you still think in Celsius because you have yet to work out what 37 degrees Fahrenheit feels like, and how much cooler, say, 35 and 36 degrees are in comparison. You're still trying to adjust to Fahrenheit (though for what purpose, you're not entirely sure, given that pretty much the whole rest of the world uses Celsius).

Today, 3 degrees Celsius feels warm, what with the sunshine and your upbeat mood. The interview went smoothly. Tony Saverino, the manager of La Candela, only asked a few questions about your serving experience. After satisfying himself with your story – how you worked part-time at a Chinese restaurant in Flushing that's always busy – he asked right away how flexible your schedule is. Your response: you're ready to work any time, including Saturdays and Sundays. He looked pleased and asked you to come in the next day.

You pass a row of cafes and record stores, imagining your future job. You've been here, to Greenwich Village, on a Saturday night and seen a long line of people waiting to get into the Blue Note Cafe. On a weekday the atmosphere is much more subdued. You start planning where to buy food if you're too lazy to pack a lunch, mentally noting a few possibilities: McDonald's, 7-Eleven, and some delis that sell burgers and dollar coffees.

You wait for the E train while listening to a street musician with an accordion. You're grateful today is going well, but then you remember the incident that disturbed you before you left for the interview. Well, it didn't really disturb you, but you couldn't stop thinking about it on the way to La Candela. A joyful day, but also a weird one. That morning you witnessed something unexpected.

At 9 a.m., as you were leaving your apartment, you saw a woman sashay out the door next to yours. You observed her from behind. She wore a violet sari with golden thread accents that showed a bit of her midriff, and her long black hair was tied in a neat braid, revealing the cinnamon tones of her neck.

You hold your breath. *That* woman.

The feral creature who was roaring so wildly last night.

You stood gaping as she strode gracefully towards the elevator. As she walked, you heard the jingling of an ankle bracelet, like music accompanying her in a dance. She stopped at the elevator and waited for it to open, arms folded. You looked down, pretending to be occupied with locking your door.

Her face wasn't visible, but at that distance she looked as if she had stepped straight out of one of the Bollywood films you'd watched so often as a child. She reminded you of those beautiful, gentle and loyal girls who'd star opposite Amitabh Bachchan as his paramour. Or one of those disconsolate mothers, tears running down her cheeks, ready to sacrifice herself for her young children. Bravely, she'd endure all manner of suffering – grinding poverty, love between castes without parental blessing, or the pursuit of a pack of criminals bent on revenge.

As soon as the elevator arrived, she hurried in. All those images of ideal women from Bollywood films gnawed at you. After she disappeared, you walked towards the elevator in a state of shock.

Your neighbour is a mystery.

You simply can't connect the elegant woman in the violet sari with the sex maniac who ruined your sleep last night.

*

La Candela, located a mere block from West 4th Street Station, is an Italian cafe that has been in business for three decades. It's not as popular as its historic neighbour Caffe Reggio, which attracts locals and tourists who want to see where famous artists have been hanging out since the 1920s. La Candela, to your knowledge, hasn't appeared in any movies and isn't a stop on any nostalgia tours. It's dimmer and more tucked away than Caffe Reggio, and you're grateful for that. La Candela fills up on weekends, like cafes all over New York, but on a typical weekday you can relax a little since it never gets overly crowded.

On breaks, you can take your lunch to Washington Square Park, a mere three minutes away. You recall the times you dropped into the pretty park to sit for a while, and how you enjoyed a garden concert and watched people saunter by in chic clothes. The *Cosmo* girls and *GQ* guys who passed by were way more stylish than the morning commuter crowd at Roosevelt Avenue Station, near your apartment. Unfortunately, in winter, the last thing you want to do is have lunch in the park. You'd rather eat in a corner of the cafe or dash to grab a burger from the McDonald's at the corner of West 3rd and 6th.

You begin to observe those around you. Tony Saverino is a relative of the cafe's owners, an Italian American family that's been in the hospitality business for generations. Some of your co-workers are university students after extra money, but others depend on their jobs as wait staff. One catches your attention because of his good looks – Fernando, originally from Peru. Your interactions begin with a geography lesson; he shows you where in South America Peru is located. You didn't know, of course.

'Are you an American or something? How come your geography is so bad?' Fernando teases you. Deftly, he points out the Indonesian archipelago.

He has thick black hair and long, curved lashes that over-shadow slightly wistful, puppy-dog eyes. Had he been a little taller, he'd certainly have been scouted as a model. Of course, you don't tell him this, even after you go out together a few times to buy lunch. His expression is rather melancholy. You don't think he realises how handsome he is, or that he understands at all how to treat his good looks as capital.

The cafe has a diverse range of customers, including women who now count as senior citizens but remain attractive and full of zest. They may well have become entrenched in New York during their glory days as hippies in the late sixties, studying at Barnard or Sarah Lawrence, refusing to leave New York for the sake of a job in Idaho. You've been eavesdropping on conversations between these ageing matrons. One group just saw a movie at the Independent Film Center, then popped in for coffee and a debate about film and politics. A crew of young people wearing skinny jeans and large-rimmed glasses seem to be discussing a project of some sort. Maybe they're writers, designers or film-makers. According to Fernando, Brooklyn is the usual habitat for hipsters.

'Everybody's moving to Brooklyn. It's the heart of New York now,' Fernando says.

'Oh yeah? Says who?'

'People who live in Brooklyn.'

There are also NYU students, of course, who frequent La Candela because it's so close to campus. You haven't worked out how they manage to study. Once off campus, tempting options immediately distract them, from eating and drinking at restaurants and cafes in Greenwich Village to browsing stores in SoHo and shopping for frivolous knick-knacks.

Many of the cafe customers are regulars. A bald man in his sixties always chooses a seat by the window. He sits alone for hours in front of his laptop enjoying decaf coffee with a splash of non-fat milk, no sugar. You remember this because you take his order each time, and he's always delighted to see you. Later you learn that people call him Bob, full name Robert Allen. He teaches in NYU's East Asian Studies Department.

One night you're surprised by a young woman with brown hair who breaks into a grin as you hand her a menu. She greets you as if she knows you. The man next to her, maybe from India, Pakistan or Bangladesh, is busy texting on his phone. He glances at you.

'Hey!' she says.

'Hello.'

'It's the red-shoes girl!'

You're taken aback for a moment and study the familiar-looking brown hair. Then you grin as well. You have indeed seen her before. She's the woman in Washington Square Park who told you about garden gnome liberators. She gets up and hugs you.

Elise, she reminds you, though you don't recall if you'd even exchanged names.

'Where are those beautiful shoes of yours?'

'At home. Do you think I want to work in high heels?' She laughs.

'I thought you'd already gone back to Belgium.'

'I was supposed to go. But,' she half whispers, 'it's really crazy. Anyway, I'll tell you later. I got a boyfriend.'

You glance at the man next to her. Elise shakes her head quickly.

'No, no. My boyfriend is still at his office. This is my friend. Let me introduce Vijay, Vijay Prasad.'

'Hello.'

The man puts his phone in his bag and smiles at you. Elise introduces him as a journalist from India. He has a fellowship to intern at the *New York Times* and is auditing two courses in NYU's Journalism Department.

Your work has ended by the time Elise and Vijay finish their coffee. The three of you chat in front of the cafe because Elise and Vijay want to smoke, then you walk together to the train station. When you'd met at Washington Square Park, Elise had only intended to spend a month in New York, on holiday. After graduating with her bachelor's degree, she had gone to work for a company and earned a decent salary, but soon got bored. She quit and used some of her savings for a trip. In New York, Elise has been living with a friend kind enough to offer her a couch. She only needs to chip in a hundred dollars a month for the water and electricity bills.

Elise met her boyfriend on a dating site. He's a young professional renting an apartment near Prospect Park (you remember Fernando's words: everybody's moving to Brooklyn). The boyfriend has asked Elise to move in, and has even encouraged her to attend school in New York. Your eyebrows knit. Can you really snag a good boyfriend on a dating site? Elise is lucky, for sure. Maybe you should give it a shot.

'Are you still taking photos of those amazing shoes?'

'Not so much any more.'

Elise tells Vijay how you took pictures of your red shoes in different places, like the flight attendant with the garden gnome in *Amélie*. Vijay, who previously seemed sedate and hasn't said much, now becomes more animated.

'Are you going to write a book?' he asks.

'What kind of book?'

'Maybe a book about the adventures of your red shoes.'

You blush. I just take the pictures for fun, you say, then change the subject. From the conversation that follows, you realise Elise doesn't know Vijay very well. He'd been invited to lecture on Elise's campus when she was majoring in Communication Studies at the Vrije Universiteit. The lecturer hosting Vijay introduced him to some of the better students, including Elise, and after that they became Facebook friends. From Facebook, Elise had learned that Vijay was in New York. Because of her boyfriend's encouragement to go back to school, Elise had invited Vijay out for coffee to ask about NYU's Journalism Department.

You nod as you imagine Vijay leaping nimbly from Delhi to New York, and then, with the aid of Facebook, connecting with an acquaintance from Brussels. Elise's professor in Belgium was a friend he'd met as a correspondent in Bangkok. For some, the world is indeed very small. But a small world such as this is not – or hasn't been – yours. So far, the world you know is vast and random.

'I'm just lucky,' says Elise. 'But Vijay here is a true cosmopolitan.'

You enjoy your reunion with Elise, though you're not sure whether running into someone you hardly know qualifies as a reunion. After that you never see her again, except on Facebook, which you open every now and then. Vijay, on the other hand, is a different story. After you get home you immediately search for 'cosmopolitan' on the Internet because the word for you is only the name of a women's magazine. A number of phrases pop up on the computer screen. Citizen of the world. Transcending national boundaries. OK, you've picked up a new word tonight.

As the three of you walked to the station you stole glances at Vijay. He was skinny and looked a little awkward behind his glasses, but it didn't take you long to arrive at a conclusion: you think he's sexy. Maybe it's because he's cosmopolitan.

You're supposed to have every Thursday and Sunday off, but today you work Fernando's shift because he's taking his daughter to the doctor.

'You have a kid?'

You couldn't hide your astonishment earlier when Fernando asked you to fill in for him.

'Yes, she's nine years old.'

'But you look so young!'

'I am young. I'm twenty-nine.'

You weren't sure whether your comment sounded like an attempt to flirt. Without additional prompting, Fernando told you that he and his wife have separated. You expressed sympathy and agreed to work that Thursday.

At three o'clock, you see Vijay step into the cafe, shouldering a backpack. He's alone and sits down in the spot usually occupied by the NYU professor, who, as it happens, hasn't come that day. You hurry over with a menu. When he smiles at you, your heart skips a beat.

You aren't sure how long Vijay will be sitting there. You tell yourself to be patient and wait until he's finished his coffee, even if it means going home a little late. But, at precisely four o'clock, he requests the bill.

'Working late?' he asks, after handing over his credit card.

'No, I'm actually leaving for home now.'

'Where do you live?'

'Jackson Heights.'

'Oh, really?' He looks surprised. 'I promised to meet somebody over there.'

'Want to head over with me?'

At this point you're sounding a bit forward, but you don't really care. Vijay waits for you to pack up. Various scenarios run through your head. Does he really need to meet someone in Jackson Heights? Maybe he just wants to go home with you. You're starting to get your hopes up.

It only takes half an hour to get from West 4th Station to Jackson Heights, but that's enough to sharpen your attraction to Vijay. He's living the life you want: travelling the world in search of stories.

Vijay doesn't know much concerning Indonesia beyond basic information about Suharto's regime and the 1998 reforms. He's visited 'only' a few countries in South East Asia, including Thailand, Cambodia and Myanmar, from when he'd been assigned to cover the Thai military coup two years previously. He makes a pessimistic prophecy about Myanmar: even if Aung San Suu Kyi is released, there will be no justice for the Rohingya. You listen reverently because everything that he says is new to you. What a strange region South East Asia is. The countries Vijay names are so close, yet so foreign.

'How does someone get to be so international?' You can't stop yourself from asking.

Vijay scratches his head. Perhaps your question sounds funny to his ears.

'Networks, maybe.'

Ah, yes. Networking. That's beyond the magic of red shoes.

'I've never done anything important,' you confess.

Vijay laughs. 'Define important.'

You ponder. When you made a deal with Devil, travel was the only thing you considered important. Leaving home to wander. Wandering, without needing to think about going home. This was more important than anything for you, and maybe for those trapped in the same city, the same house. But now that you're here, on the subways of New York where people with all sorts of stories mix as strangers, you feel that what you're doing isn't significant after all.

'Listening to stories and recording them. Isn't that important?' you ask Vijay.

'Says who?'

'You don't think your work matters?'

'Well, yes, to me. Because I write I was able to travel, my articles received some praise, and then I won a fellowship to New York.'

Again he laughs, but this time to himself.

'Stories are a curse when you hear them yet know you can't change anything.'

You don't really understand what he means.

You hope for something to happen at that moment, like a sudden train breakdown – anything that will buy time. But the train arrives as it should at Jackson Heights Station. He says goodbye in order to head to an Indian restaurant a few blocks away.

'See you later,' he says. 'Maybe at the cafe.'

'Yes, please stop by.'

You walk back to your apartment, wearing a smile the entire time.

You become the centre of attention in the cafe. Well, maybe that's a bit too strong. It's not like you waltz in and turn every man's head as if you were Marilyn Monroe. You've always known you're not the kind of woman who attracts attention in a dramatic way, but you're a magnet for some, at least. You haven't been there a month, and two men have already asked you out on dates: Fernando, the handsome waiter from Peru, and Robert Allen, NYU professor. Nice variety there, from a demographic perspective.

Fernando invites you to eat at a taco truck in front of Roosevelt Avenue Station. In fact, the station isn't his final stop. Normally he has to transfer from the E or the F to the 7, and get off at Junction Boulevard. But he's willing to interrupt his journey to steal some time with you. (Naturally, he doesn't say this, but what other reason could he have?)

'This isn't much,' Fernando says. 'I'll treat you again some other time.'

From inside the truck with its stove and steaming meat, the taco vendor leans forward and hands Fernando two tacos on a paper plate.

'What's this for?'

'For filling in for me that time.'

You brush it off.

'I'm serious. Next time we'll go out to dinner.'

You hear the clatter of the 7 train pass over Roosevelt Avenue. Fernando bites into a jalapeño, while you're still blowing on your piping hot taco.

Meanwhile, Robert – who asks you to call him Bob – starts looking for opportunities to meet you outside the cafe. At first he makes small talk every time you bring him his decaf with a splash of low-fat milk, no sugar. He asks if you're from Vietnam; your features remind him of someone he knew when he lived in Hanoi. You shake your head and say Indonesia. Bob turns out to have visited Singapore, Kuala Lumpur and Surabaya. As a Sinologist, over the past five years he has begun to turn his attention to the Chinese diaspora in South East Asia.

You chat with him longer after an accidental meeting in front of NYU's red-brick library. You've finished work and want to stroll along Broadway, and he's just come out of the building carrying a stack of books. For the first time, you study him closely. A warm cap covers his baldness, and thanks to the black overcoat that he is wearing, his belly doesn't bulge too much. His voice is soft and sympathetic. You can tell that he must have been quite handsome in his younger days. Alas, at that point you were probably still in diapers.

You realise that all this time he's been busy trying to figure out your background. He has assumed you're either a student or an artist on a tight budget waitressing for extra cash. You don't want to be too honest and say that before working in the cafe you were unemployed.

'I'm writing a book.'

You steal this idea from the question Vijay asked you some time ago. You feel claiming to be a writer isn't really a sin. Doesn't everyone write? Everyone must have scribbled lousy poetry in a diary or blog, or maybe written stories about vacation at grandma's.

Bob looks impressed. He's delighted to meet a female author from Indonesia who's working in a Manhattan cafe.

'Fiction or non-fiction?'

'Fiction,' you say. You go on to lie with remarkable fluency. 'I'm writing a story about a red-shoes adventure.'

Bob's eyes grow wider. He's becoming more and more interested in you, it seems.

'We have to chat more. Maybe we can have a coffee sometime.'

You nod enthusiastically. The attention is certainly gratifying, but you think of one name alone: Vijay Prasad. He visited the cafe again the day after your conversation on the train, but you only had time to chat briefly because he was busy with friends. No further meetings follow, but you keep thinking about him. It's all too possible to become obsessed with someone else despite – or, more precisely, because of – infrequent contact with them. You remember falling for Marcus Werner, the expat at EGW, even though the sole thing that dazzled you was when he said 'Hello, good morning, how are you?' in Indonesian. *Halo, selamat pagi, apa kabar?* An Indonesian-speaking white guy might sound sexy, because, after all, isn't Bahasa Indonesia completely insignificant? English for the Global World: that's the reality. But whatever the reason, you built up the myth of Marcus Werner every day until the Marcus of your mind far surpassed the Marcus of reality. Perhaps it's the same with Vijay. You rehearse all his cosmopolitan experience every day until you feel a growing intimacy with him, until in your imagination he has become far more captivating than the first time you met.

You start wondering. Does he think about you too?

Proceed to page 168.

The black turtleneck sweater you've worn all day clings to your body. You stand before your large mirror and comb your hair. The sweater's wool is so dark that your hair almost seems luminous in comparison. You look at the clock anxiously; it will soon be midnight. You set the comb on your bed and pace up and down before the mirror.

Your mind is made up. The mirror can show you who you are and, perhaps, your New York life before you found yourself in a taxi on the way to the airport. What sort of life did you lead? Maybe, if you remember it and retrieve your history, you'll be able to get along better in this city. Without history, no one can take a step anywhere.

So, tonight you count.

Ten. Nine. Eight. Seven. Six. Five. Four. Three. Two … Your apartment darkens for an instant. You hold your breath. Has the mirror game begun? You try to purge negative thoughts. Maybe, as in Indonesia, people here also have to deal with random blackouts. No need to panic or contact the doorman. You walk, feeling your way along the wall with your hand, moving towards your bedside table, where you grope for the flashlight stored in the second drawer. You remember having placed it there, just in case. Flicking on the torch, you try to find your phone, but something tempts you to glance at the mirror. You're afraid, but you also desire to know. You point the torch at the mirror. A face is reflected within it.

You're startled but then realise it's only your own reflection. Your black sweater renders your curves almost invisible.

You keep shining the torch at the mirror. Nothing. Instead, you become aware that the beam of light makes you look radiant. You've never seen yourself so beautiful. You smile, admiring the image that follows your movements, and remember the letter from Devil.

Maybe the mirror is telling you who you really are. You are beautiful, you are content, you don't need red shoes to run away.

Then you hear a soft whisper,

They don't know you're a murderer.

You feel a chill on your neck. There's no one behind you. The whisper has come from the mirror. You move closer. And then it dawns on you: either your reflection is too beautiful or you're looking at another woman.

You retreat slowly. You want to cry out, but your throat is dry. The woman in the mirror is still wearing your warm, black sweater, but she stays in place, no longer following your movements. Her face carries a smile, but yours has vanished. Now her eyes gaze straight at you:

'You. Murderer.'

And she starts to tell a story.

Continue to page 179.

You lay yourself down on the hotel bed. The sweater you've worn all day still clings to your body. This room is so quiet. You stare at the white ceiling, clean and sterile, and then recall your room in the boarding house back in Jakarta with its faded cream paint and the sonic assault from outside: the roar of motorbikes, the hubbub of food vendors, recitations of the Quran before Friday prayers. The trap lies not in alienation, but in the crowd. You feel as if in Juwita Padmadivya you've discovered yourself and all your hatred for the hustle and bustle of the city. What happened to her? Did she really kill herself? What was the point of her death? Is she someone who has been defeated or a martyr?

So many questions come to mind, and you want to talk to Yvette, who has curated Juwita's story. You've viewed Juwita through her lens.

Yvette's cell phone number is tucked away in your bag, but the awkward moment in front of the hotel makes you hesitate to call. The clock says eleven. You want to admit your regret in not inviting her up to your room. Had Yvette expected it? Are you embarrassed for being impolite, or ashamed to admit your own hopes?

What do *you* hope for?

You head to the bathroom and wash your face with warm water. Call her. Don't call her. Call her. No, maybe you're not supposed to. There's a difference between calling her tonight and calling tomorrow.

If you want to call her tonight and express regret for not inviting her to your room, proceed to page 157.

If you wait until tomorrow, when Yvette arrives at her office, to talk about what she has written about Juwita Padmadivya, turn to the next page.

The next day you call Yvette, but she doesn't pick up the phone. Then you call her office, but the receptionist says Yvette hasn't been seen all morning. You keep trying to reach her until the afternoon, with no luck. After two days, you decide to stop by where Yvette works, a small office on the second floor of an old building. The office appears to consist of just a few staff members. The receptionist whom you spoke to sits by the door. Again she tells you that there's been no word from Yvette. You're desperate. As you turn to leave, a woman stops you. Her name is Kristina, a good friend of Yvette.

'She left for Indonesia last night.'

You're stunned. Yvette had said nothing to you about that.

'May I see Juwita Padmadivya's documentary?'

Kristina looks taken aback by your question. She may be surprised that Yvette shared the story of the video with you.

'Nobody has ever seen the video except Yvette.' A little hesitant, Kristina continues, 'And as far as Juwita goes, I'm not sure Yvette will find her. I think it's just a game. Juwita's name doesn't even show up on the Internet.'

You feel you've arrived at a dead end. There's nothing else you can do. You say goodbye to Kristina, but as though suddenly remembering something, she asks you to wait a moment. She goes into her office and returns with a package.

'Yvette left this. She said it's a present for you.'

Confused, you accept it with a thank you and hurry out of the office. There's no point in lingering. You go back to your hotel and sit down at the guest computer in the lobby. You type Juwita's name into Google. No results.

Es wurden keine mit Ihrer Suchenfrage – 'juwita padmad-ivya' – übereinstimmenden Dokumente gefunden.

Of course not. Kristina already told you so.

In your room, you unwrap the gift from Yvette. A video camera. No card, no explanation. You cradle the camera for a long time. Yvette is avoiding you. You've received a gift again, but you feel like you've been dumped.

Berlin begins to seem unfriendly. Suddenly you feel lonely. You still don't know what you'd hoped for from your encounter with Yvette. The meetings on your journey linger for a moment before they slip away and disappear, and soon you find yourself scavenging the memories of what's left, like a loser. Just the way it has always been. Nothing strange about that.

Maybe one day you'll meet her again. But by then you'll probably have become another person.

All right, let's continue our journey. You have to get out of here, but where? Amsterdam, maybe. Or Zagreb.

If you choose Amsterdam, turn to page 204.

If you choose Zagreb, turn to page 214.

After thinking it over and over and over again, you finally pick up the hotel phone. You tap the table impatiently as you listen to it ring.

'Yvette?'

'Hey.'

Her voice is a little husky.

'Is Juwita still alive?'

'I don't know. I keep looking for her.'

Her voice sounds as it did when you went your separate ways in front of the hotel, friendly and formal, like a telephone operator.

'I'm sorry for not inviting you upstairs.'

'You regret it?'

You sigh, then say quietly, 'Yes, I regret it.'

'Do you know what will happen if you invite me?'

You fall into a lengthy silence. You don't know how to answer. Then she laughs, warmly. She doesn't say anything, just gives a long laugh, and you look at your face in the mirror on the hotel wardrobe. There's a glimmer of a smile there.

'You should come over,' you say.

'It's late, it's already midnight. And I'm not eighteen any more.'

But that night you talk on the phone for ages. You don't know how long it's been since you've done that – maybe high school or college, when everyone had all the time in the world and didn't know what to do with it. You feel like a teenager.

At one in the morning, you turn off the lights, but you're still listening to Yvette's voice on the phone. You ask her if she's ever wanted to kill herself.

'I've been through that. I chose to live.'

You wonder if this is what attracts Yvette to Juwita Padmadivya.

'I desperately wanted to die, but I was still a kid,' Yvette said. 'I was only nineteen.'

'A young woman, you mean.'

'Kid, young woman. As far as I'm concerned the difference is small. Maybe it's just sex that separates them. Sex makes you a young woman. But in other ways, you're still a kid.'

'What do you mean?'

'When you're young, you know only one kind of power: the power your oppressors hold. Power belongs to the state, schools, parents. They're all the same. In those days I thought about suicide. Suicide is the sincerest protest you can make against authority. At least that's what I used to think, but I made it through that phase. As a kid, or, if you prefer, as a youth, all you want is to be in a position to resist power. Once you're an adult, you desire power yourself, even when it presents itself in shards, or mere specks of stardust. Even the rebels you admire as a kid possess it. You crave power because there's nothing you can do without it.'

Silence. The phone receiver begins to feel hot, and you move it from your right ear to your left. You keep listening to Yvette. You feel like you're asking a lot of things, and that years later you'll forget whether the questions genuinely mattered or you were just buying time. But you'll always remember her voice, so soft and crisp, at the conversation's end.

'Time to sleep. Sweet dreams.'

Speculation about Juwita dominates your conversation in the following days. You and Yvette write out a few possibilities:

1) Juwita really committed suicide. She'd been planning it for a long time and the film was just a pretext to carry out her mission. But why wasn't her death reported in the paper? It may have been reported, you say, but the police referred to her only as 'J.P.'. If so, we should start searching archives for the deaths of people with the initials 'J.P.'.

2) Juwita didn't commit suicide. Isn't it true that after the camera pans over the white pills and the sheet of paper with the mysterious message we don't see anything else? Maybe she's leading an ordinary life now. She married a rich guy, and is living comfortably as a housewife who gets to travel the world. 'Hmm, good for her,' Yvette says. 'But that's such a boring ending.'

3) Juwita Padmadivya is a fictional character. She's the invention of a woman who made a movie about her and played Juwita's role. Maybe that person is also called Juwita, but this Juwita made a film about Juwita Prime (like A in A' – remember that lesson in school?). At this point you say: I didn't like maths. How should we refer to Juwita the Director as opposed to Juwita the Character? If so, we have to add more possibilities to the list:

4) *Juwita* is a film made by a director other than Juwita.

5) _____

_____

You discuss scenarios in detail. If Juwita's film was directed by someone else, who was it? Nadya Shafik? Yvette protests: Why not Retno Wahyuni? She's dead, you say. Even if she's not, Retno was hardly brave enough to make a film like that.

Tsk tsk. Yvette shakes her head. Don't be fooled by appearances. Maybe, in spite of her obedience to order and determination to maintain the concept of a home, Retno found Juwita inside herself.

One day, in the umpteenth cafe you visit with Yvette, you ask, 'Why are you so obsessed with Juwita?'

'But she fascinates you too, doesn't she?' Yvette says. 'Maybe it's because she returned home only to leave again.'

Juwita the Wanderer. Maybe there's a little Juwita in all of us.

Sitting at the hotel computer, you delete several emails from your sister. You always read the personal letters, though you rarely reply. But she also likes to share random information unprompted. Often these messages are forwards: 'FWD: The Beauty Benefits of Cucumbers'; 'FWD: Best International Islamic Primary Schools'; 'FWD: Beware of Formula Milk Campaign in Hospital A'. Your sister follows several mailing lists, from those for alumni of the various schools she's attended to organisations that interest her – parent–teacher associations, Quranic recitation groups, Muslimah fashion business networks, breastfeeding advocacy. You don't know if she's added your email address to a group, but you're always getting propaganda – Islamic or not – that you never open. Your sister probably realises that you immediately delete her chain emails, but that doesn't slow her down.

You casually delete the string of emails, but one subject line stops you short: 'FWD: Threat of LGBT Stalkers in Schools'.

A mother at school X reported that her son was reading a book with no educational value whatsoever. It tells the story of a child raised by two fathers. According to the book, families come in all shapes and sizes and puts forth the idea that parents do not have to be a father–mother pair alone – gay couples can be parents. School X must take responsibility for spreading this immoral material. What will happen to our children if they are infected with

the LGBT lifestyle? Of course, we have heard of sodomy
cases that occurred in the bathroom at school Y in broad
daylight. LGBT predators target schools. This news is
thoroughly unsettling. Safeguard the future of our children
beginning now.

You want to write to your sister and challenge her outright:
what do you mean by sending me an email like this?

But you're too tired. You point the cursor towards the trash.
Click. The email has found a more appropriate home.

The wall that divides you and your sister is too high to
scale. You don't know what would happen if you returned
home. Maybe you'd be turned into stone, like Malin
Kundang.

You wonder how Malin Kundang is doing now.

If you want to take another look at the story of the faithless
child, go to page 23, and then return here.

Seven in the evening. The elevator doors open and you walk
towards Yvette, who has been waiting for you in the lobby.
From a distance you see that she's sitting on the couch and
reading a book. She wears her usual red boots. You glance at
the mirror and smile seeing yourself, dressed in black, looking
slightly different tonight. More beautiful, because you're
wearing your red shoes. You stop in front of Yvette. She lifts
her gaze and puts away her book. She surveys you from head
to toe, then fixes her eyes on the shimmering red shoes.

'You also –' she stammers. '*Et tu, Brute?*'

'Yes.'

'You look gorgeous. Your shoes too. They're like Dorothy's.'

'Dorothy's?'

'You know *The Wizard of Oz*, don't you?'

You feel as if you do know. But if you need to refresh your memory, go to page 21. Then come right back.

It seems to you that you've been in this situation before. You pause to recall *The Wizard of Oz* and its familiar images: a bored Kansas girl in a black-and-white village. Later adventures full of dazzling colour, and hand-me-down ruby slippers from a dead witch. But where have you experienced this? Is this déjà vu?

'Don't go back to Kansas,' Yvette whispers.

'I want to keep travelling and travelling, without ever going back home.'

You leave the hotel and walk towards a train station. She takes you to a bar. 'There's a band from New York,' she says. 'Do you know the Rat King?'

You shake your head. Should you? What's so special about a band from New York?

'Nothing.' Yvette laughs. 'I'm just curious. And maybe also because you've come from New York. How many rats are in New York? I hear there are lots.'

City of rats. That's not your image of New York at all. But you don't know what it's like to live there since the red shoes dropped you into the middle of an adventure, and you skipped New York to travel elsewhere. You wonder what you'd have experienced if you had called off your trip to Berlin. Would your adventures have been more thrilling? But your choice has left you here, walking the city in red shoes, with someone who has her own tale to tell. You don't regret it.

It appears that quite a few people are keen to see the Rat King from New York. You begin to wonder if the band is well known. You and Yvette queue for a long time before entering the bar. Yvette says the place is always full on weekends, with or without the Rat King.

You still find the name ridiculous.

'But you know about the Rat King, right? *Rattenkönig*.'

'Is there actually a Rat King?'

The bouncer gestures for you and Yvette to go in. Yvette takes you by the hand and says a little hastily, '*Rattenkönig* – oh, you don't want to see one.'

Yvette buys you a beer. In the darkness, you can make out that the band has set up already. The stage lights soon come up, showcasing the Rat King, a band from New York that covers American songs from the fifties and sixties. Their originals also supposedly draw on older rock and roll. The vocalist, a little man with a moustache, wears white bell-bottoms and a T-shirt that reads 'Little Johnny'.

'Don't you just want to give the singer a squeeze?' Yvette whispers.

You giggle. Little Johnny, stocky and squat, reminds you of a garden gnome.

'Good evening, Berlin!'

Drumbeats, accompanied by the audience's applause, open the first song. The guitar kicks in, and Little Johnny starts prancing around. The Rat King performs Roy Orbison's 'Pretty Woman'. Little Johnny shakes his hips, does the twist, and the crowd claps. It turns out that he doesn't resemble a garden gnome. His movements are too lively, like those of a rodent. You remember what Yvette has just said about the Rat King.

'Is that what the Rat King is like?'

Yvette shakes her head. 'The Rat King is scary,' she says. 'Little Johnny is sexy.'

After 'Pretty Woman', the band perform one of their own numbers. You don't learn the title, but the music gets you moving.

'The next song is by Mel Carter,' Little Johnny says into the microphone. 'It's called "Hold Me, Thrill Me, Kiss Me".'

The atmosphere shifts from steamy to melancholic. The bright yellow stage lights have turned magenta.

'Let's dance,' Yvette says.

She takes your hand and leads you to the centre of the dance floor, near the stage. Little Johnny sings like a lover drunk on passion. You stiffen when Yvette wraps her arms around your waist. Your steps are halting. You glance at Little Johnny, and he tosses you a knowing smile and a wink.

Yvette's hair is soft against your cheek. For the first time, you gaze into her eyes. In the darkness they drag you deep into a forest. What is bewitching you – your red shoes or her gaze? You suddenly remember following Yvette into the forest in your dream. Did she pull your hand or did you chase her? You can't go home, don't want to go home. They'll curse you. You want to be kidnapped, like those who long for Snow Red.

What lies in the forest? The past, or the future?

You seek the answer in her red cherry lips.

Maybe you shouldn't let this woman cast you into a forbidden forest. You wonder who has ever stood in the dark with her.

After the show, you spend the night at Yvette's. In the morning she wakes you and invites you into her study. She opens the closet to reveal a couple of dozen red shoes in various styles arrayed inside.

'My God,' you mutter. 'I've only got one pair.'

'I have fourteen. Every year since leaving my father behind, I buy another pair of red shoes. They're sort of milestones for me.'

'You're crazy.'

You keep thinking about the previous night. Maybe everything that happened was an accident. Getting drunk makes you want to cross borders. It probably wasn't just the alcohol, but the rhythm of the music, Little Johnny's seductive voice, and the cherry lips that aroused your hunger. After that, however, not a day passes for you without Yvette. You keep meeting for coffee and are anxious when you have to go back home, like an addict: you want to drink coffee, over and over again, and you realise you crave something more. You want to crush her lips and to glance at the mirror, heart pounding, and find traces of red lipstick planted all over your nose, cheeks and mouth. You stay more often in her apartment, and in the morning you wake amid a welter of overlapping feelings: confusion, frenzy, longing. You never imagined you'd arrive at this point and feel such emotions. Maybe you've crossed a boundary, never to return.

'I have to be honest with you,' you say one morning.

You're making breakfast for Yvette in the kitchen as she hugs you from behind and kisses your neck. You tremble as you feel her soft lips and warm tongue on your skin.

'We need to talk.'

'You sound like you're in a movie,' Yvette says as she ruffles your hair.

You and Yvette sit opposite each other at the kitchen table. You put down two plates of pancakes, dripping honey, with strawberries. Yvette has taught you how to make them because your repertoire consisted only of instant noodles. In the middle of breakfast, you confess: 'I've never felt this way before. I don't know what to call how I feel. But I want to always be with you. I think I'm addicted.'

Yvette stops chewing and puts down her fork. Now her hands are on yours.

'Yvette, do you think I'm just experimenting? Pretending? Do you think I'm – ? Oh, hell, I can't even say the word, because I don't think that's me.'

'Do you think I'm pretending to want you?'

You shake your head.

'I don't think you're pretending,' she says.

'I don't know who I am. What do I call myself now?'

'Maybe –' Yvette looks at you intently. 'Maybe you should stop worrying about labels and putting yourself in a box.'

'I've never fallen in love with a woman. I don't even know if I like women. All I know is that I'm in love with you.'

'And that's not enough?'

You're taken aback. That's enough – more than enough. You've never fallen in love with anyone in this way. Yvette smiles, then she bites a strawberry. You are reminded of red lipstick and how you want traces of it all over your body.

'Come here,' Yvette says softly.

Exactly one month after your arrival in Berlin, you drag your stuff out of the hotel and move into Yvette's place. Who are you now? Together with Yvette, have you crossed over, never to return? You don't know the answer. But maybe Yvette is right. Labels and boxes don't matter any more when you always want to be with someone, hear her whole life story, or trace your fingers through her hair when you're worn out after making love.

Your visa is still valid for two months, but after that you have to go back to New York. Your residence permit for the US is valid until the fall of next year. 'Maybe we can go together,' Yvette says. 'We can live in New York, then come back to Berlin.'

It sounds like a fun plan.

In your last days before leaving for New York, Demon Lover appears abruptly. He knows Yvette is not home, so he rings the doorbell, disguised as a Domino's Pizza delivery man. He tries to tease you with hugs and kisses, then wails for you to come back, but the strategy fizzles. He is furious.

'Our contract is cancelled, finished,' he declares.

His crimson eyes blaze, and in a flash he disappears. But before he does, he spits out a question:

'Are you sure this is your best choice of adventure?'

Proceed to page 410.

Does Vijay Prasad think of you? You finally receive your answer in a most painful manner. In a word: no. He does not. He's not interested in you in the slightest, even though you've fallen for him, hope for him to show up at the cafe every day, and occasionally make him the object of masturbation fantasies on dull nights. This isn't a love that leaves you in agony. It's not even love, as you don't know if you've ever really loved anyone. Sure, sex with Demon Lover intoxicated you, but you're not exactly weeping or wailing for him, maybe because he upset you so often. You haven't known Vijay long enough to feel either intoxicated or in pain. What hurts is how the truth was revealed.

That night, after work, his presence in your apartment lobby catches you completely off-guard. You find him standing in front of the elevator. At first he's confused to see you as well, but then greets you with a friendly expression. He's visiting someone who lives in your building. You both enter the elevator, and you hit the button for the eighth floor. He does not press a button.

Your heart pounds and your imagination runs wild. Maybe he wants to see you home before he meets the 'someone'. It would be even better, of course, if there were no someone and Vijay is just making excuses to see you to your apartment. Then you can invite him in and you'll get what you've been after.

The elevator door opens. You step out, and he follows. 'Your friend lives on this floor?'

Vijay says yes.

'What a coincidence.'

'A real coincidence, yes.'

You and Vijay walk the eighth floor's corridor together. You continue your small talk, not important, but the longer it lasts, the more forced it feels. Now he looks uncomfortable, as if something has dawned on him, and his pace slows. You're on your way to the same spot.

'I'm headed here,' he says quietly.

He stops at your neighbour's door. Likewise, you stop, feeling bewildered at first, and then stupid.

He's about to visit that feral woman.

You and Vijay look at each other, awkwardly, at the door of *her* apartment. His face flushes crimson. You're each trapped with the same unbearable knowledge. Someone needs to put an end to this miserable moment. You take the initiative.

'See you later, then,' you say.

Vijay nods, smiling stiffly. You step towards your apartment. He pretends he's not watching you, but you know he won't ring the bell until you've gone in. You turn the key and hastily shut the door behind you, rescuing yourself.

There's no doubt that he was mortified.

In your kitchen, his awkward expression stays with you. He could never have imagined that you were the neighbour he'd disturbed on those sweaty nights, the neighbour who pounded on the wall, annoyed and jealous. You, neighbour as well as cafe acquaintance, have been earwitness to his uninhibited escapades with that wild creature.

Vijay was clearly miserable, and so are you. You find it difficult to accept that the porn star of your imagination is in fact Vijay, who is more on the scrawny side than a broad-shouldered, hard-muscled stud.

At your little dining table, you poke at your instant noodles. The aroma is enticing. MSG makes you ravenous even though the noodles soon feel like rubber on your tongue.

At least you can cross Vijay's name off the list of potential men in your orbit. A mental 'list' that you put together without much consideration, which is actually not something to be too proud of. Vijay has been number one, with Fernando and Bob at two and three. You sigh. Adventures don't always offer unlimited choice.

You've demolished the instant noodles and take out some Ben & Jerry's from the freezer. As you scoop out the ice cream, your mind shifts from Vijay to the wanton woman in the violet sari.

She's becoming more mysterious in your eyes. What does Vijay see in her?

The ice cream feels soft and cold on your tongue. Your teeth grind the crunchy almonds into smithereens.

Ah, wrong question. Isn't it obvious what Vijay sees in her? She's a freak in bed. One hot mama.

That night no noise penetrates the walls of your room. Vijay must have told her about his encounter with you and made a point of urging his lover to be more well mannered in her fucking.

Proceed to the next page.

The Neighbour's Love Story

It's bizarre how obsessed you become with the wild woman in the purple sari. At first, you think of her as a jealous rival would. How could she land sexy Vijay, smart Vijay, Vijay, that cosmopolitan creature? What does she have that you don't? Fine, let's say that Vijay does have particular tastes and is into women who are … expressive, even screamers, in bed. But what was it that attracted him to that slut in the first place? You remember the day you saw her from behind, walking towards the elevator. Her face was obscured. Maybe she's extraordinarily beautiful, but more likely not. Maybe she's smart and funny. Maybe she's sexy.

You shake your head, arguing with yourself. From behind she looked elegant, serene, but not sexy. It's hard to envision a woman like that going crazy in bed. You can picture her cooking in the kitchen. Knitting in a rocking chair, maybe. She'd probably look sweet in a hijab. You imagine your neighbour in a variety of identities, but sex bomb isn't one of them.

What kind of woman is she really? Is she a little dove tease or a sweet thing with an itch that needs scratching?

Your curiosity grows and becomes a much greater obsession than your idle Vijay fantasies. You want to spy on your neighbour, study her face and observe her behaviour. But that's clearly out. There has to be a safe way to do some recon.

You remember the rendang you made for Mr Zhao.

Surely no one in this world turns away a generous neighbour bearing gifts of food.

Armed with a serving container of rendang, you knock on her door. You wait a good while until she comes out. In front of you she stands, cinnamon-skinned and with freely flowing locks. Her big eyes stare straight at you.

Well, well, here she is, the woman who howled like a banshee while bonking your dream man. Bitch.

Without a sari, she's not as radiant as a Bollywood star. You stifle signs of your delight. She wears a faded grey sweater, dark loose trousers and wool socks. Thirty, maybe? She squints at you with suspicion. But she doesn't look like a predator. You smile, your expression just a little too friendly.

'Hi! I'm your neighbour.'

You don't say 'next-door neighbour' because you don't want to embarrass her (or is that anger her?). You concoct a little tale about how you made too much food and are keen to share. She frowns. There aren't any holidays this month. Christmas, Chinese New Year, Diwali, they've all passed.

'Maybe you'd like to try some Indonesian food?'

She accepts, even though your offer seems a little forced. Forced smile, forced manners.

'Thank you.'

You expect a husky, sexy voice, but it's utterly unremarkable, the sort of voice you'd hear over the phone from a customer service agent at a bank. There's nothing mysterious or glamorous about it.

You say goodbye. She thanks you again, and you return to your room with a sense of satisfaction. You've finally seen her, and she's just an average human being. Sweet enough, but certainly no goddess. Maybe Vijay's tastes aren't so remarkable. You feel like you've emerged victorious in the little competition you've created, taking the same sort of pleasure you would if you learned that your ex had ended up with someone no more attractive than you.

Her moans ring in your ears. Are they happy? You sure hope not.

*

Her name is Meena.

You discover that later. To your surprise, your first conversation is not the last. In fact, the meeting launches a series of unexpected encounters.

Meena appears a few days later at your door. She returns your container, now filled with half a dozen warm samosas. This time she is friendlier, her expression genuinely curious as she asks about your rendang.

'Did you use lemongrass?'

The question catches you off-guard. She has not mentioned her name, and you have yet to formally introduce yourself. You anticipated that she'd make small talk about how long you've lived there, what you think of the weather these days and so on. Instead she engages you straight away over lemongrass.

Blushing slightly, you confess that you used an instant spice mix because a fine rendang is so time-consuming. You don't have the patience. She nods, understanding.

'I add a little seasoning. Onion, garlic, chilli –'

'Lots of coriander?'

'How did you know?'

She chuckles. All of a sudden you feel that your question is naive and betrays you for the amateur chef that you are. You tell her how you've relied on spice mixes as you've learned to cook over these last few months. Your repertoire is limited: rendang, *rawon*, fried liver in chilli sauce, and pasta, of course. You always keep a few bottles of bolognese and Alfredo sauce in your cupboard. Instant spice mixes are your saviour, you say.

'Oh, yes, yes.' She tries to look as though she agrees. 'You cook really well. I wouldn't have known you're a beginner.'

Now you have a chance to study her more closely. Her features have a sweetness to them, and you can actually picture her as a Bollywood star. She reminds you of Kajol in the role of Shahrukh Khan's lover in *Dilwale Dulhania Le Jayenge*. You remember how the film was constantly playing on television back home.

Your neighbour asks about Indonesian restaurants in New York. You name all the ones scattered around Queens. There are fewer than five, and you've been a customer at each of them, especially before you started cooking.

'They're all in walking distance.'

Your news seems to excite her. That's when you introduce yourselves more formally, in the middle of a conversation about favourite dishes (rendang at Minang Asli, *batagor* at Mie Jakarta; both restaurants are nearby). Apparently, she's lived in the apartment for a few years. You apologise for keeping her standing at the door and invite her in. She declines politely.

'Next time.'

She's not lying.

The invitation comes on a scrap of paper slipped under the door. The message is brief: *Hello, would you like to have lunch with me tomorrow? Call me at 646-xxx-xxxx. Meena.*

She opens the door wearing a blue apron; her hair is up in a bun, strands loose at the sides. You have to admit that today she looks beautiful. For the first time, you set foot in her apartment, which is suffused with the scent of onions. It's a one-bedroom, identical to yours, but feels fuller. The main space is divided in striking fashion: kitchen, non-kitchen. Meena's cooking space is bedlam; piles of plates and pans, saucepots and seasonings, and containers of oil all bulge giddily from the cupboard. The stove is splattered with stains. You have a hunch that the kitchen sees a whirr of activity every single day.

Beyond that, the flat is smartly furnished. Next to the cooking area and its chaos stands a dining table with four chairs, in contrast to your two. A scarlet tablecloth is fringed with beads. Stepping further inside, you see a bright red sofa with two cushions that match the tablecloth. She owns a television, but it's not on. Your apartment, with its simple black futon for furniture, feels very spare. Here everything aside from the hyperactive kitchen occupies its place serenely. The absence of photos in the living room surprises you at first, but then you note the closed door of the bedroom. Ah, of course. Meena keeps her pictures there, in that room, the chamber for her delirious trysts with Vijay.

You swallow.

'It'll be done soon.'

Meena's voice prevents you from conjuring lewd images. She invites you to sit on the sofa until she finishes cooking. You move towards the kitchen and offer to help, but she tells you not to bother. You stand behind her, watching as she chops onions. Her fingers, long and agile like a dancer's, throw the diced onions in a pot. You glance at the slew of freshly used spice bottles on her counter. Reds, yellows, greens. Like a rainbow, but bolder. You've imagined her cooking, but not like this, not in such a state of chaos. You imagined a neat and orderly kitchen, not this raging mess.

The pot of steaming ruddy sauce arouses your appetite.

'It looks delicious.'

'The chicken tikka masala? Ever had it?'

'Maybe. I forget.'

You've eaten in Indian restaurants a few times but can never remember the names of the dishes you've tried. 'What's it seasoned with?'

'Garam masala.'

Meena points to a bottle of brown powder. You peer at the blend of ground spices for the first time – pepper, bay leaves, nutmeg, cinnamon, cumin, cardamom, cloves, among others. You can't remember all of what she says.

'So it's a kind of all-purpose seasoning?'

Meena laughs. 'Yes, you could say that. Like Italian seasoning.'

'What's Italian seasoning?'

Meena opens her cupboard wide, leaving you awestruck. Row upon row of bottles, of varying sizes and colours, fill the shelves. Their contents are just as diverse: powders, seeds, leaves. She points to one.

'This is Italian seasoning,' she says. 'Basil, oregano, rosemary, thyme.'

Meena smiles at your astonishment over the kaleidoscopic array of vials. Selecting one, she unseals it then brings the glass to her nose and inhales deeply.

'You must know this one,' she says, stretching the vial out towards you. 'Our treasure.'

Coriander seeds. Indian cooking uses a lot of coriander too, she says. She holds the bottle and sniffs again. Her eyes are slightly closed.

'I love the smell of spices.'

'Because spices remind you of home?'

'Because spices roam the world.'

Like Vijay.

You're a little surprised to find yourself linking her answer to Vijay.

Meena, who certainly has no inkling of the voices in your head, calmly lowers the stove's flame.

'Do you cook with coriander leaves too?'

'Coriander leaves?'

'Cilantro.'

She opens the fridge and shows you.

'Cilantro likes to travel too. You'll find it in tacos. In tom yam soups as well.'

To be honest, you hadn't noticed.

Meena transfers the chicken tikka masala to a serving bowl. You help set the table, which already has basmati rice on it. Meena offers you juice. She takes a glass and removes a container of orange juice from the fridge. Before pouring, she examines its label.

'Always check the expiry date,' she says, as if talking to herself.

You take a spoonful of the chicken. Warm taste sensations fill your mouth. The savoury, spicy flavours entrance you, leaving your tongue longing for more.

'This is amazing.' Your praise is entirely sincere. 'Are you a chef?'

She laughs melodically.

Meena, originally from Delhi, came to America to study commerce at the University of Buffalo. As an international student, she had the opportunity to work for a year in the US before returning to India and decided to intern at an online media company in Manhattan. Meena earns a decent salary, though hardly extravagant for New York, and she was also happy to finally be able to leave quiet Buffalo. She found a cheap flat through the connections of local Indian friends.

'Have you always liked to cook?'

Meena shakes her head.

Her mother taught her from childhood, but she wasn't especially interested. In America, she first cooked to survive, then to evoke memories of home. Over time, she began experimenting with recipes from all over the world, from Cajun pasta to Shanghai-style dim sum. She roasted a turkey every Thanksgiving and made a very sweet and rich Louisiana bread pudding. Cooking for her was a form of travel.

Vijay's name finally comes up over lunch. Meena mentions him first.

'Vijay says you've met.'

She sounds entirely natural. You try to conceal your agitation. Meena doesn't feel the need to say that Vijay is her lover. From the way she talks, you know she's marking territory. This is mine, that is yours.

She seems to intuit that her presence is a little threatening for you. In a friendly tone she says, 'Maybe the three of us can have a meal together some time.'

Bad idea, but you pretend to find it appealing.

'Does Vijay like to cook too?'

'Oh, yes. Just one taste and he's already worked out how your dish is spiced,' she says. 'He knows how to use his tongue.'

You feel your face flush at the last sentence, as the moans and cries that made winter feel so steamy come to mind. Now you begin to understand how to connect the cook and the courtesan. In the kitchen and in bed, she serves up a complex masala, savoury and spicy.

Is your lack of adventure starting to feel dull? Meena interests you because nothing exciting is going on. Your life in New York is turning out to be common, not like a movie, and you're struggling to find thrills. Maybe, though, if you're patient, something unexpected will appear at the end of the rainbow.

Proceed to page 198.

The Rumpelstiltskin Game

They don't know you're a killer. My room-mate Tatyana had just returned from her village in the Ukraine and she had to do the unimaginable: call 911. That night, after hours of crying, she finally managed to control herself, mourning the loss of normalcy more than the loss of a loved one. She speculated about the cause, just as people did a month ago when Heath Ledger, the Joker, was found dead in this city, and she came to the conclusion that it was suicide, pure and simple. But I know you. I said your name clearly, with a feeble sense of victory, just before you vanished. The puzzle had been solved and your name was revealed.

Throughout its interminable journey, the windows of the Amtrak Pennsylvanian reflected dull skin and a pair of tired, swollen eyes. Glass plays sadistic tricks to make you look older and less attractive. I have never liked how I look when travelling, and even more so after sitting for seven and a half hours. I've had worse: a thirty-hour plane trip including transit, waiting, delays. It's going too far for people to claim that travel is no more painful than enduring the curse of sitting around at home.

When the train pulled into Philadelphia, someone inter-rupted my daydreaming. You, stranger, so fresh and young-looking, perturbed me with your dizzying aroma, a perfume whose name I didn't know, grating, almost offensive. You asked permission to sit next to me. I had hoped the seat would stay empty because when I'm on my period, the most uncomfortable time to travel, I always find companionship suffocating. It's as if I don't have enough space, enough room to breathe. I nodded out of compulsion, to be polite, and you thanked me as you draped your red coat over the back of a seat. I thought you were from East Asia, and you might have thought I was Hispanic. I kept reading a novel, ignoring you.

You interrupted me again, asking if I was Indonesian after a glance at my book, and when I said yes, you immediately shifted languages. Presumably you imagined that we shared some sort of bond, while I still regarded you as an interloper, whatever your nationality. I hoped you would get off in New Jersey, but, alas, we were both heading for New York. You wanted to know why I had been in Pittsburgh.

'Meeting a friend,' I said.

'Me too. I've got an Indo friend in Philly.'

I hate that word, Indo. I have heard about an Indonesian community in Philadelphia, mostly from the middle class, seeking better income, even if it means overstaying a visa. I've met illegal immigrants in New York too, but we never talked to each other much beyond asking where to find spices or 'Indo' restaurants. We didn't deliberately intend to build barriers, but I can't say barriers weren't there. You did not perceive this barrier between us, and you even thought we should get to know each other better. You worked in Greenwich Village, in a cafe you called 'historic'. I answered, 'Uh-huh', without telling you that I used to visit it regularly when I first arrived in New York. The cafe made me feel nostalgic for history, or for a period of history I wanted to claim as my own. As you thrust out your hand, you mentioned a name – one that caused you to note that we should be sisters, but I knew that remembering your name would have been pointless for us both. If we hadn't been in another country, I'm sure we'd never have greeted each other. Having spent many years abroad, I don't consider meeting someone from home a thrill. And I'm quite adept at erasing faces.

'Do you work in New York?'

'A post-doc, two years.'

And that after two years in Leiden, six years in New Haven. I didn't have to explain, and you didn't need to know, that I wasn't sure what would come next. Wow, you said, though I wasn't certain you really understood what deserved to be treated as 'wow'. You asked if I grew up in Jakarta, and my nod made your eyes glow. Given the number of Indonesians here, your reaction was a bit over the top.

'Is your family back there?' You dug for more information.

'My husband.'

A little information about me was enough for you, or so I thought. Then came your turn. Your tale of melodrama tumbled on insistently with the train, past the naked trees of winter and the stark, white landscape. You quit college nine years ago, after your father died leaving unpaid debts. When your visa expired you hung out in Los Angeles, becoming a cashier at Panda Express and a shop clerk for Forever 21. (I cut you off: that's the store that was boycotted by migrant workers, isn't it? You didn't know, of course.) You married an American who took you to Chicago, then New York. After that, life entered the fast lane: you gave birth to a child but divorced after three years of marriage. You diligently saved the tips you made working at a bar, hoping one day to return to school. At least you had a green card now.

'Are you staying on here?'

'What do you mean by here?'

'New York.'

'You mean *there*. We haven't arrived yet.'

'Ah, yeah.' You laughed. 'You know what I mean. Here. In America.'

At this stage you have named and blurred 'here' and 'there'. My perfunctory answer didn't matter to you, perhaps because what you wanted to say was that you could stay anywhere, that you were always ready to leave at a moment's notice. Packing and unpacking suitcases felt so banal to you.

'Shouldn't smart people like you be the ones to go home? They need people like you, not me.'

My face flushed. I tried to change the subject and ask more about you. Hardly difficult, because you seemed very much an exhibitionist who enjoyed peeling off her layers one at a time.

Returning home turned out to be important to you because your boyfriend lived in Jakarta. You met him five years ago, 'here' (in this country, not on this train – just to be clear). You thought your dalliance would come to an end quickly in his apartment, or in Washington Square Park, where you'd meet for coffee before you left for work, but in fact you began flying to Jakarta twice a year. In between these occasional meetings you relied on the Internet, which deserves celebration; it allows long-distance relationships to be reinterpreted.

'Why not get married so your boyfriend can stay in New York?' I asked. You agreed – and have proved – that marriage is an effective way of getting around national borders, but your situation isn't so simple.

'He's got a wife.' Your response was to the point.

I looked at the portrait framed by the window. Images of furrowed trees, their sturdy roots buried beneath a blanket of snow, were superimposed on my face, wizened and weary. A question mark materialised, like calligraphy, in the distortion of the glass, a stroke of black ink that would soon fade.

As a child, when you skipped rope with your girlfriends, did it occur to you that you might grow up to be a thief? Do you take secret pleasure in hurting other women?

Shouldn't you hate yourself?

'And you?' Again you broke my reverie. 'How do you manage being so far away from your husband?'

In a world of fusion and fission, of meetings and farewells, my husband and I had different desires that led us south and north. We promised to take different paths for a fixed period of time, heeding the demands of a world that set us, or at least me, in motion. Then at some point we will meet in the middle. Maybe I'll go back for him, maybe he'll follow me here, or somewhere as yet undetermined. In the meantime, we hold on to places and times that we haggle over and manage adroitly.

I can't remember if I said more than I should have, but I heard you laugh and croon a song from the Magic Kingdom, off-key Disney. *It's a small world after all. La la la la lala lala.* Dolls of the world, unite.

'So you don't know where you'll be in, say, five years from now? That's funny.'

'Why?'

'You don't look like the adventurous type.'

I didn't want to argue, so I simply replied, 'We'll see.'

'What are you waiting for? The world to stop?'

I took it as a joke. The next minute you were busy checking your well-manicured nails. Focus wasn't your strong point, apparently.

'How do you divide your time between work and being a wife?'

Your clichéd question was too personal. I shot back, 'How do you divide your time between being a mother and being a mistress?'

You caught my sarcasm. But, without losing your sense of humour, you asked: Are there really people willing to play all these roles? They must want to die.

'You and I are a lot alike,' you then murmured.

Because we both still have ties to Indonesia?

'Our connections to Indonesia are similar. Especially when it comes to men,' you said, blinking. 'Hey, I hope it's not your husband I'm seeing.'

'That's not funny.'

'Remember the idea about six degrees of separation?' you said, your face growing more serious.

Then you talked at length about your boyfriend. He likes Mexican food, Buñuel films, and has some pretty weird sexual fantasies. I was relieved for an embarrassing reason: the man sounded nothing like my husband. I didn't even bother to ask your boyfriend's name.

'Your husband now or the one from five years ago?' you asked.

The question, posed so calmly, disturbed me. A few hours later I realised that his presence marked a new chapter in our conversation. I should not have cared. I should not have let you in.

But how does one face a question that has never existed before? Novelty betrays us.

My husband talks about clients, responsibilities, expenses, plans to purchase a new car, new furniture. But what did we talk about, and where were we, five years ago? Images of passionate lovemaking in a hotel room flashed in my head. But was that him or someone else? I can't connect the image with him. Come to think of it, maybe it wasn't even me in that hotel. Was this an older image, a fantasy, or something I dare not express?

The problem isn't just that time keeps moving, you said. Space is so slippery too, it keeps gliding away. Spaces have their own rhythm. You felt that time slowed when you stood on the Golden Gate Bridge and stared at the peaceful waters far below. The bridge, not unlike places that can be foul – Jakarta, New York, Buenos Aires, whatever – stirred you, tugged at you.

'My boyfriend loves me in a different way in New York.'

Perhaps the gorgeous glitter of Manhattan's lights, appearing in memory as fine as grains of sand, makes lovers more sensual. There's nothing strange about leading different lives in different places.

'In an email to you, he might be polite and romantic, but with me he could be an eccentric lover.'

A helter-skelter hypothesis. But your words shook the scene I had so carefully constructed and set within my little globe. Inside it, people move to the same rhythm, within the same space. Maybe it's time I became suspicious of you. Who were you and where had you come from?

I couldn't even remember your name.

Somehow I'd stopped noticing the nauseating scent of your perfume. It had taken over slowly, though of course an odour can dull after a while. As the train pulled into Penn Station, the last stop, your efforts to be a good travel companion had borne fruit. We joked about our childhoods and national television. In an era when American TV series were a luxury, we both patiently awaited *Little House on the Prairie* on Sundays. We'd forgotten the storylines but back in the eighties when we were still five or six, every black-haired girl in Indonesia wanted brown braids like Laura Ingalls. We felt nostalgia for a country that we seemed to recognise so well, for a time when space felt solid and did not slip, mocking us as it moved. Despicable as the dictatorial regime may have been, perhaps one television channel wasn't so bad, we concluded haphazardly.

I know it's a bit strange, but can we be friends?

You sounded sincere, and your farewell utterance made you less harsh.

'Nice talking with you, Lila.'

You remembered my name, and I felt a genuine pang of guilt for having deliberately erased yours.

'Sorry,' I blushed. 'What's yours again?'

There was no trace of disappointment on your face; on the contrary, you seemed elated.

'We'll turn it into a game. Invite me to your apartment and make me a hot chocolate. Then I'll tell you.'

A travelling companion who arouses curiosity, indeed. You evidently loved to play around, and I was tempted. Maybe you really were having an affair with my husband, but if not, the riddle of our relationship needed to be solved. Your game reminded me of a Grimm fairy tale that, strangely, you didn't know. So I told you: once upon a time there lived a desperate girl who, unlike women of today who can travel, was cursed to live within a sealed castle. A dwarf, perhaps an incarnation of the devil, appeared mysteriously in her room, granting all her wishes. But fulfilment of those wishes turned out to bear an extraordinary cost. The dwarf demanded the woman's baby unless she could guess his name. After puzzling and puzzling for three days and nights, the desperate girl eventually figured out her tormenter's secret. The dwarf was in the midst of prancing around with glee, certain he had won, when the woman stated his name. Like a mantra, or a curse.

Perhaps your name is Rumpelstiltskin?

'And the creature disappeared from her sight.'

You laughed and said your name wasn't as complicated as that.

'What if I remember your name while we're on the way?'

'Then I'll leave,' you promised. 'Save your hot chocolate.'

And that was that. We transferred to the A train heading uptown. Only upon exiting the subway did we discover that snow was falling again. Like a child, you delighted in the white flakes that landed upon your face and disappeared. You teased me because I was still straining to remember your name.

'What *is* your name? Sari? Devi? Wati?'

You laughed for a long time, mocking my list of common Indonesian names. 'You don't seem very imaginative.'

On the white road I scanned your footprints; your name wasn't inscribed there.

I took off my red coat and rested my suitcase, unopened, against the wall, ready for the next trip. Tatyana had not come home yet. She might have been quite anxious to learn that, unusually, I'd allowed someone I'd just met into the apartment. A stranger who, in my mind, was nameless. Surprisingly, you and I were becoming ever closer.

I had to admit that your game was both challenging and disconcerting. I was still desperate to attach a name to you as I made the hot chocolate. Was it Sri, Rani or Yanti (look it up on Google, you joked)? Maybe it's more Western (Victoria? Josephine?). Exotic (Salsabila? Mahachakri?).

You were disappointed to find no Indonesian or Ukrainian mementos in my apartment, nothing ethnic or redolent of the

Third World except a stack of DVDs on the bookshelf I share with Tatyana. Our living room is very simple. We don't have a television. You asked if you could have a look at my bedroom and started pacing about, inspecting my second-hand furniture, until you found something that appeared to make you happy. You pouted at yourself in front of my full-length mirror. 'Why buy such a nice mirror if you're only here a while?' Your remark served more as criticism than question. 'Dealing with it will be such a pain if you move.'

I told you that I'd trained myself to throw things away without a sense of attachment. You rolled your eyes. 'Liar.'

'It can't be helped if you're always moving around.'

'You can't throw everything away. Clothes, yes. CDs, cups –'

'Men?'

'Even men.' You slurped your hot chocolate while your eyes remained fixed on the mirror. 'But a beautiful mirror, no. No.'

Your explanation had a cryptic quality to it. I didn't need to take it seriously and returned to my guessing. Sarah? Maria? You bid me come closer, and we stood side by side, gazing into the mirror together. This closeness surprised me, for it made me realise that I'd been busy inspecting your curves.

'Look at me in the mirror,' you directed. 'Do I seem like a Maria to you?'

I did not respond, distracted by how old my face looked next to yours. I began to compare the two of us, foolishly and desperately, and took measure of the tone of your complexion, your small waist, your thick, gleaming locks.

'Hey.' You turned. 'Do you feel threatened? Are you worried that I really stole your husband?'

There was something strange about your body, something that went beyond my failure to conceal my jealousy. Your curves were dangerous, not because they were alluring, but because it was as though I'd seen them before. Had your lover's wife (not me, of course) ever sensed your existence?

'Come on, I'm a mom. I'm harmless.'

In the mirror you were smiling broadly. Your teeth gleamed, like the teeth of a predator.

My cell phone rang. On the screen I saw the name of June, a Korean woman who lives on the first floor with her boyfriend Andrew. I'd forgotten that they had invited me to their monthly film screening. Andrew and June had a projector and routinely invited friends over to join them.

'We have to go. I've never been to a private film screening,' you insisted. 'Maybe we can meet some sexy guys.'

'How old are you, anyway? Twenty-one?'

'You're like a girl from Victorian times. Don't tell me you've never picked up a guy at a bar.'

I hesitated, but the thought of having to introduce you to others gave me a wicked thought. This would be part of our game: you would say your name and I would be victor.

The movie had already started when we arrived. June immediately ushered us to the sofa, not wanting to disturb her other guests. She welcomed us warmly but didn't seem to care about you. I'd have to wait rather a while for a more appropriate introduction.

Andrew is a film buff. He'd play his favourite movies – classic but unique – to flaunt his vast knowledge of world cinema. That night we watched F. W. Murnau's *Sunrise*. We'd missed a few scenes and took our seats to a part in which a woman, with black hair and dark lipstick, sneaks into a settlement. She looks very fashionable, very out of place. She stops at a house and whistles to a man, clearly someone else's husband. His wife – beautiful but less stylish – is preparing dinner. The man appears uneasy, torn between the call of the temptress, and his wife, queen of the household, but, as always, temptation prevails. He leaves home to meet the whistling femme fatale. The Woman from the City, as she is called, is an adventurer. A thief. Bad girls in black-and-white movies are always made to resemble demons, and this particular bad girl reminded me of someone.

And you had left your seat.

I rose from the sofa and tiptoed towards the kitchen, thinking you were looking for a drink. From behind the curtains I heard your voice. You were talking to a blond man. Not tall, but quite attractive.

'So, Max … Max. Your name is very German.'

'And you? Is your name very Indonesian?'

'Hmm, you could say that my name is international.'

A very unimaginative exchange. New prey. He opened a bottle of beer and offered it to you. A ring encircled his fourth finger. He was into seduction, just like you.

'And what is this international name of yours?'

'If you say my name, I vanish. What am I?'

'Silence. I remember that riddle,' he answered with satisfaction. Then, wearing a crocodile smile, he added, 'But I don't want you to vanish. Not this fast.'

He didn't take his eyes off you as you drank from the bottle and started toying with your hair. Yes, some people know just when to take out their toys – people like you. I could condemn your lips and your hips, but I had a more important mission. The man was waiting for you to mention your name, while I was waiting for the conclusion of our game. Your eyes wandered until they landed where I stood. You raised your bottle, as if toasting me, and said, 'Lila. My name is Lila.'

My hands went cold. You laughed out loud at your successful dodge.

'Hey, come here.' You beckoned me. 'This is Max. He's just moved from Germany and is now teaching –'

'Political science,' Max finished your sentence as I approached. 'Hi, I'm Max.'

He reached out his hand. I greeted him with a polite smile, and, a little annoyed that my name had been poached, replied firmly, 'Lila.'

As if sympathetic to my protest and the confusion in Max's blue eyes, you smiled sweetly and corrected yourself, 'OK, OK. My name is Anna.'

'Ah, Anna.'

'No. Lucy.' Your smile changed awkwardly. 'What does a name mean, anyway? I told him my real name and he forgot.' She turned to him. 'Invite me to your apartment and you won't remember me. And you have a wife.'

Max's face went crimson. Perhaps because of my presence, he tried to make more pedestrian conversation, asking me about my work and divulging some information about himself. He had been here less than a year, on his own, and his wife would join him in the summer. His tone was placid, almost flat, and I could tell he was not particularly enthusiastic about his marriage. It didn't take long for me, or maybe for him, to realise that with you, the safest meeting places can prove dangerous.

'OK, Lila,' Max said. 'No, Anna ... I mean, Lucy.'

When you two giggled, I knew Max was obeying the rules you had set. I wondered if your affair with your lover had begun like this, in a tidy kitchen, with a beer bottle and a simple kids' game.

'So what do you do for work?'

'I move around.'

'Then?'

'Pack up, move on, meet strangers ... steal husbands.'

'I like your sense of humour. The two of you have to visit my place sometime.'

'Sure,' you answered quickly. 'We're going to start a new game. And Lila needs to win. I know she hates losing.'

I felt that Max was looking at me differently. He regarded me for several seconds and touched his hair before asking if I'd like a beer. You watched him while biting your lips, slowly. Whether it was my woollen turtleneck or the heater, suddenly I felt hot.

'Lila's a pretty name,' Max said. 'What does it mean?'

'I don't think she knows,' you said, your voice sounding softer as you drew nearer to him. 'That's why she doesn't remember my name.'

I excused myself to go back to the film. I didn't want to know what would happen between you two. When I returned to the living room, the man in the movie had taken his wife to town for a walk, trying to repair the marriage that the Woman from the City had been intent on destroying.

I thought I'd dozed off on the couch when I heard a whisper in my ear. You were leaving with the German, and I believed what I heard was a goodbye.

This should have been an ordinary morning: I found myself alone in my bed, staring at the ceiling, trying to remember my dreams. Whatever the dream, morning would straighten out any wrong turns I'd taken. I tend to be crueller to myself at night, blaming myself for what I've lost and what I've left unfulfilled, and in the morning light I forgive myself with fresh air and a cup of coffee, an opportunity to start from scratch. But on this particular morning I woke up with a sense that something was missing. I was disturbed to think that I'd forgotten how I came here. I tried to reconstruct the story. I must have drunk too much after the screening and returned to my apartment, like a zombie, unable to remember the conversations I'd had. Exhausted, I'd immediately flopped into bed. That was it; that was a plausible story.

I lifted the shade and saw the snow, already brownish on the side of the road. Maybe the screening never took place. Maybe you and the Woman from the City were just dreams. This thought comforted me because life without you is easier to bear. But something on the bed made me panic, a piece of yellow paper with neat handwriting: *I enjoyed last night. See you soon, M.*

You were here while I slept.

I grabbed the paper and flung open the door. The living room was empty. I was relieved, but then I heard a spoon clinking in a coffee cup.

'Good morning.'

The ambush of this voice, though warm and friendly, left me with a sense of fear. You were sitting on a kitchen chair wearing a pair of pyjamas. Your hair was wet.

'How did –'

'You opened the door for me, honey. Coffee?'

I caught a whiff of something that made me want to vomit – not the aroma of coffee, but your perfume. The perfume that had so bothered me upon meeting you.

M. Who was M? Did your name begin with M? I was still scrutinising the mysterious handwriting when you snatched it from my hand. I saw a smile on your face, the seductive smile I'd seen in the kitchen when you were with the blond man. Your eyes pierced me with a mischievous and accusing stare.

'Naughty girl,' you said.

'You said you left with Max last night.'

'Who's Max? The man who spent the night with you?'

'Please stop playing games.'

'Do you remember my name?'

You got up from the table almost swaggering, like a school-yard bully, and marched into my room without asking permission. You stood in front of my mirror, repeating the poses you'd made before we went to the screening, but this time your presence was more imposing. It was nine o'clock in the morning, time for forgiveness, but I didn't feel like forgiving anyone.

'Your mirror is too big,' you said, growing increasingly critical. 'It's like you need to inspect yourself from head to toe every day.'

You reminded me how I looked at my reflection in the glass as you spoke in the train. 'Obsessive,' you jeered.

'No, I'm not. Maybe when the space we're in is in motion we need to reassure ourselves that something is fixed. Intact.'

'So how did the letter land in your bed?' you asked. 'Space playing tricks, huh?'

After a long journey, a good night's sleep usually soothed my weariness. This morning was proving an exception. The room didn't have enough air. Suddenly I felt exhausted. I looked back and forth between my tired face and yours. I wished I were as beautiful as you. They say mirrors are deceptive, but distortions are often convincing.

The space we were in didn't have enough air.

I felt we'd been gazing at our reflections for hours, and then, for whatever reason, I saw tears flowing. I did not feel them, nor were my cheeks wet. The mirror seemed to be playing a trick on me. I've never been to the Golden Gate Bridge. But the tricks of space can indeed be foul.

In the mirror my lips began to tremble ever so gradually, and I felt I needed to ask a question: 'Have you ever hated yourself?'

'The way *you* hate yourself?' You laughed hideously, and continued. 'Lila darling, people hate themselves in order to feel better. Becoming aware lessens guilt. People reveal their warts because they don't want someone else to point them out first.'

I couldn't understand this, or you, or my feelings, but I knew I was too tired to be lectured to. What came next was an unbearable monologue.

'Self-hatred is the mark of a coward. If you have to confess your sins, someone needs to bear witness to it – like in a Catholic church. You must be strong and know no shame. Do you know what I want? I want the wife of my lover to be here, standing next to me. Then we will look in the mirror together, just like this, and then I can repent: forgive me because I have sinned against you. Truly, I can't bear to show you what will terrify you most. Forgive me that I have stolen your husband, your love, your prize. Forgive me for this unequal battle, and forgive me for everything that happens when you are gone. We lock ourselves up in a hotel for weeks on end, and he worships every inch of my body, adoring me like I'm a goddess. He licks my feet and gets hard as a rock when I treat him like a dog.'

My heart pounded and I blocked my ears; was this a confession or carnage? I wanted to slash your mouth with a razor blade. I fled from the mirror and glared at you. I did not want you here.

Go.

Yet you stood there, back straight, your arms folded like the statue of some cruel deity. You were so heavy, immovable, as if your form had been occupying this space for centuries, sculpted and embedded within it. I screamed, more out of fear than anger.

Get out of here, whatever your name is!

I was surprised to hear my voice, so out of control. But I was sick of seeing your face – cold, beautiful, nameless. Then came an impulse, a desperate instinct to seek justice, to shove you up against the wall and smash your arrogant head. I pulled your long hair, but you – being stronger and wily – acted first. You grabbed my hand as I was about to slap you. You held my body tight as I shouted at you to go away. Thief! Whore!

Someone stopped my curses. You planted your lips against mine and gave me a kiss, cold and long. I waited. *Something, something uncertain might change us. After this you will persecute me again.* Your face, though, was so serene. You wiped away my tears. Calm down, Lila. Don't get so hysterical. Your sweetness made me feel ashamed.

'You need help.' Your voice now sounded like a nurse's. 'But first we have to get rid of this – it shows everything bad.'

You hurled everything in reach at my mirror. An alarm clock. A book. A framed photo. A coffee cup. I could only watch this destruction in silence, unable to interpret such nonchalant brutality. I realised too late that you had drawn something out from the wreckage of the mirror. A jagged shard of glass.

I caught a whiff of betrayal. Your kindness was a sham. And that's when I recognised the smell of your perfume, a smell I'd managed to forget. Tuberose flowers. In my childhood, these so-called sweet blossoms of the night spread the fragrance of wandering spirits. But it didn't matter any more that I'd recognised the smell, because I allowed you to take my hand, to stroke my wrist, to paralyse me. I felt unsteady. Was my body shaking, or was the room in motion? Your lips were at my ear, whispering words in a foreign language. I heard not only your whispers, but the whisperings of others too, hissing. The incitements of ghosts that haunt bridges.

You stare deep into my eyes.

May I?

This space moves faster, swirls. My body sweats. I answer you, I cannot believe my own words. And so it is: one slash, so convincing, so hard to resist. Your fingers curled around the glass shard bewitch me into becoming a waterfall. Drain me, quickly. You, a bewitching ghost, wear a mother's smile.

That's when I remember. I am wrong no longer.

'I know your name!' I cry, with the last vestiges of my energy.

How stupid. Wasn't this a simple riddle? I gasp, desperate for air, but I know everything will end. I mutter, voice shattering like glass, 'Maya. Your name is Maya.'

Your face pales at once. Your smile vanishes. Blood spurts from your forehead, from your temples, drenching your eyebrows, your nose and cheeks. You crack. Your body springs leaks, it vibrates; your skin, your eyes, your entire being fills with red tendrils. Then, in an instant, you burst. The explosions are so intense that fragments – flesh, mirror, I no longer know the difference – splatter every corner of this space, fly out the window.

My carpet absorbs the red. Your blood. No, my blood. Soon I will no longer be able to open my eyes, but I have escaped. At last I have the key that unlocks all secrets, all riddles.

Lila and Maya are no longer friends.

Die, you old whore. I should not blame you entirely. Didn't I agree to invite you over that afternoon? It's just that this space, a haven on an unending journey, cannot contain both of us.

And on a merciless morning, the end of the labyrinth where I always lose my way and begin anew, remnants of you swirl among snowflakes then vanish and are gone.

Proceed to the next page.

You can feel that your apartment is brilliant with light. Are those the rays of the sun, or something else? Morning offers forgiveness for all, to killers and victims, to Maya and Lila. And who are you: Lila, or Maya? The question is no longer important. All you want is to close your eyes.

'Sleep, darling. Sleep.'

Before it gets dark, you feel light entering from the window to embrace you, whispering sweet words in your ears. The light is your angel. No, a devil. A lover who strokes your hair sings you a lullaby for the last time.

Hush, little baby, don't say a word,
Papa's gonna buy you a mockingbird.
If that mockingbird don't sing,
Papa's gonna buy you a diamond ring.
If that diamond ring turns brass,
Papa's gonna buy you a looking glass.

Who is gazing in the mirror now?

FINIS

At Meena's table, spices take you on adventures. Meena speaks not only of the aromatic masala that conjures up home but of travel as well. Of the world. She has followed in the tracks of spices, rejected national borders. She delights in using basil leaves in Thai and Italian cooking, and in discovering how sesame oil enhances Chinese, Korean and Japanese dishes differently. She reminds you that nutmeg marks your place in the world as well: the Dutch bartered with the Brits – Manhattan for Run, an island in the Moluccas, and that gives your footprints the foundation to run far and wide.

The lunch invitation is just the beginning. You express gratitude for Meena's kindness by bringing over a plate of *batagor* from Mie Jakarta. She falls in love with the fish dumplings and asks how you make them. You confess that you always buy them in restaurants because you don't know how. Meena puts her hands on her hips with a teasing smile.

'There's no dish in this world we can't make,' she says.

She challenges you to cook with her, so you search for *batagor* recipes online. Together, the two of you go and buy ingredients at Top Line Supermarket, which sells goods from South East Asia. The market is hardly 'super', more along the lines of 'dinky', but at least it's well stocked. There you buy soy sauce, shrimp crackers and ABC chilli sauce. At first it thrills you to hear people you've assumed are from China speaking in Indonesian with East Java accents. They put Blue Band margarine, Ritz sprinkles and bottled teas by the dozen into their shopping carts. The next time, you hear women in headscarves complain that the price of Munik's instant spices keeps going up. Amid these strangers, you feel like you've returned home. But before long their presence at Top Line ceases to startle you. You don't care if someone next to you is speaking Indonesian or Tagalog.

Meena browses the aisles eagerly. She buys cans of Thai curry and a block of shrimp paste. The adventurer-cook is eager to try her hand at *nasi lemak*. Crazy. She's never even been to Malaysia. Meena marvels at how the world comes together as one in the supermarket, or, more precisely, how the supermarket arranges the world in rows. You marvel more at her spice obsession.

You line up minced fish stuffing, tapioca flour, dumpling skins, spring onions, eggs, sesame oil, salt and pepper on Meena's dining table. She's reluctant to use packaged satay seasonings for the *batagor* sauce because she wants to make her own. This caused a small debate at the supermarket.

'It doesn't make a difference. You can use satay or gado-gado spice,' you said, handing her a prepared mix.

'But surely it tastes better when you make it from scratch, right?'

Spurning your instant spices, Meena went off to another aisle on a quest for peanuts.

Making *batagor* turns out to be a lot like knitting, as it creates a relaxed atmosphere with space for chat. You wrap the filling in dumpling skins and listen as Meena tells her story.

You call it a neighbour's love story.

Meena and Vijay met four months ago at a party in a Manhattan apartment. They had each gone with friends, and neither knew the host particularly well. The party was noisy, and the food was hardly special (and for people like Meena, nothing spoils the appetite like indifferent food).

'What kind of party was it?'

'What kind of party?'

'Yes, what kind? A birthday party?'

You want to know how Meena and Vijay are connected. Who is friends with who?

Meena hesitates. 'I don't remember. Probably a get-together for Indian students in New York. Yes, that sort of thing.'

The party was so boring that Meena and Vijay quickly made an escape pact. Meena invited Vijay to an Indian restaurant in Queens and Vijay saw Meena home.

'Where was your second date?'

'At Serendipity.'

'Like in a movie?'

'Yes, like in a movie,' Meena says with a laugh.

You've been wanting to visit the Serendipity III cafe located between 2nd and 3rd Avenue for a while. You're curious because the restaurant appears in so many films, like the romcom *Serendipity*. Plus, it has a celebrity clientele. You even know what you'll order: frozen hot chocolate.

'Very romantic,' you say.

'Hmm …' She smiles, seeming to weigh her answer. 'To be honest, their frozen hot chocolate might be famous, but it was pretty ordinary, if you ask me.'

'Ordinary?'

'OK. Overrated.'

You both laugh.

'And then?'

'After that we took the gondola to Roosevelt Island.'

'That's really romantic!'

Meena, reddening slightly, brushes off the remark. 'That's overrated too.'

The date at Serendipity and the gondola ride were Vijay's idea. He tried hard to make the night memorable for Meena but soon learned that, for her, 'romance' has a different meaning. They found passion in the kitchen, amid steaming cauldrons of food and the mayhem of spice bottles. At the dinner table, silence would reign as they savoured their food reverently, and only after fifteen minutes would they begin to talk.

Meena's love story makes you jealous. But it's not because Vijay chose an ordinary woman. On the contrary, the more you learn about Meena, the more remarkable she seems. Maybe you're also envious because you've never fallen in love with anyone the way Meena and Vijay have fallen in love with each other.

'Do you like the same foods?'

'We love everything that's spicy.'

Her eyes sparkle.

Savoury, she adds.

Creamy.

Sinful.

You grin. Swallowing your jealousy, you try to show how happy you are for their intimate bond. Vijay and Meena, sinners in the kitchen, sinners in bed.

You lost interest in pursuing Vijay once you set foot in Meena's apartment. After taking the time to eat with her and cook with her, you conclude two things. Firstly, Meena and Vijay are truly in love. Though you haven't seen Vijay again since the embarrassment of that night, you understand why he is a devotee of this spicy masala goddess. You can't explain it further, but you understand. Masala. That's the key word.

You draw the second conclusion for your own mental health. You have to stop obsessing over a couple united by a quasi-divine passion for food and sex. Perhaps they have a blessing from God, and, as is written on wedding invitations and in the Bible, what God hath joined together, let no man put asunder. So, let them be happy; it's time for you to go and find your own fun, and think through your future in America.

Oh, America, America. America, it turns out, is pretty ho-hum. Did you make the wrong choice? Who knows? Everyone wants to go to America. You begin to imagine that there's another version of you out there, wandering around in red shoes, having more exciting adventures in Europe.

You think of Demon Lover. He should come. You don't know what you'll do once your visa runs out. Spring is just around the corner, and he's abandoned you without a word. Shit. You ought to have known why humans shouldn't make a deal with a devil. He warned you himself.

Where is he now? Will he only come to you after you've grown sick and tired of chaos? Will he get angry if you look for a boyfriend? You never promised to wait faithfully. You're not devoted to Allah, much less to Devil.

You mull over looking for a boyfriend on dating sites, but feel you should weigh up the men around you first. Don't let a bird in the hand go fluttering away. You see two recent messages on your phone – one from Fernando, the other from Bob. Both have invited you to dinner. Do you have to choose between them? You decide to have dinner with both: this week, Fernando; next week, Bob. Nice and fair.

You and Fernando dine at an Argentinian restaurant not far from your apartment. From that evening's conversation you learn that Fernando has a complicated life, but he obviously adores his daughter. In 1999, Fernando and his pregnant girl-friend boarded a plane from Lima to New York as tourists. They never returned, and Tiffany was born in Elmhurst Hospital, Queens. At age twenty, Fernando's only considera-tion was to ensure that his baby's life wasn't as pathetic as her parents'. Maybe birth in the United States and citizenship would rescue her.

'Sometimes I wonder if my life would have turned out all right if I hadn't come to America,' Fernando says. 'Maybe I'd have gone to university. But I made some big decisions when I was too young. Who trusts a twenty-year-old's judgement?'

'Are you sorry?'

He pauses, then shakes his head.

'But if you're having an adventure you always want to know what would have happened if you chose a different road. Right?'

His remark scares you a little. He almost seems to be talking about your life.

Tiffany was born, followed by Fernando's marriage, and the arrival of his bride's mother, who joined them to be close to her grandchild. She was an attractive fifty-year-old single woman, and she soon drew the attention of a restaurant owner, who proposed not long after and asked her to move in with him. Before leaving for work, Fernando and his wife would deposit Tiffany in the grandmother's new home. Life felt slightly odd and had its hassles, but it was promising enough. Then shortly afterwards, Fernando's marriage broke up.

Now aged nine, Tiffany has a busy schedule. She is with her father on Friday, Saturday and Sunday, and on the other weekdays she stays with her grandmother because she lives in a better school zone. Tiffany's mom has moved in with a new boyfriend near Fernando. Schools in their neighbourhood, Fernando says, aren't any good. Every Friday Fernando picks Tiffany up after school and drops her off at tae kwon do. Tiffany had long wanted to learn, so Fernando granted her wish. To be precise, he grants all Tiffany's wishes.

'I'm trying to make her happy. She's all the family I have here.'

You listen carefully. The details confuse you a little, most likely because you don't have a child yourself.

After dinner, Fernando invites you to his place. You hesitate. He asks you to stop in for only a moment, and maybe nothing will happen, but you sense that your decision will determine your path from here.

If you decide to stop at Fernando's, turn to page 215.

If you decline, turn to page 219.

Amsterdam Centraal Station. You step out of the train and follow the other passengers as they cram onto the platform's escalator and then scatter like ants upon reaching the concourse. You scan the stores to your right and left in search of an information desk. Equipped with directions, you take the tram from Centraal towards Niewmaarkt, the neighbourhood where you intend to stay for the next month. An ad on the Internet has led you to a two-room apartment, one of which is leased short-term. Definitely cheaper than staying in a hotel.

You ring the doorbell of an old town house and wait. A woman in a rumpled shirt opens the door, her blonde hair dishevelled. She's Maria, who advertised the room, and she has obviously just woken up even though it is now noon. There's no lift in the building. You follow Maria up to the second floor, struggling to haul your suitcase. Maria offers help, but out of politeness you decline.

'Pretty easy to get here from Centraal, isn't it?'

Gasping your way up the stairs, you nod. You pause, catch your breath, and continue hoisting up your suitcase. You feel a pang of regret at turning down Maria's offer.

'You'll be in my friend's room. Her stuff is in there, but it's all stored in the closet.'

Maria's apartment has hardwood floors. She opens the door to her friend's room; her name, you learn, is Anna. You see a bed with a light blue blanket and sheets, a small desk, and a rolling chair. Maria shows you a large closet in the corner. Stashed there are Anna's belongings in a pile of tightly sealed cardboard boxes.

Maria gives you a tour of the apartment. This is the kitchen, that's the bathroom. Feel free to use the dishes and the spices in the kitchen cupboards. There's a compost bin under the sink, and one for recycling next to the dining table. She passes quickly from one piece of information to another, and the tone of her voice, not cold but not overly friendly, reminds you of an adept hospital nurse. After she feels she has told you what you need to know, she returns to her room.

You sit on the edge of the bed, stretching your legs. You're hungry. Maybe you should shower and head out for a meal. You take a towel and some clothes from your suitcase. From behind the bathroom door comes the sound of a tap running, so you go back to your room and wait. You feel like you've drifted off to sleep, even if only for ten or fifteen minutes.

Footsteps move back and forth in the living room. You open your door, a towel draped over your shoulders. Maria has donned a knee-length jacket and high-heeled black boots, ready to leave the house. You think you're looking at someone else. Her dishevelled straight hair now curls nicely at the tips. Her eyes seem wide open, highlighted by silvery-blue blush and false lashes. She isn't wearing – or has not yet put on – lipstick.

'I have to leave,' she says hurriedly. 'If you want to go out, just close the door. It locks automatically.'

You listen to her instructions attentively and continue watching her rush about until she departs. You wonder if she'll apply lipstick on the train.

You buy a cheese sandwich in a small shop and devour it while strolling the narrow streets around you. Cyclists pass. People here must prefer bikes to trams and buses, you conclude. You stop at the edge of a canal to admire rows of old buildings with their gradations of colour – reds, oranges, browns – and the angular window lines reflected in the water. This city is as beautiful as in storybooks, though maybe, it occurs to you, it's the storybook cities that are trying to mimic what is real.

You wander aimlessly until sunset. Inside your bag is a map, but you'll only check it later, to find your way home. On your first day in Amsterdam, you don't want to be a tourist dutifully following a map, certain of your route. You want to turn yourself around and lose your way on these storybook streets.

You wake up early and make plans to visit the Rijksmuseum. Your tourist instinct has returned. You'll feel like a fraud if you go to the Netherlands and miss out on Vermeer paintings. At nine you're in the kitchen, ready to make coffee. You open the cupboards wide and study the jars of coffee, tea and sugar, and the row of spice containers. A bottle labelled *saté saus* catches your attention. The details are in Dutch. What does Maria (or maybe her friend, Anna) do with satay sauce?

You hear a door open and gather that Maria is now awake. Soon comes the sound of the toilet flushing. Maria appears in the kitchen, her face like yesterday's: blah, blotchy, blank. She says good morning and you offer her coffee. Maria looks hesitant, apparently wanting to return to bed, but then she pours herself a cup.

'Your apartment is nice,' you say, trying to make small talk.

'It's not mine. I have to move out next summer.'

Flats in the area tend to be very expensive. Maria considers herself lucky, at least for the time being. This apartment belongs to a friend of Anna's who had to go to Abu Dhabi for a year and has sublet it cheaply. Actually, the man doesn't need the cash, says Maria. He mainly wants people who'll be willing to take care of the place while he's away. Next year Maria and Anna will look for a flat in a cheaper neighbourhood.

'There's satay sauce in the cupboard,' you say.

'Satay sauce is everywhere.'

Maria doesn't know the origin of satay sauce, but she knows that the Dutch like to mix it into food. Only then do you discover that Maria isn't Dutch. She and Anna, who has left for several months to be with her mother as she undergoes chemotherapy, are from Bulgaria.

Maria bought the satay sauce after experimenting with *patat met mayonaise*, French fries with mayonnaise, which are sold as street food. You still haven't made peace with the idea of eating French fries with something other than ketchup. The thought of satay sauce mixed with mayonnaise makes you grimace. The combination sounds disgusting, and the term satay 'sauce' rather than satay 'seasoning' sets your teeth on edge. You feel obliged to explain that satay sauce is more like a peanut-based topping to accompany grilled chicken, beef or goat meat. To imagine French fries with satay sauce offends you. Maybe you need to try your hand at some Indonesian dishes, even with your meagre kitchen skills.

'Is there an Asian supermarket around here?'

'Yes, there's one right near us. I'll take you sometime.'

After that morning's conversation in the kitchen, you don't see Maria for an entire week.

You leave every morning at 9.30, and return at five o'clock. Maria is still sleeping as you brew coffee and make toast in the kitchen, and she's already gone by the time you come back in the early evening. She seems to work late into the night. Sometimes you sense that she's not even home. Maybe she stays at a friend's house.

You spend your days wandering town, spending money here and there. You buy *kaasbroodje* at a bakery in Centraal Station; elsewhere it's half a dozen socks. Shopping always makes you feel like a local. You even make a momentous decision: you'll buy a laptop. You don't know how long you'll stay in Amsterdam or where you'll go next, but at the very least, a laptop will make your life easier, seeing as you don't have access to a hotel lobby computer like you did in Berlin.

Once you've become familiar with Amsterdam, you visit other cities by train. A half-hour ride takes you to Leiden. The city is even more storybook than Amsterdam. You tote your camera around, snapping pictures of boats and bridges, canals and windmills. On another excursion you visit Rotterdam with its stunning modern architecture. Because it was decimated by bombs during World War II, Rotterdam's buildings look newer than any other city you've visited in Europe.

After tiring of asking others to take pictures of you in front of historical sites, you decide to memorialise your sparkly red shoes. They never fail to capture attention. People come up and ask a litany of questions (sometimes they start in Dutch, then switch to English):

'Are you a fashion student?'

'Artist?'

'*Wizard of Oz* fan?'

'American?'

Honestly, you have no idea what sparks that last question.

These encounters with others – perhaps fellow tourists – make you feel good. Maybe someday you'll write about your photography experience, create a FAQ for it. Comments come in addition to questions. An elderly woman offers sincere praise: 'Oh, they're beautiful! Like an angel's shoes.'

'Thank you,' you say without correcting her, but you think, 'Actually, no angel would want to wear these, Granny. These are devil shoes.'

Dozens of photos are now stored on your laptop. You name the folder 'Red Shoe Travels'. Faceless, disembodied, your shoes determine their own destiny. They're everywhere, a pair of haunted shoes roaming about Holland. You decide to rename the folder 'Red Shoe Wanderings'.

One afternoon, a little girl stretches out her legs as you're photographing your red shoes on the train. You turn. The girl, about eight or so, is wearing glittery red slippers, like yours, but without the high heels. Her mother tries to stop her from bothering you.

'Mommy, mommy! She has Dorothy shoes too!' The girl tugs her mother's hand.

She speaks in American-accented English, not Dutch.

'Honey, your legs are in the way.'

'It's OK,' you smile.

'Are you a *Wizard of Oz* fan too?' asks the mother.

'You know the story, don't you?' The little girl chimes in.

If you feel a need to read, or reread, about *The Wizard of Oz*, turn to page 21, then come back here.

'Can you take a picture of my shoes with yours?'

You grant the girl's wish. On your camera's viewfinder, the little girl extends her legs so they're close to your shoes. You take a picture and show her the result on the screen.

She's thrilled to see it, but then her brow furrows. She tugs repeatedly at her mother's skirt.

'Mommy.' Her voice becomes earnest. 'Mommy, we've met this Auntie Dorothy before.'

'Oh, come on,' the mother replies, not taking her seriously. 'Enough. We have to get ready to leave the train.'

'We met in New York!' the girl exclaims.

You and the little girl's mother exchange glances, puzzled.

'Yes, maybe,' says the mother. 'Lots of people these days like to take shoe pictures.'

'We've met! In New York, on the subway.' The voice of the little girl rises, ever more stubborn. 'Auntie, please check. Maybe the picture of your shoes from New York is still on your camera.'

'OK, OK. We have to go now, sweetie.'

The girl's mother bids you goodbye and leads her daughter off the train. They disappear immediately from sight, but the little girl's voice keeps ringing in your head. Could there be someone like you taking red-shoe photos elsewhere? Or maybe the shoes are like cats with nine lives, and they all exist simultaneously. Isn't New York also New Amsterdam? The Dutch bartered with the Brits – Manhattan for Run, an island in the Moluccas, and that gives your feet the foundation to run far and wide.

If a city can have a twin, maybe you and your shoes do too. What kind of life might your red shoes be having in New York? You press the button on your digital camera, clicking through the dozens of photos saved there. Shock sets in. Your flesh goes cold.

Amsterdam Centraal. An announcement that you've arrived at your stop breaks your reverie. You turn off the camera and stow it in your bag. Rushing along with the crowd through the station, you don't want to think about it too deeply: what the hell should you expect with devil shoes?

After a week in the Netherlands you're no longer so driven about getting up early each morning. You don't even feel it's a waste to laze around all day at home with your new laptop. You open several email messages from your sister.

First email:

Hello Dik,

Hope you're OK over there. Don't forget to bring lots of kids' books when you come back to Indonesia. Later we'll donate them to Lentera Iman Elementary, Nazwa's school.

Oh, Abah has quit the automobile firm. He's serious about becoming an entrepreneur and making a career out of organising seminars on Islamic business with his friends. Pray for his success, OK?

You still feel weirded out when your sister refers to her husband as 'Abah' in front of you or their friends. Since they got married, they've taken to calling each other 'Abah' and 'Ummi'. Your sister's husband is not your father. You don't get why you should go along with calling him so.

Second email:

FWD: Rally to Support the Anti-Pornography Law
   As we all know, Western liberalism has infected our media. Just consider the Indonesian edition of Playboy and teen-oriented films with the sort of lewd titles that the famed cleric Aa Jim has objected to. Television is overrun with obscene dancing by dangdut singers in provocative clothes. The anti-pornography law must be passed immediately in order to protect our children.

You delete the email, skipping the rest. This is one of many messages your sister shares from mailing lists. You don't understand why she sent you this email. She dislikes Aa Jim, a cleric with two wives who appears all the time on television, and she doesn't seem too concerned about dangdut singers in sexy clothes. But maybe all her friends have joined the anti-pornography front and are full-frontal anti-pornographers, or whatever it is you call them.

Another message contains sermons from religious figures. Your sister shares oodles of emails like this. You're not sure she always knows who the author is. You delete these messages after a paragraph. The entire process takes two minutes. All it takes is a glance at keywords you're allergic to: 'forbidden', 'sinful', 'infidel' or 'serving a husband'. Then it's click, delete. You wonder why you don't just delete all your sister's messages without opening them. Maybe you derive satisfaction from being able to recognise the features of contemporary *da'wah* and to reaffirm your view of your sister. Let's see. There's the judgement genre, which cites chapter and verse and likes to denounce one group or another. Then there's the pop psych genre, which throws around the word 'psychology' and quotes from doctors, to cast a wider net of more inclusive moralising appeal. Your sister is all too predictable.

You still haven't met Maria again. Actually, you heard her moving about once in the living room; the wooden floor carries the sound of steps clearly. It was three in the afternoon and she was getting ready to leave, but you were too lazy to come out of your room and say hello.

A few days later she knocks on your door. She hasn't forgotten her promise.

'Still interested in the Asian supermarket?'

Like the last time you saw her, the way she's dressed shows attention to detail. Her hair is curled at the tips once more, and her eyes are made up in metallic blue.

'I have to go to work, but we can stop by the supermarket.'

You follow her down the stairs. She takes her bike from the parking area and walks alongside it so she can show you the way.

'Is your work far from here?'

She shakes her head.

'I work at De Wallen.'

Perhaps you look a bit foolish; you're confused and unsure what you heard. Maria adds, 'Red Light District.'

'Oh.'

She speaks like a nurse who has given you a vaccine and then is calmly dabbing the blood away with an antiseptic swab. Her expression is fully composed. You try hard to act naturally although later you know, as does Maria, that you're trying too hard.

You've never been to the Red Light District.

You repeat this sentence silently to yourself while walking in Dam Square. As the birds around you peck away at bread-crumbs, you munch on the chips you bought from the Asian market. You purchased five packets of *emping melindjo*. It's not until the next day that you learn that these chips, like satay sauce, can be found in any Albert Heijn supermarket.

You've never been to the Red Light District. It's so close to your apartment, but you've only strolled along its outskirts, in broad daylight. Curiosity takes you into a sex shop to browse lingerie and sex toys, but you've yet to pass window displays of human flesh. Inside the store you fantasise about sexual escapades with the different costumes and paraphernalia. You're reminded of Demon Lover. There has been no word from him, and after your graveside meeting you're still quite angry. But anger aside, you feel pangs of longing for your trysts. The devil doesn't need you to wear Prada, a black corset or fishnet stockings. You remember how dozens of wedding invitations quote a famous poet: *I want to love you simply.* Maybe there's truth to that line. Demon Lover is traditional, a lusty Lucifer. That's always more than enough.

Where has he gone now? Why does he show up when he's not needed and disappear when you desire him? The short answer: he's a devil, and you're horny.

At Dam Square, you can't stop thinking of the display windows at De Wallen. Who really knows why you haven't visited yet. Yes, not yet. Not 'won't visit'. In your head you form a vague plan. You put De Wallen on your list of tourist sights to be ticked off, sort of like museums, churches or Madame Tussauds.

Maybe you've yet to visit because you don't want to go by yourself, and can't imagine being a female tourist gawking on her own. You feel you have to go with someone. Two people, three people. The more the merrier. Maybe better to go with guys? It makes sense, even if you feel ridiculous. After all, according to your Quranic recitation teacher, a male relative should accompany a woman wherever she goes. Then again, he probably wasn't talking about brothels.

Ha.

The reason you stay away from the Red Light District isn't clear, and maybe there's more than one. If you go there, you'll have to hide.

But hide from what?

Proceed to page 232.

Dear reader, because of inclement weather, all flights to Zagreb are currently grounded. We apologise for this inconvenience and have rebooked you on an intercity express train from Berlin to Amsterdam.

Turn to page 204.

You arrive at a three-storey house along a dirty boulevard. Fernando invites you via a side entrance to the basement, which he is renting as a studio. He lives alone. Families from Mexico live on the first, second and third floor. Fernando pulls a key out of his pocket to open a trellis gate and then guides you down the stairs.

Fernando used to live with his family in a two-bedroom apartment, but after his divorce he moved to this much cheaper basement studio. The room itself is spacious, maybe as big as a typical one-bedroom. Actually, basement rentals like this are against regulations, Fernando says. There's no window. During the day, the only way to get natural light is to open the door. A bit of sun then filters in from the stairs leading to the side courtyard. The effect is claustrophobic. But with so many people eager for a cut-rate basement studio, deals are always going on under the table. Fernando has a large bed and a futon that his daughter sleeps on when she stays over. After he and his wife split up, she stayed in their old place but let Fernando take several items, including the futon, which had been in their den.

You and Fernando sit on the futon, chatting and sipping Chilean wine. You go home the next morning.

You thought that night would be the end of it, once you made love, since you know you can feel curious and horny at two in the morning. You thought that you were only scratching an itch. But in the following days, Fernando spoils you with attention. He comes to your apartment and cooks for you. At first you just planned to sleep with him a couple more times, perhaps out of a slight desire for revenge on Vijay and Meena (you're not miserable, because you're getting laid now too, even if the sex you're having isn't as hot and wild as theirs). Fernando, however, is persistent. He accompanies you shopping; sometimes, he'll be busy sweeping or tidying your place while you laze in bed. Bob has also been inviting you out but you haven't had a chance to respond because Fernando is always around. He can bore you, but he listens to all your stories attentively. Although he may not make every crevice of your body tingle like Devil did, a man who listens is a rare creature.

Ah, Demon Lover. Nobody makes love like a demon.

Fuck. If he really wanted you, he'd be here, right now.

You certainly don't feel that you've fallen in love with Fernando, but the guy is handsome and really sweet. He's willing to be your slave, albeit in a very different way. You can't understand why his wife dumped him.

As time goes on, you become more and more used to Fernando's presence in your life. You also come to develop a genuine fondness for Tiffany, who is apparently nice to both her mom's boyfriend and her dad's girlfriend. With Tiffany, you learn that children can be surprisingly mature and you start to discover similarities between the two of you. Unlike her friends who are content with books and movies about princesses and princes, or boy-meets-girl stories, Tiffany prefers more exciting tales. She reads the Choose Your Own Adventure series, and of course loves to watch *The Wizard of Oz*. Fernando and Tiffany start stealing your time and your heart. You don't even realise that your neighbour Meena has moved.

One day, as you're throwing out the trash, you spy the building doorman putting some sparkly objects into a black bag. You think that you recognise them.

Your red shoes.

'Sir, just a moment,' you say, trying to stop him. 'I think those are mine.'

The man keeps his back to you, ignoring you. He ties up the black bag and places it with the other ones. You're flustered when you hear him speak. 'I let you play around, but I didn't expect you to have such lousy taste.'

You say nothing but study the man carefully. Although he resembles the doorman you see regularly, something isn't right. His ears are pointy and covered with fur.

Devil.

'You're fucking up big time.'

The man stares at you, his crimson eyes a giveaway. Demon Lover in disguise ...

'Betraying me was the first mistake.'

'But you never even visited me. What's happened to make you show up now?'

'The second mistake.' Devil continues to sit in judgement. 'How dare you cheat on me with a man who has no future!'

'You're not my father! Easy enough for you to talk about the future. Why did you give me a visa that's only good for a year?'

'So that you'd find your own way, darling.'

'OK, fine. I found my own way.'

'What, by dating a low-class loser?'

Your voice rises. 'Are you talking about immigration status? I never knew you were such a conservative. You should be ashamed of yourself!'

'This isn't about politics. What if he gets deported?'

'Are you trying to say he has no rights in this country?'

'National borders are too trivial for a devil to deal with,' he says, brushing you off. 'I just think you're making things difficult for yourself.'

'Oh yes. That's my style all right. Making my own life difficult.'

Devil looks even more upset. He shakes his head, as if there's no use talking to you. He starts to go but then turns around.

'The shoes.' He points at the pile of garbage bags. 'They're not yours any more. Our contract is over and done with.'

You just glare at him as he leaves, not bothering to give chase.

Once he's gone, you open the black bag that he's tossed away. No shoes. You check the other bags, but there's nothing in any of them but trash.

Continue to page 407.

Anything could happen if you accept Fernando's invitation to his apartment. Your relationship may enter a different stage, and you're not ready. Fernando looks disappointed, but he sees you home and says goodbye sweetly.

Fernando is handsome, but his personal life is too complicated. Besides, maybe you should look for a boyfriend who can help guarantee your legal status in the future. It's becoming ever clearer that you can't rely on Devil. And really, who of God's creations is dumb enough to hang her life on some demon? If men as attractive as Vijay are hard to come by, you should probably be more strategic in your boyfriend hunt: date those who can get you a green card. At that moment, you make up your mind. From here on you're playing by new rules.

You reject the second, third and endless dinner invitations from Fernando. Finally he gets the hint that you're not interested. Instead, you start considering Bob more seriously.

Proceed to the next page.

Nyai

Your relationship with Bob makes you think of Marcus Werner, the English teacher from Germany, and his student turned lover.

You forget which one of your co-workers first came up with the idea of calling her Nyai. What's clear, however, is that although the nickname stuck, you and the other English teachers at EGW weren't really imagining an indigenous woman who became a Dutch colonist's wife. You called her Nyai because you all considered her face very 'native', a polite way of saying that she looked like a hick. She was petite but always sported seven-centimetre heels. She had big eyes, lustrous brown skin, and hair that tumbled straight down to her waist. You and your fellow light-skinned friends felt more beautiful than her. None of you could fathom why Marcus Werner, Mr Handsome Expat, would be attracted to Nyai, with her village looks. She hadn't even passed Basic English. The only explanation could be that Nyai was exotic. Some of your friends cynically called her 'whitey chocolate', the sort of dark Indonesian look that only Caucasians liked.

Yudi, your exploitative Marxist, knew about all of this. He knew that you envied Nyai but he never felt jealous over your earlier obsession with Marcus Werner (Yudi saw himself as too sophisticated for that). On one of your dates, he asked, 'If you all hate her so much, why do you lift her image by calling her Nyai?' Then he talked about the character Nyai Ontosoroh in a Pramoedya Ananta Toer novel, a brilliant woman who symbolised colonial resistance. At that point you had yet to read Pramoedya.

Only after all these years do you realise how terribly mean you and your friends were to Nyai. You were like Cinderella's stepsisters fighting for the attention of your white Prince Charming. But now you're not much different from the woman you looked down upon: Nyai Werner, rather than Nyai Ontosoroh. With Bob, it's as if you're wearing the seven-centimetre heels that belonged to Marcus's girlfriend.

The first time you went out to dinner with Bob, you felt very self-conscious. He invited you to a pricey Asian restaurant near St Marks Place. You were wrapped in a knee-length black dress that you'd just bought at H&M. Cheap but not cheap-looking, even tending towards demure and sweet. But you caught a different take on the situation from the eyes of the waiter serving you. He was very friendly, but his eyes were busy making calculations. Sizing you up, even if he wasn't judging you. It was quite clear. You'd entered the restaurant with a white man old enough to be your father.

For the waiter, of course, that would be the definition of exotic.

Exotic, a euphemism for a woman, a young ward, or a combination of the two from the Third World: a sugar baby.

After a series of dates, you don't care any more. There's no point fighting off those looks. If you and Bob were in Indonesia, maybe your light skin would keep you from being considered whitey chocolate, but you'd certainly be accused of being a gold digger, chasing after a white man with money, even if he is bloated and bald. Maybe you're like Nyai after all. Not having to worry about the cost of dinner or a movie definitely sits well with you. Besides, Bob is an engaging conversationalist. As far as insight and taste go, Marcus Werner now seems like a mole in your eyes compared to Uncle Bob, blob that he may be. You don't know any men smarter than Bob, except maybe for Devil.

Bob tells you about the twists and turns his life took before he became a scholar of Chinese culture. As a graduate student in the seventies, he felt that too many of his colleagues were researching South East Asia, including Indonesia. He chose another path. As you get to know him more, it dawns on you that he's always wanted to be different; he's an ex-hippie with hipster tendencies. You listen enthusiastically. From Bob, you learn that Indonesia used to be important to the First World. But that was back during the Cold War.

Bob eventually became a Sinologist and found a position at New York University. In the late nineties, as China's economy took off, the study of East Asia became more and more popular. The field was crowded and competitive, so he spread his wings into South East Asia. In contrast to the seventies, by the new millennium South East Asian Studies had become quiet territory. Maybe the subject wasn't important any more.

How come the US gets to determine whether your home is important or not? you wonder. After all, as Fernando said, Americans were notorious for their lousy geography.

Bob continues his story. Wanting to expand his scope of expertise from East to South East Asia, he took time off from university and lived for a year in Vietnam. The vagaries of his personal life seemed to follow the path of his career. He's been divorced twice. His first wife came from Taipei; his second, from Hanoi.

Next project: Jakarta, you say silently.

'Why Asia?' you ask.

'Going to live in Asia was the best decision of my life,' Bob says, taking a swig of Cabernet.

From a young age Bob felt sorry for two groups: firstly, Americans who were comfortable living in the same state their whole lives. They never had a need to see another world. The second were tourists who travelled constantly in order to collect photos or souvenirs (American tourists, they say, are most easily duped into parting with money). They toted cameras to obvious places – the Eiffel Tower, the Leaning Tower of Pisa, the Great Wall of China – only to produce images that hardly differed from those in travel magazines.

Bob strenuously avoided these two groups that deserved his pity. He travelled to a place to live with its community. He wanted to feel as one among them.

'Yes, but why Asia?'

He just laughs and asks back, 'How about you? Why New York?'

'Aspirations of the Third World. Cheers!'

'Cheers!'

Your glasses clink, and he laughs louder. You laugh too, even though you know that your answer is serious. After all, the beautiful lovers of Bollywood always head to London or America (yes, London or America – maybe New York or Kansas aren't so different).

You don't want to think about how sex with Bob feels. If you had to give an account, to a psychiatrist maybe, you wouldn't want to explain it for long. Cold. Scaly. Like touching paper. When he reaches climax, odd sounds come from his throat, almost as if he is out of breath. Sex with him always goes too fast for you, and often the two of you agree to leave the act unfinished, suspended, which keeps you on edge all night.

At first this disappoints you, but sex has stopped being a priority in your life. Far more exciting is your penetration of Bob's world: waking up in his apartment in Greenwich Village and feeling the First World in your whole body. Bob's New York isn't about taking the 7 train from Jackson Heights, crammed with passengers fighting over seats and annoying others by playing loud music or manspreading. With Bob, New York means attending the Tribeca Film Festival, queuing at an artisanal coffee shop near campus (Starbucks? For the plebs), and buying organic products, from vegetables to soap. There are no ethnic supermarkets whose workers are unable to answer questions because they can't speak English. In the morning, he wakes up first and occasionally prepares breakfast for you before walking to campus. You go to La Candela as usual, then at night he escorts you to the theatre. With Bob, you see a neatly packaged New York, a New York that welcomes artists from all over the globe, not mini-gladiators scrambling to take a bite of the Big Apple before they are eliminated.

Bob's world.

For you, this is the definition of exotic, the City of Dreams.

You don't want to dwell on who is using who, whether Bob is dating you because he has a thing for Asian women, or whether you are hunting for a green card and voluntarily entering a bourgeois Caucasian cosmology so comfortable as to be almost sterile. Bob hasn't made you tumble into love, let alone thirst for sex. You're not looking for a daddy figure either. But with Bob you don't feel lonely. You're pleased to find that how you dress and speak doesn't embarrass you when the good professor bumps into acquaintances at the theatre.

Spring comes to New York, and you settle contentedly into your new routine. From Thursday to Sunday, you stay at Bob's. Sometimes you do nothing but hang out at home, Bob at his desk, and you on the couch watching movies on your laptop. You're walled in by bookcases that reach the ceiling, and you can read any book you want. Apart from books, Bob's apartment is decorated with large wall maps, calligraphic scrolls from China, and half a dozen crystal snow globes lined up on the bookshelves. Often, instead of reading, you prefer to take a snow globe and shake it so that white granules flutter down upon the small world in your hand.

You remain close with Meena while all this is going on. On Thursday evenings, she invites you over to adventure with her in her kitchen. She makes you Thai beef with basil leaves, teriyaki chicken, Hungarian mushroom soup, dishes from around the globe. The aroma of spices lingers in your jacket after you return to Bob's.

'You smell of grilled meat,' Bob comments when you arrive at his apartment. Then later he will say: 'Onions.'

Often he can't guess. His eyebrows knit.

'Hmm, smells …'

'Ethnic?'

The varied fragrances tease him, so he demands: 'You have to invite me to meet your friend the cook.'

You nod, even though the plan never materialises.

Before your first dinner with both Meena and Vijay, you imagine that it will be a mild form of torture. Vijay may still have not fully recovered from the shame of meeting you that time; he looks awkward. He obviously knows you heard their passionate oohs and aahs. Meena, on the other hand, is totally at ease, either pretending not to know, or knowing but unashamed and feeling that no comment is necessary. Her composure establishes a safe space for you and Vijay, for the three of you.

Maybe you're still a little jealous, but before long you feel happy, amused, even amazed watching them dine together. Much of their conversation revolves around spices, which at times they treat almost like fictional characters. 'Do you know that spices are con artists?' Vijay asks. 'They sit sweetly in the cabinet, but while we're asleep they visit their brethren in Asia or Africa. They're not content with the kitchen. Like Meena.' Vijay looks at his girlfriend, teasing.

Meena shakes her head and shoots back: 'And what are they up to in Asia and Africa, then? Holding Non-Aligned Condiment Conferences?'

'Could be,' Vijay says. 'They oppose the hegemony of salt and pepper.'

The weather remains cool at the end of April, but sweat beads on Vijay's forehead as he savours Meena's spicy cooking. Every now and then he sighs. Meena's hair becomes a little dishevelled and her face grows red. You restrain a grin watching the scene before you. Dinner has never felt so pornographic.

Your relationship with Vijay and Meena is strange. Being between them often makes you feel lewd. The picture of Vijay, overcome with the succulence of Meena's spices, intertwines with your imaginings about the heat of their bed; he rocks his hips, mouth open, above – or below – Meena. But of course, you and Meena don't talk about sex, let alone with Vijay present. Sex only rears its head once, when you and she pass Draupadi, a shop that sells saris and Bollywood DVDs, which leads you to talk about the *Mahabharata*. In my country the Pandavas' wife is named Drupadi, you say.

Drupadi gets romanticised a lot in India and Indonesia, but nobody thinks about how incredible her management skills were. 'She must have had a secretary,' you say. 'Can you imagine what a nightmare it would be arranging your schedule with five husbands?'

'But the division is perfectly logical,' Meena responds. 'Drupadi has one year exclusively with each husband. Before changing, she walks on fire to become holy and has her virginity restored.'

'She becomes a virgin again for each husband?'

'Yes,' Meena says, grimacing, as if in pain. 'Not very nice, is it?'

You both laugh. That's your one conversation that deals with sex. You both despise these fantasies about virgin wives, but also agree that the *Mahabharata* is a thrilling early epic of adventure. From the *Odyssey* to the *Mahabharata*, travel is the most ancient human desire.

Your relationship with Bob, meanwhile, is no less odd. He seems aware that you don't love him, but he also knows that being close to him gets you excited – about life, if not him. In spring, for the first time in your life, you begin to feel happy. But as befits a journey, happiness is a terminal, not a destination; nobody stays there too long.

Continue to the next page.

Death of Cherry Blossoms

Spring wraps death in beauty. We're bewitched by pink cherry blossoms on trees previously naked and dry. The clear azure sky and the soft rays of the sun, all the luxuries that we're deprived of during winter, distract us from the ephemerality of cherry blossoms. Garden lawns become carpets of pastel, petals falling, so sweet and fresh that no one thinks about their demise. We willingly deceive ourselves into believing that cherry blossoms sound a beginning, not a warning. By the end of spring, trees have become completely green without our noticing. Their lushness, a sign of the passage of time, makes us forget that we sought life in trees flowering with pink.

Amid the beautiful death of cherry blossoms, Meena is preparing another death.

You forget precisely how Meena's saga came to be exposed. You assume that Meena hadn't wanted to share her story with you because you weren't that important in her life. You just happened to be there, playing the role of a neighbour who faithfully attended her adventures in spice when her lover wasn't present. She never intended to befriend you. But we are often with someone because we have no choice.

That Thursday evening, as you savour her caramel bread pudding, she tells you a secret. The sweet caramel smell lingering in the oven has left you relaxed, unprepared.

Meena didn't meet Vijay at a party. Her husband, Raj, had put them in touch via email before he went to England for dissertation research.

You gasp. Raj. Sudden entrance, stage right, an unknown name.

Meena met Raj after he moved from Buffalo to New York. A friend had introduced them. Raj was then a PhD student at Columbia. He had been born and raised in Arizona, but had visited Delhi several times with his parents. On one of those visits he met Vijay, a cousin.

Meena and Raj married after dating for a year. Everything seemed fine. They were compatible, as were their families. Raj's parents owned a store back in Arizona. They came from the educated middle class, like Meena's parents. After their marriage, Raj gave up an apartment near Columbia so they could move into a bigger and cheaper space together in Jackson Heights. Meena liked this decision because she could readily walk to Indian supermarkets and restaurants.

You suspect that Raj must be a brute, perhaps prone to domestic violence. Maybe you just need a compelling reason to explain Meena's betrayal of her husband, but this proves a vain hope. Raj is gentle and faithful.

I woke up one morning and wanted to change directions.

Meena's statement slashes into you. Betrayal may be unavoidable on a journey. But Meena never left her kitchen. Those spices. Yes, maybe they didn't feel at home? Was she provoked by masala? Something had to be to blame.

You chew on the bread pudding for so long that your teeth hurt. Breaking up in adolescence is easier. We fall out of love (and we believe, naively, that all those feelings are real), or we can curse ungratefully: slut. But sitting with Meena here, in a kitchen suffused with the sweet smell of caramel, you don't know who she should be with. You were never in her place, in a world shaken by an encounter with her husband's cousin. You haven't been on the journey that made her stop and question the previous turns she took.

'What about Vijay?'

Meena offers you coffee, but you refuse: you've already had two cups today. You ask if she has juice. She replies that it's past its expiry date.

'Vijay will go home in June.'

'And then?'

'Life goes on.'

You don't know whether to believe her.

Meena doesn't finish her pudding that day. You're reminded of the trees that are now fully green. There are no longer any traces of cherry blossoms to be found.

Before going to sleep you discover several email messages from your sister. In addition to a personal note, as usual she forwards information from the mailing lists she follows. Your brain operates like a paper shredder. Trash. Trash. Trash. Spam. Trash. But then a message catches your attention. The title, all in caps, reads 'FWD: NO TO AA JIM'S TALK AT LENTERA IMAN ELEMENTARY'.

You've always wondered how the two of you could be siblings. But if you have anything in common, it's your shared loathing for the cleric Aa Jim.

You read the first paragraph of the message:

Assalamualaikum Fellow Moms,

As we know, Aa Jim will attend the graduation cere-mony of Lentera Iman Elementary. Many moms do not approve of Aa Jim's decision to engage in polygamy. A few months ago, Aa Jim's first wife announced her inten-tion to seek a divorce. Polygamy clearly hurts women. Inviting Aa Jim to speak at Lentera Iman Elementary will set a bad example for our children.

You smile. You know that your sister is an active member of Lentera Iman Elementary's PTA. She must be actively trying to sway the political attitudes of the mothers (who are eager to call themselves moms). All of a sudden you feel greater affection towards certain memories of your sister. A couple of years ago, the two of you sat in front of the television watching a gossip show reporting on Aa Jim's second marriage, a woman who became known as Sister Tini. Previously he'd been a favourite with moms: sympathetic, young at heart, always projecting the image of a loving, monogamous family man with his wife, Sister Dini. Yep, Tini and Dini. The single letter difference must have annoyed at least one of them, probably both.

'Masya Allah, how heartless,' said your sister. 'How must it feel to be Sister Dini?'

'Probably a hell of a lot like plunging into a sewer,' you said.

Your gratuitous remark caused your sister to glare. But she was genuinely furious with Aa Jim. Shortly after he married Sister Tini, mothers in hijabs burned his photos and books. Your sister cheered. You wouldn't have thought these mothers had the capacity for running riot, but Aa Jim united them, just as he united you with your sister.

You hate Aa Jim passionately, but you can't be angry with Meena. Meena has no desire to be a Drupadi with two husbands, or five. She doesn't want her husband. You want Meena and Vijay to be together. *Go*, you think. *Run.*

You wake, after dropping off to sleep in front of the TV. On the screen you see a music group playing in a studio, black and white, like on *The Ed Sullivan Show*. The vocalist is a bald little man with a thick moustache. He wears a shirt that reads 'Little Johnny'.

That man. You sit up and rub your eyes. You've seen him. In dreams.

What is Johnny doing on television?

The band, whatever its name is, performs an old Mel Carter song, 'Hold Me, Thrill Me, Kiss Me'. Your eyes are glued to the movements of Little Johnny's lips and moustache.

Little Johnny sings like a seductive lover. His thick moustache looks funny, but his voice stirs up strange feelings. There's something about him that you find a little – sensual, maybe.

You can't find the exact words. His voice makes you want to hold him tight and nibble his ears.

Applause from the studio audience. Still at the microphone, Little Johnny winks. Like Casanova, he says:

That song goes out to one beautiful lover in particular … Meena.

What? What did he just say? This is no coincidence. Little Johnny knows about them, about Vijay and Meena. You rise from your seat and slowly approach the television. Little Johnny's gaze hypnotises you, making you want to enter the rectangular box. Then, losing control, you ask:

Why don't they choose –

To run away?

Little Johnny asks back at the camera, back at you. Shock. No doubt about it, he's not just breaking the fourth wall, he's talking directly to you from inside the television.

Go, and destroy everything? Not everyone has that luxury. Unless you're a rat king who can send pestilence. Hey! Do you know where all the rats went?

You can, you insist. You can take on the whole world.

You don't know why you're speaking to him as if you've known him for a long time. Maybe Little Johnny isn't a stranger. Maybe he has indeed lived inside you, in some distant past.

You're happy, you say again.

They are too. In their flight. In their dreams.

But –

Shhh. Little Johnny shakes his head.

When you wake up, your dream will be passed its expiry date.

Shhh! Little Johnny shakes his head harder. Enough talk. Sleep. Time for a little Roy Orbison.

A guitar strums, and he sings again.

In dreams I walk with you.

Continue on to page 240.

Market

Maria never intended to invite you to a coffee shop for a chat. Your relationship is clear, uncomplicated. You're a tenant in her flat, and flatmates don't need to be friends. Her invitations come because she happens to be passing by a certain place, like the Asian supermarket, or because you take the initiative to follow her, like today. She has risen early, so you run into her in the kitchen. You know that she's planning to go out because she's wearing a turtleneck and jeans. Her hair is up in a ponytail.

She's on her way to Waterlooplein, a large open market that sells all manner of goods, new and used, from household appliances to goth clothing.

'Can I join you?'

She hadn't made the initial offer, but she doesn't mind you tagging along. You ask her to wait while you quickly get ready.

'Let's go.'

She gets up and puts on her shoes. You thought Maria would apply some make-up or lipstick, but she doesn't. Without make-up, her face looks naked. Suddenly you feel that your own pink lipstick is flashy and that you've made yourself up too much.

'Am I overdressed?'

She shakes her head.

'I'm just staying away from make-up,' she says. 'My skin needs to breathe.'

Who knows how many tent stalls there are at Waterlooplein and how many shoppers. You wouldn't call it packed, but it's one of the most crowded places you've seen in the Netherlands.

You follow Maria in and out of stalls clutching your bag. She has warned you to be on the lookout for pickpockets.

Your travel companion is choosy. She can linger over a five-euro scarf, inspecting it all over, and in the end decide not to buy it. You, on the other hand, are readily tempted and come away with a new pair of gloves and a new hat.

'The scarf was nice,' you comment on the unpurchased item.

'Yes, but I'm very picky. And stingy. Maybe it's from being a vendor too.'

'A vendor? Where?'

'In the flesh market.'

Again, she handles your innocence in a clinical tone, like a nurse.

On an ordinary day, a visitor to Waterlooplein will only find ordinary items at ordinary prices, just like in the ubiquitous Hema shops, but those who are diligent and lucky can find bargains on unique items. After searching in vain, Maria asks if you want to stop by a thrift store not far from there. The atmosphere isn't as frantic as Waterlooplein, and you find the choice of clothes and shoes more selective.

'There's lots of good vintage stuff here,' Maria says. 'Shops like this always remind me why I like being an expat in Amsterdam.'

You struggle to suppress a smile at the word. Expat. Maria's thin eyebrows arch slightly.

'What? I can't call myself an expat?'

You hadn't intended to offend her. You tell her about Marcus Werner, the English teacher who caught your eye. Since then, he has become the quintessential expat in your mind. From a developed country, earning more than locals, living in an apartment in the centre of the city.

Expatriates are people who leave their homeland to work abroad, Maria says. By that definition, as far as she is concerned, she is more than qualified to be an expat.

'Why did Marcus get called an expat?'

'Maybe because –' You pause. You're not sure your answer is correct, but you try to explain, 'He was a foreigner hired for special skills.'

'And that doesn't apply to me?'

'No, you're right.'

You have no desire to cast doubt upon Maria's professional expertise.

FWD: Fitnah.

When you get home from Waterlooplein and check your email, a message from your sister startles you. You never imagined she'd send such a note. The email contains an article from a kiai named Muhammad Hasan.

Fitnah

In Arabic, fitnah *means a test, temptation, bewitchment, incitement, provocation. The notion of* fitnah *is often attached to women because their bodies are considered tempting. Men whose bodies tempt women are never censured, although there is an interesting tale from the time of Caliph Umar bin Khattab, recounted by Abu Uthman Amr al-Jahizh in his book* Rasail al-Jahizh.

When Umar toured Medina, he heard a woman singing:

Is there a way to a whiskey bar?
Let me drink there
Is there a road to Nashr bin Hajjaj?
Let me be with him

The woman must have been drunk. And indeed she was drunk – drunk with desire for a man named Nashr bin Hajjaj. Umar summoned Nashr, who turned out to be extraordinarily handsome, and ordered Nashr to shave his head. But because Nashr remained handsome even thereafter, Umar sent him into exile in Basra, Iraq. Alas, his beauty drove women mad there as well. The governor of Basra expelled Nashr to Persia. The problem recurred. Handsome Nashr drove women hysterical with desire. Concerned, the governor of Persia wrote to Umar, who ordered Nashr to be sheared once more and hidden away in a mosque. After Umar died, Nashr returned to Madinah and stayed there until the end of his life.

The story of Nashr is horrifying if we imagine Caliph Umar's strenuous attempts to control Nashr because of the frenzy he aroused in women. More frequently, though, people feel amused by it: how unlucky to be such a handsome fellow. We also remember Prophet Yusuf and his willingness to be imprisoned in order to avoid the fitnah of Zulaikha.

But the story of a man who invites fitnah is rare. For every Nashr whose body is censured, we hear of thousands of women blamed for posing a challenge to faith. Because fitnah is the female body itself. When a woman is raped, people raise a question: if you didn't want to be raped, why did you show off your body in the marketplace?

A market is not safe. Women who cover themselves continue to be victims of rape in markets, in alleyways, on the streets, on public transport. In a world of patriarchy, women must be locked in houses and kept tightly under guard. To be sure, we inhabit a world that makes little sense.

You read the kiai's writing line by line in amazement. Your head is filled with questions. Who is this scholar? Do many people think like him now? Why did your sister send you this article?

She must have known you would appreciate it.

Suddenly you become a little sentimental. You don't know how long you have been constructing a wall separating your world and hers, but now you feel a strange urge to share stories with her, just as you did when you shared a room and would lay awake together in the dark. Earlier, before the wall was erected, you would talk about anything. Teachers who made your blood boil. Friends who cheated. Maybe now you can write to her about Amsterdam, or about Maria.

Your fingers cling to the keyboard, and you find it impossible to type a single stroke. You have no story for your sister. Too many divergences on your paths, no way home. But, for the first time, you reply to one of her messages. Briefly.

> Hi Mbak,
> Thanks. I liked that.

*

You gather Maria's story as the pieces spill out bit by bit, on the way home from Waterlooplein and later, in random meetings in the kitchen. You put everything together in your head, as if arranging a jigsaw puzzle.

She arrived in Amsterdam as a naive young girl eager to be on the move. Until then her life had been perfectly fine. She wanted to earn money, sure, but that was only one of the reasons why she had come. When we're young, we always want to be elsewhere. Always.

Not everyone who travels enjoys a share of luxury.

'I've been lucky enough,' she says. 'Not everyone in a business like this is lucky. I know women who've almost been beaten to death. But not here. Here, we're all safe.'

The only thing Maria complains about is the fee for her cabin. Just to pay off eight hours' rent, along with taxes, she needs four or five customers.

'I've never been to De Wallen,' you say honestly.

'There's no need.'

You're surprised to hear that. Maria always explains her work to you in a very professional manner. She calls herself an independent sex worker. But she repeats her words.

'There's no need. For what? A free show?'

'Does it really cost fifty euros?'

Your question is so naive that you feel embarrassed as soon as it is out of your mouth. But Maria answers you with a flat expression: that's the price for standard service.

If you're at a drinks vending machine, you can put in a euro for a can of Coke. Call that standard. But some people want cappuccino with milk, full-fat or trim, half a spoon of sugar, and maybe cinnamon powder too. For that you need a barista. Some people even need a bartender. That's not standard.

On many days Maria only has a string of customers who are more than satisfied with Coke, the economy package. Maria calls such days Coke machine days.

You imagine thirsty men standing in front of a Coke machine, and Maria welcoming them like an efficient nurse. She jabs their flesh with a needle, then nimbly swabs away any drops of blood with cotton. She is so adept that patients have nothing to remind themselves of the injection and its pain except for a bandage on the arm.

One day, after you've grown bored walking around, as you pass the time catching up on emails and reading the news online, you become curious about the previous occupant of your room. Her belongings are sealed in cardboard boxes to deter petty thieves and snoops like you, but it occurs to you that maybe she keeps some items in the desk drawer. You pull it open and find lipstick and old make-up. There are also several photos. You see Anna beneath the Eiffel Tower. She is wearing a thick coat and a knitted hat, perhaps a wintertime shot. Another photo. Anna is embracing an older man, white, chubby and bald. Her father? Her boyfriend?

The next time you see Maria in the kitchen, you ask if she has a boyfriend. It turns out that she did, someone she hadn't met in the Red Light District, but since breaking up with him she prefers to be alone. Maria knows that one young client harbours romantic fantasies about becoming her boyfriend, but she is also sure that his fantasies will vanish with age (he's only twenty-two). She adds, 'I'm not good at making people fall for me. Not like Anna.'

'Does Anna work in the Red Light District too?'

Maria's expression changes at your question, perhaps from the realisation that she's pulling Anna into her story.

'Not any more. Her boyfriend didn't want her to.'

You imagine the face of the bald old man. Evidently he is indeed Anna's boyfriend.

'Her boyfriend is American. He lives in New York,' says Maria. At the words 'New York', her eyes brighten a little. 'But they just broke up.'

'Why?'

'How should I know? He wants to find a respectable wife, maybe?' She adds, 'It's better this way. That man –' Maria smiles slightly. 'He's a professor. But he's not on the up and up.'

'Meaning?'

It's strange to hear the phrase from her. As if reading your thoughts, Maria corrects herself. 'OK, he's nice. I might even say that SpongeBob is very –'

'SpongeBob?'

'Oh, we call him that. From the cartoon, you know? Actually, he's more like Patrick Star ... Yes, anyway, he's kind and caring. But I think he's involved in some kind of shady business, and Anna got dragged in.'

She falls silent.

'I don't want to talk about Anna,' she says. 'I don't want to get involved. Dealing with rent and taxes gives me enough of a headache.'

She steers the conversation towards professional matters. She wants to have more money and travel. But she keeps circling back to how difficult it is to save up given the fee for her cabin.

'If it's so expensive, why not find another way?'

'Something illegal, you mean?'

She shakes her head.

'Nobody would dare, at least not among my friends. Nobody would take that risk except the Whore of Babylon.'

Continue on to page 244.

Airport

How strange things feel that night, an unbearable New York summer night, stuffy and stifling. Again you find yourself in a suffocating cab headed for the airport. But this time there is no room for anxious hopes. There is no hope at all. You stare straight ahead, not daring to contemplate what is happening behind you. You hear neither Vijay's voice nor Meena's. The taxi driver makes occasional attempts at small talk, and you engage him so the pair behind you don't have to. They may be holding hands. When the taxi arrives at the airport, perhaps Meena releases her grip first. Or Vijay does. It doesn't matter.

Vijay reaches the security gate. He has checked his bags after a lengthy wait in line. He and his lover must have wanted that half-hour to stretch on for years, but the end has come. He gives you a brief, tight embrace, then pats your shoulder. You step backwards without a word, withdrawing to give the pair space. You pretend not to notice them, even though you know they share a long, long kiss. You look away, randomly scanning a row of signs bearing airline names.

Meena walks over to you. She clasps your hand, urging the two of you away quickly, as if the world is exploding and melting behind you.

In front of the escalator, Meena stops. She looks back.

Vijay has remained standing where he was, his eyes fixed on Meena.

Somehow you knew this would happen – Meena looking back, Vijay waiting.

On that bitter night, sealed with a final kiss, you understand what Vijay has told you. Stories are a curse when you hear them yet know you can't change anything.

You are a witness to this neighbour's love story.

What follows is nightmare. Meena strides quickly, her face an utter mess. Tears that refuse to compromise cause her eyes to swell like boils. Not daring to ask what is happening, you accompany Meena on the AirTrain to another terminal. She reaches into her bag and takes out powder, eyebrow pencil and eyeshadow. In haste, she applies the powder thickly. Too thickly, as if wanting to cover her tracks.

At Terminal 8, Meena waits to meet Raj, her husband. His plane from London lands one hour after Meena's farewell to Vijay.

He approaches Meena, his face tired, then complains at length about the poor in-flight service. He takes no notice of Meena's mask-like make-up, her pocked smile.

Now you know why Meena invited you to the airport. She couldn't bear to be in a taxi alone with Raj. Once again you sit in the front, beside the driver, unable to contemplate what is going on behind you. There is no room for anxious hopes. There is no hope at all. This taxi driver is too tired to make small talk. Raj's voice finally breaks the silence. He strikes up conversation with you, trying to show his gratitude for accompanying his wife to the airport so late at night. You engage him, speaking in Meena's place. For Meena. There isn't a lot you can do, but for the moment you feel you've rescued her, even if only temporarily.

In the stuffy cab, night yields to morning, murdering with quiet cruelty.

That's the last time you saw Meena. You start staying more often at Bob's apartment. Perhaps this is also how you rescue yourself, after being made to witness the shattering of a world.

Meena never invites you over again after the return of her husband. The door is sealed tight, swallowing her whole. Your relationship with Bob, meanwhile, offers an exit. He invites you to move in with him. You can still occupy your own apartment for another month because you've already paid Mr Zhao the rent, but you have no desire to spend nights there.

When you return to your building to pack up, the doorman gives you a hefty cardboard box.

'It's from your next-door neighbour.'

'Meena?'

'They moved.'

'Together?'

The doorman shrugs. You thank him and bring up the box from Meena.

Once inside your apartment, you open it to find a variety of spices in small bottles. Cinnamon, candlenut, coriander, chilli, garam masala.

Thanks for everything. I hope you like this little gift.
I can't run away, but of course, as we know, spices travel the world.

You open a bottle of coriander seeds and inhale its aroma, just as when you saw Meena close her eyes and breathe in deep the scents of herbs and spices, the scents of travel. You will not forget that Devi Masala, the Spice Goddess, has taken you on adventures in her small, noisy kitchen, together with spices that went a-wandering. You will not forget the day you observed her with awe, curiosity and envy as she walked towards the elevator. Meena never wore a sari after that, at least not in front of you. But you know that she's a goddess, whether she wears a sari or not.

As you leave the building, you glance at the row of garden gnomes. For the first time you are reminded of Devil's gift. The Christmas tree is long gone, but the gnomes remain in the lobby.

Not all of them, though.

The smallest gnome, the one the size of a wine bottle, has disappeared.

Perhaps a gnome liberation activist has kidnapped him, saved him from the curse of watching over homes.

You have a hunch that the liberator is Meena.

Without Meena, New York seems emptier. You feel like you've become trapped in a once tempting option that you no longer want. Is there an emergency exit? You really don't have any choice but to find it. Turn to page 248.

Shop Display

The fateful night comes. You melt into a crowd filing slowly and methodically past a series of display windows. You want to lose yourself among them, to stay safe. You don't want to be found. In the crowd, it's hard to distinguish serious shoppers from inquisitive tourists like yourself. You suspect there may be a few women like you, there out of curiosity, unless they're also customers, that is. The presence of some vapid-looking men entertains you – they stop unmistakably in front of cabin windows, eyes bulging, mouths agape, as much ridiculous spectacle as spectators. Others skirt the crowd rapidly to avoid being trapped within it. They appear indifferent. Maybe they see all this as part of a drab daily routine, and are just keen to hurry home.

After a round of calculations, if not exactly a confirmation, over reasons why you should visit De Wallen, you have arrived. You couldn't come up with an excuse, so you flipped the question: why not?

The reversal makes it easier.

Why not?

Your entire life you were forbidden to eat pork. The first time you felt an urge to try it, you asked: why not?

Maria's story piques your interest. For days you wrestle with whether curiosity is justification enough to visit. In the early 2000s you really wanted to go to New York to see the ruins of the Twin Towers. But if you'd had the opportunity to visit, what then? What does curiosity mean for those left behind?

The Red Light District isn't as complicated as that, you argue with yourself. The place is not so different from

Disneyland. It's even widely promoted by the city government. The women are legal workers who receive health and safety assurances. Maria herself said so.

Why not?

So, here you are in this alley, passing window after window showcasing women lit by multicoloured neon. Like everyone else, you stroll slowly for a fuller, more vivid experience. Some women pose provocatively, others look bored. You admire perfect bodies. See-through outfits with sparkly beads, as if tailored for the wearer. Soon you're experiencing a welter of emotions. You start to feel envy. You no longer see each woman as a whole because your eyes are too busy focusing on body parts. You'll never have breasts like this girl or a butt like that one, unless you submit to a scalpel and implants. Your thighs are too big. Your boobs aren't as firm. In your mind, your own body becomes fragmented.

Most of the women are white, but other bodies have different hues. Your attention is drawn to one brown-skinned woman in pink lace lingerie. She looks Indonesian. Maybe she is Indonesian, or maybe Filipina. She is more petite than the others, but her body is so fine, so beautiful. What if her body was yours? You feel an urge to run your hands over it, ever so slowly, inch by inch.

Then comes hatred. You hate that they have to be here, valued at fifty euros. If your body were that perfect you wouldn't sell it for fifty euros. Neither would you offer it up free for an audience; onlookers should have to buy a ticket for the privilege of admiring you nearly nude. This place is crimson, cheap and cheerful. Secure revelry, well guarded by the police. No spectator here is allowed to create a disturbance.

This is no jungle. There's nothing mystical here.

This is a zoo, not because of what is displayed within but because it is too neat and orderly. A soiree waited upon by institutions and bureaucracy.

You're a spectator dazzled by flesh, glass and light, a spectator admiring and jealous of the women there. What you see amazes you and makes you wonder. The boundary is clear. They're in a display window, and you're on the street. You and they are different women.

Something is wrong with being a spectator.

Spectators participate in this zoo. Spectators help construct a world that separates the women on either side of the window.

Now you know why you want to hide. Maybe you fear your own desire and your hatred.

You sense that a brunette in a display window is watching you. Maybe she is wondering what you are doing there. Peeping? The woman's eyes make you realise that it is not only the spectators here who peep. The women behind the glass also peep at you. The watchers are also being watched, and you are not in hiding.

Then you sense that you have spotted Maria. You approach a woman in a window lit in dim green. Her hair is in blonde curls, like so many women here. Her nimble movements have made way for slow, bored gyrations. She is different, but you're sure it's Maria.

Why, of the entire spectrum of colours, does she choose green? She looks like a whore from outer space.

You gasp when her eyes find yours. The brief seconds of the encounter leave you shamed, paralysed. She stares straight at you, flatly and drily, before finally turning in the other direction.

You keep walking. Voices fill your head. Is she comfortable there? Tired? What kind of day are you having, Maria? A Coke machine day?

You walk fast. Faster. You run away, as if fleeing a disaster.

'You're judging me.'

She says it in the morning, in the kitchen, right after you've finished making coffee. Your morning hello receives no response. She walks towards you, her expression indifferent, then pours coffee into her mug before you offer her any. She has now metamorphosed from iridescent green whore from outer space into a woman with tired eyes and a dry, slightly scaly face. In the display window, there is no place for wrinkles and pores. Standing near her leaves you feeling awkward. Somehow her presence is slightly threatening. She sips her coffee.

'I can see it in your eyes.'

'You're imagining things.'

'Every woman in my situation can tell. We're trained for it.'

You pour coffee into your cup and add sugar, stir, trying to look busy. She takes her coffee into her room, like a hunter offering pardon and releasing its prey. But Maria never pardons you. That is your final kitchen conversation. You still have a week and a half in the apartment, but after that you don't meet again. Maybe she avoids you, just as you avoid her.

You haven't yet digested your experience in the Red Light District, and now you can't understand the basis of her anger towards you. How strange. She seems to hate having seen you in her workplace, like a curious tourist. But don't millions of tourists go there to satisfy their prurience – or, as many people say, to enjoy the scenery? She certainly knows this after years of standing in the display window. Why should you be any different?

The kitchen feels lonely. Maria leaves her room to go to the toilet, but soon returns and shuts her door. Tight.

Someone like you. Tourist. You never thought being a tourist could be so complicated.

You don't have an answer for why Maria hated seeing you in the Red Light District, but you can flip the question around:

Why not?

After three weeks of you and Maria sharing stories, the question feels valid. Why not?

Continue on to page 309.

Emergency Exit

In autumn, your relationship with Bob grows more serious. He introduces you to his family and even invites you to attend his niece's wedding in New Jersey. There you meet his ninety-year-old mother, his younger siblings, and his two children with his first wife. Before the event you had already met Angela, the younger, who lives in New York and works as a programme manager at an Asian cultural foundation. At first you thought she'd regard you cynically and be unable to accept that her father was dating a woman her own age. But, to the contrary, Angela is very sweet towards you. Once or twice she even gives you theatre tickets.

Everyone in Bob's family warmly welcomes you, except one person, his elder child, Richard. Unlike his sister, he is largely silent. But you know – though initially unsure – that he's watching you; his eyes study you to the point of making you uncomfortable. He behaves like a nineteenth-century researcher investigating how you speak, how you eat, and how you move, all for the advancement of science. He almost seems to be estimating your height and head circumference. On your second glass of wine, he approaches you, wearing a forced smile.

'My dad says you're a writer.'

Somehow his overly soft voice feels slightly threatening. You nod, nervous.

'What's your book called? Maybe I can google it?'

'Oh, it's not published yet.'

His eyebrows arch. The corners of his lips rise slightly, as if he is holding back a sneer. Your innocent confession appears to please him. 'Ah, really? Have you ever taken one of my father's classes?'

'No.'

'Then you met when he was doing research?'

'We met at a cafe, near Washington Square Park. I work there.'

'Oh, he must have been doing some cafe ethnography then.'

He chuckles, but you don't find anything funny in the remark. Richard seems satisfied to discover that you're a nobody. You scan your surroundings, looking for an escape route. Where is Bob? Seriously, you don't want to stay long in this man's company.

'Sorry, I've forgotten. Where are you from again? Guangzhou?'

'Jakarta.'

'Oh, right, right. Sorry, I thought it was Guangzhou. That was his last girlfriend.'

He apologises repeatedly but you don't think he's very sorry. That was surely deliberate. Guangzhou, Jakarta. What's the difference?

'My father likes to collect antiques from abroad.'

His soft voice pokes you mercilessly.

Of course. He collected souvenirs here and there on his expeditions, and even married one of them. That's how *you* were born.

Oh, how you long to launch a sharp retort at this fresh-mouthed man, but you can't. You just bite your tongue. You don't want to hurt Bob, and you don't want to destroy your own hopes either. So you shut up and smile, like a praiseworthy child, full of understanding.

A blonde woman finally rescues you from this snare. Jennifer, Richard's wife, comes over and offers you dessert. Richard really is not like his father.

On the way home, Bob holds your hand. He knows.

'Just ignore Richard. I get fed up with him too.'

Apparently, Richard's attitude is a known modus operandi: he always treats Bob's girlfriends like trash. You don't ask details, even though you want to know what happened with the woman from Guangzhou, for example. Instead of complaining about his son's behaviour, you change the subject.

'My visa's about to expire.'

You're a little surprised at your own bluntness. But you're pleased because you consider the problem more urgent than having your feelings hurt by some obnoxious man.

Bob's reaction surprises you even more.

'Then let's get married.'

He speaks lightly, as if he's ready to take you to Vegas on the spot. But he's not joking. One week later, he presents you with a diamond ring.

If you still want to marry Bob, turn to the next page.

If you need to think it over, turn to page 254.

You firm up your resolve to marry Bob. After living with the professor over the past few months, you can't see any reason not to. Green-card marriages are common enough these days, and, anyway, doesn't marrying for love only happen in storybooks?

At Bob's suggestion, you stop working at La Candela, not because he wants to force you to become a housewife, but because he feels you should concentrate on writing and finish your novel. He clearly worries about your habit of relaxing at home after work on the excuse of being tired. As a professor who has published four books and dozens of journal articles, it makes him edgy that he never sees you writing. You're happy to quit, and Bob is happy when he finds you sitting at your laptop. He doesn't need to know that all you've written is one crappy paragraph and that you've spent more time browsing clothes on eBay.

'Maybe someday you can be the first author from Indonesia to make the *New York Times*' 100 notable books of the year list.'

'But I write in Indonesian.'

'We can find a translator.' Bob's voice rises. 'I'll ask a friend who knows lots of fiction publishers.'

Suddenly he becomes very serious. He wonders who the prominent Indonesian writers are and why he's never heard of any of them. You don't read much Indonesian literature, but you can name at least a dozen favourite books.

'Then why don't we hear of Indonesian writers outside the country?'

You shrug, but mutter to yourself: hey, if people here don't hang with the cool kids, whose fault is that? My friends?

Bob is still jabbering about how important it is for Westerners to discover the treasures of Indonesian literature. Representation is critical, he says. 'Chinese writers are already well known, Hong Kong writers are well known, Indian writers too. We don't hear anything from Indonesia, Indonesia needs to be given a voice.'

You ask, 250 million people are supposed to be represented by *me*? Wow, just like the Doll Castle at Ancol Dreamland, Dolls of all Nations, one doll for each country. Well then, if you're going to become a famous writer, representing Indonesia around the world, you'd better get your ass in gear and buy some nice outfits. Half listening to Bob as he pontificates, you open eBay and scan a number of patterns on offer: floral, polka dot, tartan, leopard print.

Bob's world is preparing keys to doors that lead who knows where, and you've long known you want in. Yes, it's an unequal economic relationship, but you hardly see yourself as a victim. He's a good man, and you never complain of being near him. All members of his family accept you – even if not with great enthusiasm – apart from Richard who continues to belittle you. But you don't need to worry about him. Let him talk trash. He can't do anything. Whether he likes it or not, he'll become your stepson.

Bob informs his family about the wedding plans. He feels that he doesn't have to invite friends to the reception, but his most important family members do need to be there.

'Maybe we should get married in Indonesia?'

'No! You'll end up having to invite a whole village, including a dukun and a *pawang hujan*.'

'A *pawang hujan*? What's a *pawang hujan*?'

'A rain master, to control the weather.'

'OK, OK, maybe we can just bring your parents to the US?'

You've never thought about it. Now you wonder who you'll invite to your wedding. You don't have friends here. Suddenly you realise that you're entirely alone. How are your father and mother? Not once have you thought about them. You are clearly a faithless child. Malin Kundang.

If you want to hear (again) the story of Malin Kundang, turn to page 23.

You have returned from page 23 (or maybe you never visited it?).

You hope to wipe out your footprints, but one shoe always gets caught behind you. You feel as if you want to break all ties, become an orphan, like a character in adventure books. Recently you received a short email from your sister:

Your new niece was just born. Her name is Nazeera Dafa Zhafira. Don't forget to bring a gift for her when you come back to Indonesia, OK?

Another new baby, another Arabic name. So much for Dewi, Wati and Sari. You don't get it. Your sister already has two children, one of whom is named Nazwa Salsabila Azzahra (or is it Nazwa Karima Maghfira?). Why doesn't she just quit already?

You reply to the email with a short note of congratulations. You don't ask for news about her first or second child or your parents. If there's no news that they're sick, that's good news. It means they're fine. That's enough. You don't need to invite them to your wedding. Maybe later, if you get tired of being on the road, you'll bring Bob to meet them. Father, Mother, congratulations! You have a white son-in-law.

You think of Devil. He won't be happy to hear of your wedding plans, but you have no choice. He's abandoned you without so much as a word about visas or money, so he's played a role in this decision. It's not only the devil who can be imperious.

Continue on to page 255.

What do you mean, think it over? Do you have time? You no longer have a place of your own. Your bank balance is a worry. Without Bob, there's a good chance you'll end up on the street.

Forgive the imperiousness of this adventure, but you know that sometimes life takes away all options. Choice is a luxury. Marrying Bob is your emergency exit.

Return to page 251.

A few days before your wedding, you're startled by Richard's presence in Bob's apartment. You've just finished dressing and are getting ready to go out when you see him reclining on the couch, cradling Bob's crystal snow globe. You gasp. You didn't see him come in, and you didn't hear the doorbell. Does he have a key? It doesn't feel as if Bob and Richard are close enough for that.

'I came here to congratulate you.'

He sets the crystal snow globe down on the sofa and strides towards you. You're still standing at the door of the bedroom, gaping.

'Bob will be on campus until tonight.'

'Yes, it's okay. I'm not here to see him.'

He folds his arms as he leans against the wall. His gaze remains fixed on your face, making you uncomfortable. You challenge his stare because you refuse to let him think you're weak. You have to admit that he's handsome. Maybe this is how Bob looked when he was younger. If Richard weren't your prospective stepson – and if his attitude didn't make you want to gag – you might find him attractive.

'I wish you happiness.'

His words surprise you. His voice is gentle and sincere, as if he wants to make amends.

'Congratulations.' He blinks. 'You've snagged an ageing orientalist with that bogus innocent face of yours.'

He roars a thunderous laugh, and his every movement suggests how much he despises you. Your body tenses. He stands closer to you. Too close. Your breathing roughens when his lips almost press against your ears. He whispers, 'Bitch.'

He kisses you with quick movements, insistently. You feel you should slap him, but you say nothing and wait, as if wanting to know what will happen next. The sensation of his lips isn't unknown. You feel you recognise him from somewhere. The longer you look, the more familiar he becomes. His eyes blaze bright red. His ears look odd, pointed and hairy.

'Bastard! Devil!'

You tear yourself from him. Richard's handsome features grow old and gaunt, metamorphosing into those of Demon Lover.

'You were hoping I was really Richard, weren't you?'

He laughs as if he's won a contest. Furious, you shove him away.

'Monster! You came just to judge me?'

'A woman is always a traitor,' he intones like a prophet.

You utterly reject the accusation. You swear at him. You want to claw him, but he grabs your hand. Demon Lover's eyes blaze a deeper crimson, ready to engulf you in an inferno.

'Where have you been all this time?' You find your voice gaining even more strength. 'Busy creating terror? Go eat your own damn adventure!'

You're still busy with your curses when the burning red before you fades. Devil hisses. His voice now sounds softer.

'Everything I touch falls apart.'

'No wonder,' you say scathingly. 'Were you thinking you were Midas or something?'

Devil reflects for a while. 'I didn't think you'd settle for a dull marriage. So this is the end of your adventure.'

'Who says?'

You caress his pointy ears. He looks at you hesitantly. You put his hand on your waist, and your lips seek his. 'You're still my slave.'

Demon Lover returns your kiss, but then he turns away. His eyes narrow.

'What are you trying to say?'

'Be my lover.'

'You're just after sex!' Now he pushes you away. You're surprised and faintly amused.

'When did you turn into a prude?'

'I'm destined by God to feel constant envy,' says Devil. 'I don't want to be some secret lover for a woman whose husband is lousy in bed.'

He takes the jacket and hat he hung on the door.

'Sorry, I can't be your slave any more.'

'So we're through?'

The devil turns to you. His eyes are dim, angry and sad.

'Yes, it's over,' he says. 'Give me back the red shoes.'

You shake your head.

'The shoes are mine.'

'You're going to regret it.'

He opens the door of Bob's apartment and slams it behind him. You trudge to the living room and throw yourself on the sofa. You grab a crystal snow globe and look at it while pondering Devil's last words.

You're going to regret it.

Maybe you shouldn't let your relationship with Devil break down. If you're not seeking divine light, who can you turn to? Now you've lost your slave, a lover who adored you even if for him love always comes with a hellish side.

Feeling pensive, you flip the crystal snow globe back and forth with your right hand. Your left hand strokes the sofa slowly, and your fingers land upon a piece of paper. You turn. A letter from Devil. You sit up in a hurry to read it.

Darling,

Maybe you're worried at the moment. Being a sceptic, you need time to think. You want to run away from me but there's no denying that I'm your destiny. I'll give you a second chance, though of course you know that, with me, love always comes with a curse.

If you want to travel by yourself with those shoes, go. But don't expect me to be your lover. I'll become your nightmare, and you'll pray to God that we don't meet again (I'm not sure he'll hear you, though, since the supplicant queue is awfully long these days).

But you still have a second chance, another emergency exit. Run away with me instead. Put your red shoes in front of the door. We'll be together again, start a new life, and I'll shower you with love and damnation, with passion and fear. And I'll worship you in the fashion of a most elegant devil.

If you want to go back to Devil, put your shoes in front of the door and turn to page 386.

If you're determined to have your own adventure without Devil, continue planning your wedding with Bob and turn to the next page.

Ar-Rohmah Mosque, Astoria, Queens, November 2008

Your wedding takes place in the Ar-Rohmah Mosque in Astoria, a refuge from the temptations of an accursed devil. Though truth be told, you don't know what spirits are present there. You steal glances at Richard who watches everything, looking haughty. Is he Richard or Devil, or both? Only God knows for sure.

You and Bob decided to marry in a mosque after a long debate that you found a little absurd. Bob cut ties with Christianity decades ago, so he refused to have a church wedding. He follows Eastern spiritual teachings but is unwilling to proclaim himself an adherent of any religion.

'OK, let's just get married in City Hall,' you said. 'All we need is the signature, and that's that.'

But Bob was against your proposal. He didn't want the marriage to be sanctified by the state either: this capitalist government shouldn't determine transcendent matters. Debating with Bob can drive you a little loopy. Finally you accepted his suggestion of an Islamic ceremony. An Indonesian colleague of Bob's officiates. You don't know him. Whatever. The important thing is that it's all over and done with. Only later do you learn that Bob's weddings have always observed the practices of his wife's culture. He's never had a Western-style ceremony, Angela said. If possible, he wouldn't marry in the West.

'I'm so delighted,' Angela says after the ceremony, once the formalities are over. 'Dad is going to be happy with you.'

You smile. She's very sweet, but it's the kind of pleasant cliché anyone could offer.

Your response is disconcertingly chirpy: 'Yes, but I think he'd be happy with anyone. With that last girlfriend, for example – maybe they'd have been happy in Guangzhou.'

Angela looks startled. She must find your joke outrageous.

'His last girlfriend wasn't from Guangzhou. Dad met her in Amsterdam. She –'

Angela stops. She seems reluctant to finish the sentence.

'Oh, it's not important,' she says quickly. 'Anyway, as far as I'm concerned, you're the best woman for my father.'

You don't enquire further because others join as you all depart from the mosque to celebrate at a Chinese restaurant in Manhattan. You forget your conversation with Angela, or maybe you don't care. At least Bob's daughter gave you a special blessing, and you feel honoured about that. But a problem remains. After your plain yet exasperating wedding and reception, it turns out that you and Bob still have to go to City Hall to take care of the paperwork to validate your marriage. In other words, you still have to deal with the state.

So all this isn't official yet.

Dismayed at the news, you immediately give Bob a whack. The situation is totally ridiculous. Getting hitched to a white guy and ending up in an unregistered marriage?

'Bob, I don't want to know. We have to make things official as soon as possible!'

'Yes, darling. We'll take care of it,' Bob says, stroking your hair.

How strange this man is. You don't love him but he can always calm you down.

'Patience,' he whispers. 'The important thing is for us to have a honeymoon first.'

Planning your honeymoon distracts you from the issue of registering your marriage and gathering the necessary documents. Your thirst for travel lets you forget about the passage of time. You can spend hours on tourism websites.

'Bob, I've never been to California.'

From behind his laptop, Bob nods. Maybe we can travel along the West Coast, Bob says, from San Francisco, down to LA and then to San Diego. Next year we can go to Europe. The notion delights you.

But Bob can't go immediately. He has to attend a conference in Frankfurt for a week. He's not thrilled about having to go to Frankfurt – industrial, too expensive, a little boring – but he's already accepted an invitation to be the keynote speaker.

'You go first. I'll catch up later,' he says.

You protest a bit, but he reminds you that autumn will be over soon. California is certainly warmer than New York, but by December, it might be too cold for walks on the beach.

You don't reject the idea. Maybe Bob knows that, honeymoon or not, deep down you prefer to travel alone.

'Can I fly in to LA?'

'San Francisco makes more sense, if you don't want to backtrack.'

'But I've wanted to go to LA for ages.'

You weigh up the two options. In your mind, America was always Los Angeles – wide boulevards and rows of palm trees. *Beverly Hills 90210.* Your pilgrimage will feel incomplete until you've been to LA. But you've also heard that San Francisco is a beautiful city.

'Well, where would you like to start? LA or San Francisco?' asks Bob. 'I can meet you anywhere.'

Your busyness making travel plans marks the end of one act. Today, you feel calm, almost without hurdles in your comfortable new existence as a professor's wife. Enjoy it. A new journey will soon begin, and you don't know where it will take you.

Before deciding which city to visit first, you should read some travel tips. Turn to the next page.

Tips for a Cosmopolitan Adventure

No matter who you are – a tourist planning summer holidays or an expat moving abroad – keep in mind that travel sucks up time and energy even before you reach your destination. If you're from the Third World, or a country identified with terrorism, expect the hassles to increase. A visa application is a mirror, reflecting back at you the distortions of international relations. And just think of all the fun that awaits!

If you're planning to go overseas, be aware that a year is no longer 365 days, but eleven months or less. Set aside a month for a whole heap of entertaining diversions: filling out this form and that; arranging visas; queuing at embassies; exchanging currency; hacking your own ATM card; handling friends' packages without strings, complaints, or courier fees; buying tickets; buying souvenirs; making lists of necessary items; making lists of unnecessary items; packing luggage; unpacking luggage; and researching how to smuggle contraband (e.g. ethnicky, strong-smelling spices).

If you're travelling for a number of weeks:
- Learn a word or two of the local lingo.
- Make this saying your own: wherever your feet tread the earth, your shoulders hold up the sky (i.e. when in Rome, do as the Romans do). Make yourself one with the universe. If necessary, go incognito.
- Have faith in the divinely ordained circulation of global capital. No need to work yourself into a tizzy about souvenirs for friends and family when you can just pop over to the local mall and come away with a mini Statue of Liberty or Eiffel Tower.

If you're travelling for a year or more:

- Don't buy new furniture a few months before departure. You'll sure regret it later when you're tossing that IKEA mirror in the trash!
- Pack at least two weeks before departure. By your big D-day, you'll always find you have too few of one item and too much of another.
- Upon returning home, deal with jet lag right away, and for heaven's sake, cut the jet brags too. Don't start conversations with the sentence: 'When I was in …'
- Throw away things you don't need, including unsupportive boyfriends or girlfriends. Being cosmopolitan means training for the afterlife. Don't let yourself be bound by worldly ties.

If you're living on the move, purge the following items:

- Your Glass Menagerie
  Get rid of glass displays (ditto metal, wood and any other heavy material) that offer little return as investments, unless you're a pharaoh and the afterlife you're heading to has a five-star guarantee.
- Books
  No question, an overflowing bookshelf at home makes you look a true intellectual! But books are a luxury that weigh down the global nomad (literally). Don't saddle your suitcase with any reading material you can download, legally or illegally.
- Music
  Stop being so romantic about the hundreds of favourite CDs, LPs and cassettes you're leaving behind. The hobby of collecting is nostalgia for childhood.
- Shoes
  See above: collecting is nostalgia for childhood. Shoes? Only Imelda Marcos was consecrated with the blessing of time and space necessary for a shoe collection.

You close the travel magazine and think about your honeymoon once more. The first choice is the itinerary Bob suggested: fly to San Francisco, then rent a car, drive down to Los Angeles, and continue on to San Diego. Second choice: LAX–SFO–LAX–SAN.

If you want to start in San Francisco, head to the next page.

If you want to fly to Los Angeles first, turn to page 297.

Hotel Madeleine

Dusk sets in as the taxi escorts you from San Francisco International Airport to an art deco hotel in Nob Hill. A sign lit with the establishment's name – Hotel Madeleine – is already in full twinkle. As you pass through the wood-framed glass entrance, you hear strains of jazz from the lobby and glance at the piano player before you approach the reception desk. Under subdued lighting, you tread white geometric patterned tiles. A young man stands behind the desk, his bright smooth skin, rosy lips and handsome face suggesting a statue in a wax museum. His eyebrows invite particular attention. He seems to have shaved them and applied pencil at great pains. They dip gracefully like dancers and leave you nearly awestruck.

'Ah, Indonesia.'

The receptionist smiles upon seeing your passport. His perfect eyebrows make you want to check yourself quickly in the mirror. You feel that your own are bushy and unkempt. He enters an office to xerox the front page of your passport. When he returns to give it back to you, he glances towards the hotel entrance. A man in a grey suit and a fedora hat is rolling his suitcase up to the reception desk. You can't see his face clearly because his hat is pulled so far down.

'Ooh, a dandy,' murmurs the receptionist.

His right brow rises and he tilts his head slightly. The man in the grey flannel suit has now arrived at your side. He removes his hat. With his tie, slicked hair and pencil moustache, he looks dapper indeed. From Latin America, perhaps, or maybe Asia?

'I have a reservation,' he says. 'Husein Ramli.'

Ramli. A Malay name. His pencil-thin moustache endows him with more than a passing resemblance to P. Ramlee, the Malay film star of the fifties. He hands over his passport, and the receptionist examines it forthwith. You're beginning to feel rather put out. You were here first. Why is the receptionist acting as if he's been bewitched by this moustachioed fop?

'Excuse me,' you say, 'I don't have my key yet.'

'Oops, sorry!'

The receptionist opens the drawer and pulls out a magnetic room card for you.

'Sorry, I was amazed because this gentleman is from Singapore.'

'So?'

'Yes, and you're from Indonesia, right?' he says, apparently indifferent to whether you're tired of waiting or not. 'Singapore, Indonesia. And guess where I'm from.'

'The Philippines?' ventures the man in the grey suit.

'Bingo, a Pinoy!' The receptionist laughs merrily. 'We're all neighbours!'

The man next to you seems equally pleased to have met a comrade from a nearby country. He then glances at you and greets you in Malay.

'How are you? Where are you from: Jakarta? Jogja?'

'New York.'

'Oooh ... I love New York!' says the receptionist. 'Hey, this is a real coincidence! Three South East Asians meeting in San Francisco.'

'A coincidence,' the man in the grey suit repeats. 'Usually, a coincidence is a sign.'

'A sign! I know what it means. There will be a fiesta!' the receptionist says with a dramatic flourish.

'Hmmm, could be.'

'Just kidding! Only Pinoys likes parties. Singaporeans don't like to party. They like business.'

'Oh, that's just a stereotype! What do Indonesians like?'

'Going to the mosque,' you say, getting ready to leave.

The receptionist laughs and says, 'If you need anything, feel free to contact me. My name is Noel.'

You politely excuse yourself and withdraw from this ASEAN mini-caucus. After six hours of flying, you're too tired for chat, let alone a fiesta. That night you don't go anywhere, preferring instead to soak in the tub and head straight to bed so you can explore tomorrow. You speak with Bob briefly. He's on his way to the airport, heading for Frankfurt.

At eight the following morning you wake up hungry. Without washing your face or putting on make-up you go down to the restaurant for breakfast, intending to smuggle a coffee back to your room afterwards. The Singaporean Malay you met yesterday is sitting in a corner, again in a grey suit. His fedora lies on the table, next to a black coffee and a half-eaten sandwich. He is looking towards the floor gloomily, but as soon as he notices you a broad smile lights up his face.

'Good morning.'

You return the greeting and place your breakfast tray on the table next to his. He mentions his name again, Husein Ramli, and attempts some small talk. How did you sleep? How many hours is the flight from New York? At first he speaks Malay, perhaps out of respect for your shared cultural heritage, but it turns out that the differences between Malay and Indonesian make the conversation a little clumsy. Finally, you speak English; he speaks Singlish. He asks if you like the hotel.

'Yes, I do. It's small, but nice,' you say.

'Look at the floor,' Husein says. 'It's perfect, lah.'

You study the black-and-white tiles at your feet. Geometric motifs stretch as far as your eyes can see. You blink. The longer you look, the dizzier you get from its repetitive patterns.

'Yeah, it's beautiful. But I don't want to look at it for too long.'

'Like finding a labyrinth in your head, isn't it?'

The sentence unsettles you a bit, but Husein, in a friendly tone, changes the subject. He asks if you'll go sightseeing today. Chewing your ham and cheese, you listen to him chatter about a number of areas worth visiting.

'You ought to go to Chinatown,' he suggests.

'OK. But we have a Chinatown in New York too. Maybe tomorrow, if I still have time.'

'Ah, I see.' He nods. 'Forget it, Jake. It's Chinatown.'

You frown and wonder what it was about your answer that offended him.

'I meant –'

Husein chuckles at your confusion.

'You don't know the lines?'

'What lines?'

'*Chinatown*!' he says. 'Watch the film, then let me know whether you think I'm like Jack Nicholson.'

That morning you learn that Husein has worked as an art curator in Singapore, but he loves San Francisco more than any city he has ever visited. He lived here for a few months many years ago. 'Maybe a few months wasn't long enough,' you say, 'for you to get bored.' You mention that tourists perpetuate myths about New York, but as you've seen for yourself in your neighbourhood, Jackson Heights, the city isn't as glamorous as you'd once imagined.

'The problem is,' Husein says, 'I have a history in San Francisco.'

Husein doesn't continue the conversation. He has to leave, but he offers to accompany you tomorrow. Maybe he's just making more small talk. You smile, say thank you, and return his pleasantries.

You go back to your room with your smuggled coffee. Bob will have just arrived in Frankfurt and will still be busy, so you don't try to skype him. You flip open the guidebook again. Some of the places that Husein mentioned are there, and you weigh up starting your walking tour at Lombard Street.

You open your suitcase to prepare your exploration outfit. Exploring. How fun. You glance at your red shoes poking out from under a pile of clothes. The shoes haven't seen the outside world for a long time.

You step out from the hotel in a knee-length black dress and your red shoes. Noel, the Filipino receptionist, is smoking a cigarette beside a rubbish bin. He lavishes praise on your shoes, and you thank him warmly. His eyes never leave your feet, and he can't contain himself.

'Ayayay! Those shoes would make Imelda Marcos jealous!'

'She probably has ten pairs.'

'No doubt. Have fun, sis!'

Back in the 1920s Lombard Street was built so that it twisted because it was too steep for cars, your tour guide informs you.

At eleven o'clock, when you reached Lombard Street and its famous curves, you stumbled coincidentally yet again upon Husein in his grey suit. He volunteered his services as a guide willing to regale you with tales of the city. When you arrived, he was standing hushed, almost as if in shock, gazing down. This is the third time you've run into each other. He seems to be everywhere. You hope he's not a ghost.

He then speaks of coincidences. 'My life is full of them,' he says. 'And maybe our run-ins are the latest instalment. Why do we keep bumping into each other?'

You shake your head, saying that you were just following one of his recommendations. Maybe, he says, the receptionist was right. It's a sign that there'll be a fiesta.

For a few moments the two of you lapse into silence, staring at the rows of houses lining the road. You walk down, Husein following. And as you head back up, you recall that Husein said he was busy today.

'I thought so, but I can accompany you for a while.'

'For a while' means traipsing around the city together for the next three hours.

'You've lived in San Francisco, right?' you ask. 'Why are you sightseeing like a tourist?'

'I'm not a tourist.'

'No? What do you call yourself then?'

'A *flâneur*.'

'And what sort of creature is that? Not some kind of tourist?'

He is momentarily taken aback.

'Probably a tourist too.'

You're not interested in continuing this rather confusing conversation.

'I met someone once, here on Lombard Street, accidentally.'

'Who?'

'Have you ever been followed by a ghost?'

'Hmm … No, not a ghost. But by a demon, maybe.'

Your words amaze him, as if you've given precisely the right answer to make him put his trust in you.

'Someone is haunting me,' Husein says.

'Ha, I like ghost stories.'

'Do you want to hear mine?'

You pause for a moment. The man seems overly animated, as well as a little tense. Are you sure you want to hear his story?

Continue on to page 272.

Unfortunately, you don't yet fulfil the criteria needed to hear this story. Please explore San Francisco on your own. When you get bored, fly down to Los Angeles.

Turn to page 297.

You may become privy to this tale after answering two questions.

Question 1:

How would you react if you read a novel and found a character almost identical to someone from your past?

The answer depends on how you see yourself. Are you: a) pragmatic, b) romantic or c) obsessive?

If you're a pragmatist, you'll say that the world is filled with patterns and repetitions. There's no need to treat every coincidence as sensational. If you're a romantic, you'll extend the invisible thread between yourself and the author, a mystery that transcends continents and languages. The author never needs to know.

This story, however, is for those who favour c, the heavenly option. If you're obsessive, you'll take the path of our friend Husein, even though you know it won't lead you anywhere.

Question 2:

Have you ever done one of the following?

a) Visited a city that fascinated you so much that you wanted to be a part of it. You tried to imitate its inhabitants and how they talked, walked and played, until one day nobody realised you were in disguise, including yourself.

b) Upon a first meeting, claimed to be someone else, either to impress or to avoid that person.

c) Worn a wig.

d) Dressed up for a costume party, Halloween or carnival.

e) Been born and raised in Kansas, felt depressed and wanted to leave.

If you answered yes to any of the above, you may continue listening to the story. If not, please return to page 271. If you're still unsure, please consult the FAQ text box below.

Frequently Asked Questions:

Q: I'm pragmatic but sometimes romantic. May I hear the story too?
A: I'm concerned that you won't understand our friend Husein, but of course you may.

Q: I'm not in the pragmatic, romantic or obsessive category, but I consider myself possessive. Do I get to join?
A: Sure thing! But I won't add a fourth type.

Q: My life is quite a happy one, so none of the five categories in Question 2 apply to me. Who has ever experienced such silly stuff, anyway?
A: Obviously something is wrong with you. Go back to page 271.

If you're still here, turn to the next page.

Wigs

San Francisco, 2005

Karina appeared like a ghost on Lombard Street at 10 a.m., on a lonely spring morning as I gazed down, looking for where the road ended and thinking about its curves. Bends are necessary because whatever is steep is dangerous. Often you need to take the sharpest turn before you finally arrive safely at home. Or at least so I thought until that morning.

She stood not far from me, frozen, staring at the road from behind her sunglasses. Until then I'd believed myself to be alone. She wore a sleek classic grey pant suit, its style from four decades earlier. Her hair especially caught my attention: straight bangs of dark brown that remained motionless even in the breeze, like the hair of a mannequin.

'Good morning.' She finally removed her sunglasses and smiled at me. An Asian face, beautiful. 'First time in San Francisco?'

Somehow she knew. I don't carry a camera because I hate to be considered a tourist.

'Nobody except a tourist lingers on Lombard Street,' she said, as if she could read my mind.

'So you're sightseeing too?'

She shook her head. 'My family is in Kansas, but I've been here for three months. I come here a lot, for some basic therapy.'

'Therapy?'

'I'm afraid of heights.'

Her self-treatment didn't exactly qualify as challenging. Nobody falls on this road. Its bends are regular. Rows of houses and flowers on the left and right have turned it into an urban park. Safe, domesticated.

'We have to start off easy. Places that aren't scary,' she explained. 'The Golden Gate Bridge comes later.'

She invited me into her car, so I could see what it felt like to drive down Lombard Street. The experience, I have to admit, was hardly special, no more memorable than a lunch at Fisherman's Wharf. She accompanied me because she didn't have any plans for the day. I wondered if I was lucky or facing danger. After all, it's not every day that such a beautiful creature abruptly materialises, with no other plans, volunteering to become one's tour guide. I hoped she wasn't a serial killer. But the information I learned later convinced me that she was no criminal. Her name was Karina Lam and she was a second-generation Vietnamese immigrant. Her parents came over as boat people right after the war. It certainly sounded to me like she spoke English with an American accent (or, to borrow the American term, 'without an accent'), and she said she didn't understand Vietnamese at all. She was twenty-six and had just stopped working at a publishing company because she'd had enough of her job.

'How does it feel to go to Vietnam but not speak the language?'

'I've never been,' she said, shaking her head. 'The only other language I speak is French.'

She'd graduated with a degree in French literature and read Balzac in her spare time.

'What do you do in Singapore?' she asked, after I told her that I was participating in a cultural exchange programme in San Francisco for four months.

'I used to study fine arts, then I became a curator,' I explained briefly. 'What do you do now?'

'Fun stuff.'

'Like therapy for fear of heights?'

'No,' she said. 'Like singing in nightclubs.'

She handed me a card with the address of a lounge in Haight-Ashbury. She would be singing later that night, at nine o'clock, performing songs from the seventies. I'll do my best, I said, because that night I'd been invited to a party hosted by the foundation that was funding my stay in San Francisco.

Maybe I sounded as if I was playing hard to get, but I really didn't want to give the impression of being overly intrigued.

'No problem. I'm sure we'll meet again.'

I felt like I was listening to a magic spell. At eight that night, at the party, I drank a glass of wine and chatted with artists while stealing constant glances at my watch. After greeting a few people I considered important, I hurried outside and took a taxi to the club where Karina was singing.

*

Chapter 2

Saigon, 2001

10 p.m. at the nightclub. Jeffrey Winston arrived late. Karina Le, in a sparkling silver chemise, was singing her last song. Her straight dark brown hair framed her face, a little too neatly.

Jeffrey chose a seat in a corner of the bar. He was still panting, trying to catch his breath. He had just been in a cafe with Trung Nguyen and a colleague of his, held back in discussion about their theatre project. They had talked for hours, but, as ever, Jeffrey was neither willing nor able to cut short a conversation when Trung was involved. Trung eventually departed for a family gathering, leaving Jeffrey to hear further details from his colleague. Though keen to go hear Karina perform again, Jeffrey stayed on, knowing how much the project meant to Trung.

Now Jeffrey allowed himself to become immersed in infatuation like a teenager. Karina stared out into the audience at him, though later he wondered whether her eyes were fixed on him or another man sitting behind. He wanted to break her stare, but the opposite occurred. Karina's gaze left him fragile, transparent, simple to read.

After her last song, Karina descended from the stage, the audience's applause trailing after her. The club's lighting grew dimmer, but Jeffrey's adoration remained bright. Ever more clearly he saw Karina sway in her sparkling chemise, striding towards him. Jeffrey felt sure he had never met a woman as beautiful as Karina in all his life, but something in her appearance evoked a sense of intimacy, as if he had long dreamed of her. He ransacked his brain for words that would sound smart and sexy. When Karina arrived at his side, he managed a nervous smile and blurted out:

'Your hair is nice.'

*

San Francisco, 2005

'You know this is a wig, right?'

I should have known from the start. Her hair was too perfect, but I didn't care, because it was impossible to separate her hair from her whole being.

'I'm imitating my muse, my inspiration. Anna Karina.' Then she added, worried I didn't recognise the reference, 'A French star of the 1960s.'

'Yes, I know. But why? Because you have the same name?'

Without answering, she turned and greeted the bartender.

When she had a martini in hand, I asked her another question. 'So, you've been travelling the world and having all sorts of fun?'

'All sorts of fun? Where?'

'Monte Carlo?'

'Oh.' She laughed, realising I was referring to the song she had just been singing. As far as she was concerned, Charlene's

'I've Never Been to Me' was a conservative, if not sappy, narrative about travel. Its message: your adventure is meaningless without returning to a home, or more precisely, to a household.

'That's not what you want?'

'What? To return to Kansas and marry some random white guy?' she said with a sneer.

'Then why do you sing that song?'

She sipped her drink, then stroked my cheek. 'It's so retro and it's fun, darling.'

*

Singapore, 2007

All characters appearing in this work are fictitious. Any resemblance to real persons, living or dead, is purely coincidental.

It wasn't the legal implications that Isaac Ginsberg was thinking of when he inserted this cautionary note in his novel. I believe he was covering up a living, breathing plot that existed outside the book I held in my hands. And if you knew Karina, you'd understand how he intended the note to be read. As an invitation.

'Think about it,' Karina said one day. 'You're standing on the balcony of a tall building, and a warning notice reads "Don't lean against the railing". What do you want to do? Lean against it. Because of the sign, a danger that hasn't even crossed your mind now has a name.'

When Isaac Ginsberg declared that everything was fiction, contrary to his expectations, he invited me to think otherwise. Not everything is fictional, not everything is coincidence. And apparently there was a truth that he wanted to keep for himself.

*

'With me, you'll never be safe.'

Such was Karina's warning. And because the warning was an invitation, I knew that being with her was the one and only thing I wanted.

The warning came when we were walking in the grounds of the Palace of Fine Arts for the third time. At first I tried hard not to see her again, because our meeting on Lombard Street made me realise that she was more dangerous than a serial killer. Travel often greets me with surprises, temptations and the unusual. But in all my experience, nothing dangerous. And going back home is returning to what belongs to you. There's nothing extraordinary about it, but at least it's yours.

Karina wasn't dangerous because she was foreign; on the contrary, I felt like I'd known her for a long time. I'd always had her in my imagination, conjuring up her life, composing how she thought, how she talked, how she walked. That frightened me. And unfortunately, I succumbed to Karina whenever I heard her voice on the phone.

'When I go home to Singapore, I'm getting married,' I said as we strolled. A desperate effort to protect myself.

'I see.' She didn't sound surprised. 'You don't look like the marrying type.'

'I'm not. But I'll try.'

'Is that so?' She blinked, but her expression remained as cold and impassive as a statue. 'Let me guess. A clichéd little tale of the naughty boy who finds true love. You found the girl who finally rescued you.'

'Partly right. On the one hand she did save me.'

'Helped you find a home and a sense of security?'

'Something like that. But, on the other hand … ' I paused for a moment, later cursing my honesty. 'I don't love her. I've never loved anyone real.'

From a distance we stared at the lake and its reflection of the domed rotunda, a relic from the reconstruction of the city after the great quake of 1906. The lake, slowly and cunningly, transformed itself into a murky-looking glass that brought forth Karina's face. For days afterwards, and in the years since, I would look into a mirror and find the image of her face reflected there. Sometimes she splits, becoming two, sometimes three, and eventually infinite.

The holy book has warned us not to build houses on the sand. Unfortunately, there are no warnings about buildings on water. Let alone on mirrors.

'People say there's no place like home,' Karina ventured.

Yes, I agreed, amen. But after that, for the first time, I kissed her. She returned my kiss savagely, forcing me to close my eyes. In the dark I felt her embrace me, then push me hard. My feet found a foothold, but I fell, fell far. A river. I tried to swim but my body immediately became heavy. Quicksand was all around me, dragging me down.

Gasping, I asked, 'Where is your home?'

'I told you – Kansas.'

She was still kissing me, but her voice faded, as if she were on another plane of existence. Half dreaming, I heard my own voice, 'Take me there.'

Karina stopped kissing me. That's when she issued her warning. I was still gasping for breath as she said, 'I'm no lifeguard. I can't swim.'

This is the message I sent to Isaac Ginsberg through his personal website. It was entirely likely that his agent would receive it and delete it. But it couldn't hurt to try. Maybe he was kinder than he needed to be.

Dear Mr Ginsberg,

A close friend sent me your novel as a gift. I couldn't put it down. Once I finished, I immediately became your newest fan.

I apologise in advance for my presumption in sending this letter, but something in your novel keeps bothering me. I am well aware that, as you state, all the characters in your novel are fictitious. But I know an American woman of Vietnamese descent who, as in your novel, is also named Karina. To be sure, I did not make her acquaintance in Saigon, where your story is set, but in San Francisco. And the Karina in your story has the family name Le, while the Karina whom I know is Karina Lam. But aside from these similarities and differences, one thing makes me feel as though all this is not coincidence: wigs.

She never let me see her real hair, which she said was a wavy black and difficult to manage. But I never asked why she didn't dye and straighten it so that she wouldn't have to bother with a wig. Rather than focusing on wigs, I preferred to torture myself by imagining the other men in her life, past and present.

We never spent time at her place. She didn't allow me. We always stayed at my apartment, or – when a friend crashed at my place for two weeks – in a cheap motel. That's where, when she was dressing in the bathroom, I found a notebook lying on her side of the bed. On the last page I saw a row of email addresses. There wasn't a single female name among them, I'm sure. She caught me, then snatched up the notebook. I'd never seen her so angry.

'What's this for? Collecting email from fans, huh?' Filled with jealousy, I barraged her with petulant questions. 'Are you still in touch with them?'

'Why are you so possessive all of a sudden?' She stared at me sharply. 'Can you imagine me without fans?'

'You belong to me. You're my fiction.'

After uttering these words, I knew that my fears had been realised. Karina was a story I kept in my head, without beginning or end. For years I'd tried to make every woman I met resemble her. But I'd believed that she never really existed. The story would have been safe if I hadn't met Karina. But it was too late. I had started it. And now, an end that I couldn't imagine was slowly unfolding.

Karina, meanwhile, looked unsurprised. As she put her things into her purse, she commented, 'Interesting. What if I'm not your fiction, but someone else's?'

But *whose*? How could Karina be the product of anyone else's imagination, and for so many years? The mere thought of a rival seemed absurd.

'I can't be your secret lover.'

'Why not?'

'I'm too high-maintenance.'

Now she was ready to go. Before opening the door, she kissed me. 'Go back to your fiancée.'

That's what I thought I did. But I knew, after meeting Karina on Lombard Street, that there was no way home.

Unexpectedly, the author replied to my letter two days later from an odd email address: thenoirfictionist@gmail.com. Far from ignoring me, his note was friendly enough and sympathetic.

> *Dear Husein,*
>
> *Thank you for your message.*
>
> *Regarding your question about the statement that 'all the characters in this work are fictitious', you and I know that such a declaration isn't to be believed. Real people are conjured into characters, just as we insert fictional characters into real life. There's nothing unique about that.*
>
> *If I can rearticulate your note, though, your main question becomes: who is Karina? I can't answer, because even though I quite understand your anxiety about her, it's not the right question to ask. Almost, but not exactly. I will explain things to you, explicitly, hiding nothing – if you can put forward the right question.*
>
> *Everything is in my novel. Pay attention to what isn't present. After that, write to me again.*

*

Isaac Ginsberg's message moved me to reread his novel, but my efforts produced nothing but a plot summary. To simplify, it's the story of Jeffrey Winston, a young American, neurotic and – in my opinion – insufficiently rebellious (he comes from an educated white family with the resources to put him through Harvard). Keen to investigate history and establish his own political attitudes, he applies for a Fulbright scholarship to Vietnam. In Saigon, Jeffrey becomes a close friend of Trung Nguyen, a young actor and director who aspires to go to America. At the same time, he falls in love with Karina, a nightclub singer. Although Jeffrey imagines Karina's life behind the stage, envisioning a melodramatic story à la *Miss Saigon*, even at the story's end we never learn who Karina really is. Jeffrey doesn't share his obsession for Karina with anyone, including Trung, who is thoroughly uninterested when he hears Karina's name.

There was nothing illuminating in the novel. It was as though the narrator, who only allows us to enter Jeffrey's thoughts, had conspired with the author to hide Karina.

I wrote again to Isaac Ginsberg. Honestly, but impatiently, I admitted that I couldn't find any clues in the text. This time I revealed more details about the Karina I knew, hoping that he would sympathise with me and want to divulge more about his Karina. I recounted how we met on Lombard Street, our first kiss at the Palace of Fine Arts, and wrote about other places from the history of our relationship. He replied briefly:

Read it again. Do not give up.

His short answer angered me. He was ignoring my experiences, so real and intense, for the sake of playing his own game. Fiction writers can be exasperating, if not exactly cruel. They work hard to create labyrinths, look for easy targets to lure inside, and then sit back and enjoy their victims' suffering over a cup of coffee and a doughnut.

Since Ginsberg was completely unhelpful, I decided to take a different route.

Are you still with me? Do you want to know about the route that Husein took? I'm concerned that you're getting bored. This route, as I mentioned early on, led Husein to a truth (he likely considers it so) that is painful. A route that only further agitated him and failed to lead him – as it might fail to lead you – anywhere. If you don't want to waste time, feel free to skip what follows and continue on to page 288. If you genuinely want to know, however, please turn to the next page. Just a word of advice: beware of your curiosity. You're becoming more and more like our friend.

Karina never knew that a few days after my fit of jealousy at the hotel, I snuck her notebook out of her purse and copied down all the email addresses. There were eight. At the time what I did was nothing more than an act of obsessive behaviour; I honestly believe that I was the only man Karina met while in San Francisco. I simply saved the list of addresses for record's sake, and had no interest in contacting their owners one by one to ask about their relationship with Karina. But after losing Karina and then rediscovering her in a novel two years later, I felt a need to examine my notes again.

I sent a letter to eight addresses. I was prepared to be ignored, to be seen as crazy, but two of the men answered my email.

From: johannXXX@gmx.net
To: huseinXXX1974@gmail.com

Dear Husein,

I'm taking the time to reply to your letter because I sympathise with you. My sense is that we have had the same experience. This may sound quite painful, but it looks like you've been deceived. The woman who said her name was Karina has stolen from you, like she stole from me in Seoul three years ago.

If you're really serious about hearing my own Karina story, we can talk over Skype.

*

Seoul, 2004 (reconstruction of the story of Johann's encounter with Karina based on a Skype conversation)

After years of wanting to get out of Konstanz, his home town, Johann finally landed a good job in Berlin. His company then sent him to Seoul for two years. There he occupied himself with work and having fun. Every Friday night he'd go out drinking with his Korean friends in the Hongdae neighbourhood, sometimes joining them for karaoke. One night, a woman in a dark brown wig appeared among them. Her name was Karina. She sang the old song 'I've Never Been to Me'. Her face was sad.

Johann escorted the woman, full name Karina Lee, in a taxi to her hotel. She came from Hong Kong, and wrote for a travel magazine that was covering one of Seoul's springtime festivals. Johann ventured to ask why she looked sad when she sang. Karina answered that she was weary of circling the world and that she'd never been to herself.

They separated in the lobby, but the next day Johann couldn't keep himself from meeting Karina again. I'm married, Karina said suddenly, a signal that she was shutting the door.

But Johann felt the door open again, just wide enough for someone to enter. The two had gone out for a coffee and in the taxi Karina revised what she had said before. She didn't circle the world; the world circled her constantly, crushing her. Her life was composed of scattered fragments, sometimes adrift, sometimes colliding and crashing. Johann was swept along with the flow of Karina's story and sent into turmoil – her story provided him with his own.

Johann met Karina every day from then on. She played with strings of words that he often didn't understand, but he was sure there was a space for him. Karina wanted to let him in. That's what Johann believed, until the seventh day, when they stood in front of her hotel room. As Johann tried to kiss her, Karina closed the door.

The next day, the hotel receptionist gave him the bad news. Karina had moved on. But the game of opening and closing doors had not yet finished. Johann sent Karina a long email, to which she gave a brief reply: *Dear Johann, thank you for the wonderful time in Seoul. Hope all is well, Karina.*

*

From: steveXXX@yahoo.co.uk
To: huseinXXX1974@gmail.com

Husein,

I'll get straight to the point: A few years ago I met someone at a costume party in London. She wore a wig. I think her name was Karina, but I wouldn't rely too much on my memory. I was really drunk that night. She was drop-dead gorgeous, wore a Japanese schoolgirl costume and claimed to be from Tokyo. Quite convincing, but to be honest I don't care where she came from. What's certain is that she fulfilled my wildest anime fantasies. After the party we ended up at her hotel.

Sorry, but I don't feel comfortable going into further detail about the experience, but obviously I was blown away. That night changed a lot of things that I'd believed. I didn't expect it at all. She was so beautiful. Even now I don't understand why I didn't stop myself when I got to know her.

Warm regards,
Steve

Continue on to the next page.

With Karina, many things happened for the first time in my life. That kiss, for example. Never before had I drowned in a kiss. And, as if coincidentally, after that kiss, a strange incident occurred. Karina fell into the sea – in the real sense – when we were taking a walk along San Francisco Bay, near Fort Point. She slipped in her high heels. I immediately remembered her confession that she couldn't swim, so without thinking I took off my jacket and jumped in to save her. With difficulty I managed to get her out of the water and carried her to her car. Her lips had turned blue, her eyes were closed tight. Seeing her wig soaked, I almost cried, hoping she was all right, hoping I could preserve her perfection.

That day was my first experience with left-hand drive. I brought Karina to my apartment. One hour later, she came to. That same day was the first time we made love.

At midnight in my room, I finally stopped staring at her lying beside me.

'Surreal,' I murmured.

She turned, asking me to repeat what I'd said.

'Surreal,' I said, more loudly. After our lovemaking, I couldn't find any other words to describe her. 'I'm obsessed with you.'

'You'll stop at some point.'

'When?'

'Imagine us together, in our daily routines. I'll become very boring for you.'

'You'll never be boring.'

'How can you be so sure?'

'Because of your promise. With you I'll never be safe.'

'How can you believe something that's, like you said –'
She turned her back to me, pulling the blanket around her.
'What?'
'Surreal.'

I rose from the desk after my eyes grew weary of staring at the computer screen and lumbered towards the bathroom. I washed my face in the sink and looked in the mirror, seeking my earlier self, the self that had existed before Karina disrupted my world. I'd forgotten it; after San Francisco, I never appeared in the mirror again. Karina had taken control, given birth to clones of herself.

I tried to seek salvation in crowds. I decided to go to a bar alone and get drunk. Onstage was a female singer. Her eyes were small, like Karina's. But she wasn't wearing a wig. And I kept returning to the superfluous questions in my head.

What did Karina want? To travel the world and deceive others, including me?

I heard Karina whispering to me, as she had when we talked in the club: *It's so retro and it's fun, darling.*

The next day, I received an email I didn't expect. It was from Isaac Ginsberg, the novel's author.

Husein,
   I haven't heard from you. Are you lost? I trust that before long you will put forth the correct question about Karina. Look for what is absent.
   Warm regards,
   Isaac

*

'What do you really want, Karina?'
   'I want to become …' She tapped her martini glass with her slender fingers. 'An author.'
   'Write a novel?'

'Maybe. The main thing is to create fiction.'
'About what?'
'About a beautiful woman named Karina.'

Who had that conversation? Karina and Jeffrey, or Karina and me? I'd now memorised every trace of the Karina in the novel. I could readily recall each of her conversations with Jeffrey, since my memories of the dialogue, movements and even the spaces occupied by Karina in the book overlapped with my memories of San Francisco.

Jeffrey remained in constant awe of the woman before him. A woman who wore a wig, a woman whose home he had never visited, a woman who aspired to create fiction.

I only needed to replace Jeffrey's name with mine, then Karina would migrate from Saigon to San Francisco.

It is easier for me to show Jeffrey as Jeffrey, the naive young American, when he interacts with others – Trung Nguyen, in particular. I always skipped over the passages where Jeffrey meets with Trung. They were tedious.

'I'm sick of talking about post-war trauma,' said Trung, throwing himself on the sofa. Jeffrey was at the table, preparing ice cream for dessert.

'The reforms of Doi Moi mean I have to talk about other things. About desire.'

Jeffrey scooped vanilla ice cream into a bowl. He moved from the table to the cupboard, looking for a bottle of honey. 'Desire for what?' He set bright red strawberries atop the ice cream.

'All sorts of things. Desire to travel. Desire to shop. Sex.'

Jeffrey swallowed. He poured the thick golden honey over the ice cream and strawberries.

'War trauma is what old avant-garde artists are obsessed with,' Trung continued, complaining. Jeffrey kept listening. Sitting beside his friend, he dug into his ice cream.

'*But history remains important,*' *insisted Jeffrey.* '*You can't just ignore memories.*'

'*Oh, you and your white-boy guilt.*'

Trung glanced at the vanilla ice cream, garnished with strawberries and drizzled with honey. He took the bowl from Jeffrey's hands.

'*I want to create a European text,*' *said Trung.* '*Make a journey to the North, that'll be my revenge. Maybe I'll take Flaubert as my starting point.*' *He spooned some soft ice cream into his mouth.* '*Or Balzac?*'

Trung looked into the ice cream bowl. He removed a strawberry, then held it out in front of Jeffrey's nose.

'*Open your mouth.*'

Jeffrey was startled but did as he was told. Trung lowered the fruit, dribbling honey, into his mouth. The strawberry felt cold on his tongue. He chewed slowly.

'*I don't like strawberries,*' *Trung said.* '*Where were we? Oh, right, Balzac. What do you think about Sarrasine?*'

I closed the book. Reading page after page filled with Trung Nguyen's dreams, his passionate (self-)obsessions, felt like listening to a sermon. I hated each time Trung showed up in the novel's pages. I enjoyed all the parts when Karina appeared, because the man would be absent.

Because Trung would be absent.

Look for what is absent.

After staring at the computer screen for a long, long time, I typed in Isaac Ginsberg's email address. I asked a short question:

Who is Trung Nguyen?

*

From: thenoirfictionist@gmail.com
To: huseinXXX1974@gmail.com

Who is Trung Nguyen? Your question is not quite right, but this time it's not because you don't know. Ask me what you really want to ask, or maybe, make me a declaration. I'll tell you everything. But out of fairness, I'll answer your question briefly now. Trung Nguyen is indeed my friend, an actor. He wants to direct Sarrasine.

From: huseinXXX1974@gmail.com
To: thenoirfictionist@gmail.com

Why did Karina show up in San Francisco?

From: thenoirfictionist@gmail.com
To: huseinXXX1974@gmail.com

Asking this question requires you to take a step back. But the question can mean two things: one, that you really are desperate; two, that you know the answer. Are you still keen to play semiotic games?

I didn't answer the email for weeks. I hoped my silence was a sufficient answer. But then he prodded me once more:

From: thenoirfictionist@gmail.com
To: huseinXXX1974@gmail.com

Sorry, I'm compelled to write to you again after rereading your messages. She's afraid of heights? How interesting. Did you walk around the Palace of Fine Arts? Go to Lombard Street?
    And in the end did she take you to Mission San Juan Bautista?

From: huseinXXX1974@gmail.com
To: thenoirfictionist@gmail.com

Yes, to everything. How could you possibly know?

From: thenoirfictionist@gmail.com
To: huseinXXX1974@gmail.com

With no disrespect intended, have you ever seen Vertigo?

＊

She left me one morning in San Francisco. When I opened my eyes, she was no longer at my side. She left behind a note:

Darling,
I adore you, but I can't be with you. If you want to meet me one last time, come tonight to Mission San Juan Bautista. If you don't find me, that means I've already gone. I have to catch a plane, and definitely not to Kansas.

I tried calling, but only reached an answering machine. Like a madman I contacted a car rental agency and soon was driving two hours to the destination Karina had mentioned.

Of course, I didn't find her.

Only years later, after Isaac Ginsberg's final email had given me a slap of reality, did I realise why Karina had asked me to go. There, in Mission San Juan Bautista, my story should have ended.

Everything was scripted, very clearly from the start. Karina deliberately left little clues, all those coincidences. She wanted to be caught out.

I don't know who to blame for my suffering these last three years. The clues that I read too late, or myself, who never gave up the story even when it was over. I only know that I've never been able to blame Karina, my true love who possesses everything.

Except, perhaps, a sense of compassion.

Turn to the next page.

Yes, this story ends here. Don't say you weren't warned before-hand. And because you're stubborn, you ask:

Then what happened to Husein? Is he still looking for Karina?

Nobody cares about Husein, but you, it seems, are very sweet. Find out for yourself.

If you want Husein to stop his futile search and straighten out the chaos that is his life, continue on to the next page.

If you want him to keep looking for Karina, turn to page 296.

After San Francisco, there was no way home. My obsession with Karina destroyed everything. One night my wife exploded, reciting a litany of the sins I had committed since our wedding (being a workaholic, constant daydreaming, forgetting birthdays, never taking her out socially, indifference to her parents, chronic impotence, blah blah blah).

But maybe I needed to believe in reconstruction, as San Francisco did after the quake of 1906. No one is the same after a disaster, but I had decided to return to square one. Going back home is returning to what belongs to you. There's nothing extraordinary about it, but at least it's yours.

So that night I apologised to my wife, hugged her tight and wiped away her tears. I bought us two tickets for a vacation in Bangkok. After that I struggled to be a good husband. We've been blessed with two delightful kids. Yes, sometimes I stray, but I do it for the sake of our household. Otherwise I'd die of boredom. Karina is hardly the sole master of disguise. My efforts to mimic what is considered happiness have been so strenuous that in the end, I think, I have truly become happy.

What is it now?

Still not 100% satisfied?

You have to learn to take responsibility for your choices. OK, fine. But you can't say you weren't warned. Turn to the next page.

You really do resemble our friend, after all.

Saigon, 2008

After San Francisco, there was no way home. My obsession with Karina destroyed everything. One night my wife exploded, reciting a litany of the sins I had committed since our wedding (being a workaholic, constant daydreaming, forgetting birthdays, never taking her out socially, indifference to her parents, chronic impotence, blah blah blah).

She gave me one more chance to patch things up. She planned a vacation, our first after two years of marriage, seeing as we'd never gone on a honeymoon. I said yes, in order to avoid hurting her pride. But by that time everything was clear to me. I didn't want to save anything, including myself.

My wife wanted to go to Bangkok, but I suggested another city. Even on my last chance with her, I sabotaged her plans. We landed at Tan So Nhat International Airport, in Ho Chi Minh City.

There, I traced the touristy streets of Hay Ba Trung that Jeffrey passed through in Isaac Ginsberg's novel. I looked for signs, though not what lay behind them. A coffee shop on a street corner stopped me in my tracks. It was a local equivalent of Starbucks, but its name leaped out at me. Trung Nguyen Coffee.

Later I learned that there were many Trung Nguyen in Vietnam. You can even buy Trung Nguyen coffee beans to take home.

And of course, Trung Nguyen, whatever his real name is, wants to direct *Sarrasine*.

I left my wife, who was still busy looking for souvenirs, in Ben Tanh Market. You can imagine how furious she was. But this was nothing compared to my previous crime. I had left her long before, in San Francisco, three years ago.

Entering the shop, I ordered a cup of coffee, seeking protection from the terror of a face that appeared in every mirror.

Continue on to page 299.

Hello, Los Angeles.

Jakarta in the nineties. You marvelled for the first time at the avenues of Pondok Indah; they delighted you – the empty, clean, quiet streets, the rows of palm trees, the nice cars, and the multi-storey houses. Here dwelled the rich. There were no traffic jams, and pollution had yet to spread depression. Now, in Los Angeles, a far more spectacular Pondok Indah, specifically designed for drivers, you finally see the Mecca to which Suharto's New Order had oriented its prayers. You've read that Jakarta is one of Los Angeles' sister cities. It makes total sense to you, especially since relationships between siblings come in so many forms. Take your relationship with your sister, for example, with its mingled loathing and longing. Jakarta, city of your childhood, is a Third World Los Angeles.

Neither Los Angeles nor Jakarta is friendly to those who can't afford a car or who don't know how to drive. You're in the second category. You should rent a car to get around the city, but, woe be unto you, you can't. Loads of people in New York don't know how to drive, and that just makes them true blue New Yorkers who grew up in a subway culture. In Jakarta, you shook your head shyly when asked if you knew how to drive. It's clear cut, either you do or you don't. Nobody gives a crap about 'a little bit' or 'studied once'. It sucks how Los Angeles reminds you of things that you've always treated as congenital defects. Unlike New York, in this city you can't sit and mind your own business on the subway and get where you need to go quickly. *New York, New York, if I can make it there, I'll make it anywhere*. Bullshit. You can't survive outside of New York. Here you have to wait for unreliable buses. Maybe if this had been the first city you visited in the US, you'd be more forgiving.

When Bob skypes you from Frankfurt, you moan non-stop about transport. He urges you to be patient. He'll arrive Saturday and then you'll rent a car. In the meantime, you order taxis through the hotel to go to the beach, see a movie, and visit the Hollywood Walk of Fame.

Los Angeles definitely awakens memories – and the trauma – of growing up in Jakarta. Not being able to drive in Jakarta puts you in your place, a place for the hoi polloi, a place unfriendly to women. You still remember how it felt to be jostled on the bus and to have a man deliberately rub his penis against you from behind. Los Angeles cabs make you think of taxis in Jakarta. Once you were earning a salary, you took them more often than the Metro Mini. You felt as if you'd received a boost in class status. It meant building a world freer from stares, catcalls and unwanted contact.

You look forward to Bob's arrival. But on Saturday, a week after you left New York, he doesn't show up. The day before, you sent an email, asking when he would get to LA, but he didn't respond. At first you assume he's busy. Oh well. Another day of sightseeing without wheels. When Bob doesn't arrive on Sunday either, though, worry sets in. You call your mother-in-law in Minnesota and Angela in New York. They haven't heard from him either.

Three days pass. You're reaching the conclusion that something bad has happened. Your husband is missing. Vanished. There's no gentler way to put it. You hurry to the police.

You report your missing husband calmly. Amid all this you check in with yourself about your feelings. Worried? Absolutely. Sad? You're less sure. The feeling is actually quite rotten. You only know that you can't stay quiet. And in the police station, you hear about a club that will change your life.

Continue on to page 317.

Over the course of two days, in various locations, you hear Husein's stories of this female fraudster. You piece them together as you sit side by side on the cable car, walk the path below the Golden Gate Bridge, and enjoy roast duck together in Chinatown. You've never met anyone so obsessed. Does he still nurture the story about Karina in his mind? Who is Karina, really? For Husein, it doesn't even seem to matter any more.

'Why are you sharing your stories of Karina with me?'

'Maybe because you look like a traveller in search of stories.'

He's probably right. You're so absorbed in his tale that you don't stop to ask why Husein has so much time to wander the city with you. Neither do you ask why he always wears a grey suit and fedora until two young men, who look like card-carrying fashionistas, greet you on the road. One wears a corduroy jacket of mustard yellow paired with maroon slacks; the other sports pinstripe pants, suspenders and a white shirt.

'I like your style,' says the owner of the corduroy jacket.

'Nice shoes,' his colleague compliments you.

You merely smile, while Husein offers praise in turn.

Suddenly it seems as though you've joined a costume party.

'Do you both feel like you were born in the wrong era too?' asks Señor Corduroy. 'My boyfriend loves 1920s fashion. I'm more into the sixties.'

'Sometimes I dream of having a time machine,' Husein says.

To find Karina again, you think to yourself.

'But I really can't imagine living in the sixties though, and going through the Stonewall Riots,' Señor Corduroy responds more seriously.

'True,' nods Husein. 'The sixties were hard times for Singapore.'

'Have you been to the vintage clothing store down the road?' asks Mr Pinstripes.

He points the way to his favourite shop. Husein tips his fedora and thanks him. The young couple go away, hand in hand. They look happy, even if they do appear to have stepped out of different decades.

'We're not going to that shop, are we?'

'Why not?'

The store in question is close by. As you step inside, you're greeted by the musty aroma of second-hand clothes mixed with scented candles. The rhythms of jazz from an LP remind you of the Hotel Madeleine. You peruse a rack of coats and jackets, but lose your enthusiasm when you see the three-digit price tags, and wander off to another corner to browse some antiques, from typewriters to 1970s Kodak cameras. Husein follows, but then stops. You turn and see him standing before a carved mirror hanging on the wall. The mirror reflects the image of a mannequin facing the window, a wig with straight bangs set on its head. Husein looks pale.

Karina. The name ambushes you. Damn. So this is what it feels like to be stalked by a ghost. After San Francisco, Husein has never seen his own face in the mirror. Karina always takes control, spawned offspring.

Which woman does Husein see? Karina Lam, Karina Le or Karina Lee?

You try to come up with the most precise term for Karina. She's a consummate con artist, claiming to be a different person with each man who falls victim to her charms.

She's an impersonator, not a con artist, Husein protests to you repeatedly.

Yeah, sure, as if that makes a difference, you mumble.

You take a deep breath when you leave the shop. You feel like you've just emerged from a booby-trapped playground in which Husein has hoped to discover a time machine. But, as if suddenly remembering something, he goes back inside, asking you to wait a while. You shrug and enter a nearby chocolate shop.

Two days isn't long, but you already feel intimate with Husein. Aside from the story of Karina, you share fragments of another tale with him. You tell him you're married. There is much you omit, including the fact that you're on honeymoon, and that your husband is more than twice your age (you don't want him to make groundless assumptions). But the story of Karina the impersonator, an ever-present third person, has brought you together. Occasionally Husein refers to her as 'the kidnapper'. He feels as if his body and soul have been abducted, shackled in a cave, and left to sleep on and on without seeing the light, like a bat.

At one in the morning, after your second full day in San Francisco, you return to your hotel room, exhausted and with blistered feet. The city's hilly topography has made walking in the red shoes torture. You conk out without trying to call Bob.

'Late night?'

Bob's face fills the computer screen. In contrast to the venerable Hotel Madeleine, Bob's hotel room in Frankfurt has minimalist decor, its colour palette a stark white. Bob is neatly dressed because he needs to head out to dinner soon with colleagues, fellow academics. You rub your eyes. It's ten in the morning. Bob has already tried to reach you a few times but you've only just woken up.

'Yes, I went to the theatre.'

'Oh. What did you see?'

'*Miss Saigon*.'

'There's a production of *Miss Saigon* on?'

'Eh, yeah … sort of an amateur production.'

'Did you go on your own?'

You lie. You weren't alone, and you didn't go to the theatre. You feel a little guilty, but you don't want to make Bob anxious by telling him that you're wandering the city aimlessly with a man you met in your hotel. It sounds bad, but really, nothing has happened. Before long you and Bob will be together in Los Angeles. Husein will only be another scrap of your story, a stranger who became a temporary companion, whom you'll never meet again. On a journey, we often meet others who never enter our personal histories because we take no note of them.

Maybe. You hope so.

'What have you seen so far? Do you like San Francisco?'

'I've just been walking around. I feel kind of bored.'

Who knows why that pops out of your mouth. You don't feel bored at all.

'OK, I'm just about to go to dinner,' Bob says. 'Take care of yourself over there, hon.'

You close your laptop. At twelve o'clock, you go down to the hotel restaurant for lunch. You steal a glance at the other guests. Husein isn't among them. Shortly thereafter, you see Noel the receptionist walking your way.

'Our Singaporean friend left this for you.'

Noel places a wrapped parcel on your table.

'It's from Husein?'

'Ah, yes. I forgot his name. But you remember, of course.'

'Thank you.'

Noel doesn't withdraw immediately. His right eyebrow is arched, and he seems to be suppressing a smile. You look at him quizzically.

'Is something the matter?'

'It's nothing,' he says, turning around. 'Be careful.'

Back in your room, you open the gift from Husein impatiently and your fingers brush against something smooth. You tear away the wrapping to find a dark brown wig sheathed in clear, glossy plastic. A card is attached to the bag.

Thank you for being my travel companion and listening to my story. This is a gift for you. From your beautiful red shoes, I've gathered that you like playing and going on adventures. Will you go out with me tonight? In the wig, perhaps? I'll also dress in appropriate costume. No special meaning. It's so retro and it's fun.

You think of the wig crowning the mannequin in the vintage clothing store. Husein must have bought it when he dashed off and left you to browse around the chocolate shop.

You hurry to the mirror and try on the wig. Your face looks different. Funny. Like a mannequin. You imagine wandering the city in the wig and red shoes, becoming someone else. More beautiful, sexier, maybe.

Will you wear the wig and go out with Husein tonight?

Contemplating it gives you butterflies. But you hesitate. If Husein really wanted to give you, say, a friendship gift, why not flowers, or a souvenir with a picture of the Golden Gate Bridge? You're so unimaginative. Husein is not like that. You feel you're beginning to know him well. You can imagine how today, without you, he is strolling around in his grey suit and fedora. What do you expect from a man who insists upon such attire every day? He's no ordinary chap.

You put the wig on the bed. It tempts you more and more. Maybe there's no harm in wearing it and joining Husein one last time. You'll take care to behave, and will remember that you're Bob's wife. You surprise yourself with your genuine loyalty to the professor. But what if Husein isn't a good man? What if he has mommy issues, or, rather, 'Karina issues'? What if he's a little crazy?

A good man. What does that mean? Obviously, Husein wants to invite you into the fiction he's creating. But what sort of fiction is it?

If you agree to go out with Husein, turn to page 313.

If you sense that something isn't quite right and choose not to go, turn to the next page.

Every mirror reflects Karina's face. Sometimes she becomes two, sometimes three, sometimes infinite.

Husein wants you to look like Karina, an idea you reject. Women shouldn't replace other women (or men) who are more ideal but unattainable. You don't have time to listen to all of Husein's obsessing over Karina and then have a moment arrive when – you can easily imagine it – he confesses that he's falling in love with you, and your face turns into Karina's. You're no doormat. The more you think about it, the more it seems that Husein might be dangerous. Maybe after first transforming the women he meets into Karina, he dates them and murders them one by one.

You're not keen to take part in a madman's games.

You call Husein's room to make an excuse: you can't go because you've just arranged to meet a friend. He doesn't answer. You stare at the ceiling, forming plans. Best if you stay in your room tonight. If you leave, you might run into each other. Your image of Husein grows steadily worse: what if he really is crazy and gets angry, and then comes to kill you? You consider switching hotels. Yes, switching cities, if necessary. After all, you're growing bored here and want to go to Los Angeles. You make up your mind to go and see Noel in reception.

'The main thing is to tell him I went out with a friend tonight,' you say to him.

Noel nods with alacrity. 'And you wouldn't go with just anyone, right? Yes, yes. That's the right way to get rid of a man.'

His tone sounds nonchalant, but with a hint of mischief. You smile. After a few days here you notice that Noel is starting to act overly friendly, but you like him.

'So that's your trick, huh.'

'Oh Jesus!' Noel rolls his eyes. 'Can you imagine me not having a line of men to deal with?'

'One more thing, Noel –'

'Oooh, you remember my name. I'm flattered!'

'Noel,' you say firmly, 'do you know where I can rent a car cheaply? I want to go to Los Angeles. But I can't drive.'

'A place to hire a car plus a driver?'

'If that's too hard, maybe I'll just take a plane.'

Noel thinks for a moment.

'I'm planning to drive to LA this weekend,' he says. 'I can be your chauffeur. But you have to pay for the gas.'

'Wow, OK!' you exclaim, delighted. 'But how do I know you're not a psycho?'

'Ooh la la, Imelda, do I look like one? No, right? And don't worry, honey, I'm not into chicks.'

Noel jots down his phone number on a piece of paper and gives it to you. 'Call me, OK?'

You put it in your pocket and head to the elevator but soon turn back.

'Noel, do you know of any other hotels near here?'

Two days later, Noel picks you up at another hotel. You moved there immediately after your conversation at the reception desk. Noel gets out of the car and greets you without removing his sunglasses.

It's strange to see him in something other than the slick suit he wears at the Hotel Madeleine. His purple V-neck T-shirt and tight jeans confirm his gym rat's discipline. The change of outfit feels like a sign that you're entering another world, whatever it may be – certainly not a retro-themed fiesta.

Nimbly, Noel helps lift your suitcase into the trunk. You get in the car and ask if Husein has been looking for you.

'Curious, huh?' he teases. 'But let's go to the gas station first, please.'

'OK, OK. Anyway, I said I'd pay.'

'Just kidding!' Noel laughs. 'Yes, he asked twice. When I said you were gone, he looked disappointed. Eh, but I hope you won't be the one who's disappointed.'

'Me, disappointed? Why?'

'A missed opportunity.'

'Noel, I have a husband.'

'Oooh, nice. I want one too. A Western Union daddy.'

Noel steps on the accelerator and pulls away from the kerb. And so, you leave Husein's story, rather than your heart, in San Francisco. You won't dwell on it again because after this your life takes a sharper turn than any bend on Lombard Street, even if there are occasional nights when you wonder idly about your choice. What would have happened if you'd put on a wig in San Francisco and gone out with Husein? Would your life have changed?

Noel drives towards I-5, the interstate highway that leads to Los Angeles. He tells many stories during the several-hour trip, one of the most memorable being about cars. You tell him that you regret never learning how to drive. Neither you nor your friends had access to automobiles, unlike the bourgeois clique at your school, who were practising with their parents' cars by the time they finished junior high.

'I just got my licence,' said Noel. 'Even though I started learning in middle school too.'

'Seriously?'

'Yeah, a year ago.'

'Should I be worried?'

'You have my permission to pray for your safety.'

But Noel drives carefully, and you forget to pray because you're too enthralled by his long story, and the string of love–hate relationships bound up within it. He names this tale his 'Driving History'.

Turn to the next page.

Driving History

Noel has a long driving history. His father tried to teach him to drive a stick shift at age fourteen. But at eighteen, he still couldn't drive. Nor at twenty-one. Noel's frustrated father, observing his son's flawless porcelain complexion, thought he wasn't manly enough. 'Look at that skin of yours. You can't drive because you're not an adventurer. You've never caused any mischief. You look too much like your mother.'

Noel came from a Mestizo family with Spanish blood. All his relatives had light skin and looked as if they belonged to the elite, but his striking resemblance to his mother made him gleam brightest of all. Mama, as everyone knew, was a true beauty. And Noel was Mama's boy. Doted on by Mama. As beautiful as Mama. But if most men in the neighbourhood proved their existence by acting like roguish adventurers – and jerks, if they could get away with it – being as pretty as Mama was not something to aspire to.

Noel took up learning to drive again, this time with his boyfriend, at age twenty-four. Noel can't forget the man: an Asian Jean-Claude Van Damme, only a little smaller and shorter. Noel was crazy about movies, and the first time he saw him, he was immediately reminded of Lino Brocka's *Macho Dancer*. Except he swore his boyfriend was even sexier than any of the actors in Brocka's film. When the two slept together for the first time, his lover looked in vain for scars on Noel's body. At the time Noel was thin and his skin as white and creamy as milk. There were no traces of mischief. No traces of adventure. He was even too beautiful to become a macho dancer.

'You really are precious. I'll always protect you.'

Noel's boyfriend, possessive and ready to battle like a knight on his behalf, said, 'You have no talent behind the wheel. Manila is a city for a real driver.' He took to chauffeuring Noel everywhere, to work, to parties, to French courses. At age twenty-six, Noel still couldn't drive.

'And I'm a real what, then?'

'You're a real beauty, darling.'

Noel wasn't a display item. He left his lover just as he had left his father. At twenty-seven, he made a momentous decision. If you've failed to die as a legend by that age, you have no choice but to make sure your life isn't too pathetic. Noel left for Boston with his new boyfriend, an American, and searched for whatever job he could find on a tourist visa. This disappointed his family: Noel was an Ateneo graduate, and not one of his relatives had ever been a migrant worker.

Noel liked Boston because you didn't need to drive. His life changed again when, at age twenty-eight, he broke up with his boyfriend. Once more he decided to start afresh and moved to the West Coast.

In California, everyone had to drive. Noel was dead.

His landlady, a petite grandmother, said one night, 'Has anyone ever told you how beautiful you are?' The little old lady owned a faded green seventies Jaguar. On its rear window, a sticker read *Good girls go to heaven, bad girls go everywhere*. She was the best driving teacher Noel had. Go Granny, go Granny, go Granny go.

And so, at age twenty-nine, Noel drove down the freeway from San Francisco to San Diego.

He can only drive automatics and maybe he can't handle a city for real drivers. But he drives. And he is happy because he is as beautiful, and his skin as flawless, as ever.

Continue on to page 326.

Whore of Babylon

And upon her forehead was a name written, a name of mystery, BABYLON THE GREAT, THE MOTHER OF HARLOTS AND ABOMINATIONS OF THE EARTH.

Revelation 17:5

Before your visit to De Wallen and before your relationship with Maria cooled, she told you about the Whore of Babylon. In the Book of Revelation, a passage states that the Whore of Babylon rides a seven-headed, ten-horned red monster. But it's more or less impossible to know who or what this woman is; she might stand for something that has nothing to do with sex. The Whore of Babylon signifies a betrayal of Christ. Prostitutes, and women in general, are often used as symbols for something beyond themselves.

From colleagues, Maria had heard a legend about a woman who is called – or calls herself – the Whore of Babylon. Like the Great Whore in the Bible, the Great Whore of Amsterdam is a mysterious figure, who only appears in gossip. In short, she is a high-class escort and madam with an extraordinary reputation. Maria didn't call her a sex worker when she spoke of her, because she thinks this woman is too wild to be confined by professional or legal terms.

They say that the Great Whore of Amsterdam always wears a mask. There are even men who have sworn that she doesn't take it off during sex, and is all the more mysterious and arousing as a result.

Does she work in De Wallen?

Maria laughed: Do you think a woman with so much power would want to work in the Red Light District?

Conversations about the Whore of Babylon often had a hypothetical flavour: if we were the Whore of Babylon, we wouldn't need to rent display windows and become Coke machines. In the Bible it says she's the mother of prostitutes. The women in her network are her daughters. They can work when they want and don't have to pay tax. Sex workers in the Red Light District are protected by the state, while the whores of Amsterdam-Babylon are protected by the loving mother.

The Whore of Babylon surpasses us all.

You peppered Maria with questions:

'So, who exactly is she? How can she be outside the law?'

'Nobody has ever seen her,' said Maria. 'She shouldn't exist. Really it wouldn't be fair for the rest of us if she did.'

'Not fair?'

You've never forgotten what Maria said next.

'We – maybe even you – possess a little authority. But no one like us has power to the extent of being that erotic. Even if someone did, that person isn't me, isn't any of my friends, and certainly isn't my mother. If the Whore of Babylon is the mother of all prostitutes, that means she is seen as representing us all, although our lives are very far from being sexy and powerful. She doesn't even operate a Coke machine. So what would be a better term for her – the One Per Cent?'

Turn to the next page.

You spend Christmas and New Year alone. Maria isn't at home, nor has she told you where she's gone (maybe on holiday in Bulgaria?). She only said that she will return on January 2, two days before your lease runs out. You've found a new place in Haarlem that is much cheaper. Meanwhile, you hang around Amsterdam with no clear purpose. You go to Centraal to see the big sparkly Christmas tree, but after that you no longer know what else to do. You have no friends, and Maria has made it abundantly clear that she has no interest in being your friend.

After days of contemplating how Maria's attitude chilled, you give up on trying to understand the reasons for it. But you come to the conclusion that you should help her to leave De Wallen. Maybe you're overthinking the legend of the Whore of Babylon, or maybe your thoughts are all too simple: Maria will be happier if she stops collecting change from a Coke machine.

Red shoes. That's the answer. Devil's red shoes will take her away, somewhere, who knows where, but it will be better than where she is now.

Since she doesn't want to talk to you, you'll place the red shoes in the kitchen before leaving the apartment. You'll depart early in the morning on the day you move out. Maria will wake up around noon, open her room door and go into the kitchen (or maybe she'll head to the bathroom first), and she will find a pair of red shoes and a house key on the table.

You repeat this scenario over and over in your head. But something makes you pause. No, it's not regret about letting go of the shoes that have accompanied you all this way. Who knows if Maria needs shoes? Are you fancying yourself her saviour?

If you want to give her the shoes, turn to page 325.

If you leave without giving her the shoes, turn to page 328.

You sit on the sofa in the lobby. The Hotel Madeleine pianist is, as usual, playing jazz. Tonight you're wearing a grey dress, red shoes and a dark brown wig. The wig is spectacular. You've lost count of how many men have stolen glances in your direction. You feel extraordinary, or rather, you feel delighted to be impersonating an extraordinary woman. Noel passes you with eyebrows raised; then he winks.

'Oooh ... so there really is a fiesta?' he asks in a teasing tone. 'You look gorgeous. Like Faye Dunaway, Kim Novak and all the femmes fatales of the world rolled into one.'

'Not Imelda Marcos?'

'Honey, don't go shooting yourself in the foot.'

After Noel passes, you glance at your watch. Husein is late. You're staring at the hotel floor with its geometric black-and-white pattern. You're getting dizzier and dizzier. Damn floor. It really does create a labyrinth in your head. You fix your gaze on the glass door. The street lights are so dim that the people outside almost seem like shadows.

Then you see the silhouette of a man in a hat. Husein?

The lobby door opens, and he appears. You feel relieved. Unusually, tonight he's wearing a dark blue suit with his tie and fedora. He hurries towards you.

'Sorry to be so late.'

'No problem. Where are we going?'

Husein doesn't answer immediately. He stares at you without blinking. You snap your fingers, and he awakes from his reverie. You look gorgeous, he says. You knew he would say this. A little nervous, Husein pulls a key from his trouser pocket. It turns out that he has rented a car for the evening. You get up from the sofa and follow him.

Husein invites you to dine at a Vietnamese restaurant. He holds the door open for you, and you feel his hand resting on your back.

'Is this a magic wig?' you ask and begin perusing the menu.

'What do you mean?'

'Everyone seems to think I'm hot.'

Husein chuckles.

'I'm serious,' you say. 'I should have worn one long ago.'

'Is it too late?'

'It depends.'

He looks at your face again, then asks, 'Did I already tell you that you look beautiful?'

Husein's fingers touch yours. You pull your hand away. Husein looks surprised.

'If you pull any crap, I'm taking off the wig,' you growl through your smile.

'But you'll still be beautiful.'

That night you drink two glasses of wine. You don't feel drunk, but you say more than you intended to. You don't know how it starts, but you tell him about your comfortable marriage with Bob. Comfortable, because you don't love him, but he gives you space. Husein replies that you've never loved anyone like he has.

'But you've never loved someone real.'

'You're real,' he says.

He's trying to be seductive, but you wonder who he's flirting with: you or Karina? Your shoulders feel heavy. You hope you're not being possessed by Karina's ghost. You have to stop drinking wine.

After dessert, Husein invites you to another spot. Where? you ask. He doesn't want to tell you. It's a secret, he says.

*

As you leave the restaurant, you glance again at your watch. 11 p.m. There's no harm in going for a stroll. But in the car, you grow nervous and think of Bob. The place Husein has in mind seems to be far away. You've left the San Francisco city limits. In front of you there is only dark, deserted road. You feel sleepy. Maybe you shouldn't have drunk so much. When you open your eyes, you catch a dazzling yellow light moving towards you. You scream. Everything goes black.

A car travelling in the opposite direction has collided with you.

In the final seconds you sense Husein swerving the steering wheel towards the other car. An accident? Or something else? You're too weary for assumptions. A series of images flickers in your head: flashing neon in front of a hotel, a silhouette of a man in a hat, a geometric floor pattern that resembles a labyrinth. Everything is so much like a slow-motion film that you wonder who could possibly be stretching time.

Do you have regrets?

Who'd have thought you'd come to such a useless end, trapped by a *deus ex machina*? But you've had many stories. You have chosen your own red-shoes adventure.

Hopefully, when the police find you in the morning, you'll make a beautiful corpse in your grey dress and red shoes. Is that asking for too much? You want to assure yourself that your head, hands and feet remain intact. But you can't feel your fingers. Let's just fantasise about tomorrow morning. Noel the receptionist might read about the accident in the newspaper, trembling. His perfect eyebrows won't move, but his face will grow ashen and he'll swear an oath never to utter the word fiesta again.

Oh, and how is Husein? Why is he silent? You wonder if he's still dapper or now unrecognisable, body crushed and torn, eyes agog, staring upward. You conclude that he wanted to take you to Mission San Juan Bautista. That's where his search for Karina comes to an end. In bringing his fiction to life, at least, he has been unswerving. Sadly, though, the woman in the wig, as the curtain descends, is not Karina.

Images continue to appear randomly, one after another, until finally you see nothing more than whiteness, a void. Will an angel come? You sense a familiar figure coming into view. Devil? Where are we going?

FINIS

The Solidarity Club of Lost Husbands

Dressed in black, everyone, yourself included, sits in a circle. You commit a few of the others' names to memory: Carmencita from Mexico, Soonyi of South Korea, and Andy, born in Boston. Doña Manuela, a tall, sturdy Argentinian woman of sixty-five, is the society's founder. She listens throughout as she wipes photo frames, a music box and her collection of miniature houses. Everyone in the club except you lives in Los Angeles. In Doña Manuela's living room, however, you must cross borders on the way to the past. The Solidarity Club of Lost Husbands is an international body that traces memories from Tijuana to the Yellow Sea.

You never imagined that a city with such an awful transport system could have led you there. It's not Los Angeles that you're indebted to, though, but the police station toilets.

A policewoman had recorded details about your husband's disappearance, knitting her eyebrows when you mentioned several traits (sixty-two years old, white, fat, asthmatic). She scanned the front page of your passport, as if trying to convince herself that you'd yet to turn thirty, and occasionally stole a glance at your beautiful scarf. Upstanding public servant that she was, though, she finished her report and said warmly, 'We'll do our best.'

In the toilets, you ran into an elderly woman of perhaps eighty, with grey, bobbed hair. She flashed a friendly smile, then greeted you somewhat clumsily, '*Dari Indonesia, ya?*' She goes on to say that she herself left Malang in the 1960s and has never returned home. For years she lived in The Hague before moving to California.

You answered that yes, you're from Indonesia, and then admitted that you'd just filed a report about the disappearance of your husband. You and he had been planning a honeymoon from New York. You flew first to Los Angeles because he had to attend a conference in Europe, but now, three days after he was scheduled to arrive, he has yet to catch up with you. All communication has been cut off.

The old woman nodded, looking more attentive than sympathetic. She rummaged in her bag and offered you a card. As she washed her hands, you took note of an odd name printed there.

'This is a club I used to be active in. You might find it helpful. Just say that you heard about it from Yunita.'

'You're here because your husband is missing too?'

'Oh, no! I lost my wallet.' She turned off the tap. 'My husband died over forty years ago.'

Yunita rotated her wrinkled hands under the dryer. Your condolences were swallowed in the machine's roar. She looked in the mirror and smoothed her short hair.

'Well, I'll be on my way. I hope you find your husband.'

The Solidarity Club of Lost Husbands doesn't aim to find those who are lost, but to bring life to loss. Nevertheless, Doña Manuela is always ready to share her contacts – police, private detectives, activist networks – as well as tips on dealing with the state apparatus. Her principle: let's not become victims twice over. She belonged to several groups demanding justice for victims of Argentina's Dirty War, and her mother-in-law was a member of the Asociación Madres de Plaza de Mayo.

'I have some pictures I haven't shown you yet.'

Carmencita's voice is husky. She opens a tiny Dell laptop in a purple case to share the photos.

Carmencita and her husband had visited Paris three years ago, in spring 2005, to shoot some pictures before their wedding. They attached a padlock reading 'Carmencita &

Pablo' to the bridge of love, the Pont des Arts. A photographer friend immortalised Carmencita in Pablo's embrace. She wore a white dress, cropped in front, trailing behind. She looked like the star of a telenovela.

But after their wedding in Los Angeles, Pablo went off to a Walmart late one afternoon and never returned. Even now, his clothes remain stored neatly in the closet.

'The lock will be there forever, like our love.'

At Carmencita's side, Andy Horowitz rolls his eyes.

'Oh, how romantic! I hope some lunatic doesn't go wild and set the bridge on fire.'

'You're so cruel!'

'As far as I'm concerned,' Andy says sweetly, 'only morons attach love locks.'

'I know a couple from Guadalajara who did it, and they're both authors!' Carmencita retorts.

Andy didn't believe in many things, including marriage, until he had a nasty accident that required surgery. Greg, his partner of a decade, wasn't legally considered a family member, so Andy's mother flew out from Boston to sign the consent forms. After Andy recovered, he thought a lot about the legal issues. If he were ever in a coma for months, he wanted to be euthanised, and he wanted Greg to be able to make the final medical decisions for him. But before euthanasia could separate them, Greg disappeared. The last time he called Andy, he was about to sail across the Hecate Strait in Canada, which was prone to storms and bad weather.

Members of the Solidarity Club of Lost Husbands remember those who are absent by repeating their stories. They can start from any point, in linear fashion from the beginning until the loss of their husband, or via flashbacks. Some choose to plunge in medias res.

Thoughts of old age triggered Andy's decision to marry in Toronto (in 2006 same-sex marriage was not yet possible in California). Andy's story then moves further back in time, to the art gallery where he and Greg met. He's a film editor and works in enclosed spaces; Greg was a photographer and loved nature.

When it's your turn to speak, you retell the timeline of your loss as if you're back in the police station. Carmencita, looking sadder than you, asks, 'What do you remember most about your husband?'

You look around as you clutch at memories. A little nervously, you say, 'Can I tell you another time?'

Your companions nod, though they appear confused. Then comes Soonyi's voice, slow and frail, just like her movements. Her face is sweet, though she is certainly older than Doña Manuela.

'It's OK. I don't remember a lot about my husband either.'

All sorts of things were scattered about after the Korean War and the US withdrew most of its troops. Grand events like wars often leave scraps of debris in their wake, useless and dirty, like syphilis and babies.

At age seventeen, Soonyi gave birth to a black-skinned child from a soldier she called husband even though they never wed.

'He never contacted me. Even his address was fake,' Soonyi said, her voice still soft. 'But there was no reminder more real than Jihoon, my son. Because of Jihoon I was treated as a whore. Because he had no father and because his skin was black.'

The participants fall silent. You intuit that this happens every time. Some stories never dull through repetition – in fact they always stab.

Doña Manuela breaks the hush. 'Next?'

You begin to understand how the members have come to cherish their loss. Memory becomes a shrine that must be polished to a sparkle, like each corner of the photo frames that Doña Manuela burnishes with painstaking care. Some other women knit. Carmencita paints her nails. Soonyi always prepares bibimbap (which seems to you like a combination of rice and gado-gado) for the members to share. Only Andy, the editor, feels that he doesn't need a handicraft of some sort, because such is his daily routine: cutting, rearranging and splicing stories.

Some days, the knitting is rent asunder and nail polish stains the skin.

It is on one of those days that you arrive early and bump into Soonyi at the door. Looking unwell, she rushes home. Shortly afterwards you come across something on the bathroom floor. Someone has hawked up a lungful of phlegm.

'I'm sorry you had to see that.' Doña Manuela approaches you. 'Sorry. It must have been Soonyi.'

'Is she sick?'

'Her heart is weak, yes. But the spitting – she stopped a long time ago,' says Doña Manuela. 'It used to be an addiction. She'd do it in places that are guarded, like government offices and city libraries.'

You can't imagine how it must have felt to have an illegitimate black child in post-war Korea.

Soonyi was determined to escape. A brief marriage allowed her to finally set foot in America in 1975. Since then she had often been struck by an intense desire to spit in public facilities. She was apprehended by a security guard once, then released because she was assumed to be ill. After all, her sweet face harboured no malice.

You remember her bibimbap. A foul sensation develops in your mouth upon seeing Soonyi's phlegm.

While helping to clean the bathroom, you hear more about not only Soonyi but also Doña Manuela and the loss of her husband during the military dictatorship of the late 1970s.

'Obviously he's dead. But how he died, I don't know,' she says. 'It probably wasn't very different from what happened to Yunita's husband.'

The roar of the hand dryer in the police station toilet comes back to you.

Yunita, says Doña Manuela, never knew whether her husband was shot or butchered.

'She's not even sure whether he died in Java or Bali.'

There's no dryer here, but your throat feels parched.

'In my country, people were disappeared in different ways,' she continues. 'Some were stripped naked and thrown into a freezing river, or forced out of a helicopter. Every day we choose our own nightmare.'

In the bathroom, you hope for the roar of a hand dryer. But all you find is a roll of toilet tissue, clean and mute, which can't rescue you.

'You must love your husband very much, Doña.'

'Does that matter?'

She asks if you love your husband. You don't answer.

'It's obvious that the state oppressed me,' she intones. Now her voice is slow and strange. 'The Bible says: Whoso sheddeth man's blood, by man shall his blood be shed.'

Doña Manuela, sturdy and calm, seems to you like a volcano, keeping her fury in check through painstaking, trivial acts. You dare not imagine when and how she will erupt.

You've already stopped visiting the club by the time Soonyi dies. An event has forced you back to New York. We'll come to it shortly, but, to be brief, you're at Bob's apartment when you hear about Soonyi's death. In the name of solidarity, you fly to Los Angeles to attend her funeral. You see her for the last time in church, her corpse done up for the casket as beautifully as a pixie's. Carmencita has applied her make-up.

You remember your disgust over the bibimbap, and the day at the club that changed everything. From then on, everyone finished Soonyi's bibimbap, and when her health deteriorated, Doña Manuela would visit her home simply to help cook.

That day Carmencita and Andy had bickered. The term 'Lost Husband' needed to be redefined, Andy argued, because it didn't apply to Carmencita. Evidently, her husband wasn't lost, he was an escapee.

'Oh, wake up and smell the coffee, Carmencita. We all know what happened. Your husband is here in LA, living with his new girlfriend!'

Andy's cynical barb made Carmencita burst into hysterical tears. Doña Manuela shot him a glare.

'Sorry.' Andy looked mildly apologetic. 'I think all of us could use a little slap from reality.'

'People aren't here to be slapped,' Doña Manuela declared.

Soonyi, who had been silent, spoke up.

'Andy's right. We need a slap,' she said. 'My husband – I found him. We met again in 1980.'

All eyes turned towards the diminutive woman. Doña Manuela's jaw clamped shut. Her broad shoulders rose and fell. The abrupt appearance of new information, a year after Soonyi had joined the club, left her feeling betrayed.

'That's quite interesting, Soonyi.' Doña Manuela's tone was icy cold. 'So now, after all these months, we learn that your husband wasn't missing after all.'

Soonyi bowed her head for a long time. Then you heard her voice, so calm. 'He wasn't missing. I made him go missing.'

A storyteller must also erase.

In 1953, the father of Soonyi's baby left Korea and married a woman in America. By the time Soonyi finally located him, he had been widowed. He swore he didn't know he had a child in Korea, and asked Soonyi to marry him and forget all her past suffering.

Two days after their wedding, Soonyi put a suitcase into the trunk of her car and drove far, far away.

'I miss him. Sometimes, even now, after decades, I feel he's still lying next to me.'

Soonyi wiped her teary eyes.

'Maybe that's what I kept in the suitcase.' She paused for a moment. 'Not him.' And then: silence.

At that point Doña Manuela stood up and served the bibimbap.

Now, dressed in black, you and your compatriots go to a Korean restaurant after the funeral. Your husband still hasn't been found. Maybe you don't love him, but that doesn't matter. Losing someone and a sense of loss – each brings a different emptiness, slippery and enigmatic. Sometimes they intersect in miraculous ways, as you learned from Doña Manuela, Soonyi and the Solidarity Club of Lost Husbands.

Turn to page 329.

You place the shoes carefully in an empty shoebox, which you found in Anna's closet, and set them on the dining table. You leave the key to the apartment and a note: *Thank you for your kindness. Please accept these shoes as a memento. Happy adventuring!*

You button your coat and pull on boots. Without looking back, you open the door and walk down the stairs. A sharp gust of wind strikes your cheeks as you exit the building. You close your eyes and take a deep breath, as if freed from a cage. In your mind, the cage resembles a shop display window. You imagine Maria traipsing about elsewhere in red shoes. Not in Bulgaria – she doesn't want to go back there. Maybe as a teacher in Botswana, or as a social activist in Baltimore. Sounds like fun.

Continue on to page 341.

Noel chauffeurs you to the hotel lobby. He helps take your bags out from the trunk and hugs you warmly as he says goodbye.

'If you need anything, just give me a call.'

You smile and nod. You don't envision calling him any time soon.

Once in your room, you immediately open your laptop to check for email from Bob. No news. Maybe he's on his way. You've given him the hotel's address, naturally, and he can take a cab from the airport. Meanwhile, you kill time visiting tourist sights in Los Angeles. Getting around LA without your own vehicle turns out to be a real pain. You can hardly wait for Bob's arrival on Saturday, so you can rent a car to travel around.

But Saturday comes and there's still no sign of Bob. Maybe his plane has been delayed, you think. Maybe he had to postpone his trip. You can't reach him. On Sunday, you wake up without any news. Anxiety sets in. You call LAX information and ask if a plane from Frankfurt has arrived.

'Can you please give me the flight number, ma'am?'

'Eh ... I don't know what it is.'

'The airline then?'

The conversation makes you feel like an idiot. You don't even know what flight Bob was on. He never told you, and you never asked. What kind of marriage is this? You call your mother-in-law in Minnesota and Angela in New York. They haven't heard any news. You continue to wait.

On Tuesday, you reach the conclusion that something bad has happened and decide to go to the police. A policewoman records details about your husband's disappearance. She knits her eyebrows when you mention several traits (sixty-two years old, white, fat, asthmatic). She scans the front page of your passport, as if trying to convince herself that you've yet to turn thirty, and steals glances at your beautiful scarf. Upstanding public servant that she is, though, she finishes her report and says warmly, 'We'll do our best.'

Your report completed, you feel so tense that your hands and feet have gone cold. You want to go to the toilet but immediately jettison the idea. The most important thing is to go back to the hotel and settle your nerves. You walk unsteadily towards the exit. A click of heels follows your steps. Someone calls to you softly, and you turn to see a woman in a red blazer and sunglasses.

'Did you just report your husband missing?'

You nod, a little dazed.

'I'm the detective investigating your case,' she says. 'I'll be in touch soon.'

Again, you nod. The woman's chic appearance stands out in a room filled with officers in dark blue uniform. But you're too tired and confused to dwell on it. You walk to the bus stop and wait almost half an hour for a bus to take you back to the hotel.

You sit all evening on your bed in a state of utter turmoil. You've never felt so lonely, so lost.

You ask the hotel operator to connect you with Noel in San Francisco.

'Noel, it's me.'

'Hey, sis! How's it going? Enjoying LA?'

You're silent for a long time.

'Hello?' Noel isn't sure you heard him. 'Hello?'

'Noel.' Your voice begins to tremble. 'My husband is missing.'

Continue on to page 337.

You stand for a long while in front of Maria's room. You want to knock on her door and say goodbye, but you know that won't fix anything. Maybe there's no need, because nothing is broken or scratched. Her apartment is just a transit point, a temporary stopover that has brought two travellers together. Maria, an expat, and you, a tourist.

Maria doesn't need a saviour. For you to assume she wants to be saved can make it seem you're judging her a second time. You don't even know if she wants to leave all this, and she doesn't need you.

Continue on to page 345.

This is the incident that occurred during your time with the Solidarity Club of Lost Husbands:

That evening, after hearing Doña Manuela's story in the bathroom, you returned with all sorts of feelings that you didn't recognise and that shouldn't have surfaced. Your head was buzzing with questions on the bus back to your basic motel. Once it was clear that Bob was missing, you'd immediately moved out of the three-star hotel where you'd been staying. Without him, you had to be frugal.

Rain was falling, drops clinging to the foggy bus window. You caught glimpses of people passing by in the sodden city. They appeared for a moment and then seemed to evaporate, to go missing. Missing persons. Did Yunita ever imagine how her husband had died? Perhaps it's better to be 'missing' – vaporous, gone without a trace – than a battered corpse that can be photographed, archived, remembered. But what right did you have to compare the two cases? You didn't know. You never truly understood how Yunita and Doña Manuela had put their lives back together. In contrast, you felt lucky. Your loss was easier to deal with because you'd never loved your husband.

Twilight in Los Angeles, and you felt utterly alone. You stared at the cars rushing past and the city lights as they started to come on. The fluorescent glow made your eyes water.

Maybe it wasn't the lights making them damp.

You tugged the yellow cord by the window, signalling the bus driver to stop. With a thank you, you hopped off onto the sidewalk. Rain raked your face, chasing you. You longed to flee far away, anywhere, but you felt heavy, with a tightness in your chest, and your legs were too weak. Everything around you seemed to slow to a crawl.

As you entered the motel lobby, the receptionist told you someone was waiting for you and pointed to the sofa. You looked at him in confusion; you hadn't expected a visitor. The receptionist didn't know what it was about either. You walked slowly over to the sofa, where a woman in a red blazer and sunglasses sat, legs crossed. You glanced at her stiletto heels. Who walks in the rain in shoes like that?

'Can we talk? This is about your husband.'

Her voice was crisp and clear. Before you could answer, she introduced herself as the detective investigating your husband's disappearance. You nodded. Previously, the police had come to your hotel room, and you were called to the station. They questioned you about many things, ranging from your last conversation with Bob to whether you had a good marriage. Perhaps the police thought that everyone had a motive to eliminate Bob. A rift had appeared in your relationship with Bob's family. Even Angela, who'd always been nice to you, began to keep her distance. You imagined that they blamed you somehow for Bob's tragic disappearance or even suspected you.

Unlike the uniformed police officers, the detective in front of you was dressed impeccably. The black umbrella she carried, neatly folded, was completely dry, as was she. You felt that you looked awful, hair soaked, cheeks wet, while she looked perfect in a mesh fascinator that obscured her face. Her nails and lipstick were scarlet. She was too beautiful for a detective, except perhaps Cybill Shepherd in *Moonlighting*. You felt as though you'd seen her before, but your thoughts were in too much chaos to reconstruct where. She lowered her sunglasses slightly and looked towards the receptionist. In a half-whisper, she said, 'Maybe we should go outside.'

'But it's raining.'

'It'll be better that way. You won't need to wipe away your tears.'

You fell silent.

As if knowing what you didn't dare ask, she continued: 'Your mascara's running. You look like a raccoon.'

Without waiting for you to respond she stepped outside, certain you would follow.

In front of the motel she opened her umbrella, black in colour and large enough to shelter you both. You complied when she asked you to hold it. She took out a silver lighter and a slim tobacco filter from her handbag while she walked. She tilted her head as she exhaled smoke, making you cough.

'Forgive me for delivering bad news,' she said. 'I'm afraid your husband won't be found.'

She conveyed the findings of the investigation. A private jet from Amsterdam to Hong Kong had disappeared mid-flight, and it was probable that the plane had crashed into the ocean. Inside were a pilot and the two who had chartered the jet. One of them was Bob.

You shook your head in disbelief. Bob had been in Frankfurt, not Amsterdam.

'How much do you know about your husband?'

You struggled to answer. Every time you talked to him on Skype, he'd been in a hotel room. You'd taken it for granted that the hotel room was in Frankfurt, but the interior would have looked the same anywhere: New York, Frankfurt, Amsterdam.

'What was he doing in Amsterdam? Why was he going to Hong Kong?'

'All I can tell you is that your husband was more than a fat, boring white guy.'

Bob had another life that you didn't understand. Of course. No need to be angry since you'd never tried to understand him. But maybe you felt angry now because you were alone and Bob was missing, quite likely dead. Your head throbbed. You paused, and the detective rushed to grab the umbrella as you staggered.

*

You must have fainted for a moment. The woman beside you continued to speak, but you could only make out distant sounds. You needed a long time to wake (maybe 'wake' isn't the right term, but you really felt you had dozed off in mid-stride). All you heard clearly was her final sentence: 'You are at a crossroads.'

You stared ahead, dazed. Roads converged from four directions. The pedestrian light turned green, and people hurried across. Where were they going?

Where were you going?

'Return to New York and pack up. Start a new life.'

'Why should I believe you?' you asked stubbornly. 'Maybe Bob will come back. He's not dead yet.'

'You don't have to believe me. By all means, wait for Bob if you want. But you need to start a new life.' The woman continued, this time more firmly: 'You can't keep those shoes forever.'

Your body went stiff. You weren't wearing your red shoes. How did this woman know? Who was she?

Something in you urged you to take flight, and you sprinted away from the detective. But when you turned a corner, there she was again with her black umbrella. You covered your mouth to keep yourself from screaming. The woman's face was pale, her lips too scarlet.

'The shoes used to be mine.'

Your throat felt parched as you asked: 'Who are you?'

'Call me Hecate.'

Shock set in, and her name echoed in your ears like a mantra. She was the witch that Devil referred to. You now realised that he had lied. Not only was this woman not dead, she was quite likely deathless.

'Those shoes come with a curse. You'll never stop travelling.'

You retreated a step.

'You're telling me to go back to Indonesia?'

'I didn't say that.'

You looked at the passing cars. You felt tired, but you didn't want to stop. Maybe you were addicted to adventure. You had to move on.

'Then where?'

You turned towards Hecate, but she had disappeared.

You bought a plane ticket to New York and returned to Bob's apartment. You still didn't know where you'd go next. Maybe Bob was dead, but maybe it was Hecate who was wrong. Someday Bob could be found. But when would that time come? You refused to wait in this apartment, depending on Bob's family, whose attitude towards you was growing colder by the day. You had to start a new life, whether Bob stayed in your thoughts or not. Maybe you should go back to Indonesia and wait for Bob there until you couldn't take it any longer, and then give up. But was going home the best choice? *Were* there any choices? You decided to follow your intuition: pack first, then buy a ticket, rather than vice versa. Who knew, you might change your mind.

You hoped to find some hint for guidance as you packed your things. There wasn't much, no more than what fit into a large suitcase. As you sat cross-legged in front of your bag, you sensed a pair of eyes watching you.

That woman. She was standing at the door to your bedroom in her red blazer and lipstick, just as when you'd first met in Los Angeles. You heaved a sigh.

'Could you please not surprise me like that? Some of us can die young, you know!'

You didn't ask how she got in. After the appearance of 'Richard' that time, you realised that spirits had their own skeleton keys for Bob's apartment. She looked sincere in her apology.

'Is there anything I can do to help you out?'

Hecate wasn't alone; in her right hand she carried a dog. It now dawned on you where you'd seen her. She was the woman who found your missing shoe. That woman, as you recalled, had also been holding a dog.

'You're everywhere, aren't you?'

'I'm more reliable than that demon boyfriend of yours.'

She'd always known that you had her shoes, but she'd let it go. You couldn't arrive at a crossroads until you began to travel.

'You didn't have a dog in LA.'

'I left it at a pet hotel.'

You leaned in for a better look at her dog. A chihuahua. Its fur was sleek and glossy. 'What's its name?'

'Cordelia. Cordelia, Regan and Goneril.'

'Cordelia – what?'

'Cordelia and her sisters, Regan and Goneril. She's a three-in-one. A purebred.' She smiled proudly.

Hecate released her dog so she could hop down onto the carpet. You shrieked. Cordelia scampered around your feet. There was nothing wrong with that – except for the small matter of her three heads. As Cordelia tugged at your trousers, Regan and Goneril were busy yapping. They might have been keen to nip at your legs too, but three heads on a single body didn't allow much leeway for any complicated manoeuvres.

Your phone rang and Hecate commanded her pooch to let you go so you could answer it. Cordelia returned to Hecate's arms obediently.

From the receiver you heard a hoarse female voice. Doña Manuela. A few minutes later you turned to Hecate.

'I have to go back to LA. Those people are family to me.'

'Is something wrong?'

'Soonyi passed away.'

Your eyes felt hot and you looked down.

Hecate approached you and stroked your hair. *Inna lillahi wa inna ilaihi raji'un.* Who'd just quoted the Quran? You, or the witch?

*

After Soonyi's funeral, you and your friends stand in front of a Korean restaurant with umbrellas, waiting for the rain to subside. Andy, Carmencita and Doña Manuela continue chattering non-stop even though you've already talked for hours over galbi and soju. They still miss you, which makes you happy.

'So how do you plan to "start a new life"?' asks Andy.

He raises his hands, making air quotes. They are a habit with Andy because, for him, everything is 'as if'. At the Solidarity Club of Lost Husbands, you all know that starting a new life is a slippery concept; no border separates what comes before and what comes after loss. When will your new life begin? What marks it? A new life entails living with a ghost, and you have to be prepared. Even now Greg is present when Andy spends his nights with black coffee in the editing suite. And Carmencita, despite a sexiness that turns every man's head, continues to terrorise Pablo and his new girlfriend with curse-filled emails and texts. She even plans to upload a photo of her rival onto a website for women who've been cheated on. The site lets users share the other woman's identity along with a warning: watch out, this slut might steal your husband.

Of course, after yet another fight with Andy, Carmencita doesn't follow through with her plan.

'Honey, don't go around fulfilling stereotypes,' Andy says.

'Latina stereotypes, you mean?' Carmencita retorts.

'I mean stereotypes about women who have no self-respect.'

'Bullshit. Racist!'

'Don't blame other women if your husband is a bastard,' Doña Manuela interjects.

Andy and Carmencita fall silent. Her sharp admonition is sufficient to put a stop to their quarrel.

Doña Manuela asks you, 'And while we're on the subject of a new life: why don't you move to LA?'

Her question initially sounds ridiculous, but you start to weigh up new choices. Yes, in Los Angeles you'll be helpless because you can't drive, but maybe it's time for a rebirth. New York, though foreign, has probably now become your comfort zone. Here you'll find a job, learn to drive, even buy a car. In your imagination, there is no Prince Charming to rescue you, no green card. Only your hair blowing in the wind as you sit behind the wheel of a convertible. Your Orient Express.

If you want to start a new life in LA, turn to page 352.

If you feel the prospect of starting from zero in LA is too radical, maybe you should go back to New York and take more time to think things over. Turn to page 356.

Noel comes to see you almost two weeks after your farewell in the hotel lobby. Again, he wears a V-neck and tight jeans, but this time he's dressed entirely in black, as if to show respect for your missing husband. You are each wearing sunglasses, but as soon as he sees you, he takes his off and hugs you tightly.

'Thank you, Noel.'

Your gratitude is heartfelt. You've never really been friends as such, except on the road, but he's driven down from San Francisco to Los Angeles specifically to see you. He squeezes your hand.

'Sorry I couldn't come sooner.'

You go to an IHOP located not far from your hotel. You're bored with it, because you keep going there when you don't have other restaurant ideas, but you're too tired to come up with an alternative. You take your seat and remove your sunglasses.

'You look shattered!' Noel exclaims.

Maybe he thinks you've been crying all night, but you're already past that stage. Now you're dealing with long, sleepless nights filled with questions. What if Bob really isn't found? What will you do with your life? Does your adventure end here?

'Any more word from the police?'

'No.'

Noel only needs the latest updates because he's been following what's been happening from the start. You've spent hours on the phone telling him how you contacted the airport and Bob's family before finally going to the police. Noel also knows you're staying on at your hotel, waiting for news.

You've communicated with Bob's family several times, but you sense that their attitude is changing. Bob's mother and Angela have known for days that Bob didn't give you the flight number or departure time and that you didn't ask. At first they thought you were irresponsible towards your marriage. But now they seem to harbour suspicions that you lie behind Bob's disappearance somehow.

A few days after you file your missing person report, a couple of police officers come to you. They poke around your hotel room and ask several questions. What did you and Bob talk about in your last Skype conversation? Who did you meet in San Francisco? Is your marriage all right? It dawns on you that you've become a suspect, perhaps as a result of pressure from Bob's family.

'What – do they think you hired a hit man or something?' Noel shakes his head. 'This isn't a film noir.'

'I have no idea. Maybe they think Bob was kidnapped, or that he ran away. And I could be involved, right?'

'So? What did they find?'

'Nothing. They only questioned me for a while and left. But –' You pause. 'The detective finally contacted me. I don't know whether to believe her or not.'

'Detective?'

'Yes, a woman in a red jacket at the police station.'

'Hey, you haven't told me about this yet,' Noel says.

'I met a detective at the police station. Two days ago, she approached me in the hotel lobby. It was really weird – she was wearing a red blazer and a fascinator. Red lipstick. She seemed totally out of place, from a different era or something. She looked at me and said, "Mrs Allen?" Nobody's called me that even after I married Bob. And who says "ma'am" these days?'

'Hmm …' Noel appears to be digesting your story. 'Then what did she say?'

'That they're still investigating my husband's case. But, she said …' You swallow hard. 'She said I had to prepare for the worst.'

'Why?'

'Apparently Bob didn't go to Frankfurt for a conference. He went to Amsterdam. The detective didn't want to explain, but Bob might be involved with some crooked operation.'

'Oh, Jesus! What? A drug cartel? Human traffickers?'

You shake your head and grow dizzy. You realise that you never really knew Bob, but now, being so completely in the dark leaves you fragile.

'That detective sounds really strange,' Noel mutters. 'Fascinator, red lipstick … Are you sure she's a real detective?'

'What, a detective can't be beautiful?'

'That's not what I mean. Can you really trust her?'

You look down. Trustworthy? You're not sure. You know at least one thing, though. Bob may show up again someday, but until that vague time, you have to continue your life alone.

Noel is supposed to meet up with a potential new boyfriend in Los Angeles, but he decides to keep you company the whole evening. After your meal at IHOP he takes you for a ride in his car. When midnight comes, he says farewell at the hotel lobby entrance.

'What will you do?' he asks finally.

'Go back to New York, maybe.'

You fall silent. You're not sure about your choice. You have neither a job nor anyone to return to there. Maybe you'll keep in touch with Bob's family, but your relationship won't be as it was. They'll probably continue to blame you for his disappearance.

'I honestly don't know. My visa has expired.'

'But I thought you had a green card. Your husband –'

'It's a long story,' you say. 'We had a wedding ceremony in a mosque but didn't take care of the official paperwork.'

'Oh, Jesus. Another hassle.'

You grow quiet again, lost in thought.

'Why not stay here?' Noel asks. 'I can keep visiting you.'
'But what would I do?'
'Look for work, wait for news from Bob.'

You're taken aback at Noel's suggestion. There's a part of the conversation between yourself and the woman in the red jacket that you hadn't related. She said that you could wait, but that you needed to begin a new life. You asked if there really was no hope. She didn't answer, but you keep pondering her words. You have to start over, whether Bob is in your head or not. Even if you return to New York, you can't go back to his apartment and depend on a relationship with his family that might become increasingly bitter. If you stay in Los Angeles, you'll be trapped because you don't have a car and can't drive. But just maybe, a new adventure will start here, and someday you'll drive a convertible as your hair flutters in the wind. The image amuses you and you muster a small smile.

'Noel,' you finally say, 'I have to turn a new page, and I can't take my shoes. I want you to keep them.'
'Those beautiful red shoes? But those shoes are too good –'
'Noel,' you cut him off. 'Don't argue. I can't keep them.'

The shoes have lost their power. If you want them to create another miracle, you'll have to turn to Devil, and at times like these, you're sure he'll just make trouble. You hope that he isn't behind Bob's disappearance. But who knows. Isn't he behind all the world's chaos?

After protesting for a while (the shoes are too good, you're too kind, etc.), Noel finally accepts them. He promises to take good care of them for you. What will your life be like now?

If you want to go back to New York, turn to page 392.

If you are determined to follow Noel's suggestion to start a new life in Los Angeles, turn to page 352.

You're now renting a room in a two-storey house in Haarlem, owned by a woman in her seventies named Victoria who lives alone. Her husband has passed away and her children lead their own lives. She has a bedroom on the ground floor, and you're staying on the first in her son's old room. Every now and then she invites you to eat dinner with her, but the thought of bothering her makes you shy. More frequently, you explore on your own or spend time on your laptop in your room. Your sister has responded to your email.

> *Dik,*
>
> *Alhamdulillah. I'm thrilled to get a reply from you. How come such a short note, though? Are you very busy?*
>
> *I'm attaching the latest photo of Nazwa and Raihan. They're posing with this funny grandfather statue. I forget his name. We just bought it at the florist's. He's a cartoon character, isn't he?*
>
> *How are your studies going? You're on vacation in the Netherlands now, right? Don't forget to send pictures of tulips.*

You open the attached photo. The computer screen displays your niece and nephew wearing big grins, like child TV stars. They flank a dwarf statue with a surly expression, a replica of one of the Snow White dwarves you watched as a kid at your friend's house. His name is Grumpy, and grumpy he is. His face radiates clear displeasure. Maybe he doesn't like standing guard over your sister's house.

Yes, I knew you'd like the piece by Kiai Hasan. It's good as an introduction for you to his writing. I like some of his material, but not all of it. A lot of his ideas bewilder the Muslim community. In another piece he states that the obligation to veil has to be understood in the context of early Arab society. What's he trying to say? That the hijab isn't mandatory? Scholars who question what's obvious confuse me.

Sighing, you close the email window and go to the Google home page to look for celebrity gossip. Sometimes you have the illusion that the wall separating you and your sister has eroded slightly. Maybe your sister entertains the very same delusion. How sweet – siblings who cling to hope.

A chime, the opening notes of 'Für Elise', startles you. You know that it's Victoria's doorbell and that she's out of the house. Sluggishly, you rise from the bed and go downstairs to see who has arrived. Through the peephole you spy someone in a yellow-and-black uniform. Maybe Victoria is expecting a package. You open the door.

'Hello.'

You gasp at the man in front of you. Before you even realise what's happened, he's already barged in. He closes the house door tightly and removes his yellow hat.

Devil.

Without the hat, you can see that his eyes are ablaze, growing wider and wider. You feel like you're being scorched. His voice is hoarse, angry. 'You can't give away the shoes. Only I get to determine who's next in line.'

'Maria,' you murmur. Suddenly you worry about her. 'Is Maria OK?'

'She's fine. You're the one who's in trouble.'

Devil's voice signals danger. You step back, as the crimson fire in his eyes fades a little. He takes a deep breath. 'Your friend doesn't need some social justice warrior to save her.'

'She deserves a more appropriate job.'

'Yes, but did she ask to be rescued?'

To your surprise, Demon Lover grabs your hand and kisses it slowly.

'I'm sorry, darling. I don't want to punish you. But I already told you, the shoes came with a curse.'

His soft voice leaves you dizzy and off balance, and his face blurs in your vision. You can't tell whether he's staring wryly at you or smiling viciously. Your head hurts so much. Your body grows shaky, just like when you first put on the red shoes.

Your eyes open slowly. You're staring at a low ceiling; from it hangs a neon light that glows pink. Your hands grope the surface your body is lying upon. A bed. Whose home is this?

You rise, staggering a little as you take in your surroundings. You're in a small room containing only a bed, a window covered with pink curtains, and a mirror. The place is strange, like a doll's house. Your head still feels heavy, but you struggle towards the mirror. You see your face reflected there, ghastly pale. You're dressed in pink lace lingerie. In a panic, you return to the bed and sit for a moment, trying to understand what has happened. You walk to the window and draw the curtain back slightly. Out there: streets. A crowd.

You're in a display window.

You dash towards the door, the only exit. It's locked. You bang on it, terror-stricken, but no one answers.

Have you exchanged places with Maria?

This is surely Devil's doing. You'll never forgive him.

You think hard, seeking a way to escape. Where's your coat? You might freeze to death if you dash out into the cold air dressed like this. Even if you succeed in breaking out, someone may be keeping watch.

Then comes a knock at the door. You're aghast. How can all this be happening? You wait a moment, hoping you've misheard, but the knocking persists. Fuck! You stiffen. There's nowhere to flee. The knocking grows more and more insistent, and you begin to pray.

Continue on to page 374.

You enjoy the new room you rent in Haarlem from a woman in her seventies named Victoria. Her house is medium-sized, consisting of two floors; all the walls are papered in a yellow sunflower motif. Your bedroom is on the first floor, Victoria's is on the ground. Before you came, she lived alone. Her husband has passed away, and her children are busy with their own families. When you tell her that you're from Indonesia, she exclaims, 'Ah, the Indies!'

'Indonesia.'

'All the same, *toch*? The former Dutch East Indies.'

'Yes, but –'

'Are you from Java?'

You may as well be back in the colonial era. You nod awkwardly at the word 'Java'. Jakarta is on Java, of course, but you've never identified as Javanese.

Victoria is an eccentric woman with a striking sense of fashion. She always wears brightly coloured overalls with floral prints – quite similar to her wallpaper – along with round hats bedecked with flowers or ribbons, flesh-coloured tights, and Mary Jane shoes, like a schoolgirl. Her appearance is exaggeratedly young and cheerful, and is likewise more suited for warm weather. She takes a coat when she leaves the house, but you don't understand why she insists on cotton clothes in winter. It's as if she's stepped out of the tropics.

The Dutch East Indies.

You are puzzled about Victoria's background. She doesn't look Dutch. You're not sure what colour her hair used to be, since it's now all white. But clearly her skin has a brownish tone, and she wouldn't be regarded as Caucasian. Her eyes have a vague slant. You hasten to correct yourself: not all Dutch citizens are white. Don't be racist.

She always speaks English with you, though she says some words in Dutch that she finds hard to translate. But you understand *brandweer*, *bioscoop*, *parkeer*. Those words made it into Indonesian, as did *tante* and *oom*, aunt and uncle. She asks you to call her Tante Victoria, even though as far as you're concerned she's closer to a grandmother. Oma would feel more appropriate.

'*Maytje*, come eat at home tonight, OK? I'll make steak.'

'Yes, Tante Victoria.'

She calls you *maytje* – 'lassie', as she pleases. Sometimes she uses similar terms, such as *lintje*, *tientje* or *dietje*, all those cute diminutives ending in '-tje' that make you feel as though you're being treated like a child. You let it go because you're not inclined to argue with old ladies.

Victoria cooks for you so frequently that you begin to feel awkward. But maybe she needs a friend, someone willing to listen to her stories about her late husband. A handsome man who wore a neat suit everywhere, and who people said always looked elegant, Victoria recalls. But of course, people back then dressed more nicely than the youth of today.

Another time she tells you about her granddaughter, who seems to be your age. She lives in New York.

'My granddaughter is writing a novel. Are you like her, a descendant of Scheherazade?'

'Scheherazade?'

'Yes, like in *One Thousand and One Nights*. A woman who is a spinner of tales.'

'I don't know,' you say, a little confused. 'But in my travels, I encounter a lot of stories.'

'I hope they're happy stories! My granddaughter likes to write weird stories. Horror stories. Uh, no. Adventure stories. Well, something like that.'

'Wow, cool,' you say, feigning enthusiasm.

'Ah, ever since she was little she's loved to daydream,' Victoria chuckles. 'She used to want to become a pilot and collected toy planes. She idolised Amelia Earhart.'

The name isn't familiar to you, so Victoria explains: Amelia Earhart was a famous aviator, the first woman to fly across the Atlantic. In 1937 she set off on a great adventure. The plane was never found.

But beyond your dinner-table encounters, you rarely see Victoria at home. Maybe she's an elderly socialite, always going out, or she's so quiet when she's in her room that you don't know whether she's home or not. Her presence often startles you. Once, as you're about to open the door and go for a walk, she calls you from the living room. You'd thought she wasn't home, but it turns out that she's been knitting in her rocking chair.

'Maytje!'

'Yes, Tante.'

You turn back from the door and approach like an obedient child.

'Going out?'

You say you're planning to wander around Amsterdam for the day, but she doesn't seem to hear your response. She lowers her glasses a little and stares straight at your feet. She asks you to come closer.

'Your shoes are lovely.'

'Yes, I bought them at –'

'I've been looking for shoes like that for a long time.'

You're just about to lie but she cuts you off, indifferent to your words, her eyes fixed on your red shoes.

'May I try them on?'

You're surprised. An odd request, but why not? Victoria always wears outfits and footwear more suitable for young women, so it's not such a shock that she's attracted to your red shoes. Despite some hesitation, you nod. Victoria stares intently, as if enchanted by the shoes. Her eyes look slightly wild.

Just as you're about to take them off, she suddenly shakes her head and signals for you to stop.

'No, no need,' she says. 'Go. Be careful, maytje.' She smiles sweetly, sounding a little nervous.

The rocking chair marks Victoria's presence at home. In the morning, as you make your way down the stairs to the kitchen for breakfast, you can already hear her humming. '*Als de orchideen bloeien, hmm hmm hmm* ... Maytje, come. Do you want bread with *hagelslag*?' She rises from her rocking chair and goes to the dining table. She spreads Blueband butter on the bread, then adds chocolate sprinkles. *Hagelslag.* Your usual breakfast in Indonesia.

Sometimes Victoria sits in the rocking chair puffing a cigarette. Does her doctor allow it? you wonder. She opens the window wide, letting smoke out as cold air rushes in. You shake your head. Granny has a seriously rock 'n' roll lifestyle.

Outside it is zero Celsius, and you're concerned about her health. What if she were to suddenly drop dead?

The rocking chair is as quirky as its owner. Sometimes it swings on its own when Victoria isn't there. Maybe Victoria has forgotten to close the window, and it's swaying in a furtive breeze.

One night, as you're getting ready for bed, you hear strains of music from the ground floor. The rhythms seem familiar. As the music continues, you feel that you recognise each song being played and open the door.

Nina Bobo, oh Nina Bobo
Kalau tidak bobo digigit nyamuk

A children's song. But the astonishing thing is that it's 'Nina Bobo', in Indonesian. Why is Victoria listening to it? Curious, you go downstairs.

You see an LP spinning on a turntable in the living room. Beside it is a record sleeve, showing a Dutchwoman in a *kebaya*. You read the singer's name and the album title: Wieteke van Dort, *Weerzien met Indië*. There is a list of songs in Indonesian, or a mix of Dutch and Indonesian: 'Tlaga Biroe', 'Hallo Bandoeng', 'Geef Mij Maar Nasi Goreng'.

Does Victoria have a connection with the land she calls the Indies? You feel a small sense of excitement and turn towards the chair by the window, rocking away. Maybe Victoria is listening to music. Maybe she fell asleep during the 'Nina Bobo' lullaby. You want to ask about the Wieteke van Dort album, so you approach slowly.

The chair is empty.

Where's Victoria?

'Tante?'

No answer. Nobody is there. The voice of Wieteke van Dort is so sweet, and the living room is as quiet as a cemetery. You tremble.

On Sundays, Victoria attends church. She invites you once, but you decline on the grounds that you're Muslim. (You don't say that you never go to mosque.) She waves dismissively, 'Do you really think I'm Christian?'

'You're not?' You're surprised.

She chuckles.

'The main thing is, I believe in God,' she says. 'You too – believe, child. Believe in God so that you don't go wandering when you die.'

'What guarantee is there?'

'Eh, guarantee?' She seems to mull over the question deeply as she adjusts her glasses. 'There isn't. But why haggle with God like a pawnbroker? In any case, the cathedral is very beautiful, built in the sixteenth century.'

In the end, you agree to go with her on a Wednesday afternoon, when there are no services. Even so, the cathedral still receives many visitors from near and far.

You put on your red shoes and join her. Those who have come to admire the building's beauty turn their eyes towards your feet and whisper. You feel a pang of guilt about showing up to a church in your red shoes.

You take a seat in a pew and stare at the organ pipes, which extend all the way to the ceiling. Next to you, Victoria whispers, 'Do you know where the Shoemaker is buried?'

You shake your head.

'Should I?'

Without answering, she glances at your feet. Again you see that look, the wild-eyed look that appeared when she wanted to try on your shoes. She smiles broadly, revealing a row of half-rotten teeth.

'Let's go.'

Victoria gets up, and you follow her obediently. Her steps are so nimble that she almost seems to fly. She leads you down a corridor, past a small chapel on the left and a row of pillars on the right. Your red shoes tread across a floor of black flagstone, upon which several names are engraved.

'Whose names are these?'

'Those buried here. You're stepping on their graves.'

You pause. The names are accompanied by dates and words you don't understand, maybe prayers, maybe something else. You feel very uneasy. Your parents always reminded you not to step over graves. Respect the dead, they said. If ghosts are disturbed, they might haunt you and make you sick.

You step hesitantly, offering respectful greetings as you go: *assalamualaikum*.

You tread more carefully, but the clip-clop of your shoes can be heard. No one is there but you and Victoria, but you don't hear her footfalls. She continues on until you arrive at a section of floor bearing the image of a pair of shoes. Step on the shoes, Victoria says. You obey. Victoria laughs.

'He's buried here, right beneath you. The Shoemaker, the one who made your red shoes.'

You stare at your feet.

Victoria moves closer. Her voice hoarse, she tells you a secret tale.

Continue on to page 378.

You decide to begin a new life in Los Angeles. You find a cheap apartment and start searching job listings. Noel visits you regularly for the first two months, but he's busy with his own life. As time goes on, he stops coming. You don't complain. Noel has done an admirable job of carrying out his role in your story. On a journey, nothing lasts forever.

Meanwhile, you develop a job-hunting strategy. You seek out an Indonesian community mosque and become friendly with those who attend. Your tactics bear fruit. One worshipper manages a restaurant, and she offers you work. As soon as you've secured a job, you stop going to mosque. Maybe this explains your bad luck: you treat a house of God as an employment agency. Pretty trashy.

One day, after a long time with no news from Noel, a package arrives in the mail from overseas with his name as the sender. You open it and discover a funny yellow toy car and a note.

Hey sis,

Sorry for not making it back to LA. A lot has been going on lately, and one day, I just felt really sick of my life. I didn't want to be where I was. So I left.

And now, my life has become a series of miracles.

A letter can't do justice to all my stories. Come visit me someday. I'll tell you everything. For now, though, let me just say thanks for your beautiful shoes. My own gift might not be fancy, but I hope it'll always remind you not to get discouraged about driving. I'm enjoying

*the sunshine on Bondi Beach these days, and I picture
you driving around like a woman set free.*
   Big hugs,
   Noel

You look at the return address. New South Wales, Australia. Did the red shoes take him there?

Life goes on for you in Los Angeles, devoid of miracles. Before you even realise it, two years have passed. Maybe someday a marvel will bring Bob back. You're still waiting for him, but you're also ready to accept that he's dead, buried on land or in a watery grave, or vanished without a trace.

Of course, life isn't completely dull. In the end, you take driving lessons and buy a used car. Every time you feel ready to give up, you cast a glance at the yellow toy Noel gave you. You remember his own history of driving, the story he told you on the journey from San Francisco to Los Angeles and the little old lady whose car had a sticker that read *Good girls go to heaven, bad girls go everywhere.* Even though you still get nervous driving, at least you now know how. A stunning achievement – especially considering that you haven't achieved anything meaningful in your life.

Does your story end here?

Without the red shoes, maybe there are no longer any adventures ahead. But you remain more than capable of creating your own trouble.

If you're happy living in Los Angeles, without Bob, and finally able to drive, end your adventure here. Write the word FINIS below. Stay where you are in America, and don't move. Change doesn't always bring happiness. Seriously.

If you want a final adventure that might only create a spectacular mess, turn to page 405.

After you decide to start a new life in Los Angeles, you manage to find a cheap apartment and start looking at job vacancies. Some members of the Solidarity Club of Lost Husbands visit you regularly for the first two months, but over time your friends stop coming to see you. Everyone is busy with their own lives. You don't complain. They've carried out their roles well in your story. On a journey, nothing lasts forever.

Meanwhile, you develop a job-hunting strategy. You seek out an Indonesian community mosque and become friendly with those who attend. Your tactics bear fruit. One worshipper manages a restaurant, and she offers you work. As soon as you've secured a job, you stop going to mosque. Maybe this explains your bad luck: you treat a house of God as an employment agency. Pretty trashy.

Life goes on for you in Los Angeles, devoid of miracles. Before you even realise it, two years have passed. Maybe someday a marvel will bring Bob back. You're still waiting for him, but you're also ready to accept that he's dead, buried on land or in a watery grave, or vanished without a trace.

Of course, life isn't completely dull. In the end, you take driving lessons and buy a used car. Even though you still get nervous driving, at least you now know how. A stunning achievement – especially considering that you haven't achieved anything meaningful in your life.

Does your story end here?

Without the red shoes, maybe there are no longer any adventures ahead. But you remain more than capable of creating your own trouble.

*

If you're happy living in Los Angeles, without Bob, and finally able to drive, end your adventure here. Write the word FINIS below. Stay where you are in America, and don't move. Change doesn't always bring happiness. Seriously.

If you want a final adventure that might only create a spectacular mess, turn to page 405.

You say goodbye to the Solidarity Club of Lost Husbands before returning to New York. You know, even though you exchange promises ('Stop by next time you're in LA!' 'I'll be sure to visit!'), that it's a final farewell.

It's also the end for the red shoes.

Late one sunny afternoon you will walk in your shoes for the last time in New York. After putting on make-up and your favourite dress, you head to your favourite station, Grand Central. The rush-hour frenzy of workday's end allows you to melt in among the crowds travelling beyond New York City, to Connecticut or elsewhere. Upon exiting the station, you walk towards Bryant Park. Off your shoulder hangs a faux-leather bag roomy enough for a pair of short boots. You'll walk until you're tired, take off your red shoes and replace them with the boots. You don't know yet what you're going to do with the shoes. There's a good chance you'll just leave them in Bob's apartment for someone else to find one day.

'Those shoes are perfect for dancing!'

You turn. An old woman knitting on a park bench waves to you. She may be seventy, or eighty, but she looks vivacious. She wears a long, light yellow jacket and a matching beret adorned with a sunflower. Her legs are wrapped in cream-coloured tights and red shoes with straps, like a schoolgirl.

You nod, say thank you, then continue walking. But praise alone doesn't satisfy the woman. She asks where you got the shoes, and you approach her out of politeness. A gift from a friend, you say, which is true enough.

'Ah, a friend.' She lowers her glasses a little and studies your shoes. 'There's a shoemaker where I come from who makes red shoes.'

Granny turns out to be from the Netherlands. She's on holiday in New York visiting her granddaughter.

'My name is Victoria,' she says without being asked. 'Just call me Tante Victoria.'

'Tante … ?'

She stretches her hand towards you. She seems a bit impatient.

'In Dutch *tante* means aunt.'

You know that. You call all your parents' friends Tante and Oom, although of course you don't remember that those words are a leftover from the colonial era.

Granny (who prefers to be called Tante) wants to chat. A few details won't hurt you. You ask if her own shoes are from this Dutch shoemaker. She shakes her head and replies, 'The Shoemaker is dead. He's buried in a church not far from my house.'

Oh. You nod. Buried, in a church. The conversation's turn leaves you feeling a little ill at ease.

'My granddaughter might be the same age as you. She's writing a novel,' she says. 'Are you like her, a descendant of Scheherazade?'

'Scheherazade?'

'Yes, like in *One Thousand and One Nights*. A woman who is a spinner of tales.'

'I don't know,' you say, a little confused. 'But in my travels, I encounter a lot of stories.'

"I hope they're happy stories! My granddaughter likes to write weird stories. Horror stories. Uh, no. Adventure stories. Well, something like that. Ah, I don't know. The two are quite similar, right?'

She laughs. You're not sure why, but you don't see anything funny in what she says. The blurring of the boundary between horror and adventure frightens you slightly.

'Yes, that kid really likes to daydream,' she says. 'What's your favourite toy?'

'T-toy?'

'Yes, toy!'

'Um … trains.'

'My granddaughter likes airplanes. She idolised Amelia Earhart.'

Victoria then tells you a little about Amelia Earhart, a famous aviator in the early twentieth century, the first woman to fly across the Atlantic. One day, she decided to embark upon a very ambitious journey. The plane went missing.

'Missing?'

'Never found, to this day.'

You're taken aback. Suddenly your husband flashes before you, along with Doña Manuela and the Solidarity Club of Lost Husbands.

'My granddaughter has lived in New York for years,' continues Victoria. She shakes her head. 'Ah, young women nowadays. They always want to go far, just like Amelia Earhart.'

'Don't you like to travel, Tante?'

'I'm old,' she says, but then her expression changes. 'Hmm, yesterday, though, I took the train from Grand Central towards Bronxville. You know, the city is very beautiful …'

She natters at length about leaving the city on her own and upsetting her granddaughter. Although sorry to have worried her, she appears proud of her solo adventure in a foreign city. Now it's your turn to shake your head. Seems like grandma and granddaughter aren't so different.

It's getting dark. You bid Victoria goodbye, having already chatted with her too long. She puts her knitting into a bag and you pause, a little reluctant to leave her alone as night falls. She gestures for you to go. No need to wait for me, she says. My granddaughter will come. You nod and walk towards Bryant Park Station. Once you descend the subway steps, you've reached a decision. You will return to Indonesia – without your red shoes.

In the midst of the crowd waiting for the F train, you hear a familiar voice.

'I already warned you. You'll regret it.'

A man in a suit and a black hat stands behind you. Devil.

'Where are my red shoes?'

'They don't belong to you.'

'Return the shoes, and your story will end here.'

You stare straight at the Devil and slowly let go of your red shoes. He looks pleased at your obedience.

No. This isn't how you want your story to end. Maybe you really do have to part with your shoes, but you don't want Devil to be the cause. You have two choices: throw the shoes onto the tracks and witness their destruction, or run off with them – who knows where.

If you want to throw the red shoes onto the tracks, turn to the next page.

If you want to run off with the shoes, turn to page 372.

You hold your red shoes in front of Devil, dangling them like you're luring him with candy. But before he can reach them, you hurl them with all the strength you can muster into the middle of the train tracks.

'All yours.'

The F train is pulling into the station, and the people around you turn. Some cry out. A woman covers her mouth in shock, as if finding it incomprehensible that someone would throw away such good shoes. You're deliberately creating a public scene, and Devil can't budge. His red eyes narrow. 'You're not the one who gets to say when my story ends,' you hiss.

Without having the chance to pull your boots from the bag, you turn your back on Devil and flee. You fight through the crowd, colliding with whoever blocks your path, and race up the stairs towards street level. Your flight feels endless, but you run and run until you're certain that Devil is no longer following you. Gasping, you finally stop and kneel in front of a small supermarket. The man behind the cash register is busy texting. He looks up, but then returns to his phone. Maybe he's witnessed too many chase scenes.

Who knows what the shoes' fate was. Maybe Devil tried to retrieve them, but he'd have needed to use powers that would have immediately attracted people's attention. It's also entirely possible that the F train was too fast, even for Devil, and now the shoes lie in a mangled heap.

There are no adventures. There are no gifts.

After throwing your shoes onto the train tracks, you decide to bestow a gift upon yourself. You buy a one-way ticket to Indonesia, dated February 1, 2009, your birthday. A small travel agency in Queens manages to find you a cut-price ticket from New York to Jakarta, using digital rather than demonic devices.

On the night of your departure, you take a moment to pray for Bob: May you be well, Bob, wherever you are. If fate is kind, we will meet again.

You weigh up whether to go to the airport by subway or taxi. The taxi will take you there faster, with far fewer hassles, but will set you back some fifty or sixty dollars. Cost, time and stress aside, taxi and subway hold different meanings for you. A taxi means reliving the first day of your adventure: finding yourself hurrying somewhere in a stuffy vehicle, unsure how you had arrived there. Your journey will be a ritual return to square one, before you leave everything behind. But taking the subway will repeat a different ritual one last time. New York's trains have been your Orient Express. Trains that are always late on weekends, packed and dirty, with b-boys doing acrobatics on the poles, oblivious men killing time by manspreading, the stench of armpits in summer – every spicy sweet feeling of the New York subway has brought you marvels and misadventures; the train has sanctified you as a citizen.

If you go to JFK by taxi, turn to the next page.

If you go to JFK by train, turn to page 371.

John F. Kennedy Airport, New York, February 1, 2009

You decide to go to JFK by taxi. There turns out to be nothing remarkable or romantic about the experience: you're stuck in a traffic jam, trapped making small talk with a garrulous driver. Going to Indonesia? Are you Muslim? Assalamualaikum, sister. I come from Pakistan. I heard that Indonesia has more Muslims than any other country in the world. Such conversations happen frequently enough to bore you. But you have to admit that membership in the international *ummah* has its perks. You've received a fifty-cent discount off your roadside coffee for responding to *assalamualaikum* with *waalaikumsalam*.

After checking in your bags and going through security, you walk to the waiting area for your flight. Finally, you can relax a while and read. Next to you, a woman is scribbling away in a notebook with her left hand. You can't read her words, but the way her script tilts to the right amuses you. She puts down her pen for a moment and removes a packet of crisps from her bag. Continuing to focus her attention on her notebook, she pops a handful into her mouth. She eats with her left hand. You remember your recitation teacher's words: eating and drinking with your left hand is satanic. Maybe a lot of demons roam this city.

Singing in a staccato rhythm makes those around you turn. *Well, show me the way to the next whiskey bar*. A man in his fifties smiles broadly at Jim Morrison's voice. It appears to be the left-handed woman's ringtone. With a sheepish expression, she presses a button on her phone to answer the call and walks to a corner to chat. Well, that's careless. She abandons her bag beside you, an open invitation to theft.

The airline clerk announces a name over a loudspeaker. The woman returns to her seat and takes her bag, coat and all the things she had left so cavalierly. Half running, she goes to the flight desk. You heave a listless sigh and return to your reading.

Fifteen minutes later, your plane is ready for boarding. As you stand up, you spot a notebook lying on the floor. It's not yours. You pick it up and look for the woman who was just sitting next to you, but she's nowhere to be found. The journal has no name on it and still has many blank pages. You put the notebook in your bag. Maybe you'll run into the owner again, but if it isn't very important to her, maybe you can use it for shopping lists.

Now in the plane's cabin, you take your allocated aisle seat; next to you sit a man and woman, a couple, it seems. You fiddle with the remote control and settle on a movie to watch.

After six hours in the air, you tire of watching. Your eyes close, but you're not able to sleep. You open the notebook that you found. The first two pages are blank. On the third, you see scrawled:

Berlin/NY
NYC > SF/LA
LA > LA/CGK

Berlin. New York City. San Francisco. Los Angeles. And CGK, Soekarno Hatta Airport, Jakarta. Is this a travel route? Maybe she's visiting these cities. How funny. You feel the route is for you.

On the next page you read:

Insert a toy piano and mirror. Visiting a haunted house?

You're startled: the sentences are in Indonesian, and they're written as if only the journal's owner would understand what they mean. Insert a toy piano and mirror where? A shopping list, maybe. But visiting a haunted house? What does that mean? You concoct a scenario. She went somewhere and shopped for a toy piano and a mirror, and after that went on an excursion to visit a house of ghosts. You smile. Maybe the woman is a tourist, just like you, even though you prefer to call yourself a wanderer now.

You turn to the next page and see:

Garden gnomes and spices.

This isn't funny. Why does she write garden gnomes here, and why does she link them to spices? No one should link the two but you. You turn to another page that contains the names of cities. NYC, SF, LA. Reading the notebook is like looking at a mirror reflecting your own image. You lean towards the passengers beside you and find them sound asleep. Somehow, though, you have to read it. Perhaps you feel a little frightened.

You turn to the next page. From that point she's written at sufficient length to fill up the next three pages. The first words that you see are at the top:

Visiting a Haunted House

You've never visited a haunted house. You sigh, mildly relieved. This is someone else's journal, someone else's life. It has nothing to do with you.

You return to the long entry and begin to read.

Continue on to the next page.

Visiting a Haunted House

This isn't your usual ghost story, you know. It's a completely ordinary tale, nothing special. My grandmother died a natural death, as most grandmothers do, four days after I turned twenty-nine. I chose not to go to her funeral, to witness the women in headscarves chanting prayers and men in *peci* heaping soil on her body, far away down yonder. I, beloved granddaughter that I was, hoped she would forgive me for not shelling out fifteen hundred dollars to see her wrapped in a shroud. There's no point in running after the dead.

I received the news of her passing in New York. I was hurrying towards West 4th Street Station when I got a text from my dad. Clutching the phone, I stopped and turned to look at a small playground on my left. A bunch of guys were playing basketball, surrounded by spectators, and a couple of pedestrians also looked on, puffing cigarettes. The game seemed to unfold in slow motion. A woman jostled my shoulder, giving a barely audible apology, and scurried down the subway stairs. It seemed for a split second as if I had fallen asleep. I felt I too should run, that way, in the direction the woman had gone, to catch my train. In my diary, I wrote a short note to my grandmother: *I'm sorry, Grandma. I can't see you off on your final train ride because I'm also on a train. My train keeps hurtling onward. It doesn't stop. Not even for your death.*

I've always liked my grandmother's name. Victoria. I don't know how she wound up with it. Maybe her mother was inspired by an incident in 1895 when Queen Wilhelmina of the Netherlands visited Queen Victoria of Great Britain. My generation was surrounded by old women, like my grandmother and great-grandmother, who'd been Dutchified. Maybe they were just trying to be fashionable, and all of us are just natives, *inlanders*, who want to be European. But I liked to say her name over and over: Victoria, Victoria. It reminded me of Victor Frankenstein, scientist extraordinaire. My grandmother wasn't a genius like Victor, capable of creating human life itself, but, having been a teacher, she knew a thing or two.

A year after Victoria's death I visited her home with my dad and an uncle. In we marched: Papa and Uncle and me, girl wanderer. Victoria's children were impatient to sell the house because none of them wanted to look after it. Who in the world would buy it? mused Papa.

Like other deserted houses, my grandmother's home seemed haunted. Someone who claimed to see spirits reported that Victoria's house was inhabited by a *kuntilanak*, a long-haired demon who lived near the well, a woman no longer in our world, but not 'over there' either. Wherever 'there' was. You could be sure she wasn't resting in peace.

Is Grandma wandering, too? I asked.

Hush! Don't talk about your grandmother as if she were a demon.

My grandmother was devout. People say the devout rest at Allah's side.

Good girls go to heaven, bad girls go wandering.

Papa and Uncle didn't want to imagine Victoria as a spirit, even though her name fit all too well with ghost stories. But I felt her gliding through these rooms, watching my every step. The *kuntilanak* had set up house by the well, but my grandmother was not the domestic type. She might have found heaven dull with its repetitive pleasures: limpid streams, a surfeit of honey, olives ripe for picking (Victoria was never a fan of olives). When she was young, she found nothing more thrilling than riding a minibus to market in a floral-print cotton dress, toting a plaited purse and wearing sunglasses. It made perfect sense that in death she'd prefer a wandering state.

A dozen years ago, before Grandma fell ill, the house pulsed with life. I remembered where she slept, and right beside it, Uncle's room, plastered with posters of Duran Duran and Phoebe Cates. (Whatever happened to Phoebe Cates, anyway?) Every Lebaran, Victoria baked *kaastengels* and layer cakes of all sorts, sinfully rich goodies laden with butter, milk and sugar. Nobody in my family baked like that any more. Who has eight hours to spend on a cake?

My father had come up with the idea of renting out Grandma's house, but it hadn't attracted any interest. It was too big and creepy. And now it had fallen into disrepair. 'Uncle really doesn't have the time to do some weeding and clear away the cobwebs?' I asked my father pointedly.

'Why would he want to do that?' Papa replied, but added enviously, 'Your uncle inherited a clove plantation from Grandma.'

Wow, a plantation. Good for him. I often fancy that only God has a garden, especially when I'm dashing around in bus terminals and airports with a backpack. God's garden is eternal; all that is transient ends up in the clutches of corporations or the state.

Victoria's house was slowly being emptied. Only recently had her children realised that most of her belongings had been siphoned off by amateur thieves. The house was begging for its own funeral; even the clock on the wall had stopped ticking.

'Aunt Leila and Cousin Rika have been here,' said Papa. They'd already taken anything of value. Antique lamps. Flower vases. The men in my family got there late. It had always been like that, really, but I'd forgotten. As the years come and go, you get fuzzy about people's habits.

'Now take what you want,' said Uncle.

'I don't want anything.'

'If you don't, somebody else will.'

Fine. At least I understood two things. First, there's no point in storing the possessions of the dead in their home. Second, there's a good chance all their stuff will be stolen, and definitely not by a *kuntilanak*.

I opened my grandmother's wardrobe. I'd lived two years in this house when I was small, and I would enter her closet and inhale the scent of her clothes. They smelled of laundry powder. I liked them better than the clothes that clung to her body, with its own scent, mingling with onion, oven-melted butter, and smoke from clove cigarettes. Gudang Garam was her brand of choice. The scent left me slightly woozy. A few clothes were still stored in her closet, some hanging, some folded, along with a prayer rug with the Ka'bah embroidered on it and a toy piano. The piano was mine. I remembered it, a light blue one, my plaything when I lived there. Papa and Uncle were still chatting. I took a tissue from my purse to wipe my eyes. Damn nostalgia.

The clothes were not the best quality, except for one grey suit that had belonged to my grandfather. The others had been spirited away. Victoria had always wanted her husband to remain a dandy, ever elegant, like when they'd first met and danced and danced. Sometimes I wonder if they didn't feel guilty for living it up in those colonial times, but back then few other dreams were available. Natives knew no ambitions beyond boarding ships, going to parties or travelling to far-off lands. My grandmother had always wanted to go abroad, but she had to make do with riding a minibus to the market in her beautiful dresses. As for my grandfather, he died in the mid-1980s, and I have few memories of him. All I remember is that he'd ferry me around town on a Vespa, light blue like my toy piano, and that he'd give me Sugus sweets, those strawberry-, orange- and grape-flavoured squares. (Do kids these days still chew Sugus sweets?)

Everyone wanted to get away but couldn't, so they set down roots at home, in the soil, in the garden.

'You have to keep what's left.'

I didn't know who was causing the fuss this time, Papa or Uncle. I wasn't paying attention.

I was more attracted to the cloudy mirror and dusty dressing table in my grandmother's room. On the table lay a small book of Islamic scripture, empty perfume bottles and broken tubes of red lipstick. Red, like the mouth of a baby-devouring *kuntilanak*. Who made herself up in front of the mirror now?

Papa's and Uncle's voices rose higher and higher, like touts at a bus terminal, more and more desperate to rescue what they could.

This one. Take this jar. This cup. This painting.

What about the wardrobe? asked Papa.

Or this. An antique chest from Bali. It used to be your great-grandmother's.

The wooden chest was like something that might belong to a sorceress. Dark and beautiful. I considered taking it. Then I would finally have something solid, heavy, venerable, something befitting a Sumatran matriarch like my grandmother, or my great-grandmother, or Aunt Leila.

'But where would I keep it? I don't even have a house.'

'Take it to New York,' said Papa.

'That'd be so expensive! And who knows where I'll move afterwards. Sydney, probably.'

'I can hold on to it until you come back home.'

'Back home? Home where? When?'

Something loomed in the cloudy mirror. I turned away. The question returned, but now it disturbed me: who made herself up in the reflection now?

A *kuntilanak*.

I didn't want to find a *kuntilanak* in the mirror. I wanted to see Grandma's spirit. Victoria. I wanted Victoria, whose body I hadn't seen as it was being covered with earth. I would smash a mirror to hold her in my arms. I stepped in closer to get a good look at the woman's face. My knees trembled and, at that moment, I realised that my grandmother was no wandering spirit, at least not in this house. The wandering spirit was me.

My feet do not tread the ground anywhere. I have no home, I know no love of any soil. But what is a home? The house had long since rotted away, long before the *kuntilanak* arrived; it was disintegrating along with Victoria's maggot-infested corpse. Taking what was left behind would rescue nothing. Papa and Uncle didn't know that. But I knew. For my feet do not tread the ground.

I decided to take a memento: the toy piano, which at least was actually mine. A souvenir from childhood turned airplane stowaway, because there was no grave to bury it in. It wanted to transit with me through Hong Kong.

My flight left three days later. Maybe if I go back in a few years I'll find the house. Victoria won't care because she'll be in New York, Tokyo or Paris with her flowery cotton dress and sunglasses. (Did I mention that she wasn't an olive fan?) Maybe it's Amsterdam that she haunts, since she was fond of speaking Dutch. Then we'll meet, in another dimension, if not in this material, visible world.

Good girls go to heaven, bad girls go wandering. See, Victoria? I really am your beloved grandchild.

Turn to page 399.

You walk to West 4th to take the E train to John F. Kennedy Airport. The carriages are quiet because you're travelling against the morning commuter flow. You transfer at Sutphin Boulevard Station and take the elevator for the AirTrain, which will bring you to the terminal from where your plane departs. There's nothing special about the journey. You try to rouse romantic memories since this will be your last time on the subway, but the trip is so long that you start to feel bored. As soon as you plant your butt down on the AirTrain, you close your eyes. You seem to have dozed off for five or ten minutes, but when you wake, the train door is open. In a panic, you rush to drag your suitcase out the carriage, but as you arrive at the bottom of the escalator, you realise you're at the wrong terminal. You look around, confused. How stupid can you get? Where do you need to go now?

Turn to page 27.

You refuse to surrender your red shoes and their fate to Devil. Clutching them against your bag, you push through the crowd of people waiting for the train and run. Some swear at you, but you don't care. You must flee from Devil, as fast and as far as possible. You sprint up the stairs, shoving aside anyone in your way.

When you arrive at the top, your knees start to feel weak. Your lungs ache, but you have to keep running. Where? You think you hear a voice.

'There!'

You turn. In the distance, you see the woman you met in the garden waving in your direction. Victoria. She knows you're being chased. She motions for you to turn right.

'Thanks!'

'See you later, honey!'

You dash towards a hallway and spy a black signboard hanging in front of you, with a round red symbol and the number one in the middle. You use your last iota of strength to race on.

Once you finally feel you've run far enough, you look back. Devil isn't following you now.

Why is it so quiet here? What number was that just now? 1? The 1 doesn't stop at Bryant Park Station, only the B, D, F and M trains. Lines with orange icons.

Suddenly you realise something. You didn't see a number 1 but the letter I. You went wrong because the 1, like the 2 and 3, always has a red circle as its symbol.

There is no I train in New York, there never has been.

You've been tricked. But by whom? Your mind conjures up the figure of the granny in her yellow jacket and beret decorated with a sunflower. The woman in the park – why did she point you to the I train, a train that never existed?

You hear the sound of ceramic cracking. The floor in front of you gives way, collapsing, and a roar deafens you as you slip into a long tunnel.

Continue on to page 414.

You don't know what to do. You lie silently in bed, clenching yourself tightly. You have no idea who's knocking, but you refuse to open the door. You will stay here, motionless, in this room with a pink glow. Playing dead, like kids in their games.

Someone is pounding on the door, hard. Your heart is also pounding. You close your eyes. One person – or is it two? – somehow forces a way inside.

You open your eyes slowly and find yourself lying on a velvet sofa, under a blanket. You're wearing pyjamas but you last remember being in a display window in lace lingerie, trembling with fear. Who dressed you in pyjamas? You step on soft carpet. You find yourself in a large living room; in front of you is a small table with a teapot and two cups, a rocking chair and an old-fashioned fireplace. Your gaze lands on four gnome figurines flanking the fireplace, each wearing a pointed cap.

You're trying to remember what happened to you. Two men, their faces masked, somehow broke in and covered your mouth with a handkerchief. You remember nothing after that. No doubt about it: you've been kidnapped.

You hear footsteps descending a staircase. You clutch the blanket tight. A figure in a long black robe approaches, his appearance slowly becoming clearer. What sort of devil is this? He wears a white mask with a pointed chin, like the kind one might wear at a carnival. You edge to the far end of the sofa, eyes downcast. You panic: a kidnapper in a strange costume? Or a pimp who now controls your life?

'My apologies for having to bring you here this way.'

You're startled. Not a male voice, but female, soft and sweet. You summon the courage to lift your head, staring at the white mask.

'You kidnapped me.'

'I sent some friends to save you,' she says. 'I don't kidnap humans. At least those who encounter me don't feel like they've been kidnapped. I only kidnap garden gnomes.'

She points towards the four bearded figurines. They remind you of the dwarf your sister bought to look after her house. The gnomes and all her words make you even more confused. Why are you here, and why is this woman masked? Then you remember the woman that Maria talked about.

The Whore of Babylon.

The woman saved you because she is the Whore of Babylon, a powerful mother figure.

She laughs mockingly from behind her mask.

'Honey,' she says, 'that's just a myth.'

She removes her disguise. Her face is stunning – so beautiful and so familiar. You've seen it. She pours the tea, ready on the table, and invites you to drink. Then she sits in the rocking chair by the fireplace.

'The Whore of Babylon. She protects prostitutes.'

'Oh, I'm not that heroic,' she says. 'I hardly ever meet them. The ones that I do are at a crossroads, in any case.'

Crossroads. The word rattles you. You've heard about this woman, or maybe even seen her. But where? You struggle to recall. Berlin? You feel you've come across her more than once. This woman inspires dread.

Is she everywhere? The rocking chair now pitches back and forth. She smiles enigmatically, letting you cast around for her in your memory. She glances at your bare feet.

'Lose a slipper, Cinderella?'

That voice. The beautiful woman who found your shoe at the airport.

'You're the one who found my shoe.'

'The one who found my shoe,' she parrots, making you feel like you're hearing an echo in a cave.

Her voice has a scoffing tone, but she isn't mocking you. You remember Devil's letter: your red shoes are an inheritance from a woman who has died.

'Who are you?'

'My name is Hecate.'

You hold your breath. She's that witch, an abductress. Your throat is dry, and you begin to cough. Hecate hands you a glass of water while repeating her statement: she doesn't kidnap. She only comes to those who are on edge and at borders, at crossroads.

'But why do you kidnap garden gnomes?'

'That's another matter. They're cursed to stand watch over homes.'

She kidnaps gnomes because they should be left free, not enslaved as garden watchmen. Sometimes, if she's feeling kind, and the gnomes need a break from the road, she returns them to their owners for a lengthy stay.

'Your shoes were mine.'

She calmly pours herself tea. 'The shoes come with a curse. You can't stop travelling,' she says. 'But now you can determine your own steps.'

You stare at her chair as it rocks back and forth. You feel as though you are beginning to understand. Your adventure will end soon.

'I don't want to go home,' you say. 'I don't want to go back to the same house, the same city, that dull life.'

'I'm not telling you to go back,' she replies. 'Home is never the same, anyway.'

When you wake the next day, Hecate's house is empty. You feel relieved that she didn't send you back to Indonesia. But that goes without saying. It's not as if she's a government with the authority to deport immigrants. Hecate has left an

OV-chipkaart so you can take the train back to Victoria's house.

After that, there are no shoes, no Devil, no Hecate in your life. You are determined to stay in the Netherlands and find work. For a year, you work odd jobs, from being a cashier at a Jumbo supermarket to waiting tables in an Argentinian steak-house. Thanks to your jobs, you manage to save up money to travel around Europe, staying in cheap hostels, without red shoes.

Then, one day, you make a major decision. You have yet to explore all the nooks and crannies of the world, but you've seen more than enough for now. It's time to go home. This is neither compulsion nor defeat, but you do feel nervous. And you understand why – for those who have been away for so long, or too long, going home takes courage.

Continue on to page 401.

The Secret of the Red Shoes

*All those girls
who wore the red shoes,
each boarded a train that would not stop.*

Anne Sexton, 'The Red Shoes'

It's not right to wear red shoes to a grave, especially if the deceased is your own mother.

Here the Shoemaker lies buried. One winter, hundreds of years ago, he made a beautiful pair of red shoes for his wife when she was seriously ill. He hoped that she could wear them when she recovered, in the spring, when the air was warmer and people didn't need to wear heavy boots outside. His wife said, 'If I die, sell them to a woman who likes red shoes.'

The Shoemaker wanted to protest, but fell silent when his wife began coughing uncontrollably, covering her mouth with the shawl that wreathed her neck. The shawl, also red, hid the drops of blood.

They often wondered who would die first. 'I want to go before you. I don't want to witness your death,' said the wife.

The Shoemaker rebuffed her. 'No, I'll die first, and I'll haunt you if you flirt with the baker and the butcher next door.' Even after thirty years together, the Shoemaker was jealous of every man who went near his wife. In his eyes, she was so beautiful that all men of this world would approach her, given the chance. His wife was often offended by his outrageous jealousy. The neighbourhood butcher and baker? Really, I'm not attracted to fat, bald men.

Although they often quarrelled, neither wanted to bear the pain of dying in second place. Their love for each other was so unrelenting that even God must have felt jealous. Before the shoes were finished, the Shoemaker had lost his wife. He found her one morning, having breathed her last. She had left, without any sign, without any message.

The Shoemaker's assistant, Tom, a young man of seventeen, came every day to help. Throughout January, the coldest month of winter, Tom watched as the Shoemaker slowly drove himself to ruin. He sat in a rocking chair, eyes blank, raving about his wife and how she liked to wander about. He believed she had only gone on a short trip to the market in her new shoes, and would soon return.

The Shoemaker left the house during a blizzard. To go out on such a night was crazy, but he opened the door without locking it behind him and trod through the thick snow blanketing the road. He wanted to stay out in the storm for as long as possible, then freeze to death so he would be found the next day, buried in the snow. As he walked, he saw red, a bothersome red, like a drop of fresh blood on a white carpet. The red grew brighter and brighter. The Shoemaker saw a woman in a long red cloak sweeping across the ice.

The next day, the Shoemaker was back in his bed. Tom and several townsfolk had found him lying on the road and had taken him straight home. Nobody could say how long he had lain in the snow. The only thing Tom knew was that after the event, the Shoemaker was never the same again. Tom no longer saw him sad. In fact, he looked neither grief-stricken nor joyful. He showed no emotion at all. Every day he sat in front of the fireplace, cobbling away. His face was pale and his eyes were large, red and unblinking. By spring, he had finished the red shoes for his wife.

He put the shoes in front of the window and said to Tom: whoever owns these shoes will never stop travelling.

Tom thought the Shoemaker would never sell them, but he was too afraid to ask. He glanced at the man. Next to the scarlet shoes, his face looked bloodless. He felt that the man beside him was a stranger who had returned in the Shoemaker's place, after he had gone out to brave the snow and met whoever it was, or whatever it was.

Soon a girl arrived who became the stuff of legend, the girl obsessed with red shoes.

She appeared in front of the Shoemaker's house in shoes made from red velvet fabric, which were too tight. People said she wore those shoes at her mother's burial because she was so poor that she had no other pair. After her mother died, a well-to-do woman adopted her. Now the girl could afford good clothes, but she still went everywhere in the red shoes, even though they were wearing out.

The girl left the Shoemaker's house in new red shoes. She admired their beauty so much that she wore them wherever she went, including church. Her steps were so nimble and seductive that the eyes of all – the congregation, the black-clad priest, and even the saints in the paintings – were fixed on her. Neighbours whispered. How inappropriate to wear such shoes to church.

Upon hearing this unsavoury gossip, the girl's adoptive mother reminded her to wear plain black shoes. But the girl's heart felt heavy at the thought of parting with her red shoes. They seemed to call out to her. The more they were shunned, the more brightly they sparkled. Since her mother was near-sighted, she kept wearing the red shoes to church anyway. An insolent lass, indeed. The ungrateful child lied to her mother. Truly, she was no better than faithless Malin Kundang.

She would be cursed like Malin Kundang, who liked to travel and was finally turned into stone (see page 23, then return here).

In front of the church one day, the girl in red shoes met a soldier who looked at them with a strange, slightly savage gaze. 'Those shoes are perfect for dancing!' he said.

So dance the girl did. Her obsession with red shoes grew even more passionate. She was less and less inclined to sit at home and read the Bible. She would pull the shoes from the closet and fling the house door wide open as she danced. She danced in the yard, in parks, in the streets. The townsfolk turned their heads, scandalised, clutching their hands to their hearts. Over time, she grew tired. She would pause briefly before the cemetery. But the red shoes seemed possessed by a demon. Her little feet continued to frolic, refusing to finish their dance. Now her steps stuttered, as if following a swift, staccato rhythm, a panicked rhythm; she danced aimlessly, circling dark forests, gambolling over graves.

Help! Help! She ran, but the shoes tightened further about her feet, making her heels blistered and chafed. Noon and night passed her by in scorn. Day after day, her feet remained fettered. She ran, possessed, into the church, pleading before the priests. But the men of religion were powerless.

Cut off my feet. Let me repent.

And so they shackled her, and amputated her at the ankles.

The girl lay on the floor like a piece of meat at the slaughterhouse table. God, forgive me. She sought light, but the red shoes refused to enter heaven. The blood-soaked chunks of flesh that were her feet fled, abandoning her to dance their mad dance far from the church. The girl had finally returned home, turning her face to God. The red shoes that knew no rest, however, chose adventure and went missing.

When the Shoemaker left his house to freeze to death amid the blizzard, he brought the red shoes with him to give to anyone who could show him which way his wife had gone. But the shoes were devil shoes. They ran away from their creator, who now rested peacefully at the Heavenly Father's side. For hundreds of years they have gone from one girl to another, stirring up inappropriate desires. And girls in red shoes never return home.

'Leave your shoes here,' Victoria says.

You look at her, unblinking.

'Here, at the Shoemaker's grave. Return them to their maker. Then you will be free.'

Transfixed, you stare at the carving of the shoes in front of you. Suddenly you imagine a future that you can't bear. You don't know where the red shoes will take you. You are terrified. But the shoes have brought you here, and you don't want to stop.

'You don't have much time.'

Victoria turns and leaves you. The lights dim, and the church darkens suddenly. You call out to her, but she has vanished. Your voice echoes against the stone walls.

If you obey Victoria and leave your shoes at the shoemaker's grave, turn to the next page.

If you choose to run away with your shoes, turn to page 398.

You take off your shoes and place them directly atop the Shoemaker's tomb. And then you run, as fast as you can, your feet frigid, passing dark corridors and the dead lying beneath the floor of the cathedral. You stare ahead into blackness seemingly without end. You feel pairs of eyes watching you – the eyes of those below your feet, or perhaps buried inside the walls. There are whispers behind you. Distant voices call you. You refuse to turn around, and the path feels long, far too long.

Finally, you see light. Somehow the cathedral door opens slightly. You make out the faint sound of people passing and of bicycle bells. Your legs feel exhausted, but you must keep running. The door, and the outside world, may not always be open to you.

You burst forward and tumble onto the cathedral steps. People in overcoats and hats walk past you. One or two turn around, but immediately look away. You're gasping. Your chest aches from the exertion of flight.

'Maybe you need these?'

Directly before you, you see a pair of black boots, like army boots. You look up. A beautiful woman in a red overcoat smiles at you. Her right hand holds a pair of shoes, while her left cradles a chihuahua.

'Hello, Cinderella.'

You've heard her voice. You've even heard her utter the same sentence. You and she have met.

'Yes, you know who I am,' she says. 'And you could get frostbite.'

She drops the boots beside your bare feet.

The tips of your toes are going blue. You quickly slide your feet into the shoes. She puts down the dog, removing a pack of cigarettes and a lighter from the pocket of her red coat, and inhales. You look at her chihuahua and nearly keel over in shock. What a bizarre-looking creature.

The woman chuckles.

'People always expect my dog to be bigger. But it's a pain in the ass to go around nowadays with a mutt the size of a wolf cub.'

'Your dog –'

'Oh, the three heads? OK, OK.' She pats the dog. 'Meet Cordelia, Regan and Goneril.'

Three chihuahua heads sway to and fro, barking in unison.

'The Shoemaker longed to be kidnapped,' the woman says. 'He offered me the red shoes so he could follow his wife. But then they got stolen. The man who returned home and sold the red shoes wasn't him.'

'Then who was it?'

'You can't guess?' She puffs on her cigarette and exhales slowly. 'I thought you knew your boyfriend better than that.'

You fall silent. Really, you don't know what to do except keep quiet and think. Cordelia and her sisters – who are now going Dutch on a single body – are silent too, even though they don't exactly appear lost in thought. For a long time you stare, dazed, at the streets and the people passing by, as the woman in the red coat smokes her cigarette.

'Does my adventure end here?'

She laughs. 'Well, that's up to you. You don't need shoes, or a devil.' She winks. 'Write your own adventure.'

She tosses her cigarette on the sidewalk and crushes it with her foot. She picks up the three-headed chihuahua.

'So long, Cinderella.'

She smiles and walks away. You watch her, a figure in a red coat who walks on this cold but snowless night. You want to call her back and ask more questions, but you can't even string the words together.

'Thank you,' you mumble. 'Hecate.'

Turn to page 391.

Ar-Rohmah Mosque, South Jakarta, July 2012

A crystal snow globe shoots out onto the green carpet that lies in front of you. You feel as if you've woken from a long sleep. Two small children apologise, pick up the globe and dash away. You fold the prayer rug and get up, following a woman in a hijab who is leading two daughters. You're with your sister and her two daughters, Nazwa and – what's the other one's name? The two look much bigger than the last time you saw them. How many years have passed?

Where did you last see a snow globe?

You're in a majestic mosque with lofty ceilings and marble floors. The floor is cold, but your feet are protected by socks and your long, flowing abaya. You pause. The clock hanging on the mosque's white wall reads 9 p.m. Where are you? Why, with all the world's people, places and creeds, are you in a mosque, and with your sister? And doesn't she have three kids?

'Where's Raihan?' you ask.

'Don't tell me you forgot,' says your sister, still walking in front of you. 'In the male section, with the men.'

Why are you here wearing this outfit? Your eyes scan around you, looking for a mirror, impatient to know how you look. But there is no mirror, no door. You finger your clothes and pat your head. You're wearing a hijab.

'Mommy, Daddy is taking a long time, isn't he?'

Your niece's voice sounds unfamiliar.

'He'll be here in just a bit, hon,' answers your sister.

You continue trailing after her, bewildered. She walks out of the mosque, towards the shoe storage area. She turns to you.

'Let's just wait here. The men can take a while once they get to chatting.'

You nod, then follow her to the shoe rack. There you see your red shoes, lined up with other simpler pairs. They look too beautiful, flashy, misplaced. You immediately retrieve them and go back to where your sister stands. You wonder why she hasn't taken her own from the rack. It turns out that she put her good shoes into a small bag and brought them into the mosque.

'You.' Your sister shakes her head. 'Leaving shoes like that outside in the rack. What if they get stolen? Only a madwoman leaves a pair of Louboutin in front of a mosque.'

'These aren't Louboutin.'

These are Devil shoes.

Devil, where is Devil? Where were you before this, and where are you going? Again, you're thoroughly disoriented. Your sister takes out lipstick and a small mirror from inside her bag. You make out the name of a famous designer emblazoned on its case.

'So, has Teddy made a decision?' your sister asks, applying lipstick. 'Your husband has lots of supporters, I must say. The real question is whether he'd want to be mayor of Depok.'

Husband? Why is she talking about a husband?

'I still can't believe it,' your sister continues to chatter on. 'It seems like only yesterday that he popped the question. But what am I saying? *Hidayah* comes after you take the veil. It's true, isn't it? You've ended up married to a successful, handsome, pious cleric. Loyal to you. Not polygamous. Masya Allah. All women want an imam like that.'

You can tell that your eyes are bulging. Polygamy. The word sparks certain memories. You remember how you and your sister used to vent about polygamy. You both hated religious teachers who justified the practice. It was one of the few things you could bond over.

You keep trying to excavate memories. What else do you need to remember?

'God willing, Samara will continue, Dik.'

'Samara? Who? What?'

'Samara. In your household. *Sakinah mawaddah wa rahmah*. Sa-ma-ra. Familial tranquillity, love and mercy.'

Your sister's words are causing panic to set in. You're the wife of a man named Teddy, a religious leader. In what world is this even possible?

'Ah, there's Teddy, on his way with Abah,' she says. 'You're coming again for the Tarawih prayers tomorrow, right?'

From a distance you see your brother-in-law – Abah – walking with his son (that must be Raihan, you think). Next to him is a handsome, well-built, light-skinned man with glasses. The three of them wear white robes and caps. As soon as Abah approaches, your sister goes to him and kisses his hand, the gesture of a virtuous wife. The man next to your brother-in-law walks towards you, smiling warmly. The closer you get, the more handsome he looks, and the deeper the panic that descends upon you.

In the car, you remain silent. The dashing, elegant cleric who is evidently your spouse drives a BMW. As his wife, you likely live well. But in the passenger seat, you feel anxious. What brought you here? You try to remember what has happened to you.

The snow globe in the mosque is the key. When was the last time you saw one?

Bob's apartment. That's it. Devil came, offered you a second chance, and you took it. You placed your red shoes in front of the door. After that you remember nothing else. Bob, New York and everything that belonged to you has been lost some-where. Then where is Devil? There could hardly be a dirtier trick than dropping you here, as the virtuous wife of a cleric with a BMW. You sure as hell would never have made a life choice like this.

'I found the magazine at the bookstore.' The man next to you finally breaks the silence. 'I bet you're proud of me, darling.'

Everything about him is a bit over the top. He's too good-looking, his voice too suave, and he speaks like an actor in a soap opera. You feel nauseous. You say nothing. Apparently, that isn't the desired reaction. Your husband opens the glovebox and takes out an issue of *Time* magazine. He turns on the car's interior light so you can have a good look at the cover. You see three turbaned men – all handsome, clear-skinned and wearing spectacles – looking stylish for the camera: your husband, the famous Aa Jim and another cleric you don't recognise. Above their photo is the title 'Wealth and Taste: Young Muslim Celebrity Preachers in Asia'. You feel dizzy.

'I want to get out,' you say.

You refuse to be a celebrity cleric's wife. This choice is one you've never made, never would have made, and it has to end this very moment. The man next to you bursts into uproarious laughter. His guffaws are prolonged and terrifying, making you cringe. Then, his handsome face begins to wrinkle. It dawns on you: your husband's ears are pointed and hairy.

'Devil!' You yank off his cap and tug his hair forcefully. 'Damn you, Devil!'

'Pleased to meet you again! Glad you guessed my name.'

He keeps laughing heartily, and you feel an intense desire to strangle him. The only thing that stops you is that he's driving and you don't want to die in a stupid accident.

'I'm famous now. Awesome, huh?'

'You motherfucker! Why are you pretending to be religious?'

'Pretending? Pretending?' Devil cackles. 'It just so happens that the devil has always been tight with religious types.'

'Your jokes aren't funny.'

'This is no joke, baby. We're having ourselves a brand-new adventure.'

He presses a button to turn on the car stereo. Samba percussion and rattling maracas come through the speakers. You recognise the Rolling Stones song that's playing, but you've never really listened to the lyrics until today. '*Please allow me to introduce myself ...*' Devil, in his guise as a cleric, taps along to the song on the steering wheel with gusto. A man of wealth and taste, indeed.

Ten in the evening in Jakarta. You look out the window at the boulevards and buildings passing by. For the first time, an air-conditioned luxury car makes you feel trapped. Where will you go after this? The night is still young; you will demand that Devil returns the lost years, or at least tells you where those years went. And this horrifying joke had better only be a temporary whim, Devil's brief jest. If not, you'll find a way to escape, escape abroad, to the moon, to hell, anywhere. Anywhere but here.

FINIS

Then what about you? Will you stay on in the Netherlands, wandering without purpose? Or settle in one spot for a while? Will you buy a ticket and return to Indonesia? How does your story end?

Nobody has the right to determine your adventures, including an author with arbitrary whims. Hecate is right. It's time for you to write the end of your own adventure (maybe it will never really end):

_____

_____

_____

_____

_____

_____

_____

_____

_____

_____

FINIS

Upon returning to Bob's apartment, you gather your things into a suitcase. After a year away, there's not much to collect but your case quickly fills. Your movements are fast, almost robotic. You don't want to think. You don't want to flit around.

You kneel in front of your bag, your shoulders sore. What else can you pack? You scan Bob's entire apartment. The desk. You'd often see Bob working there, his back to you, while you sat on the couch watching a movie on your laptop. You usually wore headphones because you didn't want to disrupt his concentration. Bob's large map remains in place, as do the calligraphy paintings and half-dozen snow globes. You glance at the bookcases that line the walls, left and right. Just take any book you want, Bob always said. You took a novel from a shelf once or twice and cracked it open, but you never made a serious attempt to read them.

Your eyes have grown hot.

You feel empty, as bare as your apartment in Jackson Heights when you decided to move to Bob's. Move, purge. You've been cleansed of everything: Bob, apartment, New York. You are spacious now. Someone could probably run around inside you.

New York. You don't know why you want to stay. Because you're used to queuing for kebabs at the Halal Guys truck in front of the Hilton on Sixth Avenue? Because you know how to save time on the train from Jackson Heights to West 4th? Go to the front car so you can get off by the basketball court near La Candela, not at the other exit. Flimsy reasons. You cast about for something firmer, and your eyelids start to droop.

You don't know what time you wake. Is it morning? You feel thirsty. You stumble towards the kitchen. Your eyes widen when you see that the refrigerator door is open.

Shhh …

A diminutive man puts his finger to his lips. He pops the top off a bottle of Bob's beer. It's been sitting there since before you left, before all this happened. You rub your eyes.

Little Johnny.

Where did you meet him? On television? In dreams?

He nods, as if he can read your mind. He looks up, downs the beer.

Yes, in dreams.

He starts dancing. You seem to hear music. Little Johnny holds the beer bottle as if crooning into a microphone: *In dreams I talk to you* …

You stand frozen. Why does he keep appearing uninvited? Is he an incarnation of the devil?

I'm your guardian angel.

Raqib or Atid? When you were studying recitation, you memorised the angels' duties. Two angels always follow us, jotting down our good and bad deeds.

Little Johnny giggles.

I'm not that kind of angel. I don't like taking notes. I'll leave that to writers.

Little Johnny continues to prance around. You don't know what to do, and stay motionless as you watch his odd little jig.

Don't go. Stay here.

This isn't my home.

Really? he asks. What language do you dream in?

You follow his steps from kitchen to living room. He stomps on Bob's carpet, romps on his couch, still acting as if he's holding a mike.

New York, New York. Everyone wants to claim New York, but New York isn't anyone's property. It belongs to a rat pack. New York is your home because you're a queen.

Queen? Queen of what?

The little man laughs uproariously. Before he disappears in the dark, you hear his question, so warm and familiar:

Where have all the rats gone?

Suddenly you feel cold.

You see a thermostat on the wall. 74 degrees Fahrenheit. You think in Fahrenheit. You shouldn't feel cold. Maybe the heater isn't working. You walk towards the radiator near the window, and put your hand near it. Cold. That's when you notice a strange smell, as if something is rotting behind it. You shift it a little.

You scream. Behind the radiator lies a giant rat carcass. Not just one, but several – eight, ten – bound together, their tails intertwined, entangled. Flesh, fur and grime, inseparable. A huge, revolting lump of rodent.

On Sunday morning you wake with your emotions in disarray. Your dream last night was really weird. You have no desire to see what you found behind the heater ever again. You feel disgusted, but the giant rat ball rouses an unexpected sentiment: you will stay here. Nothing can drive you from your home. You've found an answer to Little Johnny's question after all this time.

Where have all the rats gone?

You will go where the rats go. Because you are a queen.

And so, to Queens you return. You leave Bob's apartment and take the subway to meet Mr Zhao – the E train, the train that brought you home for the first time.

Wei has graduated from NYU and now works as an immigration lawyer. He lives in Astoria, a ten-minute train ride from Mr Zhao's home in Elmhurst. On Sundays, he visits his parents and occasionally helps translate for his father.

'Wei, do you know of any jobs I can do?'

Wei thinks for a moment.

'My aunt's restaurant in Flushing needs workers,' he said. 'But the restaurant is too …'

You wait. He looks hesitant.

'Have you ever eaten at a Chinese restaurant in Flushing?'

'No.'

'They're too busy. Crowded. Chaotic.' Wei seems to be searching for the exact term to describe his aunt's restaurant. Finally he hits upon it: 'Hard core.'

You feel your resolve shrivel.

'Work in Flushing definitely wears you out. Do you want to go back to La Candela? You can call Tony.'

You think of La Candela, the cafe that introduced you to Bob and the world you wanted to enter. But full of confidence, you say, 'Flushing. I choose Flushing.'

You stay on in New York. Maybe this is your way of living through paradox, simultaneously waiting for Bob while forgetting Bob. He might come back, he might not, but you will stay. Your old apartment in Jackson Heights is now too expensive for you, so you live in Flushing, on the third floor of a house owned by Mr Zhao, and every day you walk to work at Kam Lun Restaurant.

No rich American guy arrives to rescue you, but you feel no need to be rescued. You develop tight friendships with several Indonesian girls who work as nannies, but their friendships bore you over time because their main goal is to marry a white man. For you, adventure means enjoying the corners of the city that take you beyond banal fantasies of New York – not as a tourist in Times Square, or the girlfriend of a white intellectual at NYU or Columbia, or a hipster in Brooklyn. Flushing is a wilder side of New York. You work at Kam Lun Restaurant for a few years, setting aside money on a regular basis. When you've saved enough, you'll continue your education at the New School and study Creative Writing. You imagine that one day your modest room in Flushing will give birth to a book about a red-shoes adventure.

Your story ends here. But before we part, do you want to know what happened to your red shoes?

If you want to know the fate of the red shoes, turn to the next page.

If you don't want to know the fate of the red shoes, well, who gives a damn? Turn to the next page.

Noel finds himself in a taxi. He doesn't know how he got here; he's not wearing his usual tight shirt and jeans, but a light blue dress and white stockings. Noel sees his reflection in the rear-view mirror. He's wearing an auburn wig, pigtails tied in blue ribbons. Is this a dream? Why is he dressed like a young girl? He sees people passing by on the road, wearing all sorts of costumes. Some wear pink fur shawls, beaded black velvet masquerade masks and purple organza wings. Wings? He has a feeling he's not in Los Angeles any more.

He gets out of the cab and steps into the crowd. The sea of people is moving towards a road: Oxford Street. His glittering red heels click on the pavement. They sound loud and sexy.

'Hey, Judy Garland!'

Shouts and whistles can be heard from the roadside. A group of shirtless men wave. Their muscular frames make Noel grin. He finally understands and responds to his admirers' greetings by putting some sass in his step. Dorothy and her magical red shoes have landed in Oz.

Sydney Mardi Gras. A fiesta is about to begin somewhere over the rainbow.

FINIS

You refuse to part with your shoes. You race as fast as you can, leaving the Shoemaker's tomb, down the corridor in search of a way out, past the chapel and unlit candles. You pass some empty pews facing the altar and turn. Again, you follow a dark corridor. You run for a while but then come upon the same scene: the same altar, the same pews.

You stop, gasping for breath. You are circling in a labyrinth.

You shout, but the sole response is your own echo. In this church, your only companions are mute statues of Jesus. You run further, more panicked, groping every wall, desperate for an exit. The cathedral is pitch-dark.

You continue your flight until you return to your starting point: the tomb of the Shoemaker. Suddenly you hear the sound of stone crumbling beneath your feet. You leap backwards as the cracks spread in each direction. The Shoemaker's tomb yawns open, sucking you inside.

You see nothing but darkness as you tumble into a tunnel. You manage to scream, but you have fallen too far. You will never be found.

Your story is coming to an end now. To learn your final fate, turn to page 414.

Soekarno Hatta Airport, Jakarta, February 2, 2009

Upon disembarking, you're assailed without warning by tropical air. You look at the *joglo*-style ceiling and wood carvings in each corner. Under dim white lights, you see the same shades of brown, the same tiled floor. The airport remains unchanged, stuck in an eighties time warp, although you could call it exotic. Your skin feels sticky as you line up in front of an immigration officer. You remove your jacket. As you enter baggage claim, a large poster on the wall greets you, bearing a sugar-coated slogan for migrant labourers: 'Welcome home, foreign exchange heroes'. Your suitcase is among the last to arrive on the carousel. You uplift it and pass straight through customs. Without your red shoes, you have nothing of note to declare, anyway.

Before looking for a taxi, you go to the airline office. You're keen to hand over the nameless woman's notebook. It's not a matter of being a good Samaritan: you don't want to keep it, and hope someone else will throw it away to spare you the guilt. After reading the piece about the haunted house, you'd turned to the next page. Written there was a single word:

TAMAT

For no clear reason, you hated seeing this Indonesian word, indicating that you'd reached the end. Maybe the framing letter 't' made it ring poorly in your ears. A palindrome: like a dead end. On the plane, you picked up a pen and scribbled over it with as much energy as you could muster.

The airline clerk takes the notebook and asks you to wait a moment. Maybe he wants to write a report. There is no name printed on the notebook, making it nearly impossible to return. He must simply be following protocol. And really, you don't care whether the notebook makes it back to its owner or not. If it's important, the owner will search for it. Maybe the clerk will keep it for several days and then throw it in the trash.

To your surprise, he returns with a large plastic bag that reads 'duty free'. Your jaw drops when he hands it to you. Apparently, just fifteen minutes ago a woman reported the loss of a notebook and asked the clerk to call her at her hotel if someone returned it.

'What's this?'

'She said it was a present,' the clerk says. 'A gesture of thanks.'

Bewildered, you leave the office. As you queue for a cab, you open the bag. Inside is a light blue toy piano and a card, unsigned: *Thank you. Hopefully we'll meet someday at a crossroads.*

Continue to the next page.

You take a taxi to your sister's house in Bintaro. From behind the glass you stare at rows of billboards and giant malls sheltering beneath a dull grey sky (you dare to wager that new malls have been built since you left). On the overpass, the flow of vehicles scarcely moves. The driver's repeated haphazard braking makes you feel like vomiting. You force yourself to nap because the trip to your sister's house can take two hours. Welcome to Jakarta!

As happens so often in this city, though, you have miscalculated. The taxi arrives at your sister's house three hours later. Instead of napping, you shifted position constantly, restraining your urge to pee. Your stomach complains bitterly as you emerge from the cab, with sensations that lie between nausea and hunger. In front of your sister's house, a Kijang is backing into a parking space. Your sister waves at you with a glance from behind the wheel, but immediately returns to her rear-view mirror, looking tense. The car lurches forwards, backwards, then forwards again. This is a novel sight. The family Avanza has metamorphosed into a new Kijang. And now she, who has never driven in her life, sits in the driver's seat. She must have somehow squeezed in time to learn while looking after baby number three.

Then comes a bang and a squeal of brakes. Realising that she has hit something, your sister switches off the engine and flings opens the car door. You run after her and see a shattered statue of a chubby figure with a pointed hat. You're speechless. It's the garden gnome that you've seen in the photo.

'*Astaghfirullah* …'

Your sister looks utterly mournful as you stare at the garden gnome, now in pieces. The grey-bearded head has been separated from its body. Sorrow steals over you. You're looking at your sister again, face-to-face at last after thousands of kilometres of separation by land and sea, but this is no happy reunion. How miserable the fate of this garden gnome, who travelled so far to arrive here, only to be kept prisoner, watching over a house and finally scattered in fragments. His journey was of so little renown that no gnome liberation activist came to his rescue.

'Oof, the car still isn't straight. Never mind, I'll just wait for Abah to do it later.'

Then your sister's voice brightens considerably. She hugs you, full of emotion.

'*Subhanallah*, Dik! How are you? Put on some weight, huh?' And that is the first thing she says directly to you after so much time apart. There's no mistaking it. You really are back in Indonesia.

Returning is very strange. Your sister's house doesn't feel like a home. To be honest, you have little right to express such thoughts, as morning, noon and night, the house is filled with the delicious smells of food being thoughtfully prepared by your sister and her helper, the laughter of little children having fun (Nazwa, Raihan and – what was the baby's name again?), and the sound of a television that is perpetually on. A house filled with warmth. Maybe too warm. In fact, you feel hot. Now you understand what the Devil meant in his letter. Your home isn't there, but it's not here either.

Time passes slowly. You've been at your sister's a while now, a week or more. Your only entertainment is playing with her kids, especially Nazwa. When Nazwa isn't bragging about how many medals she's collected from memorising long verses of the Quran, she's a smart and pleasant child. She keeps inviting you to play Lego and Monopoly and asks about all the things you've seen while you were abroad. Sometimes this wears you out, and you hope she'll sit quietly in her room, shut her mouth and do her homework.

'Nazwa doesn't have homework.'

'What? Her school doesn't give homework?'

'Lots of international schools are like that these days,' your sister explains. 'They say kids in Finland don't get homework.'

Clearly, you're behind on the latest trends.

As your sister nurses her baby, she tells you about her busy life as a working mother. She still finds time to serve as a breastfeeding advocate, to write articles for the website Moms and the City, and to take care of her increasingly successful Muslimah fashion business. Yes, her business is growing rapidly, as you can tell from the new car, latest cell phone, and flat-screen television, twice the size of the previous one. You hear the word 'entrepreneur' repeatedly in her house. Her husband, Abah, is even busier. He's on the management team for a celebrity cleric named Ustadh Teddy Mubarak.

'What does a preacher need a management team for?'

'Ustadh Teddy runs a lot of motivational workshops.'

'Motivational? Motivation for what?'

'Lots of things. For example, how to succeed in business – but in an Islamic way.'

Oh, you really are out of touch.

Abah is perpetually in front of the television, a laptop and two mobile phones with different network providers at his side. The laptop has a window open with Facebook visible at all times, and his phones receive one text message after the other. He is also busy handling Ustadh Teddy's personal website.

You can hazard a guess at what Teddy Mubarak, celebrity cleric, is like. So far you haven't been taken with the many religious leaders on television, since most of them use verses from the Quran to advocate for specific interests (polygamy, for example). Only a handful, like Kiai Muhammad Hasan, write material that you like and read frequently. You ask whether he's also a celebrity cleric. Your sister and her husband exchange glances.

'He's considered part of the syphilis group. Hard for him to have broad appeal,' says Abah.

'Syphilis?' You frown. 'Why should private health issues be other people's business?'

'No, no,' says Abah. 'Syphilis is a sort of acronym: secularism, pluralism, liberalism. Kiai Hasan often puts forth controversial ideas, like allowing leaders not to be Muslim, or letting women go out uncovered. A lot of people don't agree with such a vision of Islam.'

'Then what vision of Islam should we have?'

Abah and your sister don't answer.

Your sister's house is full of technology, moving fast, and everyone speaks constantly about the business potential of social media. Your trip feels a bit like science fiction, as if a time machine has flung you into the future.

Late one afternoon, your sister and her family are rushing about getting ready to attend a lecture by Ustadh Teddy Mubarak at a five-star hotel. 'Keep an eye on the house, OK?' says your sister, in a hurry. 'We have to leave now before it gets too trafficky.'

'Are you sure you don't want to come?' asks Abah.

You smile broadly. After they leave, the house is temporarily quiet. For the first time, you feel a sense of peace. You've been here too long. It's time to go.

Continue on to page 418.

San Ysidro Port of Entry, 2010

And it's true, you've messed up your life. You sit waiting on a cold white iron bench. In front of you, an officer in a dark blue shirt paces with a sniffer dog. Out of boredom, you eavesdrop on his conversation with a colleague. The group was totally reckless, says the officer with the dog. His colleague asks how so. The dog handler then tells the story of a bunch of young people riding in a sedan, two of them hiding in the trunk. They had driven from beyond Tijuana, so the pair who were packed like sardines in the back must have been going through torture. The officer next to him shakes his head. How steep the road to Lady Liberty's house.

You look at a clock on the wall. Next to it, large letters read 'U.S. Department of Homeland Security'. You've been stuck here for two hours, witnessing people stranded and unable to enter. Some are forced back. Maybe you'll be allowed to re-enter America, maybe you'll be deported. Your situation is unclear, balanced precariously on a knife edge. Anxiety even makes you say the institution's name incorrectly.

'Do you understand where you are now?'

'Yes. The Department of Homeland Insecurity.'

The officer before you shakes his head in irritation.

'Oh, sorry!'

You pat your hair softly and say to yourself: Hey, it's you who should feel insecure, immigrant.

How did you get here?

Cynthia. You came with Cynthia.

Where is she now?

You and Cynthia drove from Los Angeles to San Diego. The whisperings of an irresponsible inner voice – or perhaps the voice of a devil – made you conspire to cross from San Diego to Tijuana, Mexico. In your adventures up until now – joyous, or cursed like your current one – you've only cared to remember a handful of names. But you'll never forget Cynthia and the story she carries – a story that brings up long-buried memories from far below.

In this tedious office of white-blue-grey you wait and wait. Yes, this is the end of your story. A journey doesn't always need a conclusion. Here, a journey is a space in between, a constant uncertainty.

If you want to know how you arrived at this sort of end, turn to page 421.

But really, you don't need to do so, because you know you will end here, on the Tijuana–San Diego border, unable to enter, unable to exit. Please stop reading, unless you want to come face-to-face with ghosts of the past.

'Dear passengers, we will soon be landing at Jorge Cháves International Airport in Lima, Peru, where the local time is 1 p.m. The weather is sunny with a temperature of 27 degrees Celsius. For your safety and comfort, please bring your seat back to the upright position, check that your seat belt is fastened …'

The flight attendant's voice wakes you. You slide the window cover up a bit and peep at a sea sparkling in brilliant sunshine.

'Soon,' Fernando says with a smile.

He is in the aisle seat, and Tiffany, now taller than you, sits between you.

The year 2017 brings this thrilling trip to Peru. It's the first visit for you and Tiffany, and the first for Fernando since he left Lima eighteen years ago. He's just said farewell to North America too.

After passing through baggage claim and customs, the three of you push a trolley full of suitcases towards a waiting crowd. Taxi drivers swarm around the freshly arrived passengers.

'It's crazy hot!' Tiffany complains in English. She takes off her jacket and fans herself.

Fernando tells her to be patient, in Spanish. 'My brother will be here soon.' Casting an eye at the sea of touts, he adds, 'Those drivers target gullible tourists and then totally over-charge them. There, have a look at that!'

He points to a cabbie who seems to have convinced two female travellers to join him. You can't see their faces clearly, but from the jackets they're wearing, it looks like they've flown in from somewhere cold.

'Yes, yes, Miraflores. Yes.'

The two women follow the driver.

In the car, observing the lanes clogged with traffic, you wonder if this is the best life path for you. Would you have made it to Peru if you'd chosen to go to Berlin from JFK ten years ago? Maybe Devil was right. Your adventure ends simply: marry a kind man and become stepmother to a sweet girl. Seven years ago, you and Fernando got married in the New York City registry office. Tiffany, Elise and several friends from La Candela attended. Tony Saverino acted as witness. Yes, married, just like that. But you went through so much to get here; your family portrait is a happy one, but not uncomplicated.

The word 'forever' was hardly in your mind when you married Fernando. You even saw the marriage as an experiment that might fail. To your surprise, though, you've stayed together these seven years. So far at least, you're enjoying each new chapter that you pass through with Fernando and Tiffany, even if they aren't the most scintillating of adventures. On Tony Saverino's suggestion, you started working at an Italian restaurant in Astoria, run by a family with ties to the owners of La Candela. You were happy because the restaurant wasn't far from your apartment or Tiffany's school. Fernando continued to work at La Candela and was promoted to supervisor, with better pay. Tiffany grew as a gifted child and was accepted at the LaGuardia High School of Music, Art and Performing Arts. You found yourself growing too. After saving for a few years, you enrolled in a master's programme in Creative Writing at the New School.

In 2016, your little family celebrated two events: you graduated with a Master of Fine Arts in Creative Writing, and Tiffany got a scholarship to study at Sarah Lawrence College. Without it, it would have been impossible for you and Fernando to afford tuition fees higher than your combined income. When you first took Tiffany to the campus in Bronxville, Fernando hugged his daughter and shed tears.

'I still can't believe it,' he murmured. 'It feels like just yesterday that I brought you home from Elmhurst Hospital ...'

'Dad!' Tiffany scolded, looking embarrassed. 'Don't be such a drama queen!'

Yes, a beautiful little snippet of the American dream. But the scene was cut immediately. In November that same year, Fernando sat on the couch, his face pale, unable to believe what he was watching on the television. The vote count for the election was continuing, but it was clear that Donald Trump would emerge victorious. Fernando turned to you with a flat expression and asked, 'Do we still want to live in America?'

In April, three months after Trump's inauguration, while Tiffany is on spring break, Fernando leaves the United States for good. His decision is easy: he refuses to live in Trumpland. Moreover, he considers his job as a father complete. Though an illegal immigrant, he has managed to see his child's education all the way through to college.

And what will you do in Peru? Who knows. But you're now proficient in Spanish, and you have a master's degree. Maybe you can teach English, or work part-time as a writer. In two weeks, Tiffany will return to being a New Yorker and Sarah Lawrence undergrad, and you and Fernando will begin travelling around South America. Life feels uncertain, and it won't become any easier, but that may in fact be why you feel happy. Without the red shoes, you will go on adventures again.

FINIS

'Dear passengers, we will soon be landing at Jorge Cháves International Airport in Lima, Peru, where the local time is 1 p.m. The weather is sunny with a temperature of 27 degrees Celsius. For your safety and comfort, please bring your seat back to the upright position, check that your seat belt is fastened …'

The flight attendant's voice wakes you. You slide the window cover up a bit and peep at a sea sparkling in brilliant sunshine.

'Soon,' Yvette says with a smile.

She sits next to you, and beside her is an obese gentleman who has dozed off and is snoring gently. You and Yvette take turns in the window seat each time you fly.

The year 2017 brings this thrilling trip to Peru. It's the first for both you and Yvette.

After passing through baggage claim and customs, the two of you push a trolley full of suitcases towards a waiting crowd. Taxi drivers swarm around the passengers who have just landed. One makes a beeline for Yvette.

Meanwhile, a voice in English catches you off guard. 'It's crazy hot!'

A girl is taking off her jacket and fanning herself. She has the rather irritating intonation of an American teenager, but strangely this makes you happy because it provides a familiar foothold in a foreign land. The man next to the teenager, maybe her father, speaks in Spanish. You suspect that the father lives in America, a first-generation immigrant from Peru, while the child is his second-generation daughter visiting her father's home country for the first time. Next to them stands the mother. She has probably never been to Peru either.

'Yes, yes, Miraflores. Yes.'

Yvette seems to have reached an agreement with the taxi driver. You both follow him. As you walk, you take off your jacket. The teenager was right. It really does feel hot today, especially coming from Berlin.

In the car, observing the lanes clogged with traffic, you wonder if this is the best life path for you. You think about Devil's question at your last meeting from time to time, but it doesn't trouble you much. Would you have made it to Peru if ten years ago at JFK you'd decided to stay in New York and hadn't chosen Berlin? Maybe if you'd chosen New York at that time, you'd have still come here, but as someone else. Maybe you'd have married a handsome Peruvian and holidayed with your family here.

You don't know if Yvette is the best possible choice, but for you, the last nine years have been the happiest adventure of your life. You've passed through so much over the last decade that you'd feel rude if you weren't grateful. Do you prefer women now? You don't know, because all this time there's only been Yvette in your eyes. You've never compared her with anyone else, male or female.

In 2008, Yvette followed you back to New York. When you opened your suitcase and took out your things, you realised your shoes were gone. Yvette hadn't seen them.

'Your Dorothy shoes?' Yvette looked at you, confused. 'I only saw them that one time you wore them.'

You searched for days, but they were nowhere to be found. Yvette tried to cheer you up. 'It's no big deal, we can buy another pair.' At the time Yvette already owned fifteen pairs of red shoes. On your birthday, she presented you with a pretty pair very similar to Devil's. You hugged her tightly. You never sought to uncover the fate of your lucky red shoes again, but you're sure Devil stole them from you. He was probably busy looking for someone else to send wandering.

Without red shoes, you had to confront real national borders. Your American visa expired at the end of the year. You considered staying on in New York illegally, but Yvette dissuaded you.

'Don't. You'll have huge problems later if you go abroad and want to come back here.'

'But I'll just stay here under the radar,' you said. 'Everything is in New York. Why do I need to go abroad?'

'You do need to go abroad, even if we don't know what for yet. And New York isn't everything. Feh.'

Finally, you decided to go back to Indonesia. Yvette joined you because she had ambitious plans. With Yvette, you started a new adventure: looking for Juwita Padmadivya.

It felt strange to return home with Yvette, like Malin Kundang bringing his foreign wife to his village. Once you had travelled, your home was never the same. With Yvette, your adventures don't feel as though they've come to an end. Of course, you never found Juwita. After following up every possibility, you and Yvette agreed to let her remain a puzzle. But one point in Juwita's account proved accurate enough. *Request Concert* was indeed performed again in Jakarta, with the same actor, Niniek L. Karim.

In autumn 2011, you registered as a film student at Freie Universität Berlin. You and Yvette returned to the cafe where you first met and agreed to make a film about Juwita Padmadivya. The film was completed at the end of 2015 and had its own adventures. It premiered at Sundance and then toured various film festivals – Rotterdam, Berlinale, Vancouver and Tribeca. When possible, you and Yvette went along to promote *Juwita* (by this point you were very grateful that you hadn't stayed stubbornly in the US after your visa expired). Journeying from festival to festival turned out to be very tiring, so after a year on the circuit you agreed to take a break. South America, here we come.

'I have a new film idea,' you say.

'About what?'

'About a woman who wears red shoes everywhere.'

'Then?'

'She meets a handsome man from Peru and they get married.'

'What, and then they have kids, and happy family holidays at the beach in Miraflores? Oh, how heteronormative can you get. Do you have any ideas that are even duller?'

You laugh. Yvette knows you're joking, but you really want to make a red-shoes movie someday. For the time being, you enjoy your holiday. Everything is perfect, except the cab from the airport. The price was absolutely outrageous. Even the most agile squirrel can fall into a tourist trap.

FINIS

You don't know how long you've been floating in the dark. Five minutes? Half an hour? You've fallen into what seems to be a bottomless black hole.

But no. There is light at its end, vague, enough to give hope. And that's where you are eventually dumped, onto a cold floor. There are no lamps. The light comes from candles burning atop pillars.

Hello!

All you hear is the echo of your own voice. Not far from where you have landed are several long, empty benches. You see a ticket window, but there is no one on duty. A large black clock stands next to it, pointing to the number 12. Its needle does not budge. What is this place?

You hear a far-off train.

This is a station.

You half break into a run as you look towards the tracks. A train is approaching from a distance, and you almost leap for joy. The train will save you. As it draws near, you can make out dark green paint and a golden colour around the train's doors. On the carriage, beneath its windows, written in a classic font, it reads: City of New York.

The train stops in front of you and the door opens. A conductor, a stocky woman with short hair, signals for you to enter. You leap in, and the doors close once more.

Inside are several passengers, all looking towards the dewy windows as you search for an empty spot. A woman in a brown leather jacket almost collides with you as she walks towards her seat. She wears a brown aviator hat and large goggles. You study her.

'Pretty cool, isn't she?'

The conductor beside you watches the woman in the hat with awe.

'Who is she?'

'Ah, kids today.' She shakes her head. 'That's Amelia Earhart, the first woman to fly across the Atlantic.'

Amelia Earhart? What's she doing here? Has she been found? You glance at the faces of the passengers. All of them are women. You behold a woman with a beret and a floral shirt. Victoria. She is also on the train. You approach her, delighted.

'Tante Victoria!'

She doesn't hear you. She is asleep. Her head is leaning against the window and her hands clasp her knitting.

Where are we going?

Victoria continues her slumber, and the other passengers also seem occupied. Some are asleep, while others are reading or staring out the window. You dart after the conductor as she makes her way to the next carriage. As soon as she opens the door, strains of jazz burst forth. A group of women sits on a shiny black leather sofa. The scarlet paint on the carriage ceiling and the golden yellow rug imbue the room with a sense of warmth. In front of the sofa are small tables and a bottle of wine. A bartender is busy mixing a drink in the corner of the carriage.

'Sorry,' you address Madam Conductor. 'Where are we going?'

'Central.'

'Which Central?'

'Does that matter, sweetie? Grand Central, New York. Amsterdam Centraal. Central do Brasil. Central is central is central. All trains go to Central.'

She smiles broadly, oddly, like a Cheshire cat. You take a step back. Central. You are not referring to the same place.

The conductor is talking about a generic Central, somewhere, but you've obviously never encountered a train like this before.

'What's the next station? I want to get off.'

This time she turns and looks at you in surprise. For the first time you notice the name printed on her blue uniform. Gertrude. Her name is Gertrude.

'They didn't tell you?'

'Who are they?'

'We come to pick people up, but no one gets off.'

'What do you mean?'

'Well, you can get off at the next station,' Gertrude said. 'But so far no one has ever done so.'

'What do you mean? We can't leave?'

'Of course you can, sweetie. I just said that so far no one has wanted to.'

'No one?' Your voice rises in a panic. 'But I want to get off. I want to go home!'

'Sweetheart.' She pats your shoulder gently. 'No one on this train wants to go home. As you can see, all your fellow passengers are looking for adventure.'

You look towards the shiny leather sofa and observe how everyone is laughing and raising a wine glass. A dark-skinned woman in a sparkling dress passes you. Her short hair is adorned in a tiara with feather accents.

'Hey, Mama,' she greets Gertrude.

'Dearest Josephine! Your show is tonight, isn't it?'

The woman, dazzlingly beautiful, give a thumbs up and walks towards the bartender. Is she a famous star? She looks very familiar.

'Josephine –'

'Yes, right. That Josephine. The Josephine,' Gertrude says. 'A fellow American in Paris. Enjoys travelling, just like you. Just like all of us.'

'Oh,' you murmur stupidly. 'Sorry, Mrs Gertrude –'

'Oh, don't be so polite. Call me Mama.'

'I have to go home!' You start to become hysterical. 'Wherever home is, I have to get there.'

Gertrude nods with a motherly gaze, as if she understands what you're going through. She then leans towards you and whispers, 'The problem is that when you get there, there's no there there.'

Gertrude again smiles broadly, enigmatically. You don't know what she means, but the statement rings in your ears like an incantation. She opens the door and enters the next carriage.

You briefly lose yourself in thought. You feel you should try talking to her again. You attempt to open the door between carriages, but it's closed tight. A sticker reads 'Restricted Area'. You step back unsteadily, slowly, and sit yourself down on the sofa. Now you hear jazz coming at a faster tempo. The passengers on the sofa rise, ready to dance. For the first time you study them carefully. Their clothing is fine, like the outfits of your childhood fantasies: women who ride the Orient Express. Your gaze drifts downward, and the resemblance increasingly dawns on you. Red shoes.

Yes, they're all wearing red shoes, and this train will not stop.

Good girls go to heaven, bad girls go wandering.

FINIS

'Have you really thought it over some more?'

'Thought what over?'

You answer your sister casually because you're occupied with lifting your suitcase into the boot of a taxi. After ten days, you know it's time to move out and find a new place to stay for the sake of your mental health. Your sister stands in front of the gate, baby in her right arm, left hand clutching her cell phone.

'I'm serious, you know. You can stay,' she says. 'What will you do, anyway?'

'I don't know. I could go back to EGW,' you hazard.

'That Global English course? Man has been to the moon, and you're still on Global English? That's not going anywhere.'

You freeze for a moment. Not going anywhere. Yes, maybe after all this you're still not going anywhere.

The taxi driver closes the boot. You take a deep breath. Once again, you glance at your sister's house and car, this perfect picture of urban bourgeois domesticity, and you feel quite sad. A ten-day reunion doesn't promise reconciliation. But we have to accept that we can't hate our families. You hug your sister tightly and wave to her kids, lined up like dwarves.

You swing the car door shut. The driver asks, 'Where are we going?'

The question gives you pause. Where are we going? Why 'we' and not 'you'? Who are we? Are we going together?

'Pejaten,' you answer.

The taxi drives away from Bintaro, entering the toll road. You look at the driver's ID on the left of the dashboard, and take your pen from your bag to jot down the details there, just in case. Miroto, 666.

'Tired of travelling already?'

The question surprises you, again. You feel as if you're being interrogated. Growing apprehensive, you study the driver, seeking his reflection in the rear-view mirror, but all you see there is your face. He whistles, adding to your nervousness. From the back seat, you realise suddenly that his ears are pointed and hairy.

'You can't keep running from me. We're destined to be together,' says the man in front of you.

His voice rings all too familiar in your ears. You're aghast. The door is locked, and the taxi continues on an empty highway. Dammit, you're trapped. You look again in the rear-view mirror. There is no one else visible. You are looking at yourself as you travel towards some unknown destination. Because each mirror is a door.

Mirrodoor.

'Make me your slave again. I'll forgive all your betrayals. Mephistopheles Most Merciful, darling, at your service.'

'I don't think I've done anything wrong,' you say. 'I don't need your forgiveness.'

'Still stubborn, I see!'

Suddenly the car shakes violently. You clench your eyes shut, preparing for an overwhelming outburst of rage that may bring your life to an end. But nothing happens. No explosion of satanic wrath, only a car that passes you without signalling at an insane speed. Taxi Driver, aka Devil, opens the window and thrusts out an upraised middle finger, 'Asshole!'

You sigh, feeling a mixture of relief and fear. Devil remains silent for a long time, his eyes glued to the wide boulevard that stretches out in front of him. His voice softens.

'So what now? Back to teaching at EGW?' he asks. 'Your red shoes are still pining for the road.'

He grabs something from under the driver's seat to fling rearward. The red shoes glitter, back in your hands once more. You look at him, confused.

'You don't want to stop here, do you? Take your shoes back. But once you wear them again, you'll forget everything. A curse, even though I call it a blessing.'

'Meaning?'

'The history of your red-shoes adventure will be erased. You won't be able to remember it. And those who cannot remember the past are condemned to repeat it,' Devil says, then hastily adds, 'That last bit is a famous line, supposedly from George Santayana. He's quoting me, of course.'

You cradle the red shoes in your lap. They look tired but thirsty for travel, just like you. You always thought adventure forced you to look back, but maybe it's also a circle – a vicious satanic circle, to be more exact – never-ending, unbroken. You'll go the same way and fall in the same holes, a constant déjà vu, but maybe, once in a while, you'll get lucky.

If you have the courage, put on your red shoes and return to page 9, the beginning of your adventure.

FINIS

Tijuana

Where were you then? Were you afraid?

You've already asked that, you said.

Yes, you said you didn't dare leave the house. As for the rest, you didn't remember. Maybe I just wanted to sweep up all the scraps of information you'd scattered. But we'd arrived at this question, and it's important to note that fact. Most people don't even get this far.

How did we get to this question?

I'd told you about the holes in my skin. I'd never told anyone about that damned disease. But on a journey people do the unthinkable. And you and I had crossed over. We had arrived in Tijuana.

The border had set us astir.

Somehow we just started talking about Tijuana, and we were bad planners. We were sitting on Pacific Beach in San Diego, our feet buried in the sand, and out of the blue you said: I'm bored. I laughed. This was already the second time since meeting you that I'd heard you say that. How could you get bored with all this, bathed by fine sand, watching surfers chase the waves? Nothing in New York could compare.

Yes, but I've been living in LA for two years now, you said.

Can we go back to La Jolla Cove? I prefer to walk high above the water too, and look down over the blue sea, the cliffs and the seals frolicking in the sand. Here everything is completely flat, not like in La Jolla where it's hilly.

But only rich people live in La Jolla, you said. San Diego is more exciting. Hey, how about getting some Mexican food?

How about going to Mexico? I said.

You thought I was crazy.

The previous day, we had driven down I-5 from Los Angeles to San Diego in your car. I was at the wheel because you were still a little scared of driving long distances. You'd finished a driving course and at age thirty, you could drive through LA for the first time in your life, in the cheap car you'd just bought, with the warm wind in your hair. Maybe this is one of my greatest achievements, you said. What are we waiting for? We have to celebrate.

We were working together in an Asian restaurant. Our manager, a sweet woman, had introduced us there. She always helped Indonesians find work, and they were always illegals, like me. We were friends too, though not overly close. You never invited me to your place or vice versa, and I never saw you when the Indonesian community got together for meals. Indos – yes, I hate the term too, but everyone uses it – always had a reason to gather and cook. Sometimes the conversations were really insipid; gossiping about famous celebrities they remembered from the nineties, long before they came to America. My main goal was to eat some Indo cooking and bring some home if I got lucky.

Then one day, when we went out for a break, you asked how long I'd been working at the restaurant. I'd lost count of the time, but it was the job where I'd lasted longest. I got decent tips there. Before that I'd worked at a clothing store for eight dollars an hour, without any chance of bonuses. That's when the words came out your mouth: I'm bored. It sounded like a slogan of rebellion.

I asked if you wanted to change jobs. Maybe Walmart, you said, because you were bored with working in a restaurant. I laughed, like I laughed at you at Pacific Beach. You're kidding, right? We get better pay here. Besides, a few years ago Walmart had to pay a huge fine for hiring illegal aliens. There's no way they'd take the risk now. Later on I learned about the ambiguity of your own situation. Your visa had expired, but maybe, if you could straighten out your marital status, you'd be able to fix that. You'd had an Islamic wedding ceremony but hadn't been able to register it officially yet. Why bother to get hitched to an American, only to end up with a marriage that wasn't recognised? Were you romantic, or just stupid? And where was your husband now?

Missing, you said.

You talked about losing your husband as casually as losing a wallet. Of course, it wasn't easy, especially in the early days, you said. You felt sad in a strange way because you didn't love him. You had tied your life to a thread, not firmly, but still you wailed when the kite broke. I listened to your whole story. No, not all of it. A lot of things confused me. You never told me how you got to New York, for example. Maybe that's why I kept asking questions. There was always something you hadn't told me.

Where were you then? Were you afraid?

When was the first time these questions came up?

As we were driving down the I-5 from Los Angeles to San Diego, you asked why I always wore long sleeves. I have holes in my skin, I said. You didn't believe me.

We agreed to San Diego because we were both bored. Maybe we just needed a holiday. Yes, a holiday, something that would give us the illusion that we were free. After that we would return to work, work, who knows why. We'd get drunk in a topsy-turvy world, but then the world would return to normal and we'd cooperate in reaffirming its order. But everyone needs a midsummer night's dream. You agreed.

You opened the car window wide to let your hair blow in the wind. Like in the movies, you said. You took off your jacket and applied sunscreen. From behind my sunglasses, I stared at the highway stretching out under endless blue sky, desert on either side. Here it was, the American road. We were like cowboys riding our horses in the wilderness – except we were women, free, in a car, rolling down the highway.

The holes, you said. What happened?

The American road – where would it take you? I'd travelled the highway many times and I'd never seen the future on the horizon. On that American road, I never turned around, but the past always managed to catch me.

May 1998. Where were you then?

You fell silent and thought. Was everyone like you, trying to remember a string of events for that month? In my head there is only one.

Rioting. That's all my father said. We rushed to cram a bunch of clothes into a small suitcase and turned off all the lights. I squeezed in a Nirvana CD, but Mother took it out and replaced it with biscuits. Father drove frantically to a hotel. From behind the windshield, we saw smoke rising. Shops were engulfed in flames. I was curious, and might have wanted to see if I could smell the fumes, but Father snapped at me. Don't open the window! I asked: the police, where are the police? We have to report this to the police! My parents didn't answer. Since then I've never looked for the police again.

For three days we ate and drank in our room. This is like a concentration camp, I said. Shut your mouth! I'd never heard my father so hysterical. Do you know what's happening out there? These are anti-Chinese riots. And like an idiot I asked: anti-us? On the fourth day, at dawn, we went to the airport and flew to Singapore.

You queried again, this time more softly:

Were you a victim of the masses? The holes – were they the cause?

They? Who are they? We're used to using the words mass, the masses – people in numbers, a faceless mob, ready to attack. Don't screw around or the masses will run amok. For years, the word masses has terrorised us. But who moves the masses – the 'they' who give orders to burn and kill?

No, I didn't have the holes then. We escaped.

Some people called us lucky. Some accused us of not appreciating how lucky we were. Chinese who got to run away.

Lucky. Doesn't that sound ludicrous to you? We were lucky because my parents had the money to take refuge in a hotel and flee to Singapore. The whole idea of luck is wrong. My aunt lost everything. Her shop in Glodok was torched. What's the opposite of lucky? Unlucky? What do you call those who were burned alive, scorched until their flesh bubbled and melted on the shop floor? Women who were raped – were they 'unlucky'? The word sounds so barbaric.

We returned to Indonesia for the most primordial reasons. My parents knew no home but Jakarta. I always thought people like them had choices. They had investments abroad and could change citizenship, but it turned out that for them home was preordained destiny.

Your home, your trap.

Neither you nor I wanted to live in Indonesia, but for different reasons. You said you were sick of being common and wanted adventure. I went through high school in Jakarta, but then I asked to be sent to Los Angeles for university. As you know, I only lasted two years. Maybe I'm not cut out for study. Maybe, like you, I get bored quickly. But I didn't think about adventure. I saw no reason to do anything, to be anything. I only wanted everything to pass quickly, to just pass, including life. My visa expired, but I didn't want to go home.

From Pacific Beach, we continued our journey to Old Town San Diego. This time you drove. I managed to convince you: it doesn't count as a holiday if you don't drive for at least an hour or two. You opened the left door of the car and sat in the driver's seat.

Take off your scarf, I said.

Why?

Do you know how Isadora Duncan died? The dancer. She was driving in France, and the scarf around her neck got caught in the car's rear wheel. It strangled her.

You immediately took off your scarf and said OK, fine. Besides, you'd learned that adventure isn't always glamorous.

I observed you from the passenger seat. You were a little tense, but over time you seemed to relax. Don't speed, I said. Your hair was fluttering, and you were laughing like a kid.

We drove around Old Town, looking at Spanish colonial buildings. America and Mexico were each visible everywhere: architecture, food, street names. A border town. We met Hispanic people wherever we went. But so far, and as long as I've lived in southern California, no one has ever greeted me and then asked *hablas español?*

Maybe my face really is Chinese.

I wanted to be anyone, Mexican, Malay, anything. As long as it wasn't Chinese.

You asked: Did you forget you were going to tell me about the holes?

No, I hadn't forgotten. We had reached that point.

When I arrived in Los Angeles, I sunbathed every day to get a tan. I'd always hated being Chinese, and May 1998 only strengthened that hatred. Then, all of a sudden, I saw the holes in my arm. I don't know exactly when they appeared. Maybe sunshine and sea air are the cause. My skin refuses to accept them because it's used to foul, polluted air.

You asked anxiously: Have you seen a doctor?

Doctors can't cure curses.

Whenever a breeze skirts across them, the pink shoots on my skin hurt. Sometimes the pain is so intense that I cry. I keep feeling cold. That's why I wear long sleeves everywhere, even under the hot California sun.

May 1998. What's your story?

I didn't dare leave the house, you said. My parents wouldn't let me leave.

Because you look Chinese?

*

They say that getting to Mexico from downtown San Diego is a cinch. Less than an hour and, bang, you're in Tijuana. But returning isn't as straightforward. The border patrol checks your passport. If they see that my visa has expired, I'll get deported. You too, unless you want to fight hard over the status of your marriage. As far as I'm concerned, you won't have a chance. You don't even have a letter.

I thought our conversation would be over and done with right there. But later, while we were having dinner at a restaurant in the Gaslamp Quarter, Tijuana came up again. You gulped your margarita and mentioned that you'd never been to Mexico.

I hadn't either.

We've arrived in San Diego. We've got to do it. *Vámonos.*

Do you want to risk everything you have?

For a long while you said nothing, staring at your almost empty glass, then you asked a frightening question:

But what do we have?

We live on the road, we have no home. When you left Indonesia, you left everything – family and friends, if not possessions. Your marriage should have been your emergency exit, your security, but it ended before you made it fail.

Is your husband really dead?

Maybe, you said. Sometimes I feel a glimmer of hope – just a glimmer, and then it disappears – that he'll return one day. Maybe he won't come home, to me, or any place. Travelling also turns out to be a waiting room. I'm not going anywhere.

You were beginning to get drunk, but maybe this city really was stirring something inside you. A border city, a city in between. You were right. This city was responsible. All it would take was a few more inches and we'd be on the other side.

A fence runs along the border between San Diego and Tijuana. You heard that the government wanted to reinforce the fence because hundreds of thousands of people cross from Mexico to America every year. Fences are a safety barrier, between home and what lies beyond, between security and threats.

I wanted to cross to the other side.

I've been surrounded by an invisible fence for my entire life, but I didn't realise it until May 1998, when the whole city seemed to unveil. Walls and fences sprayed with black Pylox: Native Muslim Property. They made fences to ward off militias, but we were out there, beyond. We couldn't enter.

Do you really want to go across?

In silence you stared out the window, as if wanting to run away. The restaurant was getting livelier and livelier, but we sat across from each other without speaking.

Maybe you don't really want to go to Mexico. It's just that limits and danger tempt you. Think it over. After this, there'll be no way home.

Afraid?

Now? you asked.

Now. Then.

The night had deepened. Again, we were in the car, but this time we kept the window closed. I stared at the highway while occasionally stealing glances at you, hazarding guesses at what was passing through your head. It was as if we were hiding, from what I didn't know, in an underground chamber. The music from the Nirvana CD that I was playing helped bury us.

Rape me, rape me my friend. I turned off the stereo. Even a decade on, I still listened to their music. There are always songs that repeat in our heads. I said to you that we're a desperate generation because we grew up on Kurt Cobain.

Not necessarily, you said. My sister was into Celine Dion.

May 1998. Your family didn't dare leave the house either. Your mother is Javanese, your father is Lahat. Muslim. But people from South Sumatra have small eyes, sallow skin. You resemble your father, so you hid in your house all day. Your sister didn't go into hiding. She was studying in Bandung and already wearing the hijab. You didn't go to school, but at the time it seemed nobody else wanted to either.

Then what happened?

Nothing. You started going to classes, as usual. When we came back from Singapore, I also hoped my life would revert to normal. I returned to school in Jakarta, but I got nothing but advice and stories. My parents repeated their mantra: look down when you walk. Don't look other people in the eye. This was how to become Chinese. And I heard lots of stories. Lots of stories. Stories of women being raped, their corpses thrown into burning shops. Stories about people being attacked, their bodies slashed, thrown away. I was forced to learn that women's bodies were so disturbing that they had to be mutilated before they could be disposed of.

We told stories because that was how we bonded, survived, learned to be Chinese. We kept remembering, secretly, because our stories weren't to be trusted. They wanted evidence. But there was no evidence because nobody dared make reports. And even if you didn't become a corpse, talking wouldn't save you. One witness was stabbed to death, so silence became the only choice.

Later, people tried to heal their own wounds. Our family's driver stopped working and didn't want to live in Jakarta any more. One day during the riots, he rode his motorbike along a deserted road and saw the corpse of a Chinese woman in the bushes. When he returned, the body was gone. Vanished. Nobody knew who took it. He even wondered whether he'd really seen it at all.

He came to doubt whether these events really happened. No one made reports, and even the corpses left no trace.

Soon he started questioning his sanity because he had recurrent dreams of bodies by the roadside. I realised that it wasn't just him but all of us who were terrorised by nightmares. And do you know what hurts more than nightmares? We were made to believe that nothing had really happened.

We were stranded in a cheap motel. The elevator door jammed and wouldn't open on the third floor. We waited a while and finally managed to get out. What kind of motel is this? you asked. We locked the door tightly.

You had a good friend in high school, Dian Carolina Halim. I could tell from her name that she was Chinese. After the May riots you hardly saw her, until a few months later she informed you that she was moving to Jogja to study at Gadjah Mada. Living in Jakarta seemed to have traumatised her.

This story emerged as you pulled out a change of clothes and a toothbrush from your backpack. Previously you'd said that nothing happened after the riots and that you went to school as usual. Did you forget your friend Dian Carolina Halim? There was always something you didn't reveal. I kept searching for more fragments.

What happened to your friend?

I haven't seen her for a long time, you said. The last time we met she'd become an activist. She had befriended women who were victims of the violence in 1965.

I was glad to hear it. In the same way I liked hearing the story of a Haji who had sheltered a Chinese family in his home during the May riots. We need stories of humanity to stay sane. It's not just the violent who inhabit this world.

After bathing I put on long-sleeved pyjamas. On the bed, you still had a book open under the reading lamp. You looked at me for a long time then asked:

What are the holes in your skin like?

I didn't like your question. You wanted to see the disease that cursed me. But for what? As evidence? Facts? Was this an investigation?

You don't trust me, like them?

I peppered you with questions. I was breathing hard, and I felt very cold. Then you rushed to embrace me and held me tight.

I believe you, you said. I believe you, and we will leave here. For Tijuana.

Vámonos.

Tijuana is a border city too, a mirror image of San Diego. We took a walk on Avenida Revolución, oh so colourful, going from restaurant to restaurant, bar-hopping like true tourists. We visited the stores for typical Tijuana knick-knacks that are on every corner. Two years ago this place was quiet, an American tourist told us. The war between drug cartels made people afraid to come to Mexico. There were even kidnappings and massacres in broad daylight. So tourists preferred to look for souvenirs in Old Town, to seek Mexico in San Diego. They didn't need to break through the mirror and enter the world where things were reversed.

We found no traces of that dark history. I was reminded of Glodok. After the shops were torched, Glodok Market was quickly rebuilt. Resuscitated, enlivened, a gravesite that had been paved over. We spent the following days in Tijuana, constantly alert. Maybe we were too careful. Although things were safer now, travelling as women kept us on guard. We didn't drink too much or go home too late.

There was no carnival. There was no midsummer night's dream. We didn't get drunk in an upside-down world. Our expectations didn't matter so much now. We had celebrated your special achievement. We had hit the road in your car as liberated women.

We had made the crossing, and that was more than enough.

How did we get here?

Hey, we both wanted to cross, right? In your car.

I mean here. To this point.

I told you about the holes in my skin.

We were in another motel, in that border city, no less dull or suspicious. But this was our final night, we agreed. Tomorrow would bring a fork in the road as we chose our own adventures.

On that last night, I swept in the last scrap of your story. We had turned off the lights. My eyes were half shut when your soft voice pierced the dark:

There's something I didn't tell you. I hid for a day inside the house, and the next morning I looked out through the curtains. There was a prayer rug hanging on our fence. My father had put it there. The mat was green, the colour of Paradise, with an image of the Ka'bah in the centre. It hung there for days, maybe weeks. Father wanted to make sure everything was safe. The prayer rug was where we prostrated, not a fortress wall. It shouldn't have been on the fence. What about those who didn't have a prayer rug? I didn't ask my father a thing. Our family never talked about it. Maybe I was afraid, not of the violent people out there, but of my own thoughts. After that I forgot, or tried to forget.

Forgive me. Forgive us. We didn't want to be burned, so we hung the prayer rug on the fence.

In the dark, I heard you sobbing.

Go to sleep.

I don't want to sleep, you said. I don't want all this to be just a bad dream and to disappear when we wake up.

I hugged you and whispered in your ear, again: Sleep. We have crossed, and that is more than enough.

That morning we separated. I would continue to Mexico City and wander there, for who knows how long. Maybe until I got bored. After that maybe I'd return to Indonesia. That's nuts, you said. All that made sense to me was this: why should I torture myself for hours in traffic at San Ysidro only to be deported? There had to be more exciting adventures, and I had no belongings and no regrets. Oh, look, you've converted me. I'm using your term now: adventure.

You said you wanted to try and return, to test the law. I thought that was pointless, as you'd never made your marriage official. True, you said. But what's the harm in trying? You'd lived through ambiguity, between accepting the death of your husband and waiting for him to return, between a longing for home and an addiction to travel. You were neither here nor there, always in a waiting room, in the borderlands.

What, we're not allowed to experiment in the borderlands? Your question, I liked your question.

Of course. Of course, we can. We'll keep on experimenting in the borderlands.

Where are you now?

I'm not afraid any more.

FINIS

How many of the story threads have you passed through? Note them down below.

1) _____

_____

2) _____

_____

3) _____

_____

4) _____

_____

5) _____

_____

6) _____

_____

7) _____

_____

8) _____

_____

9) _____

_____

10) _____

_____

11) _____
   _____

12) _____
   _____

13) _____
   _____

14) _____
   _____

15) _____
   _____

Author's Acknowledgements

Gentayangan, the title of this book in its original Indonesian language, means wandering, haunting, being in between. It often refers to ghosts who are neither here, in our world, nor there, in the world of the dead.

The novel has travelled through various in-between places. It was conceived in New York, published in Jakarta, and written over the course of nine years as I moved across continents and lived in different countries. The translation and editing process of the novel in English took place in New Zealand, Australia, and the UK. It has passed through so many caring hands in transit. I would very much like to thank Stephen J. Epstein for tirelessly crafting and polishing the translation, and for an open, fun, and thought-provoking collaborative process; my editor Ellie Steel for taking care of the book with commitment and patience; Tiffany Tsao for her help in editing the book and for providing diverse perspectives in translation; and my agent Kelly Falconer for her insights, enthusiasm, and endless support. Thanks also to Anna Redman Aylward, Katherine Fry, Rosie Palmer, and the Harvill Secker/ Vintage team who have worked very hard to prepare for the publication of this book.

I am grateful for the translation funding support that *The Wandering* has received: a PEN Translates award from English PEN and a PEN/Heim Translation Fund Grant from PEN America.

'Visiting a Haunted House' appeared in *Asymptote,* July 2017, with thanks to Lee Yew Leong and Tiffany Tsao.

Teaching has been an important lab to explore questions and perspectives around travel and displacement. I thank Malcolm Turvey and the students of 'Travel and Gender in Cinema' at Sarah Lawrence College (2015) as well as my film and global media students at Macquarie University.

Sam Cooney and Elizabeth Bryer from Brow Books and my colleagues at Macquarie University (especially the Creative Ecology Lab) have been highly supportive. I also thank friends, institutions, and communities who have supported this book in Indonesia: Mirna Yulistianti and her team at Gramedia Pustaka Utama, Eka Kurniawan, Sapardi Djoko Damono, Kartika Jahja, Gunawan Maryanto, Leilani Hermiasih, Asri Saraswati, Gita Putri Damayana, Marissa Anita, Rizal Iwan, Yudi Ahmad Tajudin, Norman Erikson Pasaribu, Alia Swastika, Gratiagusti Chananya Rompas, Mikael Johani, lit Boit, Lusia Neti Cahyani, Yennu Ariendra, Teater Garasi, Omuniuum, Paviliun Puisi, Melancholic Bitch.

Thanks to readers in Indonesia who have generously shared their reviews and photos of the novel, complete with their own maps and plenty of sticky notes.

My love and special thanks go to my daughter Ilana and my family:

My partner Ugoran Prasad has watched *The Wandering* grow – in his words – from a little creature sitting in the corners of our house to a towering monster running loose on the streets. He is the first reader and critic of this book, and a collaborator in *A Red Shoe Odyssey*, an ongoing project of collecting images of the red shoes adventure.

My mother passed away in June 2019 without having the chance to see the book travel. She will always live in the stories of disobedient women; good girls go to heaven, bad girls go wandering.

Borders are real, but some fearless women will keep on experimenting in the borderlands.

Translator's Acknowledgements

It may not take a village to produce a novel translation, but it often involves more people than readers imagine, and I owe thanks to several who helped on the journey (complete with a lost red shoe) that brought *The Wandering* into print. Most of my work on the translation occurred in my living room or university office in Wellington, but the final edits took place in Indonesia's West Sulawesi province, in Mamasa, a town with deep traditional knowledge of wandering ghosts. My thanks to its residents, especially the family of Pak Muhammad Husein, for a congenial stay.

Tiffany Tsao deserves special mention for publishing the excerpt 'Visiting a Haunted House' in *Asymptote* and first bringing Intan Paramaditha's work to the attention of Brow Books. Tiffany also brought her editing wizardry to bear on a late draft of *The Wandering* and contributed numerous suggestions that have made the final version a far better text than it would be otherwise. Virtually every page profits from her magical touch.

My thanks go to the helpful staff at Harvill Secker, in particular editor Ellie Steel; I much appreciate Katherine Fry's contribution as well. Publication of *The Wandering* has further benefitted from a PEN/Heim Translation Fund Grant from PEN America and PEN Translates in the UK.

A further tip of the hat to John McGlynn who first introduced me to Intan and her work several years ago and has done much to help us and to promote Indonesian literature generally. The team at Brow Books – most notably Elizabeth Bryer – gave us wonderful support in the initial production of the story collection *Apple and Knife*. I also thank my colleagues from the New Zealand Centre for Literary Translation at Victoria University of Wellington, and my fellow translators of Korean literature Sora Kim-Russell and Jenny Wang Medina for support. And love and appreciation to Mi Young and Sonia, always.

Above all, though, my gratitude to Intan Paramaditha, not only for creating a brilliant source text that was a joy to engage with throughout, but for being eternally delightful to work with. Intan and I have now collaborated for almost a decade in bringing her work from one linguistic context to another. I use the word collaborate purposefully, for our process differs from my other translation projects. Her own outstanding English sensibilities have improved the final text substantially, and she in turn has allowed me generous leeway to shape the translation creatively, while also attending closely to the original. Our shared goal has been to ensure that *The Wandering* lives and breathes on its own in English.

I have sought to capture insofar as possible the experience of reading the source text: fluid, witty, sarcastic, insightful and just downright fun, with its sly references to material ranging from pop culture touchstones to Indonesian legends. Inspired by the liberal use of song lyrics in the original, I developed their use in the translation. Ironically, many lyrics quoted in the original had to be dropped because of copyright issues, but elsewhere allusions made possible by the English context activate new resonances for *The Wandering*, a strategy that met with Intan's enthusiastic consent, and hopefully will with you too, dear reader. May you enjoy the journey(s) you choose through the text.

THE LEOPARD

The leopard is one of Harvill's historic colophons and an imprimatur of the highest quality literature from around the world.

When The Harvill Press was founded in 1946 by former Foreign Office colleagues Manya Harari and Marjorie Villiers (hence Har-vill), it was with the express intention of rebuilding cultural bridges after the Second World War. As their first catalogue set out: 'The editors believe that by producing translations of important books they are helping to overcome the barriers, which at present are still big, to close interchange of ideas between people who are divided by frontiers.' The press went on to publish from many different languages, with highlights including Giuseppe Tomasi di Lampedusa's *The Leopard,* Boris Pasternak's *Doctor Zhivago,* José Saramago's *Blindness,* W. G. Sebald's *The Rings of Saturn,* Henning Mankell's *Faceless Killers* and Haruki Murakami's *Norwegian Wood.*

In 2005 The Harvill Press joined with Secker & Warburg, a publisher with its own illustrious history of publishing international writers. In 2020, Harvill Secker reintroduced the leopard to launch a new translated series celebrating some of the finest and most exciting voices of the twenty-first century.

Ismail Kadare: *The Doll*
  trans. John Hodgson
Intan Paramaditha: *The Wandering*
  trans. Stephen J. Epstein
Dima Wannous: *The Frightened Ones*
  trans. Elisabeth Jaquette
Pauline Delabroy-Allard: *All About Sarah*
  trans. Adriana Hunter
Jonas Hassen Khemiri: *The Family Clause*
  trans. Alice Menzies
Paolo Cognetti: *Without Ever Reaching the Summit*
  trans. Stash Luczkiw
Karl Ove Knausgaard: *In the Land of the Cyclops*
  trans. Martin Aitken
Urs Faes: *The Twelve Nights*
  trans. Jamie Lee Searle
Ngũgĩ wa Thiong'o: *The Perfect Nine*,
  trans. the author